Katherine Scholes grew up in East Africa, England and Australia. As well as writing non-fiction books, Katherine has worked as a documentary filmmaker. She lives in Melbourne with her filmmaker husband, Roger Scholes, and their two young sons.

MAKE ME AN IDOL

Katherine Scholes

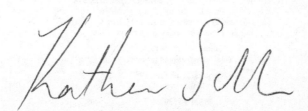

MACMILLAN

Pan Macmillan Australia

This work was assisted by a grant from Arts Victoria and a writer's
fellowship from the Australia Council, the Federal Government's arts funding and advisory body.

First published 1996 in Macmillan by Pan Macmillan Australia Pty Limited
St Martins Tower, 31 Market Street, Sydney

National Library of Australia
cataloguing-in-publication data:

Scholes, Katherine, 1959–.
Make me an idol.

ISBN 0 7329 0867 1.

I. Title.

A823.3

Typeset in 12½/14pt Bembo by Post Typesetters, Brisbane

Printed in Australia by McPherson's Printing Group

For Brian C. Robinson
who taught me so much about the enjoyment of life

Acknowledgements

I am deeply grateful to Roger Scholes who travelled with me in search of this story—sharing the long journey over land and sea and many pieces of paper . . .

I would also like thank my agent Jill Hickson, Nikki Christer and Madonna Duffy of Pan Macmillan Australia, Kay Ronai and Clare Visagie for their invaluable assistance.

I am indebted to others as well—friends and family—who helped in so many ways.

PART ONE

Chapter 1

Zelda stood on the foredeck of the fishing boat, cutting up wallaby carcasses with a butcher's cleaver. She used the heavy blade like an axe-head, lifting it high and letting it fall heavily to make a clean cut through hide, flesh and bone. She was surrounded by the disconnected pieces—heads with ears, fore-quarters with little arms, rumps with long jumping legs, and tails—all mixed up like bits of a child's game.

When the last carcass was done, she threw all the pieces into the bait bucket and carried it astern to where her father was setting up craypots.

'I wanted to get back by six, remember,' she said as she reached him. 'I'm going out.'

James glanced up at her briefly and went on baiting the pots. 'You'd better deal with that mess, then,' he replied.

Zelda watched him for a moment, then went to work tidying the ropes and nets that lay tangled on the deck. Her mouth was set in a thin, angry line. She knew that nothing she could say or do would make any difference—one way or another, James would make sure they ended up getting back late.

The sun was low in the sky, sending slanting rays over the

wavetops. Birds swooped down over the deck—big, slow-flapping albatrosses with grey shaded eyes. They flew with their beaks hanging down, on the lookout for food. Zelda eyed them uneasily. Only a few weeks ago, she had watched one snatch a baited tuna hook and fly off tethered by the nylon line. With shaking hands, she had reeled it in like a fish and struggled to remove the hook, peering into the deep red gullet while the bird screamed hoarsely and tore at her with its feet. She had been alone in the boat, with no-one to call for help. In the end there had been no choice but to cut off the line and let the bird go. It had floated on the water, holding its curved beak sideways, staring. Zelda remembered its eyes—the open, childlike look of surprise and fear.

'You'd have done better to shoot it there and then,' James had said when she told him about it later. 'It won't survive, you know. Not with a hook left inside.'

At last James went into the wheelhouse and started up the engine. They began their slow trip round a long, narrow reef, James driving in short bursts, while Zelda heaved baited cray-pots over the side. The wicker cages sank quickly, disappearing into the weed and leaving black-flagged buoys bobbing above. When the last pot was gone, James steered the boat towards the home bay: a white crescent beach, running between rocky headlands.

Zelda went to join him inside, closing the door against the spray. The space was narrow, and she leaned into one corner, wanting to keep a small distance clear between them. They stood in silence. The boat shuddered against a short, choppy sea.

After a while Zelda spoke. 'You've made us late on purpose!' She paused, but James did not respond. 'I should be able to make my own plans,' she went on, 'I'm not a kid.'

'You know this job,' answered James. 'It takes as long as it takes. Always has and always does.'

Zelda stared ahead for several minutes, her dark eyes tracing the outline of a rugged grey mountain rising up from the sea against a rosy sunset sky.

'Just tell me what you've got against Dana,' she asked finally.

James leaned across, pushing against her as he checked the fuel gauge.

'It's because of the dance classes, isn't it?' Zelda said. 'You don't like Dana because she's teaching me to dance.'

James frowned, but said nothing.

'What's wrong with it?' Zelda persisted.

'It's just a waste of time.'

Zelda took a deep breath. 'You don't like it because it reminds you of—Ellen . . .' Her voice trailed off as she said her mother's name. Ellen. The word seemed to linger in the air between them, a small strangled sound.

James kept his eyes fixed on the sea. Zelda watched his face anxiously as she waited for him to speak. But when he did his voice was calm, almost light.

'No. You're wrong. It's just not the kind of thing I want to see you getting caught up in, that's all.'

'It's only for fun,' argued Zelda. 'I'm not getting caught up in anything.'

'What about tonight, then?'

Zelda shrugged. 'Dana's got some friends over from the mainland. It's just a chance to meet some new people.'

'Great! New people from the mainland!' James said in a mocking tone.

Zelda looked down, studying her boots. She traced the patterns of dried blood and fish-scales. After a few moments she sensed James moving towards her. She felt his hand, a warm weight on her shoulder.

'Take my word for it, Zel,' he said, his voice softening. 'You don't want to bother with that kind of thing. Stick to what you know, eh?'

Zelda glanced at her father, meeting his gaze briefly. Then

she turned to face the side window, peering out at the sea through glass crusted with salt.

As soon as they reached the jetty that ran out from a sheltered part of the headland, she went ashore and made fast the mooring ropes.

'I'm taking the jeep,' she called back to James. 'I might be late. Okay?'

James began wrapping and stowing his wet-weather gear, slowly and carefully. Zelda could see he was deliberately ignoring her. Checking her watch, she sighed and turned away. She ran along the jetty, then jumped down onto soft white sand, her gumboots sinking, slowing her down.

Up ahead was a small wooden hut built in behind a row of granite boulders that bordered the sands. As Zelda ran towards it she pulled a rubber band from her hair, letting it fall long and dark around her shoulders. Then she dragged her workshirt off over her head. Underneath she wore a man's singlet, which hung low round the neck and arms and barely covered her breasts. Reaching the hut, she tossed the shirt over a drooping clothes line.

A small white shape caught her eye—a letter, propped up on the front doorstep. Lizzie must've called in with their mail, she thought, as she bent to pick up the envelope. Her gaze settled briefly on James's name and the Government of Tasmania seal stamped in the corner. She guessed it would be something do with elections, rates, fishing regulations—nothing of interest.

Tucking the letter under her arm, she leaned on the door, shoving it with her shoulder. It opened to the smell of wood ash blended with kerosene. She dropped the letter onto the table before grabbing a towel that had been draped over the mantelpiece to dry. Back outside, she crossed the yard and disappeared into the bath-hut.

The late sun filtered in through cracks in the paling walls, making a pattern on her skin as she stripped off her clothes. Bracing herself against the chill, she poured water over her body, avoiding her hair wound up on her head. Thin streams ran down over her shoulders and hips, splashing onto her feet. She ran a sliver of yellow soap over her skin, then scrubbed herself hard using a handful of small sea-sponges. She wanted to be sure that she removed every trace of sweat and salt and the lingering taint of raw fish.

She wondered if James had come up from the boat—whether she would have to face him again before she left. She felt a surge of anger. I'm twenty-one years old, she imagined telling him. It's none of your damned business where I go, and who I see. But then she pictured the look that would cross his face: the cold anger or the dark brooding pain.

'He just loves you too much,' Zelda's friends had often told her. 'It's to be expected, with just the two of you. He's had to be your mother *and* father. Everything's been for you . . .'

But Zelda knew there was more to it than that. There was another strand that ran between them, binding them together. She had sensed it over the years, growing stronger as she'd left childhood behind, emerging as a young woman—someone who looked so much like her mother that people said they could have been twins. James had never spoken of it, but Zelda guessed it must be hard for him, always being reminded of Ellen. She had finally understood how deeply it touched him when he had walked into the bath-hut one day—this same little room with its bucket shower and floor made of criss-crossed decking.

'Oh sorry,' he'd said, 'I thought you were outside.'

But instead of leaving straight away, he'd stood there, frozen. Zelda had watched his face for a moment, then followed the path of his gaze as it travelled slowly over her bare body. Her long hair, hanging down each side of her neck, almost covered her breasts; just the tips of her pink nipples were showing. Further down, the dark triangle of hair was startling against the pale skin around it. Zelda had noticed with surprise that she could just see the outline of her bikini against her fading tan.

When she'd looked up, James's eyes had been bright with tears, and his lips twisted with pain.

Now, as she thought back to that time, Zelda splashed water over her face and rubbed it with her hands, as if to wash the memory away.

It was some time before she emerged from the hut, clean and dressed. The sun had gone and the sky was darkening quickly. James had still not come up from the jetty. Glancing towards the sea, Zelda ran across to the old army jeep that was parked beside the water tank. Jumping into the driver's seat, she revved the engine loudly, then lunged off along the rough bush track.

She drove carefully along the narrow road, swerving to avoid potholes and looking out for animals in the space lit up ahead by the lights of the jeep. She tried to put James out of her mind, to escape the memory of his disapproval. Instead, she found herself thinking of Drew as well. He would call in at the hut later on, she knew, and add his own concerns about her going to Dana's house and, not wanting him to come with her. She pictured them together, her father and her lover, shaking their heads over her, puzzled and annoyed. Once, years ago, they had been rivals, hovering on the brink of open hostility. But somewhere, some time, it seemed they had decided to share Zelda. To keep her between them. Zelda swung the jeep roughly around a sharp corner as a flash of defiance ran through her. She squashed it quickly, feeling childish and ashamed.

As she reached the main road, her thoughts turned to the evening ahead. She had been looking forward to it; she'd often looked up at Dana's house, perched high on the hillside, but had never been invited there before. The only times she saw Dana were at the dance classes held each week at the Memorial Hall. Dana always waited until everyone was gone before locking up, and Drew was often late meeting Zelda with the car—so the two women would end up waiting alone together, standing talking in the pool of thin blue light cast by the single fluorescent tube that stuck out from the front of the building.

They came from two completely different worlds. Zelda, who only knew life on the island. And Dana, who seemed to wander the globe at her whim, moving in and out of the lives of different lovers, trying new jobs, changing houses for the sake of a new view. A solo navigator, Dana called herself, laughingly. Zelda envied her life—the pace, the fullness, the new faces—but she felt sure it must be lonely. 'No way,' insisted Dana. And it was true that she did seem happy.

Reaching the turn-off, Zelda began the slow drive up Dana's steep, rocky driveway. She glanced down at her white silk shirt, lying so smooth and cool against her skin. It felt foreign and adult—not the kind of thing she would have worn to go out anywhere else. A few seasons ago, Lizzie, Drew's mother, had produced the shirt from the back of her wardrobe, where she kept unwanted gifts that might be given again and old baby clothes wrapped in creased tissue.

'Your mother gave this to me,' she had said, running her rough hands over the soft silk one last time. 'It's the most beautiful thing I've ever worn. But it'll never fit me again, that's for sure! You'd better have it.' She had laid it on the bed, white and soft like a shroud. 'It's French—lots of Ellen's clothes were. See the label? Christian Dior. Strange thing, to be called Christian, as your name.'

With the shirt Zelda wore a clean pair of jeans and polished riding boots. Beside her on the seat was a knee-length skirt made of pale blue linen. Both outfits would be wrong, she thought, as she tried to imagine what Dana's friends might be like. She pictured faceless fast-talking guests in evening dresses and high heels, and wondered suddenly why she had agreed to come to the party. She wouldn't know what to say or what to do. Still, she reminded herself, she was only half-expected. She needn't go in. She could wait and see.

Just before the last bend, she stopped the jeep and continued on foot. She took off her boots and carried them, to keep them clean, picking her way barefoot over the rough ground.

Rounding the corner she paused, the house suddenly closer than she'd expected. The wide bare windows were full of warm light. She bent over and moved closer, keeping out of view. Reaching the edge of one window, she leaned round and peered cautiously inside. It was like watching television with the sound turned down. Impressions of open-mouthed laughter, cigarette smoke curling into the air, glasses of wine, and mismatched outfits as if each of the four or five guests belonged to a different story.

Immediately in front of her was a tall, willowy woman in a long red dress, her hair teased into a smooth butter-coloured mound. Looking more closely, Zelda saw with surprise that the woman was old, her face lined and furrowed beneath a coating of powder. Her hand, curved around a glass, was old too—wrinkled and marked with brown age spots. Next to her was Dana, dressed all in black. Her face was white, her lips a deep red. She leaned against the back of a chair, her loose singlet top gaping at the neck and showing her small breasts cupped in a black lace bra. Beyond her was a slim-hipped figure in a dark blue suit. Then there was a man in work clothes: khaki jeans and jumper. They appeared to have nothing in common, yet Zelda could tell that they all shared a sense of ease. It softened the angles of their bodies and lay like a calm shadow behind their looks and smiles.

Suddenly Zelda decided to retreat to the bush and head for the jeep. To drive back to the hut, to James and Drew, who'd be sharing a beer. They'd be pleased to see her. But then she tensed, listening. There were footsteps nearby. She crouched down and leaned in against the wall. The steps drew closer. Peering up, she saw a man wandering across the lawn with a glass of wine in his hand. He paused to look up at the night sky, then he turned and came straight towards Zelda. She froze, trying to decide whether to stand up and face him or bolt away. But instead of doing either, she just watched, transfixed, as he got nearer and nearer. When he was almost within reach, she hid her face against the wall like a child, as if he wouldn't see her if she couldn't see him.

She heard him place his glass down on the window ledge above her head and move away. She breathed out in relief as he strolled across to the edge of the lawn. He stood there, gazing out over the treetops towards the dark flat sea. Then he unzipped his fly and began to pee into the bush, a steady stream spattering loudly onto the dry leaves and grasses. Zelda felt herself turning red, as if she had chosen to hide here, watching. She glanced behind her, wondering if she could creep back through the shrubs without being heard or seen. But it was already too late. He was tucking in his shirt, turning round.

Moonlight bathed his face as he walked back across the lawn. He had strong, even features and dark hair, cut short. His pale grey-green eyes scanned the window ledge and fixed on the dim shape hunched against the wall. He peered closer, as if unsure what it was.

'Hi,' said Zelda, standing up. She forced a smile.

'Oh, hi,' the man replied, stepping back in surprise.

Zelda saw him replaying the last scene, his eyes widening, questioning. 'Dana invited me to tea,' she said. 'Well, dinner at least.' She moved forward, her shirt gleaming as she stepped into the glow that spilled from the windows.

The man was tall. He looked down into her face. 'I guess that's one way of coming to the door.' His accent was odd, placeless—not Australian, not English or American. 'I'm Rye, by the way,' he said, holding out his hand.

For just a moment, Zelda stared at it. Only men shook hands, as far as she knew—women just smiled. She took it lightly and briefly, feeling its warmth.

'And you are?' he asked, with a smile.

'I'm Zelda.'

'Ah! Dana's protégée.'

Zelda frowned. 'What?'

'Dana's teaching you to dance?'

'Yes,' answered Zelda doubtfully. 'Well, we have fun anyway.'

There was an awkward silence, then Rye made a move in the direction of the back door. 'Shall we go in?'

They walked side by side. Zelda looked straight ahead, sensing Rye glancing down at her. Realising she was still carrying her boots, she stopped to put them on, balancing on one leg. The grass was soft and uneven and she wobbled briefly. Rye put a hand on her shoulder. She felt it, firm against her silken skin.

'Ta,' she said, pulling on the boots with clumsy hands. She hurried on.

Dana appeared in the doorway. 'Zelda, you made it! Come in!' She turned from Zelda to call back into the room. 'She's here!' Then she caught sight of Rye behind her. 'And you've met Rye already.' She turned to him. 'Where did you find her?'

He grinned. 'She found me. I was taking a leak.'

Zelda swallowed, embarrassed, but Dana just laughed gaily and put her arm round Zelda's shoulders to draw her inside. 'I'm so glad you could come,' she said softly. 'I hope James wasn't too—?'

'He'll be okay,' said Zelda, wanting to pull back against the gentle shepherding arm. Suddenly they were facing the rest of the guests.

'This is Cassie, from America,' Dana introduced the woman in red. 'She's very famous.'

'Not these days,' Cassie laughed, stubbing out her cigarette before turning to offer a greeting. Her smile froze as her eyes settled on Zelda's face. For a brief moment she stared in silence, her eyes screwed up in a puzzled frown. Then she recaptured her smile and forced it into a short laugh. 'I'm sorry, dear,' she said. 'It's just—I thought for a minute that I knew you.' She paused to look again, tilting her head to one side. 'Your face looks so familiar. I feel sure I've met you before.' She looked to Dana for help.

'Not very likely,' said Dana. 'She's never been off the island, have you, Zelda?'

Zelda shook her head mutely.

'I never forget a face,' insisted Cassie. Zelda was aware of the old woman's eyes still fixed on her as Dana pressed on with her introductions.

Next there was a friend from Sydney who said he was a painter. At first Zelda pictured him with planks and buckets, but then Dana waved her arm towards a large, coloured canvas that hung on the wall above the fireplace. There were two other women, whom Dana described as designers. Zelda missed their names, distracted by the odd style of their clothes and make-up.

Glancing up, she saw that Cassie was still watching her, with the distant look of someone searching their memory for an elusive clue. Zelda turned away, feeling uncomfortable, as if she were being accused of concealing something. Moving to stand by the fireplace, she pretended to be interested in the collection of shells spread out along the mantelpiece. She picked up an abalone shell, tracing its familiar shape with tense fingers. Then she studied the side wall, which was covered with framed photographs. There was one of a turbanned woman standing by a camel against a backdrop of desert sands. Looking more closely, Zelda recognised Dana's face.

Suddenly she realised everyone was looking at her. Cassie was speaking. 'Zelda. Such a pretty name. I had a cousin called Zelda May.' Cassie smiled as she talked, all traces of the puzzled frown gone. Zelda guessed, with relief, that she had given up the idea that a girl from this island could possibly remind her of anyone. 'She's an absolute angel in that white shirt,' Cassie continued, 'and beautiful—Lord, just look at her. You say she can dance, too?'

'Cassie!' Dana laughed. 'You're embarrassing her. But yes, she can dance. She's got no natural faults that I can find.' She turned to Zelda. 'I've told you, haven't I, that you should be trained? You should take it up seriously.'

'Yes,' Zelda mumbled, 'but I'm pretty busy—you know, with work . . .'

'And what kind of work do you do, darling?' Cassie looked at her, a delighted smile hovering on her lips.

Zelda noticed Rye, who had stood apart from the introductions, moving closer to catch her answer. 'I'm a deckhand. My Dad's a crayfisherman. I work with him.' Looking round, she could see that this was not enough. 'We set pots along the coastline. They've got bait in them, to attract the crayfish. The next day we go and pull up the pots and take out the fish and bait them again and put them back.'

'Every day?' asked Cassie.

'Unless it's too rough. And only while the season's open, of course.' She felt awkward, guessing that they were not really interested and were using the moment to assess her in other ways. She fiddled with a strand of hair from behind her ear, drawing it through her fingers in long, steady strokes.

'Where do you work?' asked Rye. 'Which part of the coast?'

Zelda let her gaze pass briefly over his face. 'South-east.'

'I was around there just today—little place called Nautilus Bay.'

'That's where we live,' she said. 'That's our bay.'

Rye paused for a short moment. 'You live in the cottage there? Right on the edge of the beach?'

'Yes.'

'It's—a beautiful place,' he said. His voice was oddly distant, as if he didn't want to own his words.

'I was born there,' said Zelda.

Cassie had been turning from Rye to Zelda while they talked, like someone following a game of tennis. Now she took part. 'You don't mean in the cottage?'

'Yes. My mother hated hospitals. She gave them the wrong

dates for when I was due, so she went into labour two weeks earlier than they expected and Doctor Ben had to come rushing out to our place.'

Cassie clapped her hands with amazement. Zelda wished she could stop talking. She edged back behind Dana and crossed to the window. There she saw herself reflected, her face rosy above the sleek white of her shirt. Behind her, she could see Rye. He stood with one leg perched on the edge of the wood-box, a glass of wine held between two fingers. He was watching her. There was an uneasy look on his face, as if something was bothering him—something connected with her. But that was impossible. They'd only just met.

Dana began to bring food from the kitchen. Zelda quickly went to help her, examining the dishes as she carried them out one by one and placed them on the long pine table. There were plates of sliced meat, bread, salad, olives, fish, pickles, sausages—presumably brought by the guests from the mainland; nothing like this could be found on the shelves of the island's milk bar, or even in the new supermarket set up in one corner of the feed store. It wasn't going to be like a proper meal, Zelda realised, relaxing a little. Everyone was just going to drink wine and eat from the plates, choosing whatever they liked.

'Help me with this, Zelda,' Dana called from the sink. 'I got it from Mr Lohrey—already cooked, thank God. But what do I do with it?'

It was a muttonbird, barbecued black and lying cold and greasy on a paper bag. Zelda hesitated. Everyone she knew loved the fishy lamb taste of the oily-fleshed seabirds. They were best eaten fresh and hot from the fire, though still good served cold like this one. But almost without exception visitors to the island wrinkled up their noses, dropped the meat onto their plates and asked for something to wipe the smell from their hands.

'You just break it up, and put salt on it,' said Zelda. 'I'll do it.'

She pulled the body apart, unnerved by its familiar touch and smell in this place where she did not belong. She felt disloyal, preparing the bird to be spurned.

Dana carried the dish out to the table, announcing its name, like a butler.

'Dana, how could you!' cried one of the women. She went on to explain that this was a baby wild bird, dragged from the burrow while its mother was out searching the waves for food.

'Sarah!' protested Dana. 'Don't go overboard. It's just a local delicacy to try. We won't eat them out of existence!'

'You don't know that,' Sarah replied. 'I heard they take nearly all of the young each year. I don't know how they expect the birds to survive. *And,*' she paused to watch the others' faces, enjoying sharing her knowledge, 'they fly from here to Alaska and back every year. It's a miracle.'

Zelda watched from the kitchen door as the guests gathered around the plate of muttonbird. They looked at it in silence, as if faced with a sad reminder of human failing. Dana turned to Zelda with a helpless look. Zelda forced a tense smile then moved away towards the darkened window. What did you expect, she asked herself, coming here? Each to his own, remember. She looked across to the table, just in time to see a long arm reaching over from the back of the group, to pick up a leg and a wing.

Everyone turned to watch Rye eat. Sarah's eyebrows arched in surprise. 'I wouldn't have expected *you*, of all people . . .'

'Delicious,' he said, looking at Zelda, over their heads. She smiled, grateful more for the sake of the bird than herself.

Licking his fingers, Rye faced Sarah. 'And they're not endangered, as far as we can tell. Aboriginal people have been taking them for thousands of years and the population's still stable. It's not cruel either—there they are at home, next moment they're dead. It's better than farming, that's for sure. But perhaps you're a vegetarian?'

Sarah was silent.

'No? Ah . . .' He picked up a plate and began filling it with food.

There was a taut silence. Cassie threw back her head and laughed, sending long bright peals chasing through the air. 'Wonderful! I love an argument. Parties used to be full of them. Men hitting each other, people rushing out and vowing never to return, black eyes.' She let her gaze rest briefly on each guest, inviting them into her circle. 'It was exciting!' She pouted like a child. 'Things can get so boring. Dana, be an angel and give me some of that sheepbird thing.' She sparkled at Sarah and Rye in turn. 'Bless you, both of you. You're still young.'

Zelda took a plate and edged along the table, choosing pieces of food. Behind the nervous twist in her stomach was a hunger that prompted her to fill her plate with things she had never tasted. She hovered by the muttonbird, unsure whether or not she should take some.

'Try some of this,' suggested Rye, holding out a platter of raw vegetable sticks surrounding a bowl of sludgy brown paste. 'Tapenade,' he said. 'I didn't know what the hell it was, so I asked Dana and she said it was made of capers, olives . . . and anchovies, I think. It's very good.' He used a piece of carrot to scoop up a large blob of the paste. It began to fall as he lifted it up and he had to duck his head to get it to his mouth in time. He grinned while he chewed.

'Do you live in Melbourne?' Zelda asked him, hoping she sounded casual, friendly, but not too friendly.

'Now and then,' answered Rye. 'I travel around with my work. I've got a room in a flat there, but I don't seem to spend much time in it.'

'What do you do?' asked Zelda, wishing she had not had to say that she was a deckhand.

'I'm an environmental consultant,' he said. 'I get called in by various governments to make recommendations about land use and suchlike. I deal mainly with the coast; the sea.' He fell

17

silent, but kept on looking at Zelda as if considering saying something more, then deciding not to. Zelda fixed her eyes on her plate.

Rye picked up a raw oyster, tipped it onto his tongue and then began to study the shell, turning it over in his hand. Zelda ate awkwardly, with her head down.

'Would you like some wine?' Sarah appeared at Rye's elbow, looking up at him from under lowered eyelids. 'Red or white?'

Rye looked at the bottles in her hands. 'I recommend the red,' he said to Zelda, causing Sarah to turn and notice her there.

'Oh . . . hi,' Sarah flicked a smile towards Zelda as she filled her glass. 'You're certainly having a good feed!'

'It's Tasmanian,' Rye continued, addressing Zelda. 'Some new vineyard Dana's discovered.' He scanned the room as he spoke, in search of Dana. Catching her eye, he held up his glass and nodded approvingly. She smiled and raised hers back.

'Are you old friends?' asked Zelda.

'We've known each other since we were kids—I went to boarding school with her brother. Geelong Grammar.'

'You must've missed home,' said Zelda, thinking of people she knew who had been sent away to private schools in Tasmania.

Rye sipped his wine before speaking. He frowned thoughtfully. 'I missed India—that's where I grew up.'

'India.' Zelda said the word slowly. It conjured images of white-domed palaces and gilded elephants, drifting in a haze of heat and dust. 'What's it like?' she asked. 'I mean, can you remember it much?'

'Yes, I was sixteen when I left, and I go back whenever I can. I do a bit of work there.'

'In India?' asked Zelda, her voice raised in surprise.

'At the moment I'm working with local governments, developing village-based coastal conservation projects. All paid for by an American millionaire who made her money selling fast-food containers and now wants to make good.' He smiled cynically as he spoke.

'My father was an American,' Zelda said.

Rye nodded, as if it was something he already knew.

'He's Australian now, of course,' she added quickly. 'My mother was American too, but she died in a car accident when I was little.' She looked down at her feet, suddenly afraid that she had talked too long and asked too many questions.

'I'm sorry,' said Rye.

'Oh, that's all right,' answered Zelda. She studied her glass, turning it in her hand. 'I was very young. I don't even remember her.'

When she glanced up, she saw Rye looking steadily down at her. Their eyes met.

'You know, you have very beautiful eyes,' he said, so quietly that Zelda felt she'd imagined it.

While she searched for a way to reply, Dana appeared and called Rye to follow her away. Zelda stayed by the window. Hearing Rye's words again, and feeling his gaze travelling warm over her face. She reached for an image of Drew, or James, but found nothing solid to hold against a sweeping wave of joy and hope and fear.

Around midnight, when the others were still talking and drinking, Zelda prepared to leave. Sarah and the painter waved from across the room.

Cassie came over and kissed her on both cheeks. 'We must've met in a past life,' she declared. 'It's the only explanation I can think of. I'm staying with Dana for a month. Promise you'll visit again.'

Dana and Rye came with her to the door.

'I'm glad you could come,' said Dana.

'Me too,' added Rye. He looked into Zelda's eyes. 'I'm leaving in the morning. But if you're ever in Melbourne—' He smiled and shrugged.

'Look at it this way, Rye,' said Dana with a teasing grin. 'If you lived here in paradise, would *you* want to go to Melbourne?'

Rye laughed. 'I guess not. But you never know.' He turned away from Dana, towards Zelda. 'Seriously,' he said, 'I'd like to see you again.'

Zelda nodded mutely. She could think of nothing to say.

They all waved goodnight, and Rye and Dana stood chatting in the doorway while Zelda walked away across the lawn. The smell of the sea drifted in on the cool night air, enfolding her like the embrace of an old friend, drawing her back.

As she drove along the road to Nautilus Bay, Zelda smiled to herself. Gazing out into the darkness, she saw Rye's grey-green eyes, his lean brown hands cradling his wine glass. She thought guiltily of Drew, but not for long. Her mind turned back to long, hot summer days she'd spent on the beach with her friend Sharn, reading paperback romance novels that smelled of suntan oil. They'd read and reread the stories of tall, handsome strangers, people sharing long looks across crowded rooms, and love born in the moonlight. Fantasies had grown up—dreams of getting away from the island, going to far-off places with exotic names and falling in love with men they didn't already know. Tonight Zelda felt like a scout returning from a voyage to the other side. It's true, she imagined telling Sharn, her eyes shining. Love. Mystery. Romance. It's really out there. But she'd be laughing, joking, of course, just to be on the safe side.

Zelda stopped the jeep just before the hut came into view and walked down to the beach. She wanted to savour the last of the evening—to replay the moments, the looks and words, that had made her feel like someone different, someone new.

Standing near the edge of the water, she looked around her at the moonlit sand stretching away on both sides, smooth and grey, marked only by the wreaths of tangled weed that lay stranded on the tideline. Beyond the dunes, a thin line of boulders edged a dense forest of weeping she-oak. Over it all rose a steep mountain of bare rock, roughly piled into a high and jagged peak. Zelda knew its shape by heart. The way every ledge and crack stood out against the sky. This is where you belong, James had told her so many times. It had always sounded like a blessing; proof that she was safe, loved. But now the words came to her like a warning—a judgement being handed down. She belonged here. To him. And Drew. There was no room in her life for someone like Rye, coming in from outside.

A seventh wave rolled in, peaking higher than the ones that had gone before, and broke with a sudden crash. White water washed up over the sands, almost reaching Zelda's feet. Gazing out over the dark water, she watched more long swells rolling in. The sea. She wanted to reach out to it, to draw it towards her. The deep strong presence. For a moment she pictured a great tide sweeping over her, powerful and strong. A brave force bursting into her life, breaking everything open and leaving the way behind it free, uncharted—a blank page on which anything could be written down.

Turning away from the sea, Zelda walked slowly up towards the hut. In a few hours, she told herself, Rye would be gone. The bright moments of the night were no more than sparks doomed to die into darkness. Everything would carry on, as it always had, following the path that had been set.

Skeins of white smoke drifted above the chimney; pale wisps against the dark blue sky. As she drew nearer, Zelda was surprised to see a light in the window. James must be waiting up, she realised, suddenly feeling guilty; she shouldn't have stayed out so long.

Reaching the yard, she picked her way across to the window and leaned past stacked craypots, buoys and rolled nets to peer inside. There was James, sitting with his back to her, his head bent over—reading a book perhaps, or studying one of his maps. His sandy hair had been recently cut and the newly bared skin on his neck stood out, strikingly fair. At his elbow was a bottle of bourbon. The fire, burning low in the grate, spread a soft flickering glow over the peaceful scene. Zelda paused for a moment, watching, then headed for the back door.

James stood up as she walked in, his chair scraping harshly on the floor. He held a piece of paper in one hand, thrusting it towards her like a weapon. His face was pale, his eyes grim.

'What is it?' Zelda asked. 'What's wrong?' Glancing down, she saw a torn envelope on the floor—the one with the government stamp in one corner—and remembered the letter she had brought inside earlier.

James sat down heavily, dropping the paper onto the table and staring at it. There was a long silence while Zelda tried to imagine what could have gone wrong. 'Tell me what's happened,' she demanded.

James turned towards the fire. He spoke as if he were paraphrasing a formal letter. 'We wish to notify you that the area known as Nautilus Bay has been zoned as a Category 2 Heritage Protectorate.' He broke off and looked up at Zelda, his eyes red and raw.

'What does that mean?' Zelda asked carefully.

'It means that when the lease comes up for renewal they won't do it. No more lease. We have to get out. And then they pull the place down.' There was a short, sharp silence. 'They "rehabilitate" the area, so that there's no sign that anyone ever lived here.'

'Why?' Zelda frowned. 'I don't understand. I mean, they're long leases, aren't they? It'd be ages before—'

'We've got three years left,' James said bluntly.

Zelda stepped back, recoiling from his words. 'But they can't do that! Lots of people have leases. They always get renewed, that's why people buy them,' she said. Her voice sounded small and thin beside the certainty of James sitting there, hunched over with despair. 'It's our home! They can't just throw us out!'

'They can, Zelda,' James said. 'I knew something was in the

wind, but I didn't want to worry you. Charles warned me the other day, down at the council. But now—' he jabbed a finger at the letter '—it's done. *Fait accompli*. Act of Federal Parliament. It's because of the sea dragon.'

'The sea dragon?' Zelda repeated numbly. As a child she had snorkelled around the jetty, watching the graceful creatures drifting around like small pieces of stray weed. She had known they were rare, special, and had treasured their presence so close to home.

'You know how they breed in our bay and nowhere else,' James went on. 'Well, some bloody trumped-up academic recommended it for this Heritage Protectorate thing. And boom! Done! Piss off, Madison.' His voice shook. 'We don't care about you. Hell—we've got sea dragons to think of.'

Zelda stared at him, trying to make sense of his words. Someone had sent them a letter saying they did not belong in their own bay, that one day a team of men would come and take down their house and carry everything away, until there was no sign that they had ever been there at all. She swallowed on a tide of rising panic. It was one thing to dream of change, another to feel it beginning. To feel the ground beneath her shifting and winds blowing in through walls that had always been solid and safe.

She felt James's eyes fixed on her face, and searched for something, anything, to say. 'There's still three years to go. Nothing has to change yet.'

Their eyes met; they both knew the emptiness of her words—how the knowledge that they were now temporary residents cast its long shadow back, so that even in this moment, the life they had shared was already slipping away.

'I saw the bastard, too,' said James bitterly. 'They introduced me to him, when I was down at the council last month. "This is Ryc Sterling." Smile, smile. Pleased to meet you. Smug bastard.'

Zelda stared at him, a hot sweat breaking over her. No, she

thought, it wasn't him . . . But she knew it was. She remembered now how he had looked uneasy, how he had seemed to want to tell her something more. Not just that she had very beautiful eyes and that he'd like to see her again . . .

She bent her head, letting tears drop unhindered onto the old floorboards, stained with years of their dirt and spillings. What did you expect from a stranger? she asked herself.

James came to stand behind her, wrapping her in his arms. 'It's all right,' he said, as if her tears had covered his own pain and made him strong again. 'Don't cry, angel. We've still got each other.' He bent over her and kissed her gently on the top of her head. Zelda put her arms around him, grasping his strong frame, hanging on. It was true. They still had each other. That was what mattered.

'And we'll fight!' James said, breaking away and striding around the room. 'I was the toughest attorney on the block, you know. They think they're dealing with a redneck fisherman.' He laughed hoarsely. 'They'll get a bit more than they bargained for in the Nautilus Bay case. Madison versus Sea Dragon. I've won some tricky ones before—and I'll win again. You'll see.'

Chapter 2

Zelda walked slowly along the aisle of the small supermarket, her eyes scanning the familiar stacks of tinned food, jars and packets, hunting for something new. She thought back to the meal at Dana's house, with the plates full of things she had never tasted before. Weeks had gone by but the memories were still clear and strong: the deep, rich flavour of tomatoes that had been dried in the sun; the salty paste made of olives and anchovies . . . Then there was Cassie, the old woman, with her teased blonde hair; Dana, wearing black and smiling with dark red lips. And Rye, standing close to Zelda and talking of India and good red wine. But not even mentioning the sea dragons of Nautilus Bay.

Zelda frowned, pushing her thoughts aside. Reaching the jam and spreads section, she sifted through jars of peanut butter, looking for one that hadn't reached its 'use by' date. Next she selected a tin of ham and moved on towards the magazine rack. Little white labels, attached to each top right-hand corner, showed who had ordered the papers, journals and magazines. There was Doctor Ben's *Fishing World*, Mrs Carlson's *Life Magazine* and the headmaster's *National Geographic*. In a stack nearby were a dozen copies of the *Women's Weekly*. Zelda picked one up and flipped through it, stopping on a story about the breakdown of the royal marriage. There was a photograph of Princess Diana on her wedding day—Cinderella, being reborn as the princess, her young round face framed by a cloud of white gauze. In a second picture, placed beside it, she stood clutching the hands of her two small boys, looking up at the camera. Her eyes looked big and scared, her face thin and pale.

Glancing back to the first photograph—the bride in her flowing dress, with the matching flower-girls—Zelda tried to imagine the kind of wedding she and Drew would have when the time came. One thing was certain—Drew wouldn't care what she wore. Left to himself, *he'd* turn up in jeans and a denim shirt. So would James. But Lizzie would take them in hand; she'd arrange for the men's suits to be hired from Tasmania. Zelda's dress she would make herself after poring over dozens of back copies of *Today's Bride*. The box of old bridal magazines went round the island, whenever the occasion came up, along with bundles of leftover lace and ribbon. Like the baby clothes and old prams, they were passed from hand to hand—batons in a relay race that never ended.

Looking into the future, Zelda felt a twinge of misgiving. She could see it all so clearly: how she would go from being Drew's girl to Drew's wife; and then a young mum, organising play groups and helping out in the school canteen. Each month she'd place her order for her favourite magazine and count down the days to its arrival, longing for glimpses of another world, another life, that she would never take part in. But, she told herself, at least she would know where she belonged. She'd know who she was, and where she was going. And that was worth a lot.

On her way back to the jeep, Zelda paused to peer into the window of the council office. She hoped, in spite of herself, to see some relic of Rye's visit. Apparently, he had set up an office there for a week. 'He was a good bloke,' people said. 'Pity he had to do that to Jimmy's place.'

Mrs Temple, the receptionist, waved at Zelda through the glass barrier in front of her. The council secretary, Mr Jones, was standing beside her. Looking up at her movement, he lifted his hand in a small salute. They looked uneasy, thought Zelda, as if she was a victim of a new disease that might spread and touch them too. Her mouth twisted wryly. The Sea Dragon disease.

She drove home at a steady slow pace, letting the drone of the engine and the regular jolting fill her body and mind, edging out thought. As she pulled up outside their hut she noticed that James must not have been home—there was no smoke coming out of the chimney. She looked down at the box of groceries on the seat beside her. 'Get something nice,' he'd said. That meant a choice of peanuts, chocolate, dried fruit, or cheese triangles and crackers. In the end, she had bought them all and thrown in a bag of chips.

Zelda pushed at the door with her foot. It swung open a few inches, then jammed. 'Shit.' She kicked hard, using the heel of her boot, but gained nothing. Putting her box down, she squeezed her head through the gap to try and see the obstruction.

An icy panic gripped her as she found the cause. On the floor, jammed up against the door, was James. He was lying face down, his body still and crumpled. Zelda fixed her eyes on his back, searching for signs of breathing.

'Dad!' she screamed, then tried again, reaching for calm. 'Dad?' His right arm was flung out carelessly like that of a child abandoned to sleep. His other arm was curved, his hand resting tenderly against the side of his head. Beside it, on the floor, was a syringe. The plunger had been drawn out and the chamber was still half-full of clear liquid.

Zelda pulled her head back past the door, the image of the syringe with its steel-pointed needle staying with her. Words

27

circled in her head. Overdose. Drugs. Suicide. Mistake. But none of them belonged with James. It was impossible, mad, crazy. She turned, for an instant, to the safe green garden and the everyday calm of the washing line and wood pile. Through the screen of her panic they seemed oddly bright and super-real. Her breath came in short, harsh bursts, the nightmare building.

Then, spurred into action, she picked up a log of wood and hurled it ahead of her towards the kitchen window. The glass shattered, falling in long shards into the sink. Zelda swung her-self up onto the ledge and jumped down into the room. For a second she stopped, torn between hope and a gulf of nothing. Then she was on the floor, reaching for James, tears running hot down her face. She felt the oilskin, smooth and cool, then his open-weave shirt. Pulse. Pulse. Breathing. She repeated the words in her head, like a charm, as she reached round, feeling for his neck and face. Then she stopped, chilled to the core. Please, God. No . . .

He was cold. His neck was cold, and the flesh of his face. She plunged trembling fingers into his loose-jawed mouth, past hard, even teeth, to where his tongue lay wet and soft, and cool.

She edged away, scrambling backwards on her haunches, boots and hands scrabbling at the floor. She felt the wall firm and hard behind her back, and stopped there, blank and still.

Death came to her meaningless and huge, with a vicious bulk that blocked out light. She saw wombats dead on the roads, stiff and maggoty. Roos hanging like cruciforms, lashed by their long tails to the railings of the boat. Bluey, limp in her arms as they placed her in a cut-down apple box, with her bowl, her collar and her last gnawed bone. And mother dead, too. Laid out on the road—not damaged, still beautiful, mak-ing onlookers cry. Whereas James was only resting, big and heavy on the wooden floor, where daily he came stomping in. 'Hello-ooo, angel! I'm back.'

'No!' Zelda sobbed, her shoulders shaking as great gulps of pain burst up from within.

Goodbye, angel.

'No!' Her hands crowded her mouth as if to stop some vital force from escaping. 'God, send a miracle. Please . . . I can't . . . don't leave me.'

She struggled to pull James's body away from the door. Avoiding his legs, bare below his knee-length work shorts, she grabbed uselessly at fistfuls of wool and oilskin. Then she took hold of his shoulder and rolled him over—wanting to face him, as if then, somehow, she might demand that he return. For an instant, as his face swung round, she felt a surge of hope. It wasn't him. It was a stranger lying there. But then she realised that it was the swelling of his face that had formed a mask and blotted out his features. Her mind turned back to the syringe; thoughts, questions rising in her head—but she cut them off, half-formed. Sitting down beside him, she felt calmed by a sense of nightmarish unreality. She would wait, and it would end.

The sun moved high in the sky. The tin roof expanded and cracked in the heat. Flies buzzed in through the broken window and hung in small clouds, dizzy in the still air. A flock of wild geese flew past, trailing long sad cries as they headed towards the mountains.

Finally Zelda got up and left the hut, to call Doctor Ben. She rang from the airfield, refusing to speak to the men behind the counter, just staring with wide, frightened eyes as she reached past them for the phone. They listened to her call and moved to stand near her, wanting to shield her somehow. But there was nothing to be done.

Ben arrived quickly, followed by Ray Ellis, the policeman. They both rushed to James's side to feel for signs of life, as Zelda had done. After a long moment, Ben shook his head slowly. Ellis suggested that Zelda go and sit outside but she refused to leave. Instead she stood near Doctor Ben, watching as he examined the syringe, then knelt down beside James and began searching the bare skin of his legs. Gentle fingers feeling beneath the fine fuzz of hair.

'There,' he said eventually, his tone gentle and calm, 'that's it.'

For a moment Zelda felt, with another mad burst of hope, that he was about to prescribe the cure; that he would open his big black case of medicines and make everything all right again, as he had always done.

'Bee sting,' Ben said. 'Still in there—see?' He pointed to James's left calf. There was a small red lump with a tiny black spike sticking out.

'Bee—sting?' Zelda repeated his words numbly.

Ben looked up, frowning. 'You mean you didn't know?'

'Know what?'

'That he was allergic to bee stings. That he could die if he got stung.' Ben's voice rose, sharp with distress. 'I *told* him to tell you!'

Zelda stared at him, trying to make sense of his words. They seemed to come to her from some faraway place—another world.

'You're saying an allergy caused . . . this?' Ellis asked.

Ben nodded slowly. 'Severe allergic reaction. He was supposed to carry adrenalin with him at all times—specially out here. Trouble is, it's hard to administer to yourself once the reaction's begun.' He lowered his voice, but it was too late.

The words cut Zelda like a lash. She was in the supermarket, for God's sake . . . She could have saved him.

'You knew of the condition, then?' Ellis asked. He leaned over Ben's shoulder, making notes.

'Yes, it happened once before, a few years ago. Luckily he was in town and he got to me before the reaction really set in. But I told him—I warned him—he'd have died without treatment. I showed him what to do if he got stung again;

how to use the syringe.' As he spoke he kept glancing at Zelda, then looking away as if he found it too painful to face her. Little Zelda, whom he had brought into the world, right here in this room. No mother, and now no father.

'That's the way it is,' said Ellis, shaking his head. 'People don't take things seriously enough. They never do.' He bent over to examine the swelling on James's leg. 'It's hard to believe, though—just a bee sting! People get stung all the time.'

'It's not poisonous,' explained Ben. 'It's the allergic response that's fatal.' He turned to Zelda. 'It would have been pretty quick, and not painful. He'd have lost consciousness.' He straightened up as the sound of a vehicle was heard outside. 'Here's Father.' His voice lifted with relief. 'And Drew's with him.' He faced Zelda, looking suddenly tired, his hands hanging loose at his sides. 'I'm terribly sorry. I . . .' His voice trailed off into a painful quiet.

Ellis went to put his arm round Zelda's shoulders. She felt the hard shapes of his metal badges against her back. 'If there's anything I can do—or anyone at all—you know we're all here to help.'

Zelda pulled away and went to stand looking down into the dead fireplace, thinking that when those very ashes had been brightly burning logs, James had been here, with her. She saw his empty bourbon glass on the edge of the hearth and bent to take it in her hands. There on the rim were the marks of his lips. Her face was calm, but inside she was screaming, fighting for air beneath an engulfing cloud of pain and disbelief.

She heard the squeak of Drew's new boots behind her and the rustle of his denim jacket as he reached towards her. She turned and buried her face in his shoulder, breathing in the familiar smell of engine grease and wood smoke, and feeling the cloth salt-damp and soft against her cheek. Oh God, she told herself. It's real. It's true. Dad's dead. He's gone.

Drew bent his head over hers, his blond curls falling over her dark hair. He held her hard, rocking her like a baby, while his own chest heaved with deep sobs. 'Jimmy,' he said, looking up, letting his tears run back across his temples, 'Jimmy . . .'

Ellis, Ben and Father Eustace carried James to his bed and laid him there, straightening his limbs and smoothing down his hair.

'Drew'll take Zelda to his place,' said Ellis.

Ben shook his head. 'She won't leave Jim.'

There was a brief pause. The three men stood close in the small room, listening to the sound of their own breathing, the slow insistent rhythm that set them safely apart from the still figure that lay between them.

'We'll call Lizzie,' suggested Father Eustace. 'She's been like a mother to Zelda.'

'Good,' agreed Ellis. 'She can help her decide on the arrangements.'

'Yes,' said Ben. 'That's the thing to do.'

They glanced at each other before bowing their heads, observing a long moment's silence, as they always did when death brought them together.

Zelda sat on a chair in the corner of the workshop at Lindsay's service station. Not far from her, Craig and Pete were dismantling the headmaster's car. Their dog lay nearby, where the concrete floor was warmed by a patch of sun. He watched them work, mouth open and tongue flopping in the heat. Zelda gazed blankly at them.

'Zelda.' Lindsay loomed over her, holding out both hands, offering to lift her to her feet. The smell of fresh soap lay thinly over grease and petrol. Zelda looked up at him, her eyes swollen and bleary.

'You know you don't have to deal with—all this—so soon,' Lindsay said. There was a hint of reproof in his kind voice, as if it was unfair of her to come to him like this, alone and without warning, only an hour after Ellis had phoned to tell him of James's death.

Zelda gave no answer, but stood and followed him into the small office. It was jammed with paperwork and spare engine parts. There was just enough room for two chairs and a desk.

'Please—sit here.' Lindsay wiped off the seat with a rag and steered Zelda into it. He was polite and formal, treating her like a stranger, rather than the kid he'd sold petrol to for years.

Zelda looked at his bulky figure, remembering him helping her strip down the engine of the jeep only last summer.

'You're almost as good as a bloke!' he'd joked as she wriggled under the chassis. 'And you've got legs . . .'

'Normally all this is arranged by appointment,' Lindsay explained, looking down at his grease-marked overalls. 'I would've got changed.'

'It doesn't matter,' said Zelda wearily. 'I don't care.'

Lindsay paused, as if unwilling to continue. 'You know, someone else could do all this. Lizzie, or Drew. Or you can leave it all to me.'

'No, I want to do it.'

'I understand.' He reached up to a high shelf and brought down a big vinyl-covered book, like a photograph album. He opened it at the first page. There was a coloured picture of a coffin—ornate, with gold edging and gleaming red-toned wood. 'Deluxe,' he said, moving quickly on to the next page. 'This is the more popular one on the island,' he commented, showing her a new image. 'Plain, but dignified.' He looked at her closely, trying to read a response in her blank face. 'It's about middle of the range, pricewise.' He faltered suddenly. 'Look—I—there are financial things to be discussed. I really think it would be better if someone else was here. You shouldn't have to think about things like this.'

'Money doesn't matter,' said Zelda firmly. 'I don't want to decide now. I just want to see what there is.'

'Ah!' Lindsay relaxed, the folds of his red face falling into easier lines. 'Well, that's fine. Fine. Do you want anything? Drink? Smoke? Water?'

33

Zelda shook her head and took the book onto her lap. She turned the pages steadily, passing glued-in photographs of coffins, headstones, plaques and floral arrangements.

'Of course, we don't do all these lines here on the island,' added Lindsay, looking over her shoulder as if to view the range through her eyes. 'And we try to do a bit extra, a personal touch, you know like having something in the funeral that says something about the deceased. You might give some thought to that. Jimmy was American, wasn't he?' He paused as an idea came to him. 'Where was your mother laid to rest? Sometimes people like to be together.'

'Melbourne. Somewhere. But *this* is his home.'

'Yes, of course,' Lindsay nodded. 'Well, now, we'll handle everything, with Father. Ellis told me Doctor Ben's signed the death certificate, so that's straightforward. Jimmy—he's—at your place, now?'

Zelda nodded.

'I'll send someone out there right away.'

'No!' said Zelda quickly. 'No, they said I could—he could—stay till tomorrow.'

Lindsay looked at her. 'They?'

'Ellis and Father Eustace.'

'Oh well, of course he can,' he said doubtfully. 'You'll be at Drew's?'

'Probably,' she said, standing up and handing him the book. 'Thank you. I'll have a think about it.' She wanted to say, 'I'll leave it thanks', but what would she do then? There were no other choices.

Lindsay smiled, nodding sadly. 'I'll phone Drew and see how you're getting on.' He shepherded her out, past the boys who were taking a smoko, sharing the bones of a cold muttonbird with the dog.

'Hi,' they said awkwardly, without smiles.

Zelda nodded, sudden tears gathering in her eyes. She walked on, keeping her head down, until she reached the entrance to

Lindsay's washroom. Plunging inside, she bent over the basin and splashed her face with cold water. She heard the boys returning to the workshop, the chink of metal on metal as they picked up their tools. Wiping her face on her sleeve, she turned to go.

'A big bloke like Jimmy, downed by a bee! It's bloody unreal.'

'Poor bugger.'

Zelda froze, mid-step, as the voices carried through the wall.

'Tough on Zel. They reckon she'll have to move out now, too. You know, because of that sea dragon business.'

'I thought they had three years to go on the lease.'

'Yeah, but it's whichever comes first. The end of the lease. Or the death of the leaseholder.' There was a short pause. The dog whined. 'That's what I heard anyway.'

Back in the hut, Zelda noticed that a piece of cardboard had been put up to cover the broken window. It had the look of something Drew had done: neat and practical. She pictured him here, hunting around for something—anything—he could do for her. When she'd told him she wanted to be alone, he'd been hurt and puzzled. She didn't blame him—it seemed strange to her, too. It was as if she had been caught up in James's deep silence and stillness. She felt remote, cut off from everyone else.

Picking up a half-full bottle of bourbon, she took a long draught.

Then she went to stand in the doorway of James's room. Her gaze travelled slowly, from his heavy boots pressing into the soft mattress, up his bare legs, and on over the wool-padded mound of his body. There she stopped, her hands clenched by her sides, her eyes refusing to go further.

Dad? She thought in words, as if chatting at the end of the day. You should see this book Lindsay showed me! Photos of coffins, and things made of flowers . . . She began to laugh, an edge of hysteria taking hold as she imagined James swathed in oilskin and greasy wool jumpers, crammed into one of the polished boxes.

You're kidding me, she heard him say. You damn well better be!

She tried to remember if James had ever said anything about her mother's funeral or her grave. Grave. Sad lost place, like the middle of a dream. But all he'd said that she could recall was that graves meant nothing. It was memories that counted. Memories of their life—Dad and Mum, Dad and Zelda—here in the shack on the edge of Nautilus Bay. Home of the sea dragons. Heritage Protectorate, Category 2 . . .

Turning away from the bed, Zelda crossed to James's desk and began to search quickly through the drawers. Everything was filed neatly away in large manila envelopes marked with texta. She flipped past 'Fishermen's Association', 'Income Tax' and 'Zelda: Miscellaneous'. Then she found 'Sea Dragons: Correspondence and Legal'. She shook the contents out and shuffled through letters, newspaper cuttings and handwritten notes until she found a formal-looking document printed on grey government paper. She scanned the print, her eye pausing on key phrases—'rehabilitation of the area . . . removal of the existing dwelling and outbuildings . . . upon expiry of the lease . . . or the death of the leaseholder.'

Death of the leaseholder. It was true.

Zelda leaned back against the wall, closing her eyes. She saw figures swarming over the hut like ants; officers of the Conservation Department, scurrying off with pieces of roof, wall and floor. She imagined them carrying away the old toothbrushes, rulers and penknives that would be found in cracks and crevices, under eaves and below floorboards; laughing over homemade toys; reading out bits of old letters; uprooting her vegetable plants, one by one, and ripping up the herbs by the back door; prising apart the stone chimney and breaking up the hearth where she and James had sat together night after night, drawing comfort and warmth. It would not happen straight away, Zelda realised. They would wait for her to make plans and pack up and move. But the flag had fallen. Time was already ticking away.

Back in the main room she put on one of James's records, her hands trembling as she lifted the needle. Then she stood by the fireplace, resting her head on the mantelpiece as the vibrant tones of a grand aria spread through the quiet air.

For one night, she had made them all agree to leave her alone. But tomorrow it would all begin again. People. Plans. Flowers. Church. She was sure it was not what James would have wanted. It was not what she wanted either. She looked around the hut, with its handmade furniture and piles of fishing gear. The place seemed so much a part of James himself. Her eyes filled with tears. There had to be a better way of saying goodbye to it all . . .

She stood still, thinking, as the music played on. By the time it came to an end, she knew what she wanted to do. She went outside briefly and returned with a stack of plastic fish bins. Laying them out in a line down the middle of the floor, she began to move about the hut, choosing things to stow inside them. Books, tools, clothes, tackle, cups, plates . . . And special things, like the huon pine chopping board James had made with their names carved along one end: JAMES AND ZELDA 1979. A silver candlestick that stood in the middle of the table on important occasions. A paper nautilus shell, delicate and perfect, kept swathed in cotton wool. James's box of treasured, sacred maps. Lastly, she picked up an old leather writing case bound with a rose-pink ribbon. Inside was a bundle of photographs. Most of them were of Zelda—a sprinkling of captured moments that spanned her life: birthday parties, fancy dress parades, last days at school, first days at sea . . . She shuffled quickly through them, feeling a sharp jab of pain when she came across ones in which James's face appeared as well.

Near the bottom of the pile were two photographs of Ellen. Zelda knew the images by heart. They were the only reminders she had of the mother she had lost so long ago. Over the years she had searched them again and again, hoping to discover something new—something more. In one, Ellen was holding baby Zelda and smiling gently at the camera. There was something strange about the picture—a sense of stillness, as though they existed out of space and time together, like the Madonna and Child.

In the other photo Ellen stood on the island wharf, pretending to model a pair of Farmers and Graziers trousers.

'She made them look like the work of a world-class tailor,' Lizzie had once commented. 'Ellen had that special style. You just wanted to follow her around.'

She had Zelda's face, and body, and hair. And Zelda's smile.

As she looked at her mother's face, tears clouded Zelda's eyes. A dull pain grew inside her—a sense that James had betrayed her; left her to join his first love. After all, his daughter was just the reflection—the reminder—of the one who'd gone before. Zelda shoved the bundle of pictures back into the wallet, cursing as the bottom one snagged on the lining. She snatched it out. It was another familiar picture: a portrait of Ellen's father. Zelda's grandfather. A laughing man, with his daughter's bold black and white face. He had a first name—Harlan—scrawled on the back of the photo. But that was all. In the past the picture had always aroused Zelda's curiosity, but now it seemed meaningless, empty, like everything else . . .

Zelda carried each of the bins down to the jetty and stowed them away on the boat. Then she took a last look through the house, finally coming to stand beside James's bed. The evening sun reached in and touched his waxen face with a soft golden light. His hair glowed warm against his mauve-shadowed skin.

Reaching across his body, Zelda took a knife from his belt, and cut off a thick lock of his hair.

She bent over him, her tears bathing his face. 'Goodbye, Dad.' Then she turned and walked away, refusing to look back.

Outside, she took a jerry can of petrol and emptied it in a long thin line around the hut. Then she tossed the match.

Whomp!

Bright flames shot out sideways, flaring up and quickly taking hold.

Zelda stood on the edge of the beach, watching the hut burn—a flaming beacon against the sky. When there was nothing left but blackened studs and stumps, she went down to the boat and sailed out to sea.

Chapter 3

One by one Zelda pulled up the craypots and stacked them on the deck, working by the first light of dawn. She lined up the buoys, neatly coiled the ropes and emptied the buckets of bait, as if it were the end of the season. She moved with a distant sense of confusion—there was no plan, just action.

When all the pots were in, she headed for a small bay and dropped anchor in the lee of a rocky headland. Then she began the task of stowing away the fish bins full of gear she had brought from the hut. She carried them into the forward cabin and stacked them neatly on the bunk, side by side. This done, she spent a few moments checking for food or wet clothing and then prepared to close up the cabin. As she did this her gaze settled on James's map case. She took it out with her, holding it carefully between her legs as she bent to padlock the door behind her.

Back in the wheelhouse, she stood with a cup of tea, watching the sun leak over the horizon—a big golden egg yolk ready to break and spread itself across the sea. It was dead flat calm, the kind of morning James liked best. The kind that made him smile and say, 'You know, angel, I never saw a dawn until I was older than you are now. What do you think of that?' or 'I used to spend every day in an office with sealed windows and plants made of paper.' 'If you're up there, God,' he would say, lifting his face to the coloured skies, 'I thank you from the bottom of my heart.'

Zelda pictured Lizzie praying for James's soul, as she did for the old saints and martyrs. Their bodies were long gone, burned like James, or buried, but they were still alive, she said. God, thought Zelda, turning her eyes to the rising sun. Look after Dad. Please look after my Dad.

She looked down at James's map case, propped against the wall, and wanted, suddenly, to open it up—to see and touch the things that had been so precious to him. Using a penknife, she prised off the hinges at the back. She felt guilty, forcing the case open, but it couldn't stay locked forever, and James's hidden key would now be just a blob of melted metal. Inside, the top few maps lay flat and floppy from use. These were the charts for their own Furneaux Group of islands. They advised that additional local knowledge was required in order to navigate safely, and James had marked them with his own notes on rocks, seabeds, safe harbours and minor wrecks. Zelda peeled the maps back carefully, blinking away tears as the careful jottings brought back memories of shared voyages.

As she leaned to look more closely, her elbow bumped against her half-full mug. From the corner of her eye she saw it tilt. She grabbed at it and caught it just as it fell, but tipped the whole case onto the floor, scattering charts and maps. Kneeling in the small space, she gathered them up carefully. Her hand hovered over a yellowed piece of torn newspaper. It was about nothing, just a clothing sale in a shop she had never heard of. She turned it over. Shock jolted through her as she stared at an image of her own face. Her eyes, her mouth, her hair. *Her face.* There was a headline above the picture: 'LIBERTY' FINDS NEW FOLLOWING. The story itself was almost totally torn off, but just below the photo were the opening lines:

FILED FROM RISHIKESH, INDIA.
A decade after the American ballet
superstar vanished amid rumours of

Zelda read and reread the words. The picture was of Ellen, there was no doubt of that. Why did they call her Liberty? Ballet superstar! It didn't fit with what Zelda knew. And India? Was that before they came here to the island? James had never mentioned India, but then he'd rarely talked about Ellen, or the life they'd shared before she died. Whenever Zelda had asked him questions he'd become silent, sad, almost angry. The mood would last for days, spreading an ugly black pall over everything. Zelda had soon learned to leave the past alone.

It was Lizzie who'd told her most about Ellen.

'She's your mother, you should know something about her,' Zelda remembered her saying, lips pursed in thinly veiled disapproval of James. 'Ellen was a ballet dancer. A real professional dancer. She worked in New York. Danced in all the big ballets—*Swan Lake*, *Nutcracker*, *Giselle*—all of them. And things she called "modern dance ensembles" as well.'

'Was she famous?' Zelda asked.

'I don't think so,' Lizzie laughed, her eyes gentle and sad. 'But she was a beautiful dancer! I saw her once in our milking shed, dancing. She was waiting for me to come home and didn't notice me arrive. I saw something in her then, for the first time. It was as if she came alive!'

'Was I there?' asked Zelda.

'Yes,' replied Lizzie, 'I believe you were. Standing in the corner, watching with big eyes. You were just a toddler. But even you could see it. The magic in the way she moved, in her face . . .'

'Then why did she want to give it all up and come here?' asked Zelda.

'Because they had money and fun and famous friends, but they weren't happy,' Lizzie said, as if fairytales were true.

42

'You've only got to look at James to see that this is where he belongs.'

'And Ellen—Mum—was she happy here, too?'

Lizzie paused before answering. 'Not like James,' was all she'd say. 'Not the whole time.'

Zelda studied the cutting again. The photo didn't look like a posed shot—Ellen was only half-facing the camera. She appeared to be about the same age as Zelda, but it was hard to tell. Zelda read the line of text again. 'Vanished,' it said. She guessed it was referring to the time when Ellen and James left America to come to the island. (That was one thing James *would* talk about—how they left without telling anyone, burning their bridges and cutting all ties.) But 'a decade after' that time? By then Ellen was already dead. They must have vanished twice! Amid rumours of what? Zelda felt sick, a mountain of questions building over her grief. And irrationally angry, as if James had chosen to disappear and had deliberately scattered confusion behind him.

She turned the cutting over, hoping to find something—anything—more. Her eye seized on a scrap of a story, running down the edge of the advert. Only a portion of a column was there. She pieced the words together. It was a follow-up story on the shooting of Ronald Reagan. Zelda remembered it—she remembered James saying that it was a damn pity the guy was a bad shot. She'd told her teacher, who'd been shocked and outraged.

Zelda leaned back, steadying herself against the wall. It had been Miss Smith. Grade Four . . . She'd been nine years old.

And Ellen, her mother, was not dead.

Zelda knocked at Dana's front door, a loud hammering that echoed through the house. She waited for a few minutes then ran round the outside peering in through the windows. A low fire was burning in the sitting room but the house seemed empty. Reaching the window of the spare room, Zelda paused, pressing her face to the glass. The bed was strewn with silky clothes and high-heeled shoes dotted the floor. She breathed a sigh of relief—Cassie had not yet left the island.

She returned to the front doorstep and sat down to wait. Thinking back to the night of the party, she remembered how the old woman had studied her face, insisting that she had seen her before. Or someone like her. Perhaps . . .

She refused to allow herself to think further, to let her hopes build. Instead she pulled her knees up to her chest, cradled her head in her arms and tried to rest. But her stomach rumbled and pangs of hunger pierced the dull ache that seemed to fill her body, and after a short while she lifted her head and gazed around the garden. It was like a manicured wilderness, with native plants carefully arranged around lumps of the local granite. It resembled the rest of the hillside, but was somehow more perfect. Beyond the lawn was a path that led to a small pond. By leaning sideways, Zelda could just see a row of faded deckchairs set out along one side. A patch of red caught her eye. She jumped to her feet. There was a figure stretched out in the farthest chair.

'Dana?' she called out, running towards it.

As she drew close, a white-gloved hand lifted the wide brim of a straw hat, revealing owl-eyed sunglasses and red lips.

'Hello, darling! It's me!' Cassie laughed, her bright, looping laugh. 'You wouldn't recognise me under all this.' She softened her voice, confiding. 'I'm allergic to the sun. Can't let it touch me.'

Zelda stared helplessly at her. 'I need to talk to you . . .'

Something in her voice caused Cassie to remove her sunglasses and raise herself up. 'What on earth's the matter? No, don't cry.' She spoke firmly. 'You'll only mess up your face. Sit down.' She placed a cigarette in Zelda's hand, ignoring her refusal. 'It'll give you something to hold.' Then she sat perfectly calm, nodding now and then, while Zelda told her of James's death, the map box, and the torn piece of newspaper with the words that made no sense.

'Of course!' Cassie said, peering at the photograph in the newspaper cutting. 'I knew I'd seen your face before. The minute I saw you in that Dior blouse. But who'd imagine— Liberty's daughter—here, on this nowhere island?' She looked up, to study Zelda's face. 'And you dance as well!' She shook her head. 'It's just extraordinary—'

'But that wasn't her name,' Zelda broke in.

'It was her stage name,' Cassie explained. 'Like Twiggy. You know, the English model?' Zelda looked blank. 'Never mind,' Cassie went on, 'let me explain. You see, Liberty—your mother—was more than just a famous dancer. She became a celebrity.' Cassie squinted at the sky as she searched for the right words. 'I guess you could say they made her into a kind of—teen idol. In fact, that's what they called her.' Her eyes narrowed as she met Zelda's hungry gaze. 'Just marketing, you know. If they decide to do it, they just go ahead and make it real. And of course it was a long time ago. Ancient history in a fast-moving world.' She waved at the cutting. 'Even this—'

'I have to find her,' Zelda stated.

'Yes, of course you do, darling,' Cassie nodded. 'It's tricky though, if someone really *wants* to disappear. But perhaps you could start by contacting the American embassy. Send them a copy of the cutting.'

'No. I'm going to India.' Zelda's voice came out firm and loud, wiping out uncertainty. 'The place where that photo was taken. I'll begin from there.'

Cassie watched her in silence for a moment. 'I guess that's as good a plan as any,' she said finally. There was a pause while she placed a new cigarette in her holder. Then she leaned forwards and laid a gloved hand firmly on Zelda's arm. 'But listen to me now. Are you?'

'Yes.'

'Look at me. I'm not much these days, but in my time I

went from one film to another with hardly a break. I was an actress. I've travelled the world. I've got houses in places I've forgotten about.' She laughed, with a trace of bitterness. 'I'm at my peak now—with all the benefits of my experience, knowledge and skill—and I've got nowhere to use it. No-one wants to go to the movies and see an old thing up there, do they? But that's not the point. My father was a bank teller. My mother worked in a laundromat. They dreamed of owning a brick box on a decent estate—of course I've given them one—but Zelda, look at me. Do you see the daughter of a bank teller and a washerwoman? Well, do you?'

'No,' said Zelda. 'You're . . . no, I don't.'

'There.' Cassie folded her hands to signal that her point had been made. 'Go in search of your mother by all means, but don't count on what you'll find. She might help you. You might help her. You may despise each other. Just don't confuse any of this with the question of who you are.' She peered at Zelda's face. 'When did you last eat a proper meal?'

Zelda shrugged.

'Up you get. We'll eat and then decide what to do.'

Chapter 4

Zelda moved some of her things up from the boat and stayed with Dana and Cassie, feeling like someone who had gone mad and run behind enemy lines. She phoned Drew and Lizzie to tell them where she was, knowing she sounded cruel and desperate; unable to explain why it was that she wanted to be with strangers instead of friends. She agreed to phone them once a day, but refused to see them, to talk face to face. She had planned to phone Sharn as well, but changed her mind when she could think of nothing she wanted to say. The only person she saw, besides Cassie and Dana, was Ellis the cop. She sat by the pond with him while he spoke in circles, trying to avoid saying James's name, but wanting her to know that she should not have set fire to the hut. She had committed serious offences, he explained. She was just lucky that it was up to him to decide whether to take matters further. He was prepared to turn a blind eye, for everyone's sake. After all, he understood how she felt, especially with the sea dragon thing. What he didn't understand was why she was here and not down at Badger Head with Lizzie and Drew. But that was her business.

By mistake, she spoke to Rye. She was expecting the bank manager and picked up the phone.

'Zelda,' he said. 'You're still there!' As if it mattered to him. 'I am sorry—about James.'

'Who told you?' Zelda asked bluntly.

There was an odd tone in Rye's voice as he replied. 'I got a call from the Council, saying that you . . . burned down the hut.'

'Yes, I did,' said Zelda, her voice thin with fury. 'I didn't want—'

'I understand,' Rye cut in. 'They're all—we were all—surprised, that's all. Zelda, I really am sorry about James.'

'You could have said something,' Zelda burst out, in spite of herself.

'I know. I should have.'

'You knew you were going to get us kicked out!'

'It wouldn't have been for a long time, I thought,' answered Rye. 'When I made the recommendation I didn't realise your lease was so old. And of course no-one thought the other clause would be—I mean that your father would . . .' His voice trailed off. He sounded close. He could have been down at the phones by the pub, with mosquitoes biting his feet, and the smell of fish and chips lingering greasy on the torn directories. 'Look, Zelda, Dana said you're planning to go to India.'

'I *am* going. We're already organising it.'

'Oh, good.' He seemed relieved. 'You've found someone to go with then.'

'No.'

'I told Dana you can't go by yourself. It's not like a trip to Melbourne.'

'Thank you,' said Zelda coldly. 'But it's really not your business.'

'Just listen to me will you?'

'No,' said Zelda in a small voice. Damn you. 'No!' she shouted. 'Don't tell me what to do.' She meant to hang up the phone, but found herself clutching it in grim silence.

'Zelda? Are you there?' The voice was kind and worried.

'Yes,' she said. 'But I'm going. To India.'

She placed the receiver carefully down—then picked it up again, but he was gone.

A week after James's death Dana found a bunch of carnations standing in a bucket of water by the front door. Taped to the handle was an envelope with Zelda's name written carefully across the front. Dana carried the flowers and letter round to the verandah, where Zelda and Cassie were eating breakfast.

'It's for you,' Dana said, holding out the letter.

Zelda half rose as she recognised the handwriting. 'Drew . . .' A warm feeling stirred inside her. She wanted, suddenly, to jump up and run away, down the steep hillside and on across the plain towards the bay. Where Drew would be finishing his morning's dive. Probably still sorting out the boat, hosing his wetsuits. She longed for the touch of his lips on her face, his strong hands on her shoulders.

Tearing open the envelope, she spread out a single page of notepaper and began to read. *Dear Zelda, I hope this letter finds you well.*

The tone was stiff and formal, as if the need to put words into writing had forced an even greater distance between them. Zelda's eyes leapt ahead, skating over the words, grasping the contents.

Drew wrote that he had thought very carefully before sending her this letter. He understood that she wanted to go in search of her mother. But he couldn't see why there was such a rush. It didn't seem right, with James so recently gone. He was asking her not to go. She should wait until they'd had time to think. He would even consider going with her, if it was arranged properly. But—and she must see this—it wasn't right for her to go off alone. James wouldn't have wanted it. Lizzie was unhappy about it, too. It wasn't like her to act in this way. It just didn't make sense.

Zelda, he wrote, his pen pressing firmly into the paper. *I'm asking you not to go. I love you, you know that. Drew*

Zelda stared out over the garden. Neither Cassie nor Dana spoke. Silence grew around them, broken only by the sound of two small birds squabbling in the eaves.

Finally Zelda stood up and went inside. She picked up the phone in the hallway and dialled the number of the travel agent in Melbourne.

'This is Zelda Madison,' she said when her call was answered. 'My friend Cassie spoke to you a few days ago . . .'

'That's right, I remember,' a man said. 'She booked your flight to India. What can I do for you?'

'I want to go earlier. As soon as possible.' Zelda's voice surprised her. It sounded so firm and sure.

'I'll see what I can do.' There was a pause while the travel agent tapped computer keys. 'There's a seat available 15 April. That's this Friday.'

'I'll take it. Thank you.' Simple as that.

Zelda smiled into the phone with a sudden sense of relief. Now nothing could stand in her way; the journey was already begun.

'All rightie,' the travel agent continued. 'You've got everything else in order, then? Passports, vaccinations? If you were here, we'd get you to pop in.'

'It's okay, we've got it all arranged.'

Cassie had taken charge. She knew how to get everything rushed through. Darling, she'd begin. You wouldn't believe the trouble we're in here. I *do* hope you can help . . .

'It'll be bloody warm in Delhi. Better pack your sunnies!' the travel agent added. 'I was there once, I nearly died of thirst. What's wrong with good old Queensland?'

There was a short pause.

'I'm going to meet my mother,' said Zelda. She savoured the words, feeling a small knot of mixed pain and joy tightening in her throat.

'Ah,' said the man. 'That's different then. Well, it's been a pleasure, Zelda. Have a great trip.' He laughed. 'And say hello to your mum.'

Zelda replaced the phone, and stood in the hallway, alone.

Mum. Mother. Ellen.

She repeated the names, as if they would grow into something real. A face, a voice, a person. It was like the magazine advertisement that the girls at school used to look at together: a picture of a handbag lying open with its contents scattered. You were meant to try to imagine the owner by piecing together the things she carried around. Old theatre tickets, good luck charms, lipsticks, business cards, photos, tampons, condoms—whatever. Sharn used to list the things that would be found in her bag; the one she would have if she was rich, famous, far away. Zelda had a different dream. She found a mother's bag, and found herself inside. The smiling face of a precious daughter on a worn old photo with soft, ragged edges. And spread out around it were all the things that she needed to see to know who her mother had been. Only now, Zelda thought, with a surge of joy and fear, everything was changed. Now she would find the real mother. The living face behind the scattered clues.

PART TWO

Chapter 5

Remains of hotel labels hung in clusters around the handle of the case. A few were whole, with room numbers, names and crests embossed in gold, but most were just scraps of coloured card, clinging to battered eyelets. Ellen flicked them aside as she grasped the handle with both hands and swung the case up onto the bed. She leaned over to fit a small gold key into the lock, then paused, turning her head as if to catch a half-heard sound. A native goose called from the forest, the kettle hissed on the range; but that was all.

Crossing to a window, she peered out between the wind-worn branches of a she-oak. Her gaze swept across a white, curving beach, then followed the dark lines of an old jetty out to a mooring buoy. The small white shape bobbed in a quiet sea—an empty sea, with no sign of a boat.

Returning to the case, Ellen unlocked the catches and slowly lifted the lid. Strains of old perfume escaped, wafting up. She breathed them quickly away, letting wood-smoke, oilskin and the raw taint of fresh fish blood take over. Long strands of dark hair hung across her face. She pushed them back over her shoulders and began to search the case, feeling with blind fingers down through layers of neatly folded clothes. Her lips parted as she pulled out a long suede boot. She squeezed its leg and toe then tossed it aside. Moments later she found its pair. This time she reached down into the foot, burying her arm to the elbow, and eased out a narrow package wrapped in white tissue.

Over at the table she wiped a space clear of breadcrumbs and laid the package down: a small corpse, wrapped in a pale shroud. Cries of seabirds drifted in from outside, riding clear in the windless sky. Taking an end of the tissue paper, she shook the package open. A plastic doll rolled out and lay face-down on the table. A pale, slender body, naked, but crowned with a fan of long dark-red hair. A word was printed down the middle of the back—colourless script embossed in the plastic, like an old, healed scar. *Liberty.* Then in tiny letters, *pat pend.* Patent pending. Registered trademark to come.

Ellen picked up the doll, her suntanned hand contrasting with the matte peaches and cream. Slowly, she turned it over. Eye meeting painted eye. Bare dry lips against sleek red smile.

'There you are.' Ellen's voice sounded loud and hollow in the quiet room. She took the small neat head between her fingers and thumb and squeezed slowly, watching the face distort like an image in a fairground mirror. When it was thin and ugly she let it go. A startled silverfish ran out from under the tissue paper wrapping and dashed away over the table. Ellen grabbed a book and slapped it down hard, waited for a moment, then raised it slowly. The insect was squashed onto the cover, a small mess in the middle of the title: *The Antarctic Navigator.* Quickly Ellen scrubbed the book clean with her sleeve. Then she paused. There was the faint drone of an engine in the distance. She snatched up the doll, returned it to the case, tossed everything back in, then slammed it shut and pushed it under the bed.

Outside, she leaned back against the closed door and watched an old grey Land-Rover edge down the track towards her, engine whining over the steep mounds and ditches. It looked like several she had seen down at the wharf—rusted, dented, wired together, with a solid roo bar guarding the front. As it pulled up near the shack, Ellen recognised the driver by his straw hair and tanned face. She waved briefly. He lifted a single finger from the steering wheel in reply, before leaning back to yank on the handbrake.

'G'day,' he called, ducking his head sideways as he climbed out. He wiped his hands on his khaki overalls, then ran one over his hair pressing down yellow spikes. 'Ellen? I'm Tas. From down at the wharf?'

'Sure,' Ellen nodded. 'You're Lizzie's—'

'Cousin,' he broke in. He paused to pick at his teeth with his thumbnail.

Ellen looked away, her eyes following the flight of a small brown bird. It swooped low over the garden, then wheeled away, heading for the hills. The thin cry of a sandpiper drifted up from the beach.

'How's it going then?' Tas asked, nodding vaguely at the shack, the garden, the sea. 'You look pretty well settled.'

'Yes. We're fine,' answered Ellen. She looked down at the jetty again. 'Ah . . . James isn't here yet.'

'No worries.' Tas jerked his head towards the back of the Land-Rover. 'I've just got some bait. I'll leave it for him.'

Ellen followed him round. The open tray was strewn with wallaby carcasses, piled on top of one another. Random legs sticking up in the air and long velvet tails criss-crossing. Small clouds of flies hovered over glazed eyes.

'We had a cull last night,' Tas commented as he climbed onto the tray and began picking up the stiff bodies and tossing them onto the ground. He glanced at Ellen's face. 'Don't mind, do you?'

'No,' Ellen answered quickly. 'Course not.'

Tas grinned. His face pulled into fine creases like soft tanned hide. 'You can never tell. Some of the folks that blow in here—

'bloody hopeless.' He looked across to a square of bare earth at the other side of the shack. 'Vegie patch?' he asked.

'That's the plan,' Ellen nodded. 'But there's some kind of grass that runs along under the soil. I've spent weeks pulling it out.'

'Nah.' Tas shook his head. 'Waste of time. You gotta poison it once and for all. It's the only way to go.' He swung the last wallaby down. It landed with a dull thump and rolled slowly over, showing the pale fur of its belly. 'Anyway, get Jimmy onto it. You don't want to be overdoing it.' He glanced at Ellen, his eyes on her body which was draped in loose men's clothes. 'Not with the youngster on the way.'

Ellen smiled briefly.

'You wanna make sure it's a boy you know!' Tas grinned as he spoke. 'Jimmy'll be needing a deckhand before long.' He wiped his hands again and tipped back his head to scan the sky. His eyes were the same blue, like small reflecting ponds. 'There's rain coming.'

'Is there?' asked Ellen. She looked doubtful. The sun was shining strong and warm, touching the back of her neck.

'See that line of cloud?' Tas came and stood behind her, pointing over her shoulder. He smelled of gun oil and engine grease. 'No—over there.' He shook his finger towards a line of bare rock mountains that rose up steeply like battlements on the horizon. 'See how it looks soft underneath? That's rain. It'll give the tanks a good top-up. Do us all good. Anyway,' he turned back towards the Land-Rover, 'I'll be off. Tell Jimmy I'll see him down at the wharf tomorrow.'

'Sure. Thanks.' Ellen watched him back away up the track, his head craning out of the side window as he dodged the worst bumps. She waited outside, listening to the sound of the engine dwindling into the distance. Finally there was just the soft rustle of the trees, the distant slap of waves on the beach and the buzzing of busy flies.

The rain came, pounding the roof of the shack and streaming

58

off the corrugated iron in a line of thin waterfalls. Ellen rolled up a towel and laid it along the bottom of the door to hold back a creeping puddle. Then she added more wood to the fire and sat down at the table with a mug of black tea. She bent her head to breathe in the steam, hunting for the delicate fragrance of Darjeeling beneath the taint of kerosene. Her gaze travelled the room slowly. An old journey, with no surprises. Just the same dark timbers, hessian curtains, bunches of dried herbs nailed to the walls. A stack of old newspapers for starting the fire. A pile of books—mostly leather-bound and solid, but here and there a bright-spined paperback. The bare pine floor, soft with ground-in earth.

Her eyes focussed on a small mirror near the door. It was narrow and splotched with mould. She crossed to stand in front of it. She could only see one eye at a time and half a nose and mouth. Rain had sapped the daylight. The reflection was colourless and shadowy. It needs extra colour, thought Ellen, to bring it to life. A bit of eyeliner, some shadow . . . But the face was bare. Bare face. Barefaced liar. The words used to go together. But James said the opposite. Bare is good. Just be yourself. That's all I want.

Ellen leaned closer. Watching the eye grow and grow until it swallowed up everything. *That's all I want . . .*

'Huh!' She gasped, and spun round as the door burst open, crashing against the side of the shack. A tall figure lurched in, shiny with rain.

'Son of a bitch! It's damn wet out there.' Water spattered the floor as feet stamped heavy boots.

'James.' Ellen breathed his name. 'You gave me a shock.'

He turned round towards her voice. He held a large cardboard box against his chest. 'I left the boat in town and hitched,' he said, looking at Ellen through thick strands of dripping hair. 'Didn't know this was coming.' He crossed the room and put the box down on the table.

'Ah,' said Ellen wisely. 'You should keep an eye on the sky.'

James snorted. 'What would you know about sky?'

'More than you,' Ellen answered. She laughed, suddenly, tipping back her head, showing the pink roof of her mouth. 'Look at you!'

'Yeah, well anyway,' James beckoned to her, waving an arm behind him without turning round. 'C'mon over here. I got a present for you.'

Ellen went to stand beside him. A small cold feeling hatched inside her.

'Go on,' James nodded at her. 'Open it. Although it's not really for you.'

A sudden scrabbling sound came from inside.

'Oh, God,' Ellen drew back. 'If it's something to eat, kill it first.'

James laughed. He bent over, pretending to speak into the box. 'Don't listen to her. She's crazy. Who'd eat a cute little . . .' He opened the flaps of the box and lifted out a small brown puppy. 'Doggy.' He held it towards Ellen, its legs outstretched and head hanging down, eyes bulging. Ellen stepped back.

'No,' she said. 'I don't want to take it.' She folded her arms, hiding her hands. 'I'm afraid of dogs.'

'No you're not!' James looked at her in astonishment. 'Carter had that Dalmatian. You didn't mind her.'

Ellen looked at him, frowning. 'Well . . . I don't know. I just . . . perhaps it's puppies. I know, it's silly.' She gave a short laugh.

James pushed the dog at her again. 'Go on. Have a hold.'

Ellen took the puppy, closing her hands over its warm, damp body. She could feel the rib cage, a flimsy frame beneath its loose skin. The heart beating. You could crush it, she thought, without even wanting to. She held it away from herself. 'Where did you get it?'

'*Him*. I bought him from old Joe at the milk bar. He's a Queensland Heeler, called Bluey, after his dad. I'm going to train him up, ready for the baby.' Ellen put the puppy down on the floor and stepped back. He stood stiffly, afraid to move in the wide space. 'Joe was all for giving me an old water tank for a kennel. I said he'd sleep inside with us.' James grabbed a tea towel from the table as he spoke and used it to rub dry his hair. 'Do you know what he said? "Bloody hippies. You don't know what's what." For a minute there I thought he was going to ask for him back!' James scooped up the puppy. 'Come here, Bluey. Hey, little fella.' He stroked the smooth brown head, running his hands out to the tips of the ears. He looked across to Ellen. His eyes were warm and bright, his face still streaked with rain. 'We'll be a real family, Ell. Ma, Pa, dog—and then, the baby.'

Ellen went to stand by the window, looking out into the bush through a blur of rain. 'Tas came before, with some dead wallabies. They're out by the tank.'

'Good. I could do with some more bait. What else?'

'What?'

'What else happened today?'

'Nothing much.' She paused, then turned to face him. 'I went to see Ben. Doctor Ben.'

'Is everything okay?' James put the puppy down quickly and moved towards her.

'Yes, yes. Fine. But I was in the waiting room, and you know how Ben's wife gets her magazines from Melbourne—'

'Marian,' interrupted James. 'Why can't you learn people's names?'

'Well anyway, there was an old copy of *Teen*—must be from about two years ago. Just after Liberty started. She was on the cover. There were two girls from the high school looking at it.'

'And what happened?' James asked urgently.

'It's all right,' said Ellen flatly. 'They didn't recognise me. Not at all. I mean, it was so weird. They were talking about Liberty. You know, just saying she'd look good with short hair or something. And then one of them looked up, straight at me.' Ellen let out a high, thin laugh. 'She asked me the time.'

'Are you sure?' asked James.

'Yes.'

'Shit . . . What about the magazine?'

'I took it,' said Ellen. 'I burnt it.'

'Good.'

The fire crackled and spat in the quiet. 'Do I look—I mean, don't I look at all . . .?' Ellen faltered.

'I guess not!' answered James happily. 'But then who would ever think of you being here? The end of the world, next stop Antarctica. And a mother-to-be as well.' He came over and put his arm round her shoulder. 'You're free! Today proves it.' He strode across to a cupboard, stepping over the puppy. 'I think that's worth celebrating!' He pulled out a bottle of champagne and blew off the dust. 'No ice-bucket I'm afraid, ma'am.' He looked back over his shoulder. 'Oh—while I remember—I saw Dave at the milk bar. He said some of the girls are getting together to have a function for you. Someone'll be over tomorrow to tell you.'

'What are you talking about?' asked Ellen.

James shrugged. 'Dunno. Something called a shower—baby shower. Some kind of party, I guess.' He began tearing the foil cover off the cork.

'You're kidding! Well, I'm not going.'

'Sure you will. How can you say no?'

'Watch me.'

James put down the bottle and turned towards her, his face hardening. 'No. You *will* go. I'm not having you upset the whole place. We live here. Our child's going to grow up here.' He spread his hands helplessly. 'You have to get used to the idea that you're not special any more. You're just going to be an ordinary young mother, the same as they are.' His voice softened. 'It's what we wanted, Ellen. What we both wanted. Remember?' He waited for a response. 'Do you remember?' he persisted.

Ellen nodded.

'What?' asked James. 'Tell me what you remember.'

'We both wanted to get away, to make a new life together. Where we could just be ourselves.' Her voice was flat, like a child reciting a grown-up poem, only half understood.

'That's right,' said James. 'That's why we're here.'

Ellen bent over from the waist, stretching out her lower back. Her face was hidden by her hair. 'It's not that I think I'm special,' she said slowly, 'or better than them. It's just . . .' Silence grew after her words, stretching on and on.

'Well, it's not a big deal anyway,' James said finally. 'You just go along to the party and be nice. You're good at that kind of thing. Who knows, you might even enjoy it.' He got two glasses out of the cupboard and dusted them with the untucked end of his shirt. He whistled through his teeth, as he held them up to the light to look for smears. 'By the way,' he said suddenly, 'did Tas stay?'

'What?'

'Did Tas stay? Did you ask him in for a drink?'

'No,' Ellen answered quickly. 'I didn't ask him. You weren't here, and I thought you wouldn't want me to.'

James nodded. 'Yeah, I know. But with Tas—I don't want him to think we're not friendly.' He went on preparing to open the champagne.

Ellen looked at him without answering. The puppy came and sniffed at her feet. Her toes curled under, away from the wet whiskery probing. The puppy was warm and damp. She shut her eyes. A close, animal smell rose up to her and snagged like a scream in her throat.

The cork popped and shot against the roof. The puppy yelped in fear and ran towards the door.

James held up a glass. 'Here's cheers,' he said with a grin. 'To liberty . . .'

Chapter 6

The headlights swung long beams into the dark as the jeep jolted along the track. Ellen drove leaning forward, gripping the steering wheel for balance and peering ahead, trying to pick the best path between rocks, ruts and sunken tyre tracks. Suddenly a dark shape lunged out, close in front of the bonnet. She braked but had no time to swerve. A dull thud jolted the chassis, then something bumped underneath. A tremor of shock ran through Ellen's body.

'Oh, Jesus,' she moaned. Not again. She threw the jeep into reverse and backed until the headlights picked up the twitching body of a young kangaroo. Dark blood splashed the chalky gravel road. As she watched, the animal began to move, clawing its way towards the bush, dragging limp hind legs and tail. Ellen's hands stiffened on the wheel. She had to finish it off, she knew, or it would die a slow and painful death, ants and crows beginning their work too soon.

She fixed her eyes into the distance and drove straight ahead. This time the tyres met a low, yielding bump. She braked and went over it again, forwards and backwards without stopping—till the headlights showed just a red, furry mess, spread out on the road.

Ellen rested her head on the steering wheel. This is life. Real life. That's what James would have said. After all, you don't see squished raccoons on Fifth Avenue. Why? Because they've gone, disappeared. You see? The city is a dead place.

She drove slowly on. Up ahead, the lights of Lizzie's house broke through the tea-tree thicket; bright yellow stars, hanging close to the ground.

Ellen and Lizzie had met only once before, down at the fish factory. James was weighing in the week's crayfish and Tas came over to check his tally. 'Not bad for a city slicker,' he said.

'I'll get there, don't you worry,' answered James with a grin.

'Hoi!' Tas called out across the wharf. A figure looked up and came over. Close up, Ellen saw that it was a woman. Like all the islanders, her face was sunburned, her skin hardened by wind and salt, but she still looked young. Late twenties, Ellen guessed, or early thirties.

'Hi.' The woman greeted them all with an easy smile.

'My cousin, Lizzie,' said Tas. 'This is Jimmy and . . . Helen? From America.'

'I've heard all about you, of course,' said Lizzie. 'You bought the *Humble Bee*.' She nodded down towards the line of tethered crayboats.

'We'll leave you two to have a natter, then,' said Tas.

He led James off towards the office, leaving the women alone together. For a moment, they eyed one another in silence, like children caught by chance in the same sandpit.

Ellen smiled, polite but distant, as she glanced over Lizzie's face and clothes. Carter, she found herself thinking, would not like her. He'd say she was a waste of a woman. Good bones, good teeth and skin, nice eyes and lips; but overweight, with no make-up, ragged eyebrows and untrimmed hair. On top of that, she wore men's trousers, gathered in at the waist with a piece of rope, and her stained jumper had snagged threads and frayed cuffs. But the outfit suited her, strangely. So did the raw-edged cloth that hung like a cravat around her neck.

'Well that's Tas for you!' Lizzie said finally, and shrugged. 'God, I'm a mess! I've just come in from the boat.'

'Me, too,' said Ellen. 'I went out with James . . .' Her voice trailed off as she felt Lizzie's eyes on her velvet coat and silk trousers. 'I've only got these things I brought with me,' she said apologetically. 'I don't know—where do you buy clothes here? Work clothes.'

'You mean like these?' asked Lizzie. 'You don't. You pinch them from your old man.' She laughed. 'But originally they come from Farmers and Graziers.' She nodded in the direction of a short line of shops. 'I can show you if you like. Now, I mean. I'm getting a ride with Tas, and they'll be yakking in there for ages.'

'Well . . . thanks,' said Ellen. 'But I don't have any cash on me.'

'No worries, they'll let you take it on credit,' said Lizzie.

'You mean American Express?'

Lizzie giggled. 'I don't think so. No, they'll just write it down. Your old man can pay for it next time he comes in.'

They headed up the road, passing the council chambers and an old Memorial Hall.

Lizzie glanced sideways at Ellen. 'First thing, we should get you a hat. And you want to wear something on your neck. It'll fry.'

Ellen ran her hand over the back of her neck. 'Usually I have my hair out,' she said.

'So when are you due?' Lizzie asked. 'It's your first, isn't it?'

Ellen nodded. 'Five months.'

'I was sick as a dog with my first. The second was a breeze, though, till the last month, when she stuck her foot into the nerve at the top of my leg. I couldn't move!'

'I've been fine,' Ellen answered quickly. 'I barely notice I'm pregnant.' But the road wound up steeply, and soon she had to stop and rest. Lizzie waited beside her. They looked back past the wharf and out to sea, where two small islands nestled low on the horizon.

'I heard you built a place in Nautilus Bay,' Lizzie said. 'We used to camp up there, a whole pack of us kids. Those were the days,' she added cheerfully. 'Now it's all hard yakka!'

Ellen glanced sideways at her face. Lizzie looked tired, but relaxed. Someone who knew there would always be too much to do, but that there were ways and means of winning out.

'I heard you were a dancer,' said Lizzie as they began walking again.

Ellen made herself keep moving steadily on. 'Yes.'

Lizzie sighed. 'That was my dream when I was at high school. Pointy shoes and tutus. I know it's hard work really. Were you famous?' She smiled, joking.

'No,' replied Ellen. It was easy. She kept going. 'A few make it, of course. They get the lead roles, they get to travel. But I was just one of those little dancers—you know the ones, they all look the same. They dance on the edge of the stage, or right at the back. It was quite boring in the end.'

'Not as boring as splitting scallops,' said Lizzie.

'I guess not,' answered Ellen. There was a short silence. Their eyes met and they both began to laugh. They laughed long and easily together, as if they were friends.

Lizzie's house stood on the crest of a low hill, surrounded by the dark shapes of old cars. The smell of wet sheep dung rose up from the ground. A single light marked the back door. Ellen walked towards it, pulling her jumper down to cover her body, running her tongue nervously over dry lips. Near the door, she noticed a strip of clear window at the edge of a drawn blind. She moved quickly to peer inside.

Facing her was a wide bottom pressed into a pair of men's suit trousers, with ridges of underwear showing through. Beyond was a foldable card table loaded with food set out on mismatched plates. Cakes, slices, little pies, sandwiches, scones. In the middle was a cut glass ashtray, half full of bent butts. The rest of the room was crowded with women, seated on chairs and cushions—smoking, talking, but mostly laughing. Ellen ran her eyes over the faces. There was almost no-one she recognised. She felt her mind running on, taking its old track. They won't like me. They won't want me. Quickly she reached for the cure: the face of her old friend, wrinkled with sun and age. Eildon. She carried his face, his smile, like a talisman; something to bring out and hold up against the dark. But still she didn't want to go into the house.

She glanced back towards the jeep. She could leave, say she was ill. But James wouldn't accept it. He would be furious. She reached back and pulled the band from her hair. The dark locks fell in a soft and heavy mantle onto her shoulders. She walked slowly towards the door. She would have to go in— she had no choice. There was always someone hovering behind her. Madame Katrinka, with her rough old hands and voice worn thin with swallowed pride. Carter, with his lists of parties. (You *will* go, you *will* wear a Young Design, you *will* pause and smile.) And James . . .

She jumped at the creak-crash of the flyscreen being flung back. Lizzie appeared in the doorway. 'Ellen! We were wondering where you were. Come in!' She touched Ellen on the shoulder and drew her inside. 'I hope you don't mind all this. It's something we always do, and I thought—Tas said so, too— it would be a good way for you to meet some of the girls. Once the baby comes you'll need a hand, for sure—even if it's just to pass you a sherry!'

Ellen followed Lizzie into the lounge, shielded by her for a moment, then laid bare to the room. Talking stopped, cigarettes poised midway between mouth and ashtray. Eyes slid from her face to her body and back.

'Everyone, this is Ellen,' Lizzie said, eyeing her as if she, too, were taking her first look. 'You won't remember them all, but anyway—this is Pauline, who you've met at the post office; Susie you know; Kaye, the new schoolteacher; Mavis; and

Elsie—Tasman's mum; then my other auntie, Joanie; and Jan from Stacky's Marsh . . .' The list went on.

Ellen smiled, letting her gaze settle lightly but carefully on each new face.

'Now, we've kept a spot for you.' Lizzie pointed Ellen towards a high-backed armchair that was set apart like a throne, just in reach of the table of food. Ellen took her place. Glancing around, she noticed to her dismay that each guest had brought a small package. Wrapped in pastel tissue—pale yellow, green, cream or plain white—they dotted the room like a flock of nestling birds, perched on laps, or tucked away under chairs.

'We'll have the pressies now,' said Lizzie, 'in case some people have to leave early.'

'Oldest first!' A gravelly voice came from Ellen's side. 'Here you are, love.'

Elsie passed the first present over, smiling with her son's grey-blue eyes. The tissue wrapping was soft and crinkled as if it had been used several times before. With clumsy fingers, Ellen uncovered a tiny, finely knitted cardigan in soft yellow.

'It's beautiful,' she said, turning to Elsie. 'Did you knit it?' She tried not to glance down at the woman's big rough hands.

'Course, love. There's one or two more left in me as well!'

Everyone laughed. Ellen looked up uncertainly, but Elsie was beaming.

'Lashed out on the colours too—that's not baby yellow.'

'Hold it up,' said Lizzie.

From around the room, there were words of admiration. Without warning the door opened, letting in a man's head and shoulders.

'G'day, girls,' the man said with a grin. 'I don't need to ask where Mick is then . . . down the pub?'

'That's right,' Lizzie answered. 'He's not allowed back before closing time either.'

'You're a tough lady.' The man glanced around the room, frankly checking who was who. His eyes met Ellen's. She jerked her gaze away, but sensed him still looking, curious. Just like the nameless waiters, taxi drivers, delivery men; even doctors called out at night. Looking in from the outside, they always saw that she didn't belong. She could tell by the look in their eyes.

'Off you go, then,' said Lizzie firmly. And the man retreated, shutting the door behind him.

Someone reached for Elsie's cardigan and passed it round. Then the next package came forward. Two white knitted singlets with cream ribbons. Then a smocked nightdress, knitted hat, crocheted booties. Ellen smiled over each one, and tried to find new things to say. By the side of her chair, a pile of tiny clothes grew. Then the teacher handed over her present, wrapped in bright paper.

'*Wind in the Willows*,' she said, as Ellen uncovered a book. 'You probably had it yourself, as a child?'

'Yes,' answered Ellen, vaguely. She flipped quickly through it. 'The pictures are great.'

When she looked up, Lizzie's other aunt was standing over her, offering a large bundle. Inside was a set of three matching jumpers.

'You shouldn't have,' Ellen said, as she held them up one at a time. 'So much work.' Hours bent over needles and hooks and wool. For a stranger, for her . . .

'A baby's a precious thing,' the old woman said, firmly. 'And the first one only comes once.' She studied Ellen. Faded old eyes, hooded with wrinkles. 'If it's not worth some effort, then I don't know what is.'

'Everyone finished?' Lizzie scanned the room. 'Okay, now it's my turn. I couldn't find any paper, so . . .' She took a bundle of knitting from the mantelpiece and knelt with it on the floor in front of Ellen's chair. She bent over, carefully unfolding an all-in-one suit. There were legs with feet joined onto a button-through body, long sleeves with mittens on the end, and even a rounded hood. It made up the shape of a whole baby, lying there as if its owner had just wriggled away, casting off its skin like a snake.

Seconds passed as Ellen stared down at it. It was so small, only a little longer than her foot. But it stood out, pale against the brown rug. The empty hood called up the image of a face. A little boy, with the eyes of James and a small happy mouth. Ellen smiled.

'D'you like it?' Lizzie asked. 'I saw it in a magazine and made up a pattern. One leg turned out a bit wrong.'

'It's—like a baby.' Ellen said, almost without thinking.

Everyone laughed. A gentle, friendly sound, growing around her. It lingered for a time, then bubbled away into a hum of talk as people turned back to their drinks and conversations.

A plate of buttered scones appeared in front of Ellen and she took one.

'Pumpkin scones,' noted Elsie.

'Have another,' said someone else. 'You're eating for two, remember.'

The room was warm and noisy, the smell of heating sausage rolls mixing with smoke and perfume. Lizzie brought Ellen a cup of chamomile tea which she said would help her relax. Ellen asked for a cushion to support her back, and leaned her head on her hand.

'That's the idea, love,' said Elsie. 'Have a good rest now, while you can.' She turned to Lizzie. 'She'll need the whole bit then—with no family around.' Leaning close, she patted Ellen's shoulder. 'What are you going to do, dear, about a cot, pram, nappies and everything?'

Ellen looked at her blankly.

'She might want to buy her own,' said Lizzie quickly.

'That'd be a waste!' Elsie objected. 'There's plenty of stuff around. Bags of clothes. Some are a bit stained and that, but they're still good. I saw the youngest Roberts boy yesterday. He was wearing a jumper I first knitted for Bobbie. Then Sally had it. Then it went all down the line at Brownings. Must be six or seven kids have worn that little jumper.' She leaned round to look into Ellen's face. 'I think that's rather nice, don't you?'

'Yes,' said Ellen. She nodded, half to herself. It was—nice. It was a comforting thought. Safe, solid. Giving you somewhere firm to stand.

'Look at her,' said Elsie. 'There's nothing more beautiful than a mother-to-be.' She patted Ellen's hand, slowly, like a priest giving a blessing.

Ellen smiled, feeling suddenly full and warm and strong. James was right. She would be a mother. Ordinary, busy, tired but happy—just like anyone else. In the hut on the edge of the sea she would raise her children, handing out milk and cookies after school, mending torn trousers and tending scratched knees. She would love them like a lioness, brave and fierce. And they would love her back. Everything would be all right, after all.

Chapter 7

Ellen looked down at the sleeping child, her eyes wandering over cheeks rosy with warmth and dark hair curling against ivory skin. Tiny mauve veins shadowed the eyelids. The wet mouth was slightly parted. The chest rose and fell, gently and evenly.

'Zelda,' Ellen called softly, 'time to get up now.'

Zelda stirred and rolled over, without waking. Ellen traced the shape of the child's body, curled up beneath the blanket. It looked disconcertingly small, stranded in the big half-empty bed.

Glancing around the tiny alcove bedroom, Ellen remembered how the first little cot had stood in the corner—no bigger than an apple crate and surrounded by ragged piles of nappies, clothes and bunny rugs. It was strange, she thought, how the years that had passed since then felt so short, and so long, at the same time.

She looked at her watch. 'Come on, angel,' she repeated. 'You have to wake up now.' Leaning down, she grasped the thin shoulders and shook them. Eyes opened. Ellen's own eyes, looking up at her. 'Hello, beautiful. Smile for me?'

Zelda stretched sleepily, screwing up her face, flexing arms and hands. Then she grinned widely and sat up.

'Good girl,' Ellen smiled. 'Come here, then. We'll put this on you.' She held out a thick jumper.

'No.' Zelda shook her head. 'I don't want it on. It's scratchy.'

'You'll be cold without it. Come on.' Ellen pulled the jumper quickly over the child's head.

Zelda pouted, but pushed her arms into the sleeves. 'Where's my tracksuit?'

'Wet,' answered Ellen. 'You wore it to the beach, remember?' She stood back to let Zelda climb out.

Bluey padded across from the front door, tail wagging. He pushed past Ellen to greet Zelda with a lick on the face. Zelda laughed, and pulled at his ears.

'Out, Bluey,' Ellen grabbed hold of the scarf tied around his neck and tried to pull him back towards the door. He stuck his legs out in front and refused to move his feet. 'Get out!' Ellen dragged him along, his claws scoring the floorboards. As she shut the door behind him, Zelda came towards her riding a small tricycle, a hand-me-down from one of Lizzie's boys.

'Not inside, Zelda,' Ellen said, 'you know that.'

Zelda rode on, looking back over her shoulder.

'Take it outside,' Ellen said evenly.

Zelda did another lap of the room. As she passed her, Ellen gave the bike a sharp push towards the door. The bike lurched forward, then tipped, throwing Zelda off to the side. Her head whipped against the sharp corner of the wood box. The next moment she was sprawled on the floor, legs still tangled in the wheels of the bike. Her mouth opened wide, tongue trembling as she gathered breath. Ellen stood motionless, caught in the silence. Then the scream began—a high, piercing cry. Outside, Bluey began barking. Then the door scraped open and James struggled in carrying two craypots and an armful of fishing tackle.

'What's happened?' He put down his load and crossed the

room. 'Zelda!' Dropping to his knees, he picked the child up and felt gently through her hair. His hand came away sticky and red with blood.

'God, she's bleeding. Get me a towel!' James looked around for Ellen and found her standing behind him. 'For godsakes, Ellen,' he called out over Zelda's screams, 'just get anything.'

Ellen snatched a sheet from Zelda's bed. James took it from her and pressed it in a wad against the side of the child's head. She was still screaming, the sound riding over his calm voice, 'It's all right, Zelda, Daddy's here, it's all right.'

Ellen hung back, her hands useless at her sides.

'Bring the jeep round,' James ordered. 'It looks deep. We'll have to take her down to Ben.'

In the car the cries died down to small, gasping sobs. Ellen held Zelda cradled against her shoulder, one hand holding the bloody sheet in place. She gazed straight in front of her through the windscreen. The winter landscape was flat and dull. Floodwaters covered low-lying paddocks, leaving grey sheep huddled together around gates and fences.

'What was she doing?' James asked, keeping his eyes on the track as he drove fast, while picking the smoothest path.

There was a short silence, broken by the sound of the engine and Zelda's whimpering.

'I don't know,' said Ellen flatly. 'I didn't see properly. She fell off the bike.'

'You should watch her more carefully,' James frowned, glancing at Zelda.

Ellen said nothing. Her hand patted Zelda's back with a steady movement. Zelda stopped crying and put her thumb in her mouth.

They reached the surgery, an extra room built onto the side of Doctor Ben's house. James took Zelda in his arms, and carried her inside. Ellen followed slowly.

I should be there, she thought. Bending over Zelda, holding

her hands. And Zelda reaching out for me, wanting me. Only me. No-one else would do. Only mother.

When she entered the waiting room, James and Zelda were not there. Marian, Ben's wife, was sitting at the desk.

'They've gone straight in,' she said. There were several people seated in the chairs. Ellen felt them watching her.

'I know how you feel,' Marian leaned forward and spoke in a low, kind voice. 'Don't blame yourself—kids at that age are a walking disaster! If you knew how many cuts and bruises we see in here . . .'

Ellen nodded mutely.

Marian pointed towards a closed door marked Treatment Room. 'Go on in.'

The child's screams met Ellen as she opened the door. She stopped midstep. They were different cries, edged with a note of fear on top of pain. She felt herself pulling away, inside. Her feet unmoving, but the screams sucking her away. Ben turned towards her, an empty syringe in his hand.

'That's the worst over,' he said. 'She won't feel a thing.'

Ellen nodded blankly. Panic rose like bile in her throat. In her mind, she saw again Ben's hand swinging round. Long, shiny needle poised in the air. Disinfectant smell. She rushed to the sink and vomited.

'I'm sorry,' she said. 'I don't know . . .' She raised her hand to wipe her mouth and kept it there, squashed against her lips. The air seemed bright, all the lines and edges of the room too sharp. Ben, Zelda, James—figures cut out of glass and edged with light. And the wall, so cold and hard behind her, pressing the bones of her back.

James watched her silently over Zelda's face.

'It's just a few stitches,' Ben explained with careful calm. 'You don't need to watch.' He opened the door and beckoned to Marian, who entered with quick steps. 'Why don't you take Ellen inside and give her a cup of tea?'

Marian led the way across to another door which opened

into the house, the neat, white surgery giving way to the burnished tones of polished timber and oriental rugs. The door closed behind them, snuffing out the cries.

'Come into the kitchen.' Marian opened another door to a room lit with morning sun. A faint smell of baking lingered in the air. She went ahead and began boiling the kettle and setting out cups and saucers.

'Sit down there and take it easy.' She glanced at Ellen's face. 'Zelda'll be fine. Just a few stitches . . .' She talked on, working against Ellen's silence. 'A couple of hours and she'll be running around happy as anything.'

Ellen leaned back in her chair. She felt dazed, as if a migraine had just gone, leaving the memory of pain still shimmering. She tried to study the lines of copper pans hung on the wall, the checked curtains, handpainted crockery. It was a magazine kitchen, borrowed from another place, The only hint of the island was a fishing reel perched on a shelf.

'I'm sorry,' Ellen smiled, aware that Marian was looking at her, waiting. 'I missed that.'

'Oh, it doesn't matter. I was just saying, you've got no family here, have you?

'No,' Ellen answered.

'They're all in America?' Marian prompted.

Ellen looked out through French windows at a courtyard garden. 'James's folks are in Washington DC,' she said, vaguely. 'I don't have any relatives.' There was a short silence. No sound came from the surgery.

'I'm sorry.' Marian handed her a mug of tea. 'I made it myself,' she said.

Ellen tasted the tea and smiled.

'I mean the mug,' Marian added.

'It's very nice.' Ellen shifted in her seat, trying to swallow the hot tea quickly.

'My new magazines have just arrived.' Marian pointed to a pile on the end of the table. She smiled bleakly. 'I try to keep up with things, though I don't know why I bother. Sometimes I think Ben's decided to stay here forever.'

'It's a beautiful place,' said Ellen.

Marian snorted. 'If you like mountains, beaches and paddocks full of sheep. I'd rather have galleries, cafes, good shopping, music.' She paused, then launched on. 'Ben says you were a dancer. Don't you miss it all? The stage, the excitement? Interesting people?'

'Hmmm.' In the garden, a black cat scratched in the earth.

'Have you met anyone?' asked Marian. She leaned forward, waiting. 'Anyone I'd have heard of? Tell me!'

'Ah—well, you know,' Ellen frowned. 'I don't really remember . . .'

The phone rang, drawing Marian away. Ellen got up and put her cup on the draining board. Glancing out through the kitchen window, she caught sight of James standing in the garden. He held Zelda in his arms, her face nestled against his chest. Tall shrubs and trailing vines surrounded them and bright winter sunshine lay on their shoulders. It reminded Ellen of a painting in the dining room at the dancing academy, an old framed print left behind by the nuns who had lived in the building before. It showed Jesus, with long hair and hippy sandals, holding a child in his arms—a neat little girl with golden curls and straight English clothes. 'Suffer the little children,' it said underneath, 'to come unto me.'

Zelda stirred in James's arms and he bent his head to kiss the side of her face. Ellen watched them. They belonged together, belonged here. Small Zelda, browned by sun and wind, grown sturdy on muttonbird, fresh fish, farm milk. And James, tall and strong, with toughened hands. He stood with his feet apart, as if the earth was the deck of his boat, buoyed by the sea.

That night Ellen was sitting on the other side of the fireplace, watching James read Zelda a bedtime story. The tears were long gone and the stitched wound hidden by hanging hair.

'And the littlest bear said, "Who's been sleeping in my bed?"' James read in a high baby voice.

Zelda grinned, looking across to Ellen. 'Daddy's a littlest bear!'

James read on, his head resting on Zelda's. His sandy hair, grown long, lay in pale strands over her dark hair. Ellen studied their faces. She has my hair, she thought, my eyes, my mouth, my nose. There is nothing of James. She's just like me.

'And then what happened?' James asked Zelda, as he reached the end of the book.

'She lived happily ever after,' said Zelda.

James laughed. 'Just like us. Now go kiss Ellen.'

Zelda came over and laid her head in Ellen's lap. 'Sorry, Ellen,' she said.

Ellen looked up. 'What?'

'It was a bad bike, being inside.'

Night birds called, breaking the silence. Ellen glanced at James. 'It was an accident. It wasn't your fault.' She stroked Zelda's hair, drawing it away from her neck.

'Goodnight, Mummy.'

'Goodnight, baby.' Ellen took Zelda gently in her arms and held her close, drawing in her clean, warm smell. 'I love you, angel.'

James leaned over, touching Ellen's cheek with one hand while he reached under the bedclothes with the other. He found her breast, small and soft, then traced a wandering line slowly down her body.

'Wait—you're bending my book,' Ellen turned away and half sat up.

'Who cares?' James pulled her back down. 'The world is full of books.' He lay over her, flattening her breasts, one knee trying to push between her legs.

'Not a chance,' Ellen laughed. Her thigh and calf muscles, flexed, were taut and hard.

James took hold of her by one shoulder and a leg, and rolled her over onto her front. Then he lay on top of her, their bodies touching from shoulder to foot.

'Close the curtain.' Ellen spoke over her shoulder.

'What?'

'Well turn the light out then.'

'Holy cow!' James rolled off her and reached for the light switch. 'D'you think people come out here and wait in the dark hoping for a show?'

Ellen said nothing, but turned over and lay still. Firelight painted her skin a soft rose. She could hear Zelda's gentle breathing from the other side of the curtain.

James hovered over her, looking down at her pale, slender body, almost luminous in the half-light. Her eyes were big and dark. 'You're still just a little girl,' he said, leaning down and kissing her lightly on the nose. 'I bet you've hardly changed. I can see you in pigtails, with bands on your teeth.'

'I'm not a little girl,' Ellen protested. 'I'm twenty-six years old. I have a three-and-a-half year old daughter.'

'But did you? Have bands?' James asked. 'I always thought your teeth were too perfect.'

Ellen frowned up at him. 'No.'

'Are you sure?' asked James, mocking.

'Yes. I'm sure.'

'Ladies and gentlemen—it's a world first!' said James. 'Ellen remembers!' A shadow of irritation crossed his face. 'I don't know why you're so secretive. Sometimes I wonder if there's another whole part of you that you keep hidden. Another life.' He laughed shortly. 'Perhaps you're wanted by the CIA. But then you're a bit young for that.'

'I *have* got a secret life,' said Ellen, with a smile. 'I was rich and famous, remember? Beautiful, sexy . . .'

'Oh yeah, that's funny,' said James. 'Sexy Ellen, the teenage sex symbol. Smouldering eyes. Come and get me. Great stuff. Then you just lie there.'

Ellen pulled out from under him and edged away to the far side of the bed. She stared at the wall and swallowed, a loud sound in her head. 'When I used to be more—well—do more,' she said finally, 'you didn't like it. You always said I was acting.'

'You were!' said James. 'I could almost hear the director coaching your lines!'

'See? I can't win with you.' Ellen closed her eyes in the long silence, feeling suddenly old and tired.

'Hey, don't fight with me, Ell,' James said at last. 'Come on. Come here.' He pulled her over to him and began to stroke her hair. His hand ran down to her shoulder and crept round to close on her breast.

A possum scrabbled on the roof, waking Bluey, who ran to the door and whined.

Ellen stiffened.

'S'all right, just possums,' James said.

Ellen stared up into the dark. 'It's not that,' she said eventually. 'It's the dog whining, it's—' she searched for the right word, knowing how it would rise and hang in the darkness between them. She tried laughing instead. 'It's like waiting at the dentist.'

'That's crazy, Ellen.' James turned away, hunching the blankets over his shoulders. 'How're you going to tell Zelda to be a brave girl? You've got to learn to wind down. Just take it easy, hey?'

Ellen sensed him listening, waiting for some response. She breathed out a small light laugh.

It seemed to be enough. He pulled the blankets closer and relaxed with a sigh. 'Sweet dreams, then . . .'

Ellen looked at the dark mound of James's body beside her and listened to the gentle, even rhythm of his breathing. She imagined his dreams, calm and smooth. He never cried out in his sleep. He was never afraid . . . She thought back to the surgery. The sound of Zelda's fear. The hand. The needle. Then the brightness, as if she was becoming more alive. Everything more real than real. It reminded her of something.

Carter's voice came to her, clear and strong, cutting into a dazzling New York night. 'I don't like that light in your eyes.' Then he was searching through her bag, finding the tabs—little bits of blotting paper wrapped in a square of foil.

'Street score, too!' Carter shook his head. 'I'm your agent, not your mother. And I have only two rules. You don't miss appointments and you don't do drugs. Get in the car.'

The long black car with soft deep seats. You could lie there forever. And never have to go home.

Tears welled in Ellen's eyes, gathering in the corners and running back across her temples and into her hair. It was years since she'd taken acid, or anything else. She thought slowly, aware of her brain working, tracking words like mice in a maze.

There is something wrong with me. Something inside. Perhaps I'll go mad. Like Sister Annunciata. Locked up in the gardener's cottage, muttering through the days, only coming out to put her meal trays on the doorstep. Poor old Annunciata, the last of the nuns. No husband, no children to love her. Just the thin gold band on her finger. Just God.

Ellen lay still, cold fear spreading through her as she imagined what it would be like to end up living all alone. Abandoned . . . She stared into the shadows around her, seeking the comfort of familiar objects—but still her thoughts wound on, feeding her fear. Careful not to wake James, she climbed out of bed and crept into the main room. There she lit a candle and sat down, holding it in her hand.

The flame burned brightly, a warm, brave presence. Ignoring the hot wax running down onto her fingers, Ellen kept her gaze fixed on the flame. She forced herself to breath deeply and evenly. Eventually, the fear began to die away.

Chapter 8

The edges of dawn glowed gold above the mountains, but night shadows still lingered in the treetops. The beach lay like a slice of the moon, white painted with grey.

Ellen ran ahead of James and Zelda, taking long strides and then jumping, with legs and arms outstretched, head held high above a straight back. The sand was cool and hard and flat beneath her feet. She leapt again and spun round in the air, barely touching the ground with her feet before taking flight again.

She waited for the others at the end of the beach where the sand gave way to pale granite boulders coloured with orange lichen. She was breathless, pink-cheeked.

'You looked like a fairy,' called Zelda, as they came close.

Ellen stared over her head and on past James. 'I'm losing it,' she said.

They jumped from rock to rock, picking different paths, glancing down into deep cracks encrusted with small purple mussels. Near a rock pool they stopped to eat muffins with jelly, leaning over the weedy sides to see clusters of red sea anemones waving thin arms into the water.

'Tas calls them bloodsuckers,' said James. Reaching down, he poked one with his finger. It closed up with a shudder, snatching in its arms. Zelda laughed with delight and tried to copy him but before she even touched the creature she squealed and snatched her hand away.

'We should get back,' said Ellen as she watched the crumbs from her muffin falling down and floating in slow circles. 'I want to do some things outside before it gets too hot.'

'It's never too hot for me,' said Zelda. 'Is it, Daddy?'

James gazed out over the ocean, and then inland to the line of mountains patterned with wind-beaten highland shrubs. 'It's the end of the earth,' he mused, turning to Ellen. 'Like we're the only people in the world.'

'I wish we were,' said Ellen.

'Why?'

'I don't know. It'd be . . . simple. There'd be no-one to worry about. Nobody starving, or dying of cold.'

James looked at her and shook his head. 'That's what I like about you, Ell. I can never tell what you're going to say—or do—for that matter.' He screwed up his eyes slowly. 'Still waters run deep, my ma used to say. Must be a damn mine shaft inside your head.'

They walked in silence. Even Zelda stopped pointing and chattering. The sun rose higher in the cloudless sky, tracking them as they hopped from rock to rock, heading home.

Still waters run deep. Ellen looked down into the cracks between the rocks. Deep and murky. Hiding all kinds of evil. James was right. You could never tell what she might do. Suddenly she stopped and crouched down. 'Look! Come here, James.'

He came over, holding Zelda's hand as she picked her way between sharp barnacles.

'There . . .' Ellen pointed down between some rocks. In the middle of a small patch of sand was a single white shell. Against the dark basalt that walled it in, the pale shape seemed to glow, as if possessing a light of its own.

'It's a nautilus,' Ellen said. She said the word slowly, like the name of a god.

'What?' asked James.

'I read about them at Joe's museum. You only find them every seven years.' She looked up. 'It shouldn't be here. Joe said it's only four years since last time.'

James reached down and picked up the shell. He settled the graceful arch into his hand. 'It's a good omen, then,' he said. He smiled with his eyes. 'Perhaps it'll bring us seven years' good luck.' Turning it over, he passed it to Ellen. 'Feel it. It's amazing. Weighs nothing at all.'

She ran her fingertips lightly over its colourless pattern of tiny bumps. It was paper-thin. She imagined its journey; a small and fragile craft afloat in a savage sea. A deep, dark and endless place, with rocks, reefs and wild currents to fear.

'Give it to me!' Zelda reached up for it, clawing the air.

'You can look but don't touch,' said Ellen. She bent down, cradling the shell in her two hands.

'No, let me,' cried Zelda. 'I want to hold it.'

'No, you can just look.'

'Give it to her. She won't break it,' said James.

'Daddy said I could.' Zelda fixed Ellen with her dark, angry eyes.

'Okay,' said Ellen. 'Here you are.'

Zelda walked a few steps away, pretending to study the shell. She lifted it up to her ear. 'It doesn't even work. You can't hear the sea.' She held the shell out towards James. 'Here you are, Daddy.'

James took the shell and stowed it carefully in Ellen's backpack, on top of the leftover muffins and a bottle of water. 'Let's get going then. I want to be back in time to catch the tide. There's work to be done.'

When they reached the home beach, they saw Lizzie and her boys fishing from the rocks. James waved at them, but kept walking straight on towards the jetty, where the *Humble Bee* bobbed at her moorings.

85

'We can't stay and fish,' Ellen warned Zelda as they went to join their friends. 'We're just saying hello.'

Lizzie stood up as they came close. 'Hi,' she called. 'Where have you been so early? I thought you'd be here.'

'We just went for a walk,' answered Ellen. She helped Zelda cross to the big flat rock where the three boys sat bent over their lines. 'Caught anything? Sammy? Mickey? Drew?

'Nope,' the boys called back together without turning round.

Zelda pushed in between Drew and Mickey and squatted down, propping her elbows on her knees.

'I brought a thermos,' said Lizzie. 'Drew, you watch Zelda while we have a cuppa. Got that?'

'Okay, Mum.'

Ellen followed Lizzie back to where the rocks met the sandy beach. In the thin shade of a she-oak a rug was spread out, dotted with sandshoes, cricket bats, balls, towels and bags.

'Boys . . .' said Lizzie, frowning as she cleared a space to sit down. She took out a workman's metal thermos and poured two mugs of tea.

Ellen sat beside her and sipped at the hot brew.

'Look at Zelda,' said Lizzie with a smile. 'Wedged in between Mickey and Drew. She's in heaven!' Her face grew serious. 'If I knew I'd have a girl, I'd have another baby tomorrow.'

'Would you?' asked Ellen.

'Oh, yes!' answered Lizzie. 'I'd love a little girl.'

'Why, particularly?'

'I guess, to have someone that was—like me. When I see you and Zelda—I mean, she's the spitting image of you.' She looked at Ellen over the rim of her mug. 'It must be special.'

Ellen didn't reply.

'It must be,' repeated Lizzie.

'Well,' Ellen answered slowly, letting out words one at a time. 'It's strange in a way.' She lowered her voice, even though the children were well out of earshot. 'But I think she's too much like me.'

'What do you mean?' Lizzie asked.

'Oh—nothing really.'

'Yes, you do. I can tell by your face. What's wrong?'

'I don't think I can explain it.' Ellen looked out into the distance. There was a small boat, a black speck against the sea.

'Try,' insisted Lizzie.

Ellen chewed at the side of her finger. 'Well, it's like—do you believe in telepathy?'

'Yes, I suppose so.'

'Well, perhaps it's something like that. Sometimes Zelda looks at me, and it's as if she's—' Ellen's voice cracked.

Lizzie leaned round to look at her face. 'She's what?'

'Well, say she's standing up on a rock. I feel her saying "You want me to fall, and crack my head". Or, if I'm holding a hot iron, or shutting the car door. I . . . It comes from somewhere outside me. Or way inside me.' Her voice became thin. 'Sometimes I think I just pretend that I love her, like a mother. But deep down, I hate her.'

Lizzie's eyes were wide in her face. 'That's a terrible thing to say,' she said quickly. 'You don't mean it. You'll have to talk to James. Take a holiday.'

Ellen nodded slowly, picking up a piece of driftwood that was lying on the sand nearby. Years of wind and water had etched out the grain. She picked at a jagged splinter with her fingernail.

'Look, Ellen,' said Lizzie in a firm voice, 'leave Zelda with me and go to the mainland. Do some shopping, see some films. It's all right for us who were born and bred here. Others need to get away now and then. Or they go coastie.' She grinned, to signal a joke.

'What's that?' asked Ellen.

'Coastie. It's what happens to cows when they're put out for too long in the sea paddocks. The grass is short on some mineral they need. After a while they start to hang their heads on one side. They go a bit mad.'

'Oh, thanks,' said Ellen.

'Any time,' Lizzie smiled. 'Really, I do mean—' She looked up at a cry of excitement. 'Hey, they've caught something.' She jumped to her feet. 'Be careful!' she shouted. 'Don't fall in, any of you! You hear?'

Chapter 9

Sun sparkled and glittered like diamonds spread over the sea. Zelda stood knee-deep in the water, squealing and jumping as each low wave broke against her. Ellen watched from the edge of the wash, where she lay with the foamy ends of waves lapping over her legs.

'I want to practise swimming,' called Zelda.

'Daddy's teaching you to swim,' answered Ellen. 'I don't know what to do.'

'I'll show you. Come on. Please!'

Ellen got up slowly, untying her sarong and tossing it back onto the sand before wading into the water.

Zelda looked up at her naked body, her eyes moving in a triangle from one breast to another and down to the pubic hair. 'Mummies wear bathers,' she stated.

'Some do,' answered Ellen, 'but not yours. Not on our own beach anyway.'

'Why?'

'Because there's no-one to see.'

'Lizzie always wears bathers.'

'I know she does.' Ellen sighed. 'I thought you wanted to

have a swimming lesson.'

Zelda nodded and pointed out to sea. 'We have to go deeper.' They faced the horizon and waded side by side. Zelda put a hand on Ellen's thigh; outstretched fingers ready to grab if she lost her balance. 'Now you have to hold me up.'

Zelda lay in the water supported by Ellen's outstretched arms. Her skin was soft and slippery with suntan oil. Her waving limbs were pale thin shapes in the water.

'What now?' asked Ellen.

'You have to stay like that while I swim,' Zelda said. Her head was tilted back away from the water. 'Don't let me sink.' She looked up at Ellen, her eyes dark and intense. Then her face screwed up with effort as she launched into a wild, splashy dog paddle.

Ellen held her arms stiffly. She looked out over Zelda's head towards the horizon. Where the sea was cold and deep, and dark silent shapes slid beneath innocent boats.

Suddenly Zelda was gasping, struggling. Her body squirmed in the water. Then she screamed, choking on gulps of salt— fighting. Sinking. Small face tipped back, a white moon in the water.

Ellen closed her eyes. She knew what came next—it played out ahead of her like a familiar tune. Her hands pushing down on the small head, warm and hard. Hair swirling up like sea-weed. Limbs flailing, useless. Weak fingers tearing at big strong hands. Ears filling with water. The small close underwater sounds . . .

A timeless agony, in which nothing, or anything, was real.

No! Ellen stood still, frozen, as she reached for strength with every part of her being. Then she clamped her arms rigid against her sides, refusing to follow the call. Making the song go on without her.

She looked up as Zelda disappeared. The waves closed over the child's head and washed calmly by, leaving no sign that she had been there.

Zelda! The cry was buried deep, like a nightmare scream, fighting up through layers of sleep to pierce the quiet air.

'Zelda!' Ellen lunged after her. Throwing herself under the water to grasp the small body. Dragging her up—back to the air and the open sky. The small arms were still beating and the thin chest heaving as Zelda coughed up water and sobbed with fear.

'Mummy!' She cried, forcing the word out between choking coughs. 'Mummy!'

'It's all right—I've got you. Mummy's here.' Ellen bowed her head as Zelda's arms clung round her neck. She felt the small face pressing warm and wet against her breasts.

Ellen carried her out of the water and sank down onto the sand. She held Zelda close, tasting the salt on her skin, smoothing her cool soft flesh. Tears ran down Ellen's face.

'You slipped out of my hands, like a little slippery fish,' she said, in a light voice that died in a gasping sob.

'Mummy . . .'

'It's all right, angel.'

A long time passed. Sun burned their shoulders and seabirds made tracks around them. Finally Zelda grew calm and pulled away.

'Mummy? Don't cry, Mummy.'

Ellen stared down at the bright sand, the millions of grains, each cut and polished like a tiny gem. Her feet were buried, already lost. She was sinking, disappearing.

'I want to go home,' said Zelda. She began to cry, her bottom lip quivering, the tears glossy on her face. 'Come on. Mummy?' She backed away, looking.

Ellen's eyes were locked to the sand. Only her hair moved, stirring in the breeze.

Slowly, Zelda turned and walked away.

Chapter 10

'Are you sure I can't get you something?' The woman leaned round with her lips-only, skin-saving smile.

Ellen shut her eyes behind her sunglasses. After a moment of stillness she heard the woman move away, wafting a faint smell of French perfume. It was sharply familiar. Ellen made herself chase its name, hunting back . . . L'air du something. L'Air du Temps. The air of time . . .

Next, a male flight attendant appeared. He was polite and distant. 'Ma'am, if there's anything at all . . .'

Ellen shook her head. She could feel them wondering, studying her face with the hidden eyes. I forgot to ask for the right seat, she thought. This must be 2B. She kept her thoughts turning, chasing them along whenever they looked like settling. She always used to have 1B, with 1A kept empty if she was travelling alone. It was noted in her contract. Once there had been a mistake and she had refused to fly. Carter encouraged things like that, he said it added to her style. Carter. She pictured him, delighted and wary on the other end of the phone. You'd better meet me, she thought.

A hostess parted the curtain that hid Economy Class from

view and led a young girl up towards the front of the plane. Ellen turned and watched them pass, catching a glimpse of the child's face, open and bright, her hair neatly parted and drawn into straight, even plaits. Her full skirt swayed from side to side, the hem flicking along arms and armrests as she walked. The door opened briefly, revealing uniformed shoulders and blue sky. Then she was gone.

Ellen hung her head down, dark hair making a curtain that shielded her face. Her hands lay stiff in her lap.

Angel.

Tears rose misty, like a screen against her thoughts, brimming in her eyes and running down her cheeks. Ellen pushed her sunglasses aside and closed her eyes, pressing them hard with her hands. But still more tears came. And with them the images, sharp and painful . . .

Lizzie bending over Zelda's dark head, promising ice-cream and dress-ups and stories by the fire.

And then Lizzie waving to Ellen and calling, 'I'll bring her back after tea. Give you a chance to catch up with things.' A shadow of doubt dulls her smile as she searches Ellen's face. 'Are you all right?'

Ellen trying to answer, but only nodding her head.

'Look, I know what it's like,' Lizzie says kindly, 'trying to stay on top of things. Just go easy on yourself, okay? Zelda, run and kiss Mummy, then.'

The girl skips across the yard, long dark hair dancing about her shoulders. Reaching Ellen, she stops and grins. 'See you later,' she sings. 'I'm going with Lizzie, for the whole day!'

Ellen bends over her, feeling blindly for the upturned face. Not daring to breathe, or speak. Pushing her lips against the warm soft skin.

The child wriggles free and runs away.

Back at the hut, Ellen stands with both hands gripping the rough wood of the doorposts. Watching, frozen, as Zelda climbs into Lizzie's car. The windows are cloudy with dust, the faces inside vague and ghostlike; already fading . . .

The horn sounds briefly, the car moves off up the track. A patch of red appearing and disappearing between the trees. Then losing itself, finally, in the blue haze of the summer afternoon.

Ellen gasps, breathless, as if the air around her has been suddenly sucked away. Her body sags back against the door. Moments pass. Frozen, endless. Then she rouses herself, turning to face the gloom of the hut. The empty suitcase, waiting dusty under the bed. And the letter, not yet written. The blank white page, lying ready on the table.

Carter met Ellen as she came out through passport control. He drew her quickly aside and studied her for a second before reaching up to hug her close.

'Babe,' he said happily. 'It's great to see you. Welcome to New York. Welcome home. The car's this way.'

Ellen rested her head on his shoulder for a moment. 'I feel like death.'

As they drove in silence towards the city, Ellen gazed out at the passing traffic, grey and dirty. Nothing had changed. Nothing. She sensed Carter watching her.

'Ellen,' he finally said, 'if there's anything I can do. If you want to talk . . .' He spoke lightly, almost carelessly, but his eyes were bright with curiosity.

'No, I don't want to,' Ellen said quickly. 'But—thank you, and thanks for coming for me. There was no-one else I wanted to call.'

Carter searched her face for a moment, then smiled and waved one hand as if to brush her words aside. 'You don't know how many meetings I've cancelled, how many careers I have mercilessly stalled, just to be here.'

'Can you take me to some kind of hotel?'

'Oh I'm sure we can talk some old place into taking you in,' he joked. He patted her arm. 'It's all set up. You'll have a good rest, I'll send a car round at seven, and we'll go out to dinner. Just like old times.'

Ellen leaned back in the deep soft seat and closed her eyes.

The car swept into the wide curving driveway of the hotel. Doormen and bellboys, responding to Carter's signs, helped Ellen inside and up to her room.

They opened the door to a suite and switched on lights and called her Miss Kirby.

'Have I been here before?' she asked Carter.

'Yes, lots of times. It's your old suite, but it's been redecorated. And I guess that's a new skyscraper outside.' He crossed to the window. 'You used to be able to see the Statue of Liberty.'

Ellen followed him over, pausing as she caught sight of a bouquet of flowers in the bedroom. Brief jolt of hope, stillborn. It would be from the management, or perhaps Carter, or even his secretary.

'Yep, she was right there, behind that tower.' Carter pointed briefly, then turned. 'You rest up, babe.'

'Sure.'

'I'll get some Perrier sent up.'

'Thanks.'

Ellen followed Carter towards the door. A frown crossed her face. 'Oh, Carter. I need some money. I mean, there must be money, somewhere, but I don't know what happened about all that, when we left. James fixed it up.'

Carter stopped still. 'Honey, I have been *pouring* money into your account.' He held out his hand and counted off on his plump fingers. 'Royalties on the dolls. Young Designs. Commercials. Interest payments. You're rolling.' A flash of doubt flicked over his face. 'How much do you need? There's no trouble, is there?'

Ellen shook her head. 'No. It's just to live on. You know what it's like, in the city.'

'Sure do. Costs you to breathe!' Carter pulled out a handful of notes and dropped them onto a sideboard. 'Take this for now. I'll get Lois to sort things out for you.'

'Thanks.' Ellen bent to gather up the money.

'Don't mention it.' Carter paused, narrowing his eyes thoughtfully. 'So—would it be too much to ask where you've been—all this time?'

Ellen froze, one hand hovering over the green notes. She had expected questions, but not so soon. She hunted for something to say, but her mind was blank, a dark painful void. When she looked up, her eyes were shiny with tears.

'Sorry,' Carter mumbled. 'You just take it easy, okay? There's plenty of time.' He picked up a room service menu and thrust it towards her. 'You hungry?'

'No.'

A dense silence came between them. Carter shrugged it off. 'What can I say, babe? It's just great to have you back.'

Ellen's body was hidden beneath a thick layer of bubbles. She breathed in the fragrant steam and carefully relaxed her body. It was her first real bath in years. She looked around at the mirrored walls, velvet towels, plush chair, carpeted floor. This was her world. At least, it had been only a few years ago. Now it would be again. Easy. She had come and gone before, fading or jumping from one kind of life, self, to another. The deeper the cut, the more it hurt, that was all.

She sank down slowly under the foam, feeling it creep up the sides of her face, slightly cooler than the water beneath. She closed her eyes and let the white froth immerse her. Her hair floated, then sank slowly, settling in long strands over her eyes and mouth, swirling like seaweed. Cold fear grasped her. It filled her body, spreading into every nerve. God help me. The small hands beat uselessly, the mouth open, screaming. *Mummy*! Ellen stiffened, refusing to move. The pain was too great to fight. Instead she forced herself to take hold of it, baring her flesh in its searing flame. Hanging on until, at last, she felt only a dull ache inside her, then a numb and empty hole.

Ellen saw Carter stand, ready to greet her, as the waiter led her across to the table. Other heads turned her way as well—the ordinary rich, looking out for the could-be famous. Ellen sensed their uncertainty as they studied her homemade clothes, trying to decide if the look was hopelessly wrong or just very new.

Carter stared at her as she drew close. Her hair hung in long loose strands, sweeping back over her shoulders as she walked tall and steady. She wore no make-up, but her lips were pink and her skin was smooth and tanned. She watched him with even eyes burning clear.

Carter smiled but said nothing while the waiter arranged Ellen's chair, hovered briefly and then withdrew.

'I couldn't have imagined another look for you,' he said frankly. 'But, hell, you look like you were made in heaven!'

Ellen laughed, brushing his compliment aside.

'No, I mean it,' Carter insisted. 'This is it—the new-look Ellen!' He poured champagne as he talked. It was Veuve Clicquot, with an unblemished label. No silverfish here.

'And what is it—the new look?' Ellen asked, in a mock indulgent tone, covering a small knot of unease.

He winked, as if about to make a joke. 'Eve,' he stated, 'fresh from the Garden of Eden.'

Ellen laughed. 'Carter, listen to me.' She leaned towards him as she spoke—then pulled back, remembering that he, himself, had taught her to do this: to lean close, intimately, so that the person listening feels that you care. It gets them ready to hear what you want. 'I don't know what I'm going to do. I don't know about dancing, or modelling, or anything. I need time to—see.'

97

Carter nodded, reaching for her shoulder and squeezing it lightly. 'Sure you do, babe. There's no need to rush. I'll just be here.'

Their eyes met. In that moment, Ellen caught a glimpse of the old Carter—the man who always schemed and planned ruthlessly for his own ends. She felt alone and friendless.

'Ziggy—how's Ziggy?' she asked. 'Years ago—three or four—I saw her in a magazine, an Australian magazine. I couldn't believe it—' She broke off, reading a wary look in his eyes. 'Is she still working?'

'No.' Carter glanced around, as if searching for a diversion. 'She's been unwell.'

'Ziggy! She was never sick in her life!' exclaimed Ellen.

'Well,' Carter shrugged, 'she was nervous, I guess—highly strung.'

'You mean she's had a breakdown?' Ellen pushed him.

'I don't know the details.' Carter answered her in a deliberately calm and gentle voice, a man used to dealing with troubled women. 'I haven't seen her for ages myself. I believe she's staying in a clinic in New England—near where you came from, in fact.'

Ellen was silent, fixing her eyes on him, wanting more. Carter stalled, pouring and drinking more champagne.

Finally he spoke again. 'I've got her address somewhere. I'm sure I have. I sent flowers.' His face lightened suddenly, as his wandering gaze found its mark. 'Michael!'

Ellen turned to see a tall man in a creased daytime suit picking his way across the room towards them. No-one looked up as he passed between the tables, a trenchcoat slung over his arm and a battered briefcase in his hand.

'Ellen, you remember Michael Holland,' said Carter, motioning for a waiter to bring over another chair. Ellen looked up as the man drew near, and smiled blankly.

'No.'

'Sure you do—sit down, Michael.'

The man sank into the chair as if reaching the end of a long journey. 'Hi,' he said to Ellen. His attention was caught briefly by her face, but he gave no sign of recognition. He turned to Carter. 'Where is she?'

Carter faltered for a brief moment, then laughed. 'You're a character, Holland.' He motioned towards Ellen's face. 'Look at Ellen, doesn't she look wonderful? I bet you hardly recognised her.'

Michael's eyes met Ellen's. 'I'm sorry . . . I didn't. But then it's been years.'

Ellen nodded. 'That makes two of us.'

Carter called for more champagne and some menus. 'Holland, you'll eat with us, of course.'

Ellen glanced at him in surprise followed by a tinge of doubt.

'Michael wrote that Cat Man story on you for *Teen* magazine. Way back when.'

Ellen took a slow drink, her eyes lowered thoughtfully. She remembered the interview. Holland had been keen and serious, asking her questions and covering his ragged notebook with shorthand. She had been young and nervous, but already able to subdue her panic. Sitting politely, swinging her long legs from a high stool, she had answered everything that he asked her. And he had found what he was looking for. She was already a Cinderella rising star and a new Pavlova— a perfect fantasy figure for her peers. Through him, the world learned that her dancing lessons were paid for by a reclusive old man who lived in a crumbling mansion with forty-seven cats. Their chance friendship had begun with a little girl walking home from school, just like anyone . . . However you looked at the story, it had been a winner. And it was Holland who had taken her picture, pointing his camera up at her on the high stool, her eyes all dark and smudged with remembering and her lips touched by the smallest, faintest smile. Against all plans and traditions, it had made it onto the cover of the magazine. It was there that Carter had first seen her. And everyone else.

'It's still one of my best pieces,' said Michael.

'You know,' Carter jerked his head up, as if getting an idea for the first time. 'Holland would be just the one to do a story on you now. You know, "Ellen Returns".'

'Thanks. It makes me sound like a Martian,' Ellen protested. Now it was her turn to glance around, looking for an escape. Carter, she thought, you never miss a trick, do you?

The journalist was already reaching for his notebook. Ellen watched his face, guessing at how he would be sizing up the possibilities, planning his piece. He could re-use bits of the Cat Man story, do a 'then and now'. Bring up all the innuendo about her sudden disappearance. And ask why, after so many years, she had chosen to come back . . .

Michael took a pencil from the pocket of his jacket and held it poised over his notebook. He leaned towards Ellen across the table. 'You know,' he said, 'in a way, you seem just the same as you did back then. All those years ago. Where were we? Some little cafe.' He grinned. 'You ordered an espresso, and couldn't drink it.'

'Did I?' asked Ellen. 'I don't remember things like that.'

'Ah,' Michael said, 'but *I* do. Journalists never forget.' He glanced at Carter, who nodded encouragement. 'Yes,' he went on, settling back in his chair. 'I could retell that interview almost word for word. You were ten years old when my story began. And you'd not yet danced a single step. It was the summer of '59.'

Ellen stood, suddenly, pushing back her chair. 'I'm sorry, you'll have to excuse me,' she said. 'I'm very tired.'

Carter jumped up with a look of concern on his face and hurried to stand at Ellen's side. 'I'll take you back, right away.'

'No, thank you.' Ellen shook his arm off her shoulder. 'I'll take a cab.' She forced a smile. 'I'll be fine. Let me go—please.'

Outside the restaurant, she ignored a waiting cab and

crossed the road, heading for a small park. Bright yellow street lamps marked her way, but all else around her was grey: grey buildings and footpaths, dark grey roads. Even the night sky, reflecting the lights of the city, was a dull hazy grey, without stars.

She reached the park and walked in amongst the trees. She knew it wasn't safe to be out here alone at night, but couldn't face going back to the hotel—to the quiet empty room and the small pile of things she'd brought with her that looked so faded and lost on the wide plush bed.

She found a small bench, almost hidden under a drooping tree, and sat down. The noise of the traffic seemed far away, and the air was freshened with the smell of wet grass. It was almost dark. She thought briefly of Carter and Holland, bent over their meals. She remembered the journalist, now—she could recall his face—though he'd aged a lot in the years that had passed since the day they first met in the cafe. The Footlight Cafe.

Ellen closed her eyes on an image of metal chairs clustered neatly around dark wooden tables. She tried to escape from it, but the memory drew her on—and she saw herself there, perched on a high stool at the counter. Stirring a cup of dark bitter coffee that had long gone cold.

'How old were you when you first learned to dance?' he'd asked.

'Ten.'

Ten years old. A lifetime ago.

Ellen gazed into the gloom, tracing the outlines of the tangled branches, trying to make their pattern fill her mind. But the words and pictures kept on coming.

There was a little girl, with a pale serious face. She was on her way home from school. Walking alone, as she always did . . .

Chapter 11

Blossoming fruit trees bent over the narrow road and grass grew young and thick along the verges. Ellen walked carefully, avoiding the ruddy-green poison ivy and patches of mud left by a recent shower. Her socks stretched spotlessly white and unwrinkled to her knee. Her blazer was buttoned and her straw hat still sat squarely in place, though school was now well out of sight. She held a spray of laurel in her hand. As she walked she tore off the delicate white petals and pink tendrils and left them scattered on the road behind her.

She stopped to pick handfuls of tender grass for a tall brown horse that followed her on the other side of the fence. She fed him in small serves, feeling his velvet lips searching against her palm. His shoulders rose high and strong above her. She imagined him carrying her away, jumping over fences and streams, crossing roads and highways, further and further, until they recognised nothing and no-one knew who they were . . .

She jumped back as he shook his head suddenly, spreading green foamy saliva into the air. A drop landed on her sock. She pounced on it, rubbing it away with the inside of her skirt. Then she walked on, passing by the canal. Her eyes followed their usual path along the wide ribbon of water, passing aimless ducks and settling on a brown shape lying in the mud at the edge of the water. She climbed down to have a closer look.

It was a potato sack, tied at the top with string. There was a small bulge in the end. She nudged it with her foot and jumped backwards with a short cry as it wriggled faintly. She stared, a sick feeling coming over her. Something was trapped inside and struggling weakly to escape. She imagined it wet and bloody, scratching with fear. Eyes open wide in the dark and rubbed sore by the rough sacking. Ellen ran a few steps away and looked anxiously up and down the empty road. Behind her, a weak mewing began. She turned back.

'Kitty, kitty, kitty?' she called uncertainly.

At the sound of her voice the movements stopped. The sack lay still, as if watching and waiting. Ellen bent quickly and picked it up. It hung wet and muddy against her legs. Holding it out to one side, she ran back to the road and on towards a big house that stood up on the hill, surrounded by dark pines.

Her feet crunched loudly along the gravel driveway, matching the rhythm of her breathing. Down a side path she ran, pounding over layers of damp leaves and then on past a ragged tennis lawn fenced with rusty wire mesh. She took a detour, carefully skirting a large swimming pool. It was elegantly tiled with blue and gold squares, but the water that filled it was dark and dank, with overblown goldfish lurking in a slimy tangle of rotting lilies. Ellen kept her gaze fixed ahead, refusing to look down, as if afraid that the murky depths might catch her eye, and call her in.

She slowed down as she reached an old dressing shed that resembled a miniature alpine hut. Like the rest of the grounds, it was falling into decay; the little wooden shutters with hearts cut out of the middle hung drunkenly from hinges gnarled with rust.

Inside she knelt and quickly untied the sack, hurried fingers fumbling. As she worked, her eyes travelled around the small room, searching among piles of junk. Dragging out a carton, she filled it with pieces of yellowed newspaper screwed up into balls. Then she found a towel, stiff with age, still hanging from a hook beneath a perished rubber swimming cap. She paused, breathing out slowly. Taking hold of the end of the sack she shook it first gently, then roughly.

'Come on!'

A small body fell weightlessly onto the floor. It rolled over, scrabbling onto its feet and stood stiffly with its tail stuck straight out behind. Ellen stared at it in horror. Tremors travelled up and down its pitiful body, white fur clung wet against its heaving rib cage and fleshless limbs. Eyes bulged from a rat-like head with large pointed ears. It began to stagger towards her.

Ellen jumped to her feet and backed away. 'No. Get away!' Her stomach churned. The creature was ugly, clumsy and dirty. She wanted it back in the sack, flung to the middle of the canal, sinking in green water.

It looked up at her as it kept walking. One eye was clear blue like a summer sky, the other a warm chestnut brown. It opened its mouth wide in a long and voiceless cry.

Ellen moaned, her eyes filling with tears. 'Come here . . .'

She knelt by the kitten and quickly rubbed it dry with the towel, her hands moving lightly over its flimsy frame. Then she put it in the carton and ran outside. Minutes later she returned with a bottle of milk. She slopped some into an old saucer and placed it beside the kitten. Pausing briefly in the doorway, she saw the white shape stirring, leaning forward, and then a pink tongue lapping.

A warm feeling spread through her. She turned away towards the house, feeling tall and strong, like a conqueror.

Margaret was late home that night. Ellen waited for her mother as she always did, carefully seated in front of her neat homework. The stained socks had been washed and hung to dry in the attic. The muddy shoes were now clean and felt only slightly damp. A new pair of spotless white socks stretched unwrinkled to her knees. Even so, the sound of the car tyres crunching in the driveway brought a knot to her throat. It tightened as the high heels clacked across the parquet floor in the hall, thudded softly through the dining room and stopped at the entrance to the kitchen.

'Hello, Margaret,' said Ellen, without looking up. She breathed the smell of cigarette smoke and perfume. Her senses clung to the perfume. She recognised it, matching the smell with one of the flasks on Margaret's dressing table. Madame Rochas. She felt a short thrill of optimism. This was the perfume smell that had gone with them to the beach. When Margaret had bought her an ice-cream and laughed and played like a friend instead of a mother. She had worn a new bathing suit and was so beautiful that Ellen had wanted to cry . . .

But it meant nothing today. Margaret stood in the doorway, holding in one hand a long black cigarette holder and in the other an opened letter. A frown marked her smooth, elegant face. Ellen tried not to look, knowing how Margaret hated to be eyed like a mother cow. But the letter worried her, even though she was sure she had done nothing wrong.

'Good!' Margaret's lips pursed with satisfaction. 'That'll be just fine.' She glanced at Ellen, taking in her posture and dress and handwriting in an instant, accepting without approving. 'It's about next vacation.' She paused as if aware of how Ellen would hang, waiting. 'You'll be going each day to school.'

Ellen masked surprise and relief. School! Instead of long blank days of sitting in the house, clean, quiet, alone—just waiting for the holidays to end.

'There are going to be dance classes. Ballet in the mornings and folk in the afternoons. You can go to both.'

'Oh, no. Please.' Ellen looked up, horrified and disbelieving. 'I'd rather stay here. I can't do dancing, I know I . . .' Her voice died away as Margaret smiled, smoke wisping faintly from between her glossy red lips.

'Don't argue, darling. You're a clumsy child—little girls mostly are.' Her eyes flicked down to Ellen's chewed finger-nails. 'It'll do you good.'

Later that evening, Ellen stood by the window in her room, resting her forehead against the cool smooth glass, listening to the distant sound of the radio coming from downstairs. Stepping back, she looked at her face reflected against the darkness outside. Eyes too big, brows too thick, forehead too high. Pale skin and dark hair. Nothing like Margaret, or the gentle, wispy man with pale hair who stood beside her in the wedding portrait that hung in the hallway.

I am a goblin's child, Ellen thought. Switched in the cradle. Or someone from an old silent movie. Someone awkward and clumsy, like Charlie Chaplin. I won't go, she told herself. Her eyes were like dark wells. I'll stand at the back.

She counted the weeks till the end of term. Nearly two months. Eight weeks of waiting, dreading . . .

Leaning close to the glass again, Ellen looked past her reflec-tion and down through the dark limbs of the pines towards the old dressing shed. She pictured a warm kitten, curled up over a tummy full of milk. It would have been dead by now, she told herself, feeling again the small glow of strength. She held it inside her, a secret flame, something to hold like a shield against the dark.

There was no chance to visit the kitten before school the next morning. Ellen tried not to look preoccupied as she tidied the kitchen, aware of Margaret standing behind her, carefully brushing lint from another tailored suit. But her thoughts swung back and forth. Was the kitten all right? And what on earth would she do with it? She considered the idea of keep-ing it in the shed, feeding it before Margaret came home each day, and letting it wander in the garden like a stray. But Margaret would know, she told herself. Margaret *always* knew in the end.

She was still thinking about it as the car pulled up at the school. Not on the road outside, where everyone else stopped—Margaret's red sports car swept into the grounds, as usual, and stood with its engine purring outside the main office. Teachers and parents nodded greetings and Margaret handed back small, bright smiles.

'Goodbye, darling.' She leaned across and kissed her daughter.

Ellen felt herself watched and envied. Margaret was the perfect mother: young and beautiful and a successful doctor admired for her work with children.

'Wipe your face,' Margaret said in an undertone. Ellen lifted a hand to where she knew there would be the red shadow of her mother's lips. She looked briefly into her eyes as she rubbed the mark away.

'I'll be late home again,' said Margaret, peering into the rear-vision mirror, checking her face, or the road behind.

At lunchtime, Ellen headed for the library, where she looked up Cats in the phone book. Breeders. Boarding kennels. What was she looking for? Then she saw it, clear and simple, as if written for her. Cat Protection Society—Home for Cats.

After school she ran home and went straight to the shed. The kitten met her, mewing with pleasure and rubbing against her legs. She lifted it into the carton and closed the flaps of the lid.

Carrying it with her, she ran inside the house and phoned a taxi. Then she went upstairs and peeled her Christmas money from where she had glued it underneath the desktop. She moved in a daze, knowing that if she thought clearly she would never, never dare . . .

The taxi arrived and honked in the driveway. Ellen jumped, breaking into a cold sweat as she ran downstairs.

She handed the written address to the driver. 'How long will it take to go there?' she asked, in a cool Margaret voice, with a slight frown on her face.

'Ooh, it's not far—if we go by the back way, about fifteen minutes, I guess.'

'Hurry, please,' said Ellen. 'I've got another appointment to keep.'

The taxi driver grinned at her as he drove off, mock saluting, 'Yes, ma'am!'

He nodded at the box. 'Got a lost cat in there?'

'No, it's a kitten, I found it by the canal tied up in a sack.' Ellen's words tumbled out like a confession. 'It's thin, it needs food, but I can't keep it at home—I—my mother doesn't like anything that's alive. Anyway, I found this place in the phone book.' She paused, looking up at him uncertainly. 'Do you think they'll take it and look after it?'

'Oh, they'll take it,' the driver began. 'I guess they'll—' He broke off.

'What?' asked Ellen, anxiously.

'Well, they'll try and find a good home for it. That's the best they can do really, isn't it?'

'What do you mean?' asked Ellen frowning. 'What if they can't? Won't they keep it?'

'For a while. Then I guess they'd have to put it to sleep.'

'You mean—kill it?' Ellen's voice was soft with horror.

'It's the only kind thing to do,' the driver said firmly. 'You know there's always too many kittens around. If they kept them all . . .'

Ellen stared silently at the road ahead. She held the carton tightly on her knee. It was so light, she thought. The kitten was so thin. She gazed out of the window at trees flashing past, and glimpses of houses, gates, driveways. A rough sign tacked to a letterbox caught her eye.

'Stop,' she said. 'Stop here.'

The driver turned in surprise. 'What?'

'Stop. I want to get out.'

'Look, sweetheart, I think you've got the right plan. Take it to the cat home.'

'No, I've changed my mind. Let me out here.'

'Well, I'll drive you back . . .' He turned the car round.

'I'd rather walk,' said Ellen. 'I can go across the field—see?' She pointed towards the tall pine trees on the brow of the hill.

The driver stopped and let her out, refusing to take her fare. 'You just show your mom that sweet kitty and see if she can say no!' he suggested kindly. 'But you go straight home, mind!'

Ellen smiled again. She stood still, holding the carton in her arms, until the car turned the corner. Then she headed back along the road. Soon she came to a long, curving driveway. She paused by the sign on the letterbox, handpainted in peeling red paint: KITTENS. FREE TO GOOD HOMES.

The house was big and old like Margaret's, but whereas she only neglected the outbuildings and grounds, this place was falling down all over. Two cats slept curled together in the front doorway. It was a good sign, Ellen thought. She reached up and knocked loudly.

For a long time nothing happened. Even the cats declined to stir from their sleep. Ellen wondered if she should just leave the carton on the step and walk away. But she didn't want to. Then she heard soft footsteps inside and the door opened wide. An old man stood in a shadowy hallway, surrounded by dozens of cats. They swirled around his feet like a stream. The air was full of cat smell, floating hair, and the low hum of mass purring.

'Lord!' the man exclaimed, opening his arms wide as if about to embrace her. 'You've come for a kitten! Come in, come in.'

'Wait, I—'

But he was striding down the hallway, the cats flowing after him.

Ellen followed, holding the carton firmly to her chest. They passed through dim rooms decorated with long velvet drapes, drooping chandeliers, Chinese couches, Persian rugs, stuffed animals and urns fulls of dried flowers. Crystal glasses stood here and there in groups on polished tables and sideboards, as if just recently abandoned. But over everything lay a thick covering of white dust and cat hair. Wooden surfaces were scored with clawmarks, and cloths and tapestries hung in ragged strips.

They stepped out of all this into a light, sunny conservatory, furnished simply with three long tables and matching wooden benches. The windows were open and a fresh breeze aired the room. Abandoned teapots were scattered along the tables among piles of baskets, brushes, bottles, tins of flea powder and cat food.

Ellen stopped in the doorway. 'I'm sorry,' she said as politely as possible. 'But I've *brought* you a kitten.'

The man turned slowly. He peered at her from under heavy eyebrows.

'I rescued it from the canal,' Ellen said simply. 'It's starving. But I can't keep it at home. You'll have to take it. Please.' She put the carton down on the nearest table, and carefully lifted the flaps.

'Just a minute.' The man hurried over. 'Don't just let it out free—it'll run off and we'll not get near it.'

'It's all right,' said Ellen, reaching in and picking up the kitten. 'It's not scared of me.'

She held it gently, cradling it against her chest.

'Look at that,' said the man. 'It's a fairy's cat.' He stroked the thin head. 'See? One blue eye and one brown?' Ellen nodded. He frowned, making a small clucking noise with his tongue. 'Poor creature.' As he felt its body, an angry look came over his face. 'It's starving!'

'I only found it yesterday,' Ellen said quickly. 'I gave it some milk,'

'Good girl. You're a lucky kitten,' said the man gently. He took the creature and turned it over. 'It's a male. What's its name then?'

'I don't know.'

'Well, how can he be your kitten if you don't have a name for him?'

'You don't understand,' said Ellen bitterly. 'He's not going to be my kitten. I'm not allowed—'

'Oh, but he *is* your kitten. You saved his life! I'll look after him, but he'll be your kitten.'

'You mean—I could visit him, here?' Ellen asked in a small voice.

'Sure. Any time you like.' The man spread his arms again, welcoming.

Ellen smiled, her eyes widening with joy as the meaning of his words sank in. There would be no more empty hours of sitting neatly, waiting for the time to pass till Margaret came home. Instead, Ellen would come secretly after school, to visit her kitten—like other children visited their schoolfriends to eat cookies and milk in warm kitchens.

'You're always welcome,' the man said.

Ellen studied his face before deciding to speak. 'Only, it would have to be a secret.'

'Sure,' said the man. 'You can come in disguise, take a false name if you like. I'm Eildon, by the way.' He held out a hand, his rough old skin marked with red scratches.

Ellen took it, feeling its warmth. 'I'm Ellen. I'm ten years old.'

They named the kitten Perdita, 'the one who was once lost'. When Ellen came to visit after school, he would follow her around, purring and rubbing his head against her legs, while she helped Eildon with his chores. Together they fed motherless kittens, checked ears for ticks and picked burrs from long-haired Persian tails. After that, they washed cat bowls, rinsed out teapots and painted herbal flea repellent onto handwoven cat collars. And when the day's tasks were done, they sat in the dusty parlour and shared a pot of tea. There was no milk or sugar allowed; the fine china cups brimmed with fragrant liquid of clear honey-gold. Nectar of the gods, Eildon called it, and Ellen imagined it might be true. There was Darjeeling for Mondays, Jasmine on Tuesdays, then Ceylon, Assam and Russian Caravan. Sometimes, as they sipped slowly, they swapped stories about the family of cats, but often they just sat quietly together, surrounded by small kitten sounds and the hush of wind in the trees outside.

'Time to go,' Eildon always said, after the second cup. 'We don't want you being late . . .'

By the time Margaret's car turned into the driveway, Ellen would be sitting at her desk, clean and tidy, her precooked meal eaten, the dishes washed and her homework done. As she listened to the key turning in the front door and the high heels tapping across the hall floor, she would stare down at her hands, afraid that her secret might show in her eyes.

To drive out thoughts of Perdy, or Eildon, or the big, ragged house, she would make herself look ahead, beyond the coming weeks, to the end of term. The dark shadow looming. Dance classes. Ballet and folk, morning and afternoon, every day, for the whole vacation. She would call up images to go with the words, letting the darkness build. Time does not stand still, she'd remind herself, feeling the glow of her secret safely dimming. Time moves on. The days will grow colder and shorter. The end of term will come. And there will be no escape.

Chapter 12

The other girls watched as Ellen pulled on her new pink leotards, pink wraparound jumper and pink satin shoes. They said nothing but she could feel their envious looks.

Caroline was dressing beside her, pushing short, skinny legs into clingy black tights. She leaned past Ellen to talk to two girls who were whispering together behind their hands.

'Hey, take a look at Nicola.' Caroline nodded across the room to where a girl was dressing in a black suit that looked warm and woolly and had slightly baggy knees. 'Knitted—by her mom! I'd just die!' She looked down at Ellen's soft pink shoes, with their long ribbons trailing. 'Lucky thing. Your mom's the best.'

'I know,' said Ellen. She was silent for a moment, before continuing. 'Except—she doesn't let me go anywhere. I'm only here because she's at work and she wants to be sure where I am.' She looked down at her feet, as if ashamed of her words.

Caroline nodded knowingly. 'It's because you've got no dad. You're everything she has—it's natural for her to be overprotective. Or that's what my Mom said.'

Ellen looked up. 'Did she?'

'Yes,' nodded Caroline. 'Not to me. She was talking to Mrs Edwards.'

Ellen bent to tie her shoes, trying to remember the way the lady in the shop had shown her; but it had been hard to concentrate with Margaret watching, talking about little girls and how much work they made.

A woman appeared at the door, tall and straight-backed, with long, dark hair tied up in a bun. She was dressed in loose clothing and wore flat leather slippers.

'Hello, girls,' she said briskly, with a sharp smile. 'I am Miss Louise. Is everyone ready?' Her eyes swept over the crowd of milling bodies, pausing for a second on Ellen, her glance running up and down the girl's body. Her eyebrows lifted slightly. Ellen flushed and chewed at her thumb.

The woman's eyes moved on. 'You—the girl in the patterned sweater,' she said. 'Take it off. Then you may all come in.' There was silence as she turned and left the room.

Caroline pulled a face at her back and moaned loudly. 'It's going to be worse than school. I'm not going to keep coming.'

The woman was waiting for them as they filed into the gymnasium. Ellen glanced up at her as she passed. Up close, her face looked less hard. She had a black line painted along each slanted eyelid, tilting up at the outside corner. She smelled of flowery talcum powder. She smiled. Ellen looked quickly away.

'Now, girls,' Miss Louise called. 'Everybody find a place at the barre, and stand like this.' She angled out her feet and placed one hand lightly on a bar that had been installed in front of a large mirror along one side of the gym.

The girls hurried to take up position. Ellen went to the furthest corner and stood right at the end of the bar. The teacher talked and counted and made slow movements with her arms and legs. The girls listened carefully and followed as best they could. They worked with serious faces, the grins and giggling banished already by Louise's grave manner. She had a deep lilting voice with a slight French accent that transformed ordinary speech into something mysterious. The girls hung on her every word, as if she held the promise of something precious and secret.

Ellen felt bare and clumsy as she struggled to match the fluid gestures. She knew that her clothes showed up every bump and angle of her body, and wished she had worn plain gym clothes like some of the others. She wondered if Margaret knew how silly she would feel—all dressed up like a real dancer, yet so clumsy. She bent her head, looking down at her pointed toes, but even her curtain of hair was gone. Her scalp still stung from Margaret dragging her hair up and winding it tightly on top of her head, fixing it there with sharp pins.

Ellen looked up, suddenly aware that everyone was watching her.

'Ellen,' the teacher was saying. 'Come here.'

Ellen trailed towards her, hoping only that she might expel her from the class. (Really, Mrs Kirby, she imagined her explaining, it would just be a waste of my time. I'm sorry . . .) Then she felt Louise's hands, firm but gentle on her body.

'Lift . . . and now stretch. Feel that?' she asked. Ellen nodded. 'Now, point the foot, and turn out from the hip. And again. Feel it?'

Yes. Ellen's mouth twitched at the corners, a faint smile of surprise.

'That's good,' said Louise, her head nodding on her long, straight neck. 'That's very good, Ellen. Now stay here at the front . . .'

Ellen studied the woman's tall, erect form and worked hard to copy her. Now and then she caught sight of herself in the wall mirror and started with surprise. It was as if she had discovered another body, a puppet that responded to her instructions; a creature of foreign grace and beauty.

Louise came to stand beside her again, bending Ellen's arms into smooth curves and arranging her fingers.

'There', she said, 'just hold like that, Ellen. Lengthen your neck. You must become like a swan. Girls, watch her.' She smiled along the line of faces. 'You are ugly ducklings, all of you; but you can all become swans. Practise at home. One, two, three and four. In front of the mirror in your bedroom. Every night. Like saying your prayers.'

At the end of the class she bowed and clapped her hands. 'Thank you, ladies.'

The two weeks passed in a dream of strain and sweat and small, sweet moments of success. The movements were not natural, Ellen quickly realised. The arms might be raised, but the shoulders remain lowered. The neck may bend but the back stays flat. She learned how to send commands to each part of her body, accepting nothing but obedience; demanding neatness and organisation. 'Mind over matter' was one of Margaret's favourite sayings—and it worked. That was the first stage. Then everything had to be put back together seamlessly, so that movements ran smoothly like syrup. All the while the face took refuge in its own world, serene and calm and with the ghost of a smile, as toes recoiled from blisters and calf muscles cramped.

Louise kept Ellen at the front and pushed her for more, the firm hands demanding more stretch, more length, more smoothness. The other girls watched her with a new kind of envy; it was as if she had been marked out and was now being made into someone new. She was less and less a part of them each day.

After class was over, Ellen would walk home, along a road that spread before her like an empty stage. The horse would watch, nodding approval as she leapt and spun in the air.

And Eildon, with his troupe of cats, would smile and clap.

'I'm good at it,' Ellen told him.

'Of course you are,' he said. 'There's a bit of the cat in you!'

Too soon, the holidays came to an end. When the last class

was over, Louise took Ellen aside. 'Ellen,' she said, almost wistfully, as if bringing bad news, 'you have a perfect dancer's body. It deserves to be trained.'

'Will you come again next holidays?' asked Ellen hopefully. 'It was fun.'

'No, you don't understand,' said Louise. 'I've got a plan for you. There's a new ballet school that is about to open. It will be modelled on the old Imperial Ballet School in Russia: residential, full-time, all students chosen only on the basis of their potential.' Excitement warmed her voice. 'They will be an elite, selected from all over America. Everything will be taken into account. Their training will be—complete. They will be the first real American ballet dancers.' She took Ellen by the shoulders, her eyes glistening as she was overtaken by her vision. 'I'll nominate you for an audition and a scholarship. It's a chance I never had. To begin young, and to give up everything!'

'My mother wouldn't let me,' Ellen broke in. 'I couldn't even ask. I just wouldn't be allowed.'

'Don't worry about that now. If you were accepted it would be such an honour, your mother would change her mind,' said Louise. Ellen shook her head, but the woman was unperturbed. 'I've seen it happen,' she insisted. 'Anyway, it will be a few months before the auditions are held for this area. I'll arrange for you to do yours here, during school time. That way we need not bother your mother about it, okay?'

Ellen nodded.

'And one more thing,' Louise added. 'Don't do classes with anyone in the meantime. It's better if you're . . .' She frowned as she hunted for the word '. . . untouched.'

When the day of the auditions finally came around, Louise appeared in the doorway of Ellen's classroom. An excited hiss spread around the room as some of the girls recognised her. Even the teacher looked pleased to see her. He seemed disappointed when she simply asked if she could take Ellen out to keep an appointment.

They walked along the corridors.

'Don't be nervous,' said Louise. 'Or if you are, hide it. The essence of performance is the ability to control your fear. A dancer is useless without it.'

Ellen walked calmly beside her. She would just do as she was asked, neatly and politely, as she had been brought up to do. Beyond that, there was really nothing at stake, because Margaret would simply never agree to her going away to ballet school. She would punish her just for asking, for being so selfish. Thinking of what she wanted, while Margaret worked to save the lives of frightened children (removing their kidneys, giving them medicine that made them grow hair like monkeys . . .). But imagine, thought Ellen, a place where girls lived together, with all the same rules and same games. It was like the old dream of being carried off by the horse. It would never happen.

When she entered the gymnasium, three men in suits were standing waiting. Nearby was a thin, younger woman carrying what looked like a medical bag. Seeing her, Ellen felt pangs of nervous sickness. Louise brought her up to the men. 'This is the student Ellen Kirby, ten years old. Curtsy, Ellen . . .'

The men seemed restless, and anxious to get on with the next thing. Their faces said they were not expecting much.

'Ellen will just get changed,' explained Louise.

Ellen came out ready to go through the dance routines, but it became clear that this was not important. Instead, they studied her body. They asked her to stretch, twist, reach, and made comments on her flexibility. Then the thin woman opened her bag and took out a tape measure. Ellen tried not to breathe the antiseptic smell that followed the woman as she hovered, measuring the relative lengths of Ellen's main bones, and the circumference of her head, waist, hips. Everything was noted down by one of the men. He referred to some printed diagrams, then stood still, studying Ellen with intense eyes, deep-set in an ageless face. He paused on the slight mounds of her breasts.

'Has she begun menstruating?' he asked Louise.

'Oh . . .' She lifted her hands uncertainly to her face. 'I haven't asked.' She ran quickly and leaned close to Ellen, speaking in a half-whisper. 'Have you begun your—monthly bleeding?'

Ellen looked up slowly, stalling for time. There was a puzzled look in her eyes, overlaid with the sharp anxiety of someone bluntly accused.

'No, she hasn't,' said Louise.

The man nodded, satisfied. 'Now, er—Ellen—tell me about your mother.'

Ellen jumped as if she had been slapped.

'Is she tall? Fat?'

'She's—big,' Ellen began, but stopped as Louise burst into laughter.

'No she's not! I've seen her. She's tall—not too tall—and beautifully slim.'

'What about the father?' the man went on. 'How tall is he?'

Ellen kept her eyes on the floor. 'I don't know about my father,' she said in a low, small voice.

His name was never mentioned at home and Ellen had learned not to ask questions about him. Only once she had risked it. On a rare day out, when she and Margaret had been happy together, shopping for clothes and a new perfume.

'You're a big girl now,' Margaret had said. 'You can come and have coffee with Mother!'

They had sat in an elegant cafe, chatting together over Vienna coffee and a three-tier cream cake.

Now, Ellen thought, I can ask. 'Margaret, what happened to my daddy?'

A horrible silence spread over them, the sunshine draining away. Margaret's face grew hard, and terribly sad. 'Your father left when you were just a little baby. I tried to make him stay, but he said he couldn't bear being around you every day. That's what he said. Just seeing you there made him feel . . . sick and unhappy. So he went away.' Margaret had had real tears in her eyes. 'He just disappeared.' She'd sighed and Ellen had reached her hands across the table, but Margaret had pulled hers away and clenched them tight against her chest.

Louise led Ellen to the other side of the room and told her to walk back past the men, turn round twice in front of them, and then return to her.

Ellen did as she was asked, feeling the men watching her. You hate me as well, she thought, and imagined for a moment that she might wither up and vanish like a dead leaf tossed on the fire. She took refuge by hiding herself in the puppet of grace and beauty. Lift your head, lower your shoulders, turn your head and give a small, small smile. Remember you are the ugly duckling turned into a pure white swan. Everyone wants you . . .

Through the haze of her concentration, she heard the voices.

'Perfect!'

'Yes!'

'That, my friends, is the body of the Russian ballerina.'

Chapter 13

It was weeks before the letter arrived, addressed to Ellen, care of the school. The American Academy of Classical Ballet was offering Ellen Livingstone Kirby an inaugural scholarship and placement, beginning in the following term.

Ellen waited until Margaret had relaxed after work before handing her the letter, along with one from Louise, explaining what a great honour it was and how proud they all were.

Margaret put the letter down and laughed long and loudly. Watching her, Ellen began to feel afraid and wished she had dropped the letter, as she had considered doing, into the lily pool.

Suddenly Margaret stopped. There was a strange look on her face, her mouth was twisted and her eyes too wide. She seemed to be searching for something to say, or do.

'Do you want to go?' she asked bluntly.

Say no. Say no. Say no. Ellen's heart pounded.

'Yes, I want to go. I want to be a dancer.'

Margaret's face spun away from her.

'You wouldn't have to clean up after me,' Ellen went on, then paused, overtaken suddenly by a wild thought. Margaret might not want to lose her! 'I'd come home in the holidays. It'd just be like anyone going to boarding school.'

Margaret's face was unreadable. She held up the letter and glanced over it again. 'Now what do we have here?' she mused. '"Consent form . . . indemnity . . . parent or guardian sign below . . ."' She took a pen from her bag and signed the document carefully with her elaborate signature. Then she folded the paper and handed it to Ellen, glancing at her briefly with hard, bright eyes.

Ellen walked slowly upstairs, the letter like a sacred offering in her hands. She wanted to run and dance with joy. She wanted to see Eildon's face, glowing with pride. She wanted to take Perdy in her arms and hug him tight. She stumbled over the top stair, her eyes blurred with tears. More than anything she wanted Margaret, mother, to say 'well done'—to smile at her daughter with pride and love in her eyes.

Margaret came later to Ellen's room, a glass of pale spirit in her hand.

'I hope you're not packing already?' She laughed again, with the twisted mouth. 'You're not really going—you know that, don't you.'

Ellen stood quietly, knowing that some new wild card was about to be played. There always was one.

Margaret sighed. 'If it really was a full scholarship, I could hardly stop you. It wouldn't be right to stand in your way, with your talent. But, as you'll see if you read on past the glorious opener, the scholarship doesn't cover living-in expenses, or dance requisites—whatever they might be. They say it costs hundreds more each term. You know I couldn't possibly afford to take on any more expense, I work so hard as it is.' She shrugged, with a pained look on her face. 'Unless you've got some secret source of money, I'm very much afraid it's just a dream, sweetheart—going off by yourself.' She stared at Ellen, fear shadowing her eyes. Then she spun round and headed for the door. As she reached it, the glass fell from her hand. It smashed, scattering jagged shards. A strong, sharp smell permeated the air.

Ellen stood gazing after her, hearing her footsteps on the stairs. She was running—running away.

In the days that followed, Margaret came home late as usual. She checked Ellen's homework and inspected her hands and spent the evenings in her study, reading. Slowly the silence of the house returned to normal, as if there had been no letter, no mad dream to come between them. Ellen tried to tell herself that it was over, the whole thing best forgotten.

But when she visited Eildon, he sensed that something was wrong, and pushed her to say what it was. When she told him about the scholarship to the new academy his face lit up with pride and excitement. He jumped up, scattering kittens, and grasped her hand. 'Well done!' he said, squeezing her fingers. 'That's my girl!'

'But I can't go,' Ellen said bitterly. 'You have to pay for lots of things and Margaret can't afford it.'

Eildon's smile froze. 'Is that what she said?' he asked incredulously.

Ellen nodded. 'We have lots of expenses. And she works very hard already.'

'Too hard,' agreed Eildon, but with no hint of sympathy on his face. He bent to scratch the ear of a cat that rubbed itself around his ankles. 'Do you want to go?' he asked quietly.

'I want to be a dancer,' answered Ellen. 'It's something I can do . . .' She breathed in slowly. 'But she won't let me. That's that. She never changes her mind.'

'She will this time,' said Eildon firmly. His eyes narrowed, becoming hard and angry.

'What?' Ellen shifted nervously in her chair.

'I may look a bit ragged around the edges these days,' he said, 'but I've still got contacts.' There was a moment of quiet, broken only by the low rumble of purring cats. When he spoke again, Eildon's voice was light, almost casual. 'She's a very respected pediatrician, your mother.'

Ellen nodded. 'People come all the way from England to see her.'

'Yes,' said Eildon. 'I heard she was being considered for an honorary chair at Harvard.'

'She'll be the first woman to manage it,' Ellen stated. Her chin lifted, showing a tinge of pride.

'Hmmm.' Eildon's mouth was a thin line, pulled down at the corners. 'It just seems odd to me, I guess, the way she spends so much time helping other children and meanwhile you're left at home by yourself. I've never been happy about it.' He kept on stroking a big old tomcat that lay over his knees. The movement was steady but too hard, so that finally the cat squeezed free and escaped. 'Any way you look at it,' Eildon went on, 'it's a damned shame. How old are you? Ten? Eleven? It sounds like a case of neglect to me.'

Ellen stared at him, her eyes wide with shock. Her lips parted, waiting to form words. Finally they came in a flood. 'But Margaret *has* to work late. There's all those sick children. They need her at the hospital.'

'Well, it's time someone thought about what *you* need,' said Eildon firmly. 'I think I'll have a little chat with Doctor Margaret. And if that doesn't work, I'll take it up with my colleagues at Harvard. They would agree with me, I feel sure.'

'No, don't!' Ellen pleaded. 'She'll be angry.'

'So will I,' Eildon responded. He leaned forward, looking straight into Ellen's eyes. 'Look, you don't have to worry. I'll make sure it works out.'

'But you don't . . .' Ellen began, then her voice trailed off.

'Trust me,' said Eildon. 'It'll be all right. I promise.' His faded blue eyes held Ellen's until she nodded, slowly. 'Good girl,' he smiled.

Ellen bent to pick up Perdy and hug him against her chest. She looked down into his eyes, one blue, one brown.

'Margaret likes me, you know,' she said. Her voice was faint, vague, like the wisps of fur floating in the air. 'She does.'

Eildon's his face softened. 'Sure she does. But she has to devote herself to her work. It's impossible for her to look after you as well. What she needs for her daughter is a really good boarding school. And I'm sure the dancing academy would do just fine!'

'But there's still the money,' Ellen said. Her face was strained with uncertainty, torn between hope and pain.

'To hell with money!' Eildon grinned as he waved his hand towards the parlour. 'I've got a lot of valuable old junk in there, going to ruin. I'll pay.'

'You can't do that—' Ellen began, but Eildon leaned forward and placed his finger on her lips. She felt it there, rough-skinned, but gentle.

'You can have it all,' he said. 'My horse, my kingdom . . .' He clasped his hands together, mock-begging. 'Anything for a smile.'

Ellen's lips wavered. Tears filled her eyes and began to slide down her cheeks. But at last the smile came, wide and lasting, pushing out fear.

When the day came to leave, the skies were blue and the air laced with sunshine. The train station was noisy and crowded. Porters wove crooked paths between ragged groups of passengers, onlookers and friends. Piles of luggage dotted the ground.

Margaret stood near the edge of the platform, one high-heeled, ox-blood shoe tapping a tense beat against the concrete. Eildon was beside her—a big, still shape. Ellen hovered in front, turning her eyes from one face to the other. She swung her arms awkwardly around her body, feeling the stiffness of the new school uniform brushing her legs. In the pocket of her blazer was a small sharp-edged card, tucked close to her heart. On one side was a black-and-white photograph of her face, big dark eyes gazing out. On the other, it said 'Student Identity Card. American Academy of Classical Ballet'. Ellen sensed it there, hidden, like the proof of a crime.

Margaret handed Ellen's bags to Eildon with a grim smile and a nod, as if some transaction were being completed.

The guard whistled. Eildon carried the bags onto the train, then came back with a smile. 'Time to say goodbye.' He drew Ellen towards him and hugged her hard, smelling of tweed, cats and herbs. 'You take care now.' His voice was close in her ear. 'And write me, you hear?'

Now it was Margaret's turn. 'Goodbye, Ellen.' A kiss on the cheek. A touch of crisp cotton collar. Ellen jerked back, panic springing up inside her. There was no perfume. No hint of any scent at all. She stared, cold with guilt, as if it meant, somehow, that Margaret was dead. Killed. Betrayed. Left alone again.

From the window of the train, Margaret and Eildon looked small. A man and a woman standing side by side, like any mom and pop. Ellen tried to pretend that they were; that they loved each other, and loved her; that they would miss her.

The train pulled away. The two figures waved. Ellen waved back. She opened her mouth to call goodbye, but her voice could not be found.

She sat in the train, rocking with its motion, her head bumping rhythmically against the hard, cold window. Her ticket was limp and damp in her hand. Her shoulders slumped and tears rolled down her cheeks as the train carried her further and further away. She felt numb, frozen; caught between pain, fear and loss and a dim, warm hope.

Chapter 14

Ellen drove slowly through the New England countryside, pausing now and then to check the map. Carter had scrawled a fax, giving her instructions on how to find the clinic where Ziggy was staying, but the roads were narrow and winding and the way was not easy to find.

As she looked out at the scenes passing by, Ellen tried to remain remote, contained by the car, with no connection between herself and the world outside. But still old links began to emerge. She remembered the brown horse; the feel of its velvet lips against her palms. Dark red hawthorn berries, pulled from the bushes and squashed on the road. Big, damp maple leaves like umbrellas. Ducks dabbling, drifting on still water. Untended fields full of knee-high trees, fledgling forests snatching the chance to return. And the houses, looking cold and blank with their huge facades and lines of matching windows.

She turned her thoughts to Ziggy, trying to imagine her lying in bed, looking pale and ill and tense; but she could only picture her running, long blonde hair flying out behind her, green eyes sparkling, breathless with some new plan. She called

up other Ziggy faces—they came to her, fleeting and lingering, with snatches of talk and long lines of laughter. But
nothing that hinted of clinics and doctors and giving up.

They were both ten years old when they began sharing a
room at the new American Academy of Classical Ballet. It was
a small upstairs room, unheated, with a window that looked
out over the old trees that stood in the grounds of the con-
verted monastery. In winter they conspired against the
window, talking of boarding it up or nailing blankets over it.
They lay in bed with their backs towards it, feeling the chill
coming off the glass. But in summer they hung up a piece of
muslin to keep mosquitoes out and left it open day and night.
As they lay whispering into the shadows, the rustling of trees
sounded like sleep on its way towards them.

'This room was used by nuns,' Ziggy liked to say. 'Their beds
were just where ours are, but they slept on bare boards. Every
night when they knelt to pray they beat themselves with small
whips that had hooks on the ends. To mortify the flesh.'
Neither of the girls knew what 'mortify the flesh' meant, but
it sounded noble and rare.

They lived by a rigid daily schedule, with changes rung out
by the old chapel bell. They wore plain black and white clothing issued by the school—leotards, vests, jumpers and leggings
—all to be worn in the right combination, for the right occasion. At mealtimes they sat at the long refectory tables eating
food laid out lean and small on their plates. No-one asked for
more. They learned the art of silence, turning their thoughts
inward to the task of total control.

In spite of the hard work and nights of girls weeping with
homesickness and fatigue, a sense of privilege lay over the
school. They were the chosen, the elite. For the ones who
completed the journey and proved worthy, a great glory
awaited . . . We will never marry, Ziggy and Ellen swore to
each other. We will lay down our lives.

At the end of the day they would sit together beneath the

window, their heads bowed—one blonde and one dark—as they bathed each other's feet, counting their purple bruises, weeping blisters and sprained muscles—marks of honour and stigmata of their faith.

They made up new ways of working on their bodies: lowering their shoulders, loosening ligaments, increasing the turnout of their legs. They would sit with bent knees, feet tucked into the small gap under their heavy chest of drawers. By trying to straighten the knees, they could cause a stress on the instep. They sat there side by side, straining until their toe joints were red and sore with the pressure. They found new positions that forced muscles to lengthen, then took turns to push the stretch further by leaning or pulling hard on parts of each other's body. They would agree in advance on the length of time and promise not to stop before then. They learned how to watch each other's contorted faces and listen to cries and tears without being tempted to weakness. They would turn their faces away to the side. They never let each other down.

On special days—opening nights, annual picnics, Thanksgiving—the students were allowed visits from their families. On any one occasion there were always a few girls for whom nobody came. But Ellen was the only one who never had a visitor of her own. There was just her mother, she explained to those who asked, and she was very busy. Working, travelling, lecturing or living overseas.

By contrast, Ziggy's mother, Lucy, seemed to live only for her daughter, surrounding her with an almost romantic passion. Ellen remembered Lucy arriving at the school at every opportunity, trailing furs and silk scarves, her arms loaded with packages. She seemed to move with the rustle of tissue paper; those delicate layers that enfolded gossamer shirts, cocktail dresses and underslips. Endless gifts, to be unpacked onto the nuns' narrow beds.

'What does she think we do here?' Ziggy would say, halfannoyed, as she tossed them into the back of the cupboard behind the even rows of folded blacks and whites.

But on their birthdays—Ellen's as well as Ziggy's—Lucy would wrangle permission from the matron and take them out to a restaurant.

'You can eat what you like,' she'd say, delighting in her role of provider. 'Don't even look at the menu, just tell the man what you've been dreaming of!'

The waiter would stand, pen poised, taking orders for strange combinations of food that the chef would, at first, simply refuse to prepare. Finally he would shake his head and set to work. The maître d' would double the average lunch bill. Lucy would leave a huge tip on top of that. In the end, everyone would be happy.

Lucy felt protective of Ellen, whose only real family contact appeared to be a rich but eccentric uncle who had a passion for cats. He sent her odd presents—funny old scarves and brooches that Ellen insisted she liked. Lucy was touched by this but knew that the place of a mother remained unfilled.

'Call me Lucy,' she'd said, early on. 'And think of me as your—oh, I don't know . . .' Her confidence had failed her in the moment, and the relationship had never been named.

'You'll both be great dancers,' she often said, with a knowing smile. 'My girls. The first real ballerinas to come out of America.' She told Ellen and Ziggy how someone had once said she could have been a professional dancer herself. Her eyes had become distant with regret, because she had not been given the chance. Ziggy and Ellen had smiled at her, knowing that she would count all Ziggy's achievements as her own and would not be disappointed.

Then Ziggy's toes began to hurt. It was not just the ongoing pain of dancing on strains and bruises, but something more that even she could not bear.

'You'll have to tell matron,' Ellen said finally, as Ziggy stared straight ahead, tears standing in her eyes.

Matron went herself with Ziggy to visit a leading orthopaedic surgeon in New York. He took X-rays and told them bluntly that if Ziggy continued to dance she would be lame for life. There was nothing to be done, he explained calmly. The trouble was being caused by the fact that her big toes were unusually long compared with the toes next to them. Consequently, he explained, waving his pen at the X-rays to support his words, the big toes took too much strain when she was en pointe. The joints were collapsing. They are quite far gone as a matter of fact, he commented, it must be agony.

Ellen and Ziggy sat mutely, crushed by the disaster, and filled with impotent fury that after all their work, one of their bodies should turn out to be a traitor. Ziggy tried to picture a future without dancing, and saw nothing. Ellen tried to imagine dancing without Ziggy, and couldn't.

A conference about Ziggy was held in the dance master's apartment upstairs. Ellen accompanied her, holding her arm, feeling her stiff with self-control. They were ushered into a luxurious salon and seated on antique chairs with gilded legs that ended in lions' feet. They stared around them, amazed that such a world should have existed all along, just above their heads. It was such a contrast to the long cold halls and bare floors that they were used to. Then there were the soft words of sympathy from teachers and tutors who usually spoke only to demand something more. More height, more curve, more distance, more fluidity and a little more of a smile. (I must have it, girls. I must! You are hopeless. Are you a cow? The daughter of a cow?)

Ziggy was moved to a couch and made to rest her legs along it. She lay there like a corpse presiding over her own funeral. And like a dead girl, she was pale and peaceful, her lips pressed into a small waxen smile.

Then Lucy arrived, sweeping in on a torrent of anger and despair. She demanded to look at Ziggy's feet and then at the X-rays.

'But she's only got this one year to go,' she raged at the head dancing master. 'There must be something we can do. Some kind of surgery? Anything!' Her voice was sharp and thin, as if something inside her was ready to snap.

'I'm afraid not, in this case,' the dancing master said. 'There's really no hope at all.'

A dark silence fell over the room as Lucy stared at Ziggy. The look in the woman's eyes was one of near panic. Watching her, Ellen realised suddenly that Ziggy's mother would sacrifice anything, or anyone, to save her bright dream.

Ziggy saw it, too. She flinched and looked away. Fixing her eyes on the parquet floor; following the lines of wood, tracing the small squares round and round and round.

A bleak year passed. Ellen stayed alone in the small room, and had no-one to help her work her body harder, or to wake her when she cried in her sleep. She was like a creature in hibernation, in limbo, just waiting for the year to end. All her energies were spent working towards the final exams and her principal role in the graduation performance. After that, she would be launched, they said, in a blaze of publicity. The pick of the first crop of real American ballerinas.

In the meantime, Ziggy had gone home to New Hampshire, then run away to New York. Carter found her somewhere, noticing her tall, slim-hipped frame moving between cafe tables with a grace he knew to be rare. He waited for a look at her face, expecting the disappointment of acne and colourless eyes, or even middle age. But when she turned she was beautiful—tossing her hair from her eyes with a slow, smooth movement. Like a mermaid, Carter thought, surprising himself. She was laughing, her head tilted back.

She laughed again when Carter told her he would make her into an international model, worth thousands of dollars a day. 'I'll see you in Chanel, St Laurent, Valentino,' he said. 'Because you move like a mermaid.'

Ziggy's smile faltered. 'You're kidding me,' she said.

'Try me,' answered Carter. He was thinner then, and almost attractive.

Wild headlines led up to the big night of the Graduation Gala Performance: 'Test drive of the American Dream', 'Cream of a New Crop', 'Cultural Coup for Democracy'.

The inaugural showing of the American Academy of Classical Ballet was by invitation only. In media offices throughout America tickets were coveted, sold and stolen. Anyone connected with dance, theatre, youth, education or fashion—the future—just had to be there. Andy Warhol had taken photographs for the cover of the souvenir programmes and advance copies had been sent direct to archives and museums across the Western world.

In the morning, the dancers were gathered together in the solemn dining hall, faced by the same men in suits who had cast piercing eyes over their trembling ten-year-old bodies light years ago.

This is your chance, they were told. The world is watching you. Tonight you will dance your way into the glorious history of the greatest nation on earth. We have given you everything. Don't let us down.

Finally the time came to gather backstage in the theatre. The dancers were quiet, tense, unable to be still. Production people ran like mice through the corridors, checking bodies, dresses, make-up, lights. Teachers moved around, trying to spread calm, but knowing that they, too, were about to stand trial.

Meanwhile Ellen, the principal dancer, dressed and painted ready for the opening sequence, had slipped away. She stood in the lighting booth, gazing silently out at the audience.

Third row back. Twelve seats in from the left-hand side. There she was. Her hands lying on the armrests. Her face pointed straight ahead.

'See her?' Ellen called back to the technician. He came and stood behind her, looking over her bare shoulder. 'Third row back, twelve seats in. There's a white fur over the back of the seat.'

'Curly hair?'

'Yes. That's—' Ellen turned to face him, her eyes glistening bright. 'That's my mother. She's here!'

'Honey,' he said, 'everyone's got their mom out there. I bet she's proud and nervous as hell.'

'No, you don't understand,' Ellen said quietly, 'She's never come before. She's never seen me dance.'

'You're kidding!' said the technician. 'Why not?'

Ellen seemed barely aware that he had spoken. 'But this time I wrote,' she continued. 'I said, please—please come. And she has!'

The man frowned. 'Well now, I guess that's something.' He turned around as a man in a black and white tracksuit burst in.

'*There* you are! It's ten minutes! You're called!' He shot an arm towards Ellen. 'Please . . .' He paused, breathing deeply, calming himself. 'Miss Kirby, could you go to stage left immediately please? And don't run on the stairs.'

Ellen waited in the wings with a smile softening her lips. She sensed the other dancers looking at her, wondering at her calm. They didn't know that for her the night was already won; already layered with stars and scattered with gold—a treasure beyond price.

She's here . . . She came . . . To see me . . .

'Just you do your best,' said Katrinka, the Russian dance mistress, as she limped across.

'Sure,' said Ellen.

Katrinka stood behind her, gnarled hands resting on slim, satin-draped hips. A spectre of everyone's future, the old dancer's eyes were hooded with wrinkles and dim with the memory of who she had been and what she had lost. As the music began, she tightened her hold on Ellen's waist, poised with her, waiting for the moment. Then she released her like a dove into the air.

Ellen flew onto the stage in a burst of mind-spinning pirouettes. She was wild with joy, but calm and firm at the core, where her heart beat its steady rhythm of hope. She drew on all the strength and discipline of her years of training, harnessing the power that had grown with each small triumph over pain and weakness. And she poured it all into the dark space beyond the brink of the stage—reaching out to the third row back, to the one who held her love, her soul, her life.

Mother.

As she left the stage, Katrinka met her with tears in her eyes. 'You are an angel. An angel with wings.'

But Ellen brushed her aside and ran back up to the lighting booth. There was a short divertissement then she was due to dance solo again. Her piece was listed in the programme— Margaret would be waiting for it, impatient for the other dancers to get through their parts so she could see her daughter again.

Ellen peered down into the house. Third row back . . . The white fur standing out in the shadows . . .

Only, now the seat was empty.

Stagelight spilled over the front seats of the house. There was no mistake. She was gone.

As the dance moved into a new phase, the lights came up brighter. Ellen stared at the seat where Margaret had been. Her coat was gone. And the souvenir programme, with Ellen's own face on the cover, lay abandoned on the seat.

She began the next dance in numb, blank shock. Her body played the part, remote but accurate. Then gradually, a stubborn hope grew back. Margaret was in the powder room. She was unwell. She would come back. She was probably there already. Ellen's body ached and stretched with longing. It had to be true.

There was a moment of stillness, near the end of the dance.

Against all the rules, she looked into the audience. Not with the blank gaze of a performer gathering up her crowd, but with a raw naked pleading—that went on for a beat too long. It touched a nerve across the crowd and applause filled the air. Ellen danced blindly on, following the patterns she knew. When at last it was over, she ran from the stage and fell, sobbing, into Katrinka's arms.

'What has happened? What? Tell me!' She took hold of Ellen's shoulders and shook her hard.

'She's gone.'

'Who's gone?'

'Mama,' Ellen cried, 'Mama . . .' It was not Margaret's name. Never. Not Mom, Mommy. Not Mama. But she had come to see Ellen dance. To see how graceful and beautiful her daughter was, how everyone loved her. It was a new beginning. Nothing would ever be the same again.

'Come on. Stop this baby playing,' said Katrinka. 'You have to go back on.' She spoke over her shoulder to the production manager. 'Get the wardrobe mistress. Tell her to bring one of the masks, from the masquerade.' She stood Ellen up like a doll and wiped her face with the end of her skirt, soft with dust from the stage floor. 'You are a big girl, you don't have to cry.' Her voice was gentle but her hands were firm. When the mask arrived, she blotted the tears away for the last time and covered Ellen's eyes.

'Now,' she said, 'it is over. You are not Ellen. You are nobody. You are an American ballerina.'

On cue, she sent Ellen back onto the stage. Ellen danced, unable to spare breath to cry but letting tears drop behind the sequinned mask. She moved with the driving, hammering pain of shattered hope. And when she sank to the floor at the end, lowering her head until her face met the smooth wood, she felt she would never move again.

The crowd rose and clapped. Flowers fell from heaven. Programmes fluttered as people checked who she was, the name of her home town. Critics scribbled anthems in their notebooks, delighting in the irony of something that was masked and yet so naked.

As the applause swelled and broke around her, Ellen felt cold and empty. Tears blurred her eyes. She saw the image of Margaret, sitting in her seat. Then she imagined her standing, walking away. Up the aisle, step after step, without looking back.

No! She wanted to scream. *Don't go. Don't leave me. I need you. I love you.*

You're my mother!

The sign was small and discreet, black letters on gold: THE MARSHA KENDALL CLINIC. Above it was the original name-plate of the old mansion. It had been recently repainted, a layer of fresh gold covering the many that had gone before. Shangri La, it said, in letters of an oriental style. The house bore the marks of old wealth and eccentricity. There were dragon-topped pagoda roofs on the towers that stood at each corner of the building and the front door was encased by a Chinese arch made of thick slabs of grey stone. In the garden there was a small marble temple, set beside a shallow pool that reflected the tranquil sky.

Ellen walked up to the entrance, passing under the stone arch. As she drew near, the door swung open, letting the morning sun fall in onto sculpted Chinese rugs and vases of tropical flowers.

A man stood holding the door, his face discreetly blank. 'Good morning, ma'am.'

Ellen stepped inside, feeling the carpet thick and soft beneath her feet. She breathed in the smell of beeswax polish and frangipani, blended with a hint of fresh coffee. She looked around at walls lined with framed photographs—seascapes, mountains, waterfalls—all soft-edged and hazy. She could imagine the designer choosing everything to work against the sign at the gate and the pain and embarrassment that went with it.

'Would you like some assistance?' asked the doorman.

'Yes,' Ellen turned to look straight at him. 'I'm here to visit my friend. I've been told she's here. Her name is Ziggy Somers.'

'Certainly, ma'am.' A note of sympathy softened his impersonal tone. 'Please go down to the drawing room.' He gestured towards the end of the hall.

A young woman looked up as Ellen appeared in the doorway. In her hand was a calligraphy pen, poised above an open appointment book which was neatly marked with flowery script.

'I've come to see Ziggy Somers,' said Ellen.

The woman smiled gently, her eyes wandering over Ellen's face. 'Yes of course, you've been before . . .'

'No, I haven't,' replied Ellen.

The woman was suddenly tense. 'Oh, I am sorry. It's just—I thought I knew your face. Take a seat please.' She took another book from her desk and began to flick through the pages. 'We much prefer that visits are arranged,' she said, without looking up. 'We have to consider matters of privacy. Your name, please?'

'Ellen Madison. No—Kirby. Ellen Kirby.'

'Ah . . .' The woman nodded, a flicker of interest passing over her face. 'Excuse me while I just check.'

Ellen looked at a large, gilt-framed portrait that dominated the room. It showed the head and shoulders, in profile, of a handsome, middle-aged woman. She gazed straight ahead, towards the right-hand edge of the picture, with a look of unsmiling calm. Her hair was wound simply up over her head; her clothes were plain and practical; but the background landscape was dramatic, with threatening clouds and sunshine breaking through a tempestuous sky.

'Marsha Kendall,' murmured the woman, in a tone of wistful respect. 'She passed away only last fall. She was a saint.'

Glancing around the room, Ellen noticed the calm profile duplicated in silhouette, like the head of a monarch, printed on stationery, engraved on a silver vase, embossed on the leather lounge, stamped on a cup and saucer and embroidered on a handtowel. Beneath the head were initials, in curling script—M. K.

'I'm sorry,' the woman looked up with an apologetic frown. 'Your name is not listed for Miss Somers.'

'What do you mean?' asked Ellen.

'A list of visitors is prepared by the client and her family in association with the consultant.'

'But I haven't been here,' explained Ellen. 'She wouldn't put me down for visiting because I was—living overseas. I've just come back.'

'I'm sorry.'

'What?'

'I'm sorry.'

'But I know she'd want to see me! We were best friends. I've driven from New York,' Ellen pleaded.

'I understand, madam,' said the woman gently. 'I can take your name to the next case meeting. If you'd like to leave your address.'

Ellen watched her face, recognising the look of practised calm.

'The Marsha Kendall clinic enforces strict security,' the woman added delicately. Ellen imagined the impersonal doorman coming to life as a kung fu expert, ejecting long-lost lovers, sisters, daughters, sons and fathers—dragging them out under the Chinese arch and past the tranquil temple.

'Shall I take down your address?' asked the woman, dipping her pen carefully in a monogrammed inkpot.

'No, don't bother.'

Ellen left, walking steadily down the hall and past the doorman. She felt him watching her as she crossed the lawn, jumped in her car and drove out through the wrought iron gates.

A short way down the road, she stopped the car on the verge and got out. Placing her feet carefully, to avoid the poison ivy, she headed straight into the woods that bordered the road. After a few minutes she saw the dragon gargoyles sticking up above the treetops. Soon she reached a high wire fence.

Ziggy, she thought, as she began climbing up onto the lower branches of a big pine, you'd approve of this. But now I'm the one climbing, instead of waiting at the window, searching the branches.

Where have you been, Ziggy!

I got a lift into town.

You're mad. They'll throw you out.

No they won't. We're too good.

It's nothing to do with me, Ziggy!

(Smile.) But you'd die without me.

(Smile.) Be careful—please.

Ellen jumped down on the other side of the fence, smoothed her hair and clothes and strolled across the grounds towards the rear of the building. She passed an old man sitting on a marble bench, staring mutely at his hands. She passed a statue of Marsha Kendall, her stony profile softened by bird droppings and outcrops of lichen. Then she found the back door and strolled inside.

Now the plush interior carried undertones of medical authority. Beside mahogany and ivory, there was stainless steel and white porcelain. The tropical flowers bloomed but their fragrance was tinged with antiseptic. Ellen hesitated, putting her hand up to her nose and swallowing hard, before walking quickly up a long corridor. There were rooms off to either side of her; each door carrying a plaque with the name of a tree: Myrtle, Dogwood, Maple, Beech, Cyprus, Candle Pine.

Only one door stood open. Ellen paused to look inside. It was like a hotel suite with a coffee table and easy chairs. But the legs of a hospital bed could be seen peeping out from under the French tapestry bedspread, and over the windows, instead of blinds or lace curtains, was an ornate filigree of fine strong metal. There was a strange impression of roundness; the room carefully furnished so that there were no sharp corners on anything.

Ellen looked up at the sound of soft footfalls in the corridor. A man was coming towards her, his face pale and rigid. She knew it was a famous face, but couldn't name it. He ignored Ellen and she looked past him.

Muffled sounds came from distant parts of the house, their meaning lost, smothered in layers of carpet, thick drapes and solid walls. Ellen became aware of her breathing; a careful drawing in, and letting go . . .

Reaching a corner, she turned into another long corridor lined with closed doors. She tried a few and found they were locked. One opened, but there was no-one inside—just a pair of pink high-heeled slippers lying in the middle of the floor. She kept on, moving quickly, trying a door here and there. She would never find Ziggy this way, she knew, but she might meet a nurse, or a patient, and be able to bluff them into giving her some help. She stopped suddenly, her eye caught by the name on one of the doors. Chestnut Suite. The big tree outside their old room had been a chestnut. She and Ziggy used to gather the conkers scattered below, the polished brown nuts that always felt warm in your hand. She turned the brass knob and the door swung open.

A woman lay asleep on a bed, her neatly plaited hair lying in long dark lines against the white sheet. Ellen crossed the room silently and stood looking down at her. Sores covered the woman's arms and face. Only her eyelids and lips were clear, oases of smoothness. Beneath the flaky, crusted skin, however, were finely sculpted bones. She would have been beautiful, Ellen realised. As she watched, the woman stirred, a frown of distaste wrinkling her brow. Her hands reached slowly towards her face, fingers curled, nails pointing—then they stopped, held in check by straps of thick webbing. Her eyes opened, deep wells of sunlit brown. She focussed on Ellen and smiled slowly.

'I'm sorry,' muttered Ellen, backing away. 'I'm looking for someone else.'

Out in the hall, she half-ran towards a door which bore a small image of a woman's head—carefully styled to look nothing like Marsha Kendall—and a sign that said Powder Room.

She burst in, running past lit mirrors and more vases, into one of a row of three booths. Leaning over the toilet bowl she retched loudly. Nothing came, only tears stinging her eyes. She coughed; a harsh sound, like dry sobbing.

'Let it go, angel.' The words drifted languid and careless from the next booth. 'You'll feel so much better.'

Ellen lifted her head. 'Sorry? Did you say something?' she asked.

No answer.

Ellen frowned. 'Who's there?' Something stirred in her memory. *Angel*. She jumped up on the toilet seat, stretching on tiptoe to look over the top of the partition.

She looked down on a figure sitting fully dressed on the closed lid of the toilet. It was like a stick person drawn by a child. Long, bony limbs, clad in dark, body-hugging clothes, were angled awkwardly in the small space. The head was bowed, as if too heavy for the fine neck and thin shoulders. A navy beret hid its hair from view.

'Ah . . .' Ellen made a noise, to say that she was there. The head turned to one side, revealing a pale gaunt face. Beautiful deep green eyes.

For a long moment, the two stared at each other, as if neither could believe what they saw. Then the stick figure unfolded painfully and stood up on the toilet seat, clinging to the top of the partition for balance. Now they were face to face. Hand beside hand. They felt each other's breath on their skin, warm.

'God, Ziggy,' Ellen whispered, 'what have they done to you?'

A tremor passed over Ziggy's face. She sobbed once, then

her eyes closed and a smile spread over her pallid face. 'Ellen. Ellen. Ellen.' She chanted the name like a prayer. She looked up again, her eyes shone with tears. 'I knew you'd come.'

Ellen breathed out slowly and mustered up a weak smile. 'Well, thanks for leaving my name at the door.'

They stood together, beside the line of sinks, keeping a small gap between them. In the past they had always hugged and kissed, then wiped off the lipstick marks on each other's cheeks, before leaning back and taking a look. 'Hey—you look great,' they'd always said.

Now they stood in silence, the words hanging unspoken in the air between them, the hugs held back. Ellen tried not to look at Ziggy's wasted body, the bones that pushed against her loose dull skin, as if they would soon break through. She imagined touching her and recoiled from the thought. Instead she looked into Ziggy's eyes, the only part of her that seemed familiar.

'Carter told me you were here,' Ellen said.

'It's a wonder,' Ziggy laughed. 'He's angry with me. He came all the way here once to tell me. Then he sent roses every day for a week. Roses! I ask you . . .'

Ellen smiled, remembering how they had always scorned roses, especially the long-stemmed ones that came with the thorns neatly sliced off—symbols of helpless beauty. 'Is there some reason why you're in here?' she asked.

'They tell me I'm starving to death,' said Ziggy flippantly.

'No, I mean in this . . . powder room.'

Ziggy's face stiffened, her green eyes narrowing. 'I was having a pee.'

'Okay.' Ellen leaned towards the mirror to remove a phantom eyelash from her eye. 'Well, can we go to your room or somewhere?'

'Ye-es,' said Ziggy, 'I guess so. I've got a visitor, though.' She seemed to rouse herself, putting on a bright smile. 'It's Mommy. I'm sure she'd love to see you. Come on.'

Ziggy walked slowly, with one hand supporting herself along the wall. Ellen followed her, refusing to watch. They came to one of the tree rooms and Ziggy paused to let Ellen go on ahead.

Ellen crossed the room, faltering for a second as she realised the figure kneeling by the bed was hunting through Ziggy's drawers.

'Lucy!' she called.

The head swung round guiltily, blonde curls swinging. 'Ellen, darling!'

They exchanged hugs, Lucy marking Ellen's cheek with her pastel lips.

'I hardly recognised you with a tan!' said Lucy. 'You look wonderful.'

'Thanks,' answered Ellen. 'So do you. You haven't changed a bit.' But there was, she thought, something odd about Lucy's face—a lack of expression, as if some part of her had ceased to function. Unless it was a facelift. Ellen pictured the surgeon easing Lucy's wrinkles away one by one; working carefully back towards deadpan youth. She turned to see Ziggy trailing into the room.

'Ziggy—where did you get to?' asked Lucy. 'I was about to call someone.'

Ziggy sat on one of the chairs, clearly exhausted. 'Give me a break,' she said wearily.

Lucy bit her lip, then turned to Ellen. 'Is James with you?'

Ellen looked at her, unable to reply. Finally she shook her head.

Lucy eyed her sharply, holding her head a little to the side. The air seemed full of stifled, distant noises. 'Dear, dear,' she said, her face softening. 'We're all in a mess, aren't we?' And she burst into tears.

'Stop it, Mommy,' said Ziggy, without looking up.

Ellen went to stand at the window, leaning her head against the cool glass. She heard Lucy moving around behind her, gathering up her bag and coat and umbrella, hunting for her car keys. Turning to say goodbye, she felt a sudden pity for the woman; the confusion and defeat in her faded eyes, as she faced the pitiful shadow of her only child, the vessel into which she had so freely poured herself.

'See me out, Ellen,' Lucy pleaded, leaning to kiss the top of Ziggy's beret.

Ellen followed her into the corridor. They walked in silence until they reached the corner. Lucy stopped and took Ellen by the shoulders.

'She's been in and out of here for three years now. Twice she's almost died. They say there's no hope for her. Nothing to be done. There was a singer in the next room, a famous folk singer, with all the money and all the love she could ever use— she just starved herself to death. It's impossible to understand. And she was doing so well, you know. Carter had such plans for her.' For a moment hope burned in her eyes. 'Ellen, you're her best friend. Perhaps you could . . .' Her voice petered out as her optimism failed her.

Ellen nodded mechanically. She could see Lucy weighing her up and deciding that she didn't look too good herself.

Lucy managed a brief smile. 'Anyway, we're still where we were. You call us, all right?'

'Sure. Thanks,' answered Ellen. 'Oh, Lucy, could you put my name down at the front as you leave? They wouldn't let me in.'

Lucy smiled. 'I'll tell them you're family.'

When Ellen arrived back at Ziggy's room, the door was closed. Leaning her ear to the door, she heard soft voices.

'There you go . . .' Calm tones, as if speaking to a frightened child. 'Just a little jab.'

Another voice. 'She'll be all right now. She always does this after a visit from Mommie dearest. I've told her consultant that the old witch should be kept away.'

Soft laughter.

'She's probably paying the bill.'

Ellen walked out past the drawing room, glancing in at the portrait of Marsha Kendall. The young woman at the desk raised her head and nodded. The doorman smiled.

Outside, birds splashed in the temple pool, making ripples in the tranquil sky.

Chapter 15

Ellen sat in a dim cafe, pushing yellow corn chips around in a bowl of salsa. She tipped back her head and swigged beer straight from a bottle, sending a shot of icy cold against the chilli burning on her tongue. There was no-one else in the place and a Mexican waiter watched her steadily from behind the small, cluttered bar, his face framed by outsized bottles of tequila, each with a worm lying wan and pickled in the bottom.

Ellen turned towards him and held up her hand, signalling for another beer. He nodded bleakly and reached into a fridge behind him without shifting his gaze. Slices of lime appeared with the beer, and a menu marked with oily red fingerprints.

Ellen shook her head. 'No food.'

'*Yes* food,' insisted the waiter. 'Beer and food good. Beer and no food, no good.' His eyes hovered on Ellen's face. She looked down at her hands, wanting him to leave.

'Taco? Enchilada?' he offered.

'Sure. Whatever.'

'You leave to me. I bring what you want.'

He headed towards the kitchen, enlivened by his task. Ellen

stretched back in her chair and looked up at the ceiling. It was dark with smoke and age, and spattered here and there with food. She imagined lovers fighting, picking up dishes of refried beans and side orders of chilli.

We were never like that, she thought suddenly, with a stab of pain. We were calm and quiet. She remembered James, always reasonable, while she would grow distant, trapped in a paralysing silence.

And now it was all over. Finished. Only the memories were left—replaying again and again, like clips from a film she had never wanted to see . . .

First, there was the woman writing a letter to her lover, putting down the words that could never be said to his face. She has to leave. It's not safe for her to stay. She is bad, or crazy, or both. Their child is not safe. She goes on, writing it all down. Then screws up the paper and begins again. Where did it go wrong? How? Why?

Then the man comes home, too early. In the same moment he sees the packed suitcase and crumpled letter. She's frozen in panic. He spreads out the letter and reads.

'It's not true,' he says. But his eyes believe it. Still waters run deep, he knows. Deep and black. He could never tell what she might do.

'I always knew you'd leave,' he says finally. 'At least now it'll be over with.' He sighs, almost with relief. The inevitable disaster has finally come; and the pain is no worse than the waiting.

In that moment, the woman watches him crack, and shift, and let her go. She sees the remnants of his love blacken and die. What is left between them he hacks off and tosses away. Leaving only the child—the one bright light burning in his eyes.

'Get out of here,' the man says. 'Leave us alone. Don't ever come back.'

That's where the story ended. But there were still more

scenes, more moments, to be played over and over—threads leading back to the place where it all began.

Their first meeting had been in the man's office, a room panelled with polished wood and furnished with solid sea captain's furniture. They faced each other across a wide oak table; an expanse of burnished brown, marked with old burns and scars.

'And what can I help you with?' the man asks. His eyes flick down to the woman's hands, checking her ring finger, looking for a white band of tender skin, newly bared.

'It's—not much,' says the woman. 'I'd just like you to look at a contract for me. It's with my agent.'

'And who's that?' he asks. Now his gaze lingers on her face. He finds her eyes, big and dark.

She looks back at him, noticing his hair, the colour of washed sand. 'Mr Meroe,' the woman replies. 'Carter Meroe.' She speaks his name softly, as if her words of treachery might reach him, somehow—echoing down the hall and on across the city.

The man frowns. 'Do I know you? I mean—Carter's big league . . .'

'No. I've only just graduated—from the American Academy of Classical Ballet. But he saw something about me. There was an interview in *Teen* magazine.'

'Of course!' His hands slap the solid table. 'The Cat Man story! The first American ballerina!' He smiles wryly. 'Trust Carter to get in on it.'

'He's done a lot for me,' the woman says.

'I'm sure he has.'

'Yes. I owe him everything. It's just that I—'

'Of course. You must have legal advice. You need someone to protect your interests. Someone thinking only of you.' He leans towards her as he speaks, his voice gentle and kind. 'You can rely on me, absolutely.'

The woman watches his face, his mouth, as if memorising

the way the words look as they come out. She smiles and settles back in her big leather chair, it's padded bulk surrounding her like a fort. She feels safe and warm.

That was the beginning. But the moment, the time of certainty, came later. On a chill November morning . . .

The fug and racket of peak hour traffic greeted Ellen as she followed James out of her apartment building. She smiled briefly at the doorman and walked quickly on across the pavement. A mass of bright red caught her eye. She froze, mid-step. Her car was covered in roses. Hundreds of them, swarming all over the bonnet and the roof, and spilling down onto the road.

Ellen swallowed, a snake rising inside her. Charles. It was Charles . . .

James strode on until he reached the car, then he bent to put her keys in the lock. 'What's all this shit?' he asked, with a slight frown, and began sweeping the flowers away like rubbish into the gutter.

Ellen watched, overcome with guilt. She had left Charles for James. The relationship had never meant that much to her anyway—but Charles kept phoning her. He still loved her . . . still wanted her . . . still couldn't live without her . . .

They drove off. A single rose remained, caught in the windscreen wiper. As they gathered speed the wind stripped away its petals. Ellen looked at James. He whistled as he drove, one elbow hanging out of the window, one hand on the wheel. He felt her eyes on him and grinned. She laughed. That was the moment she knew that she loved him—wanted to be with him. Forever.

The Mexican restaurant began to fill with lunchtime diners but Ellen barely noticed them. She stared down at her hands, spread out on the bright woven tablecloth. Words formed in her mind and pushed forward, demanding to be heard.

It wasn't love . . . You didn't love him.

She winced at the thought, sharp and unexpected, but with the sting of something true. She had thought she loved James and wanted to be with him forever. Instead, she realised now, she'd wanted to be *like* him—strong and careless, brave and free.

Carter's face came to her, his knowing smile thinly veiled with sympathy. I told you, babe, she imagined him saying. Right at the start I knew it wouldn't work out. I tried to warn you, remember?

It had been the day of Ellen's first meeting with the man from American Plastics. Back then, Carter still worked from an office in the heart of the city. The air in his rooms was always still, cold and dead. It trapped small sounds, burying them in the thick carpet and floor-to-ceiling drapes.

Ellen had paused in the street before going in. She sensed Rex, her bodyguard, stopping behind her, his big steady shape shadowing her own. Ignoring the traffic fumes, she took two deep breaths. Then she glanced briefly up at the third-floor window and headed inside.

A secretary was waiting for them by the elevator door. She smiled brightly. 'You're Security, aren't you?' she asked Rex. When he nodded, she pointed him towards a line of vacant chairs. 'Please come with me, Miss Kirby,' she said and led the way across the foyer. Her heels clacked over the marble tiles; a quick beat, her stride cut short by a tight skirt that hugged her knees. Behind her, Ellen moved easily on long free legs encased in lime green stockings.

'Go right in,' the secretary said, with another neat smile that lingered as she backed away, looking curiously at Ellen.

Ellen stepped inside. She held her hands together to stop them from checking the back of her skirt. She knew it felt much shorter than it was.

'El-len.' Carter drew out her name, as if to fill a set space. He crossed the room and kissed her, leaning in past her hair. She felt his chin, already bristly, and smelled his musky aftershave. Smiling briefly, she moved on to stand beside a tall potted palm.

Carter hovered for a moment before returning to his chair. 'Great to see you.' There was a pause as he appraised her body, his gaze hovering at the point where her thighs met the edge of her suede skirt. 'You eating?' he asked, with a sidelong glance.

Ellen tore a long strip from one of the palm fronds and dropped it into the pot. Then she raised her eyes slowly and fixed them on Carter's bulging waist. It was held in check by an old leather belt. Every year, she knew, he allowed himself to move on to another notch. Each one was marked in biro: 1966, 1967, 1968, like New Year graffiti scrawled along the highway.

'I know, I know,' Carter grinned. 'But it's not my job to be beautiful.' He reached for a notepad. 'For godsakes, Ellen, sit down—please.' He waited while she chose a place on a long leather-covered couch. 'Mr American Plastics will be here any time now.' He leaned forward a little. 'Thank you for not being late.'

Ellen's eyebrows rose. 'I'm never late. I don't believe I've ever been late for anything.'

Carter paused, gauging whether to go on. He checked his watch. 'These days,' he said finally, 'I'm never so sure about you.'

Ellen studied the picture on the wall above his left shoulder. It was a framed photograph of a winter sun setting behind the Statue of Liberty. Long rays of golden light radiated from the spiky-crowned head.

'I know you don't like James,' she began, 'but I don't see what—'

'It's nothing personal,' Carter cut in. 'He's just not good for you. I know it. And you know I know. I always do.'

'You've hardly met him.'

Carter waved her words aside. 'I don't need to. I've heard about him, read about him. I've seen him around. Black shirt and jeans every day of the year. The famous "I-don't-give-a-fuck" attitude. Who does he think he is? Bobby Dylan?'

Ellen laughed and held a smile on her face until Carter found one too; but he wasn't finished. 'Ellen, you can't afford to have a man who attacks photographers. Those guys are your friends. Without them you'd just be a—' He frowned as he reached for his next word, 'a dancer—nothing more.'

'It was a small bar.' Ellen looked at her fingernails as she spoke. 'We went there to be by ourselves. And you—' she glanced up '—were the only person who knew where I was going.'

'Hey, hey!' Carter held up a hand. 'Don't bring me into it. If I was going to give someone a scoop it wouldn't be Smithies. I hate the guy.' A sudden snort of laughter broke out. 'I wouldn't have minded being there, seeing his face. Standing there with the back ripped clear off his camera and his film dangling round his neck.'

The phone buzzed. Ellen shifted in her seat, making the leather creak.

Carter grabbed the phone. 'Yes? Okay, bring him right in. Don't bother with coffee. And tell him Miss Kirby has been waiting.' He put down the receiver. 'He's here.'

Earl Hollister looked hot in spite of the cool air. He held out his hand to Carter as he came in, then faltered, sensing Ellen behind him.

'Si'down, Earl.' Carter waved him towards a chair. 'I don't think introductions are needed. Miss Kirby looks just like her pictures. And we know who you are.'

Earl smiled uncertainly. 'I'll get straight down to business, then,' he said, snapping open the clips of a moulded plastic briefcase. He turned to Ellen. 'Our designer has done a wonderful job. I know you'll be delighted.' He pulled out a cellophane-fronted box printed with bold red, white and blue stars and stripes. 'I thought I'd show you the male doll first—as it's all done. It'll give you an idea of where we're going with the concept.' He held up the box for Carter and Ellen to see. Inside was a doll dressed as an astronaut, standing on a printed cardboard moonscape. A space helmet was tied to the doll's hand, leaving his face open to view, showing off a confident smile. 'It's about the same size as Barbie, Sindy. Authentic NASA gear of course, right down to the last detail. Good likeness, huh?'

Carter met Ellen's eye. 'Sure is. Couldn't be anyone else. Small step for man; giant leap for mankind?' he prompted.

Ellen looked blank.

'Neil Armstrong,' Carter added.

Ellen shrugged. 'Well I guess I've been pretty busy.' She felt Earl's eyes fixed on her.

'You know, the guy who just got back from the moon,' said Carter smoothly.

'Oh, right.' Ellen nodded. 'Sure.'

'So this is the companion product to the Liberty doll,' Earl ploughed on. 'They'll be launched at the same time.'

'Let's see her, then,' said Carter.

'Sure.' Earl reached into his case again. He watched Ellen's face as he brought his hand out and held an object towards her. 'Here you are.' He grinned. 'I mean, here *you* are!'

Ellen stared at the bare, plastic doll. A long moment passed. She felt her features moving—eyes widening, mouth pinching in the corners, chin lifting—to match the painted face. She sensed the two men waiting. 'It's a . . . weird thing for me,' she said. 'I mean, it's . . . me.'

'Sure is,' agreed Earl, with a proud smile.

'Take a closer look,' said Carter, removing the doll from Earl's hand and laying it carefully on her knee.

'The hair—I have to talk to you about the hair,' Earl said quickly, darting nervous glances round the room.

154

'It's red,' Carter stated.

'Yes, it is. We realise you don't have red hair, of course, Miss Kirby. It's just that we all thought—the long dark hair—' he broke off to take a deep breath. 'It's very much the ballerina look, of course. No question about that. But the feeling in the company was, it looks just a bit too—Russian.' Muffled sounds of typing touched the silence. 'We thought of short hair, curly hair; but long hair's the thing for a teenage doll. So—'

'You want Miss Kirby to dye her hair to match your doll?' asked Carter.

'Well—I guess. Yes, she'd have to.'

'You mean all the time?' asked Ellen. 'Or just when I was doing promotions?'

'Honey,' said Carter smoothly. 'You're going to *be* Liberty, all the time. That's the idea, remember? Armstrong's a real person. You'll be one, too. We won't use Ellen Kirby any more, just Liberty.'

'A bit like Twiggy,' suggested Earl.

Carter dropped him a cold glance, then returned to Ellen. 'It's up to you, about the hair, of course—as always.'

Ellen picked up the doll and ran her fingers through the nylon hair. She parted the long strands. They were planted in small clumps, neat rows running like tracks over the scalp. Her mouth pursed with distaste.

'It's not at all a carroty red,' said Earl, leaning forward in his chair and clasping his hands together urgently. 'It'll really just mean adding a tint to your natural dark brown. We've consulted hair stylists.'

'It's not the colour of the hair,' said Ellen. 'It's the way the head shows through. It's too white. You can see all the roots. It's ugly.'

'Good,' said Carter, jumping in quickly. 'That's settled then. You just get them to change the colour of the scalp under the hair and that'll be fine. Now what about clothes?'

'I can help you there,' Earl said happily. He took out a sheaf of drawings and spread them over Carter's desk. Visions of Ellen the doll in party dresses, disco skirts, pantsuits, leather jeans and studded cowboy shirts. Round yellow daisies appeared as a motif on every outfit.

'It was a great idea of yours,' said Earl to Carter, 'getting Young Designs to do the clothes. They're making them in true size for Miss Kirby to wear as well. Later, there may even be a ready-to-wear range of Liberty clothing, pitched to the kids. But that's their territory.' He laid out some more sketches, of riding clothes, ski suits, tennis outfits and hiking gear. 'We added these, too. The idea is, you can make her into anything you want. Just take your choice and dress her up.'

'But she—Liberty—can't *do* those things,' said Ellen.

Earl looked at her, then back to the drawings. 'You mean?' A puzzled frown gave way to a tentative smile. 'Oh, you mean the *doll* can't . . .' He looked at Carter, waiting for help.

'She's right,' said Carter. 'Dancers can't ski or ride or anything. We get their legs insured, and there are lots of exclusions.' He nodded towards Ellen. 'Those are million-dollar legs. Multi-million. No-one wants to see damage. But it's not a problem. No-one out there knows that kind of thing.'

'No, no problem at all,' agreed Earl. 'Now, there was talk of a bridal outfit. Perhaps something—'

'No,' Carter interrupted. 'No brides. We're talking teenage image here. Absolutely no way. You tell them that.' He placed his hands on the desk top, ready to raise himself to his feet. 'I think that about wraps it up for now.'

Earl put out a hand for the doll.

'I'd like to keep it,' said Ellen.

'Well, I wish I could say yes—' began Earl.

'Come on,' said Carter, 'let her have it. Soon you'll have thousands to play with.'

Carter ordered iced coffee when Earl had gone. For Ellen, he made up a drink by stirring orange powder into a glass of water.

'It's new,' he said, handing it to her. 'Specially developed for the space programme. What do you think?'

Ellen shrugged. 'It's okay.'

'Better than the real thing, they say.' Carter drank down his iced coffee in four long gulps then took out a fresh sheet of notepaper. 'So, what we've got here is Neil Armstrong making footprints on the moon and Liberty the all-American ballerina dancing for the world. He's strong, brave—an achiever. She's all those things too, but feminine, delicate, beautiful.' He eyed Ellen steadily. 'It'll work, you know. No question—it'll take off. Nineteen seventy's gonna be your year, babe. You'll be a household name.'

'You mean Liberty will be,' said Ellen.

'Sure. Liberty. Freedom, success, reward for hard work. You'll be a symbol of the American way. It's an honour.' He looked serious. 'And that's why, Ellen, you have to be so careful right now. And the thing you have going with James Madison worries me, it really does. He's—anti-tradition, anti-establishment. I'll bet he's against the Vietnam War. I can put it simply. He's un-American.'

'He loves me.' Ellen spoke quietly, mainly to herself.

'For godsakes, Ellen,' Carter burst out, 'everyone loves you. Everyone wants you.' He spread his hands wide. 'You could have anyone.'

'He's not interested in dancing, fashion or anything like that,' Ellen went on. 'He's different. He cares about *me*.'

'Aha.' Carter nodded calmly. 'Honey, how many beautiful successful women do you think I've heard saying those same words? It's the wrong approach. You need to find someone who'll stand behind you, work *with* you, not against you. You owe it to yourself. Think of the years of work you've put in. You need a man who values what you're doing as well as who you are. The two have to go together. And James Madison won't do that. He's just not the right man.'

Carter unlocked a drawer at one side of his desk and took

out a slim blue folder. He softened his voice. 'It's not just my view. I've dealt with this kind of thing before. What I do is have a psychologist look into the family, observe the person, talk to colleagues and then make an assessment.' Carter placed his hand firmly on the folder, palm down, fingers spread. 'It's all here, Ellen. Unhappy family. Nervous mother. Harsh father. What would you expect? The fact is, he's insecure. He'll never cope with your high profile. He'll be threatened at a deep level by the fact that others admire—and desire—you. He'll be jealous, suspicious, possessive. He won't even like your money.' The phrases came out smoothly, in well-worn lines. He cut the flow to leave room for a response, but Ellen was silent and her face gave nothing away. Carter sighed. 'I know it may seem premature, but I have to warn you, and the sooner the better. It won't work. If you keep him, he'll damage you. If you marry him, he'll destroy your career. And remember he's not a successful lawyer for nothing. He knows how to make things happen his way.' He held the folder out towards Ellen. The air was still, silent. 'As I said, it's an old story. But read it if you like.'

Ellen shook her head and turned away. She forced her hands to lie loosely in her lap. One foot tapped against the leg of the chair.

Carter watched her for a moment, then sighed suddenly and rested his head in his hands. 'Ellen, I'm sorry. I always go too far with you. It's your fault. If I said half that stuff to almost anyone I know, they'd walk right out. But you just sit there and take it all.'

Ellen looked puzzled. 'I'm used to you going on. You lecture me about everything. You always have.'

'Yeah, I know, I know.'

'It's your job. That's what you always say.'

Carter shook his head. 'You're a mystery, Ellen. I can't work you out. That's why I worry about you. This stuff about James— I'm just trying to protect you.' His voice was low, husky. 'If I was older, I could tell you that I love you like a daughter. And that's just what I would mean.' He came round and stood beside Ellen, waiting for her to look up and give in to a smile.

A light rain began, a gentle spattering against the smoked glass window. Ellen picked up the doll from where it lay balanced on the arm of the chair. She made it dance in the air, one leg bent back, the red hair flopping stiffly from side to side.

'I never liked dolls as a kid,' she said thoughtfully. 'I had them, of course, but I didn't play with them.' She shook her head and frowned.

Carter touched her lightly on the shoulder. 'Come on. Let's go out to lunch.' He grinned. 'Before you get so famous that you have to stay inside.'

As it was, it was much too late for anything that Carter might have said about James to have any real effect. Already he possessed Ellen as no-one ever had before. In public he was casually attentive and affectionate; but at the earliest opportunity he would arrange to get Ellen away by herself. They left parties early, with most of the guests still to arrive; cut films and plays short; abandoned lavish lunches, still steaming on white-clothed terrace tables.

And when James finally had Ellen to himself, an urgent passion transformed him. He wanted her clothes off, make-up off, hair loose; stripping her as if to feed on her very core. 'I want you,' he would say while they made love—feeling inside her with his fingers, his tongue, as if searching for some further, hidden part of her. 'I want all of you.'

Ellen entered his dream, fascinated by the power of his longing. She opened herself up, baring face and body, while carefully concealing the nagging fear that when she had given all that she had, and was, it would not be enough.

Meanwhile, although their time together had only just begun, James talked of planting his seed inside her, creating a child—their child. 'We belong together, you see,' he said. 'We'll never be apart.'

Looking into his eyes, Ellen felt herself being lifted up and swept away on the tide of his bright dreams. At the same time, his arms around her were strong and firm like an encircling harbour. A place where the cold winds and ugly storms of life could never reach.

Ellen stared out through the window of the Mexican restaurant. She fixed her eyes on passers-by and tried to make herself wonder who they were, where they were going, what they had bought today. But it was no good—her thoughts ran on, taking their own path. She pictured the hut on the island, the place that was to have been their haven, far away from the rest of the world. And Zelda, the child James had wanted, who would make their life together complete.

Zelda.

She saw her, bright and happy, waving her last goodbye. She remembered the feel of her, the smell, the taste.

I love you, angel, she thought. I miss you so much.

Then why are you here? The question came barbed with pain. Why did you have to take yourself away?

Tears filled Ellen's eyes as she bent her head. The loss was too great, too heavy to bear. She clutched at another thought. A place, a name; anything to take her away.

Karl.

She closed her eyes and tried to imagine his face. Karl Steiger, the choreographer—the man who had plucked her from the cloistered safety of the Academy and launched her into the outside world. She saw him leaning against the wall, legs crossed at the ankles, arms folded, head tilted back as he studied her with steady brown eyes.

It had been just two days before her eighteenth birthday when she was summoned to the director's office to meet him. She was hot and shiny-faced from the morning's classes. The smell of perspiration lay fresh on her skin and lingered stale in her old black jumper beneath the strains of liniment and lemon cleanser.

'Hi there, Ellen,' Karl called out as she entered the room. She glanced at him while she hovered in front of Madame Katrinka, uncertain whether a formal curtsy was still required now that she was no longer a student but a visitor taking extra classes.

'This is Karl Steiger,' said Katrinka, directing her gaze towards the French windows and the empty courtyard outside. Beneath her Russian accent was a tone of displeasure. 'The Board has decided to lend you to him.'

Ellen looked quickly at his face, then down again at the floor.

'Mr Steiger is from the New York Modern Dance Ensemble,' continued the older woman. 'He has the idea of choreographing a modern dance around you.' There was a dry edge in her voice, betraying her feelings.

Listen to me, girls, she had often said. Have nothing to do with them. Dirty, bare, turned-in feet. Rolling on the ground. You are real dancers—remember that!

'You are to attend his rehearsals each morning and perform in a five-day season.' Katrinka's voice was kind and sad, like someone sending away a favourite pet to what they feel sure is not a good home.

Perhaps she knew, Ellen thought later, how he would smoke dope before class and spend half of the time not dancing or teaching but just talking and thinking, and drinking herb tea. His long, strong legs casually sprawled on the floor.

On the day of the first rehearsal Ellen went to Karl's private studio. She was surprised to find that she was the only dancer there.

'I need to begin with you,' Karl explained to her in his soft, clear voice. 'My dance is a metamorphosis. You are the classical

161

dancer, your body ruled by perfection, your personality contained by rigid style and uptight costumes. In my dance you begin to change—break free. Hey, you discover yourself! And the dance follows the change. In a way, it's just like "The Sleeping Beauty" or "The Ugly Duckling".'

Ellen laughed. She pictured telling Ziggy. You wouldn't believe it! Karl Steiger's a mad hippy! She wanted to stand and walk away, but he had shown her his letters from the academy. 'Unique opportunity', they said. 'Timely, and beneficial to both parties. We strongly support it.'

As Karl began to work her through the dance, Ellen kept her face turned away from the mirror, giving herself over to the new movements—natural and unschooled, or deliberately gawky and ugly. She imagined herself swallowing a potion that would taint her body forever. She felt betrayed by her teachers, but she also felt guilty at the thrill of joy that came with the unfamiliar movements of wild, forbidden abandon.

They continued to work alone, as if the dance were a shameful thing to be kept hidden. Finally Ellen asked when the other dancers would join them. Karl told her that he was rehearsing with them as a group, but that she and they would only come together at the performance.

'Not even at the dress rehearsal?' Ellen asked, her heart sinking.

'No,' said Karl coolly. 'There will be no dress rehearsal. On the opening night, I will prepare you and send you out. Your costume will change as the dance proceeds, but you will not know how.'

'That's crazy,' said Ellen.

'No,' answered Karl, 'it's just new.'

And so, on the night of the premiere, Ellen sat in the dressing-room wearing a plain gown, while her face was painted to match the first of the secret designs taped to the mirror. A wet brush licked along her closed eyelids in a lilting upward curve, followed by a feathery touch of powder. A line of cool glue, and then the weight of long, curled lashes lying tickly on her cheeks. One by one she eased her fingers, loosening her tight grip on the armrest. Behind her, she knew, stood Karl, leaning, as always, against the wall.

'Okay, honey, open now.' The make-up artist leaned back to study her work. Karl waited for her to nod her satisfaction before coming over to check for himself.

Ellen gazed blankly at the face in front of her. This was for the first act—the caterpillar ballerina in traditional face and dress—very clever and beautiful, but nothing unusual. It was in Acts Two and Three that she would emerge from her dull chrysalis to test and spread her new-found wings and fly off, changed forever.

When the curtain fell at the end of the performance, Ellen stood chilled and afraid, the silence of the audience surrounding her like a damp and clammy cloud. Even Karl, watching from the wings, looked tense and unsure. The curtain rose and he nodded at her to run forward. She stood there alone, the other dancers behind her. There was no partner to take her hand and invite the crowd to applaud. It had been her story alone. Karl's story.

The crowd was talking, Ellen realised, but it was not the usual gentle murmuring that begins as the clapping fades and tingling hands reach for coats and programmes. This was a low, excited swell that merged seamlessly with the first wave of applause and grew as figures rose from their seats and broke into loud cheers.

Flowers fell onto the stage. And amid the usual roses were hundreds of big yellow daisies that matched the ones printed on her stockings. That had to have been set up by Karl, Ellen realised—but the applause was genuine.

She bowed her head and let the tumult roll over her, warm and comforting. I was okay, she told herself. I was okay. But behind the sense of relief, she felt, as she always did, a gulf of loneliness opening up wide and empty inside her.

Karl led her forward, ambling into the spotlights, one hand playing casually with the mandala that hung round his neck.

'Hey, honey,' he said, squeezing her hand. 'They loved it.'

She smiled, acknowledging the audience as she had been taught to do.

'Encore! Encore!' they demanded.

'Go on,' Karl said.

'What?' asked Ellen, panicking. There was no encore prepared.

'Just begin anywhere,' he said calmly. 'The orchestra'll pick it up.'

As the crowd fell quiet and sat down, Ellen stood caught in confusion. Suddenly most of the dance felt seamless, with no clear point from which to begin. Unconsciously, she found herself going back to one of the early sequences. It was a difficult piece, but purely classical, allowing her to draw directly on the legacy of her faithful study—the six hours a day, nearly every day, for the last seven years.

As she began the first steps slowly, waiting for the music to follow her, she realised what she had done. Even Karl, standing on the edge of the stage, turned to watch her, caught up in the surprise as she performed a piece of *Giselle* with faultless precision—wearing a tight sweater in bold stripes, a plastic see-through miniskirt, a cropped wig and stockings patterned with big, round daisies.

She ended the piece with a slow sink to the floor, the stiff skirt riding up over her thighs. Bending her head to rest her face on her knee, she waited breathlessly as the curtain came down. She heard Karl come to stand above her, but refused to look up.

'Well now, that's what I call upstaging,' he said, in his familiar drawl. 'Giselle in a mini. Wild.'

Ellen glanced up at him, aware now that the clapping had started again.

Flash, wind, click, flash again. A camera—on stage? Ellen

jumped to her feet. Flash. Click. Flash. Click. She tried to step behind Karl, but he moved at the same time.

'Get him out of here,' yelled Karl, seconds after the security boys hauled someone away from the edge of the curtain. He took hold of Ellen's arm and led her across to the wings. 'It'll be in all the papers,' he stated happily. 'We'll be the talk of the town!'

'Oh,' said Ellen. 'I don't know . . .'

'You're too young,' said Karl. 'I've been waiting for this for fifteen years. You watch. It'll be, "The First Real American Ballerina Goes Mod!"' He smiled around as people shouted their congratulations. '"Giselle in a Miniskirt!"'

With a sidelong glance at the crowd of dancers, friends, critics and reporters, Karl leaned to kiss her on the mouth. He lingered longer than necessary, probing her lips with his tongue. Champagne corks ricocheted off the walls and sweet white froth showered over them.

Ellen looked around her. Karl's right, she thought. They like me. They want me. She felt a sense of hope and relief, as though these strangers, who were pressing around her with warm smiles and admiring words would be able to keep her safe and give her all the love she needed.

The waiter came bearing a large plate of food, setting it down in front of Ellen with an encouraging nod.

She looked down at it, watching cheese melting and running into yellow pools. Her eye traced the pattern of tomato, beef, sour cream and slices of green chilli against the background of pale corn dough. Thousands of calories, she noted, probably close to three days' worth.

She thought of Ziggy, hidden away in the clinic, starving— her flesh wasted, eyes sunken. Raising her eyes, she glanced at her own reflection in the glass of the window. Shadows lay softly over her golden skin, her hair curled gently around her shoulders. She looked strikingly well, as if her body acted naturally to conceal the darkness inside her.

Tearing off large pieces of the laden tortilla, she began to eat—filling her mouth so that she could barely chew without sauce running over her lips.

It's good, she told herself, taking more and more, wanting to defy Ziggy, who had, it seemed, made a choice against food and was now unable to choose again. Lucy had explained this to Ellen during a long, distraught phone call. Ziggy must have some deep-seated problem, she'd said. It needs to be brought out, discussed and dealt with. Everyone who loves her must help.

The next time Ellen visited the clinic she went straight through Reception and walked quickly towards Ziggy's room, not wanting to give herself too much time to think.

She opened the door, and took two steps in before realising she had entered the wrong room. It was dim and bare. And the window looked not over the garden, but into another room. Ellen moved closer—through the glass, she could see four white-jacketed men standing around a pale figure stretched out on a bed. Ellen froze, midstep, as she recognised Ziggy's beret lying on the floor. Then she saw the bouquet of ribbons and flowers that Lucy had left on the dressing table, and Ziggy's other things dotted around the room.

Ellen sat down on a swivel chair set close to the window. She remembered how on her last visit she had noticed a wide mirror running along one wall of Ziggy's room. It had made the place seem spacious and light. Now she knew its other function: a two-way mirror linked to an observation room.

Ziggy lay on the bed, watching wide-eyed and shaking her head as one of the men approached her with a syringe. The others leaned to hold her arms and legs—firm but gentle, their faces calm and kind. Ziggy seemed to know it was useless to cry out or struggle. She just stared at the ceiling and waited.

No, Ellen thought suddenly. Don't give up! Don't let them! She felt panic rising in her. The man with the syringe turned, his hand poised, ready. Ellen swallowed and looked away—knowing, suddenly, how the drop of amber liquid would grow up out of the hollow end of the needle and sit there ready to fall. The image seemed to come from somewhere inside her, shafting up out of nothingness and carrying with it a sense of cold dread.

Ellen's shoulders slumped as she fell back in the chair. She watched with unseeing eyes as a man leaned over Ziggy holding a length of transparent tubing. He put one end near her mouth, then laid it against her face, running it back to reach her ear and on from there down to her stomach. He seemed satisfied with the length, and after rubbing some kind of ointment onto the end, he began to push the tube into Ziggy's nose.

'Damn you!' A man's voice cut into the silence.

Ellen jolted upright, looking around her in confusion. Then she spotted a small speaker set into the wall by her knee.

'Sit her up and tip her head,' the man spoke again.

His helpers hurried to obey. Ziggy was a rag doll in their hands, not unconscious, but carelessly pliant.

'Now gimme a look-see . . .' Ziggy's mouth was pulled open and the man peered into her throat. 'Yep, there it is.' He went on pushing the tube, back and down. Ziggy started to cough, painful spasms shaking her thin shoulders, held down beneath white-trousered knees.

'Oops!' He pulled the tube back and tried again. Now Ziggy gagged and choked, her hands, free only from the wrists, scrabbling in panic.

'Bull's-eye. Hook 'er up.'

There was a disturbance—the doorman strode in, closing the door behind him and locking it with a key. His eyes searched the room. 'No-one come in?' he asked.

The men shook their heads.

He relaxed. 'Oh, good. Sorry, saw someone go round the side. Thought you might have had a visitor.'

They laid Ziggy back on her mattress and one of the men attached the tube to a bag of cloudy liquid hanging from a stainless steel stand. They stood around her for a minute, watching the liquid sliding down the tube and up into her nose.

'Who's next, then?' asked the man in charge.

'Silver Birch, Dogwood and Mahogany.'

They all left, except for one. He sat on the window ledge and watched the tube, while carefully cleaning his nails.

Ellen leaned against the glass wall of the observation room, watching the blend of salts and sugars seeping down to spread strength through Ziggy's tired body. It seemed pitiless, useless and dishonest. Why not let her go? she asked. It would be so easy to just let it all go. A new thought came to her; a tempting vision. She, Ellen, could make her own escape from the world. Why not? She played with the idea, coming up with two scenarios. In one she was rescued, surrounded by white figures, urgent and concerned. She was placed in the steady hands of her own consultant, who would not rest until he found out what was wrong with her. In the other, she actually killed herself—not by joining Ziggy's slow and ugly dance, and not by struggling, gasping, sinking into blackness . . . For her, it would be something wild and quick and wide-awake—a rush towards death. She thought of how it would feel—death invading her body like a drug. She imagined the pause as it travelled through her veins to meet her.

Goodbye, James.

Goodbye, Zelda.

Angel.

Darling.

Then the end, building and bursting like a climax.

Mummy loves you.

Chapter 16

'I came to say goodbye.' Ellen stood looking down at Ziggy, who was sitting cross-legged on the floor, wrapped in a mauve cashmere blanket that was delicately embroidered with the clinic monogram.

Ziggy glanced up through her eyelashes. 'Where are you going?'

'I don't know—I just can't take being here,' answered Ellen. There was silence. She chewed tensely at the side of her mouth and stared out through the window, her eyes drawn to the horizon. 'Not here in particular,' she added. 'I mean New York. America.'

'Are you going back to James, then?' Ziggy asked, carefully neutral.

'No.'

'Why?' asked Ziggy bluntly.

'I—' Ellen paused, longing suddenly for the strong, bright Ziggy of old. She thought of how ludicrous it would be now to fall into her friend's frail arms and bury her face. 'It would take too long.'

Ziggy snorted. 'You could always begin. See if I'm still around by the time you get done!'

Ellen glanced at her, disconcerted by her willingness to joke about her illness while it was eating her slowly to death.

'Let's go out onto the balcony.' Ziggy began to drag herself to her feet. 'At least it's outside air.'

They sat side by side, like they used to, both looking out at the trees. But now a filigree mesh lay between them and the patterns of limbs and leaves.

'Start at the beginning,' said Ziggy, her eyes half-closed as she thought back over the years that had passed. 'You just disappeared! Everyone figured there was some kind of scandal. The press were hot for it—all they could find to take pictures of was your empty house! Carter was onto me, he thought I must've known you were planning something.'

'We weren't planning,' said Ellen quickly. 'We just went. James got an agent to deal with the house and everything. We just packed a case each and got in a taxi.'

'You didn't even send a postcard,' said Ziggy, with a mixture of reproach and admiration.

'We didn't contact anyone. We didn't even talk about them, or anything back here. That's what we decided—just to break clean.'

'That's fabulous!' Ziggy's eyes lit with excitement. 'You know, I was so envious of you. Everyone talks about getting away, doing what they really want, just for themselves. But you did it! And there you were, right at the top of the tree, where we all wanted to be. How did it feel, leaving it all behind?'

'I don't remember,' Ellen answered, after a moment of thought. 'I don't think I felt anything. I guess I just followed James.' She frowned, thinking back. 'I remember the day though—my last day's work. I'd been doing a Liberty shoot. Something to do with camels.'

The long black car eased slowly through the peak-hour traffic. Ellen leaned back in the seat, watching the night lights flash past.

'Long day, Miss Kirby,' commented the chauffeur kindly.

Ellen nodded. He'd driven her for almost a year now and had earned the right to chat. I've got a daughter 'bout the same size as you, he had told her. That was why he knew all about eating proper meals, wrapping up warm, and *always* thinking about who was walking along behind you.

'Where was it today, then?' he asked.

'Liberty in Persia.'

He shook his head. 'What will they think of next. What was the set like?'

'Oh—carpets, people smoking water pipes, belly dancers, veiled ladies lying on cushions—that sort of stuff. And Liberty, of course.'

The driver swung the limousine into a driveway, easing its length carefully between the marble gateposts. He paused while the security guard checked their faces.

'I'll see you inside,' he insisted as Ellen swung her legs out of the car.

But then the front door opened and James appeared.

The chauffeur touched his cap. 'Evening, Mr Madison.'

'Hi,' Ellen said flatly. She kept her head down as she pushed past James, heading inside. 'Don't touch me, I'm still made up.'

In the bathroom she used tissues and lotion to wipe off layers of cream and powder. Then she used a man's shaving brush and soap to scrub her skin bare.

She came out an hour later, wrapped in a velvet bathrobe, her hair loose and wet on her shoulders. She dropped into a couch.

'Get me a drink, hon,' she called to James, who was in the kitchen.

'Get it yourself.'

She paused for a second, then reached for the phone and dialled. 'Freddie?' She spoke loudly into the receiver. 'Is that you, Freddie? Mix me a Wallbanger and send it over, would you?'

James came to stand in the doorway, a cigarette in his hand. 'Good day?' he asked coolly.

'No,' Ellen answered. 'Carter's messing me around again. He had some magazine crew in there doing "A day in the life of . . ." Can you believe it? They wanted to come home with me.'

'Oh, everyone wants to come home with you,' said James flippantly. He pointed towards some floral bouquets piled in the corner. 'They do, too, I guess.'

Ellen lay down on the couch and closed her eyes. 'I'm dying.'

The drink arrived, delivered by a waiter in full livery. Ellen put her single initial on the docket and waved him away.

'It's not a goddamn hotel,' James said, closing the door behind him.

'Yes it is,' said Ellen.

'Okay, you're right,' replied James. 'I guess it might as well be, for all the time we get to spend here.'

Ellen said nothing. She swallowed her drink and reached for a cigarette.

'How can you dance and smoke?' James asked, watching her.

'It's not proper dancing,' Ellen answered wearily. 'It's just posing around. But—' she laughed shortly '—Carter says right now I'm earning more money in a day than any woman ever has, in the history of the United States.'

'Well, that's something,' said James.

Ellen looked at him, unable to read his thoughts. 'Let's go somewhere,' she suggested.

'Where?'

'I don't know—out I guess. What would you like to do?'

'What would I like to do?' James went quiet for a long moment, then came to stand in front of her. 'I would like to take my case files and dump them in the bay. Then I'd like to—' He glanced at a life-sized sculpture of a dancer that stood in the corner. 'I'd like to snap the fingers off that thing.'

Ellen sat up, giggling. 'I don't like her either, pointing away at us.'

'And then,' James continued, 'I'd like to go fishing.'

'Fishing? That's nothing much. You can go fishing any-time—in that floating airplane thing.'

James went to stand by the window, looking out at the lights of the city. 'Ellen. I don't like the way we're living. It's not good for us. I think we should do something about it.'

Ellen lay back on the couch, her eyes closing. 'We've been through this before. We never get anywhere.' Her voice was soft and sad, like a child's. She looked frail, lying there swathed in velvet, with her wet hair trailing down onto the floor.

'No, this time I mean it,' James continued. 'Remember I did your contract. It's an exclusive. You can't dance or model for anyone else, but you don't *have* to work for Young Designs, and you don't *have* to do the Liberty promotions either.' He crossed the room and opened his briefcase, pulling out a large book in a brown paper bag. 'You don't have to work at all. Neither do I.' He tore off the bag, revealing an atlas.

Opening it at a double-page spread of the world, he laid it down on the table. 'We're going, Ellen. We're gonna just find us a place where there are a few things we like—and disappear.'

Ellen stared at him as she grasped the meaning of his words. She tried to imagine what it would be like to just walk away from it all. Carter. Dancing. Cameras. Crowds. The constant pressure to be bright and beautiful, brave and perfect. A vision of freedom floated before her, filling her with a sudden longing.

'Do you really mean it?' she asked, sitting up.

'Yes, I do.'

'You've been planning it!' Ellen's eyes brightened as she leaned over to look at the map. 'I like mountains,' she said.

James frowned.

'Not for skiing and things like that,' Ellen added quickly. 'Just to look at. I want to see them on the horizon, or at the end of the garden.'

'Good.' James nodded his approval.

'What do *you* want?' Ellen asked him.

'A fishing boat.'

They studied the map, moving north and south. An hour passed. The liveried waiter returned, bringing grilled sea trout on silver plates.

'This is what they call fresh . . .' James remarked.

They considered the options—too hot, too wet, too cold, too dry. Too foreign, Ellen kept saying, but she couldn't explain what she meant.

Finally they found what they knew they were looking for. At the bottom of Australia, a small island—Tasmania. They turned to a larger-scale map. There were two main cities, one in the north and one in the south. Ellen said they should toss a coin to choose.

'Wait a minute,' said James. 'Look here.' Almost hidden by his thumb was an even smaller island, about halfway between Tasmania and the mainland.

'What's it called?' Ellen moved his hand away. 'Flinders Island.'

'That's it then,' said James.

They smiled into each other's eyes.

'What will we do, though?' Ellen asked, a shadow of doubt in her voice.

'We'll get to know one another,' answered James. 'I mean really get to know who we both are.' Ellen smiled quickly. 'No, I'm serious,' James continued. 'We need to get away by ourselves, be alone together. We've been married almost a year, and we're strangers.'

Ellen looked down at the floor, at the ethnic rug so carefully chosen by Carter's designer. She was silent for a while, then looked up and smiled. 'What shall we take with us?'

'Almost nothing.'

'So you went straight to that island?' asked Ziggy. She leaned forward, listening intently.

'Yes, we didn't even stay overnight anywhere. Just changed from a big plane to a really small one.' Ellen paused, chewing at her lower lip. 'It was a beautiful place. A bit hard to get used to at first. The bush, wild animals, the sea. And I didn't really have anything to do.' She looked at Ziggy with a wry smile. 'Imagine that? Nothing to do! James was always busy. He bought a boat straight away and went crayfishing. Then I got pregnant.'

'You had a baby!'

'A girl. Zelda.' Ellen went on to tell, soft-voiced, about what it was like to have a child and to be in love with that child. How the small hands reached out to you, trusting and loving, and made you feel like a god.

'I always thought it would be like that,' said Ziggy.

'Yes, but—' Ellen frowned as she licked dry lips. 'The same things that filled me with joy—like the way she stretched her arms when she was waking up, or her little toes curling—they brought out this feeling . . .' She talked slowly, searching for the right words. 'It was like when you watch a film. The scene is normal, nothing is wrong, but there's something about the lighting, the sound, whatever—you know something terrible is going to happen. Well, it was like that. Worse than that.' Ellen shook her head slowly. 'I couldn't understand it myself, let alone tell anyone else. I had a friend—Lizzie. I tried to explain it to her but it was like she just couldn't see what I was saying. She thought I just needed a break, or something. And James . . . I couldn't—'

'No,' Ziggy broke in. 'You could never have told James anything like that.'

'Why do you say that?' asked Ellen, surprised by her certainty.

'You always had this idea of who James thought you were and you were terrified of letting it slip.'

Ellen looked at her. 'What do you mean? What idea of me?'

Ziggy shrugged. 'Same as everyone's. The great American ballerina dream. Graceful, strong, healthy, beautiful. You know, land of the brave and home of the free. Big smiles and big hearts.'

Ellen thought for a while. 'Maybe once. But we left all that behind over here.'

'Well, you would have replaced it with something else and still been afraid of stepping out of line. You've always done that. And you've always been afraid.'

Ellen glanced sideways at her. 'Where'd you get all that stuff from?'

'My consultant. That's what he said about me.'

'Oh.'

'Anyway, that's a sidetrack,' Ziggy went on. 'You didn't leave just because you were afraid of something now and then.'

'No. It was more than that.' Ellen stared ahead as she spoke. 'This . . . feeling . . . started to take over my ideas, making plans for things I would do. Not in advance, but just suddenly I'd get a flash, and I'd see myself doing something.' She bent suddenly and rubbed her face with her hands. 'I don't know where it came from. And then—' She began to cry, without tears, just sobs; her breath coming in long shuddery gasps.

'What?' Ziggy's voice was firm. 'Go on.'

'I can't.'

'Yes you can,' Ziggy stated calmly. 'You must.'

'Ziggy, it's worse than you're thinking of.' Ellen's voice was thin with pain. 'I tried to kill her.'

Ziggy was motionless and silent beside her.

'I tried to kill her—Zelda,' Ellen repeated as if wanting to make sure it was heard. 'I nearly drowned her. In the sea.'

Drowned. The word sounded like what it was: being lost in engulfing darkness, finally and forever.

'There's no point in this,' Ellen said suddenly, moving to stand up. 'I don't understand it myself. How could anyone else imagine . . .'

Ziggy leaned back, resting her head against the wall. A minute passed before she spoke. 'What I do know,' she said, 'is that things get so you just can't fix them up. Look at me. It's like waking up in the middle of a dream. At first you're relieved. It's just a dream. But then the dream goes on. It's never real, as far as you can tell, but it's there just the same . . . And it hurts just as much.'

They sat without words, the trees swaying around them, leaning close in the wind.

'Where will you go, then?' asked Ziggy finally.

'I don't know—just away.' Ellen made her voice light and carefree. 'Away from maple trees, clapboard houses, Ford cars, poison ivy . . .'

'Carter,' added Ziggy.

Ellen laughed. 'Marsha Kendall . . .'

Ziggy stared at her, lips parting.

'I was joking,' Ellen said quickly.

'Yes!' Ziggy leaned towards her. 'Let's both go away somewhere.'

'Don't be crazy, Ziggy. Look at you!'

'I'm much better.'

'You are sick,' Ellen said gently. 'You need to be looked after.'

'You can look after me.'

'I'm not a doctor. I haven't even done first aid.'

'I'm not sick.'

'You *are*.' Ellen tried being harsh. 'You're a wreck. Look at you, you can hardly stand up. They wouldn't let you onto a plane.' Ziggy took hold of her arm. Ellen felt the bones of her fingers.

'Take me, Ellen,' Ziggy pleaded. 'I have to get away from here.'

'But—what about Lucy?'

'Lucy!' A short, bitter laugh burst from Ziggy's lips.

Ellen frowned, puzzled. 'You were always so close. What happened?'

Ziggy gave no reply. She pulled herself to her feet and turned to look back into the room, her gaze travelling over the neat furnishings and coming to rest on the wide blank mirror. Her mouth twisted with distaste.

'You owe me, Ellen,' she said quietly.

Her eyes spoke: I found you at the back of the class. You didn't even know how to tell a joke, or make up secrets. You used to wait until all the toilets were empty, so that no-one would hear you pee. You used to scream in your sleep and wake up in tears. I was your friend. I stood beside you. I peed in front of you with the door wide open. I saved you.

'You'd have to start eating first,' said Ellen.

A smile spread over Ziggy's face. 'Yes, sure,' she replied.

'I mean it,' said Ellen, her voice firm. 'I'm going to sit and watch you do it.'

Looking at Ziggy, she felt suddenly calmer and steadier—fed by her friend's weakness and made strong by her pleading. The tables had turned.

Ziggy nodded, still smiling. 'Now—where shall we run away to? You're the expert.' She giggled. 'Imagine Carter's face when he finds out he's lost you again.'

PART THREE

Chapter 17

Ellen rested her head on her arm and tried again to sleep—to lose herself in the low, even hum of the engines, blotting out the murmuring voices that filtered through from the seats behind. Ziggy had not slept, as far as she knew, and neither had her companion. Instead they twisted and turned in constant restless movement, as their mean-fleshed bones pressed painfully into the padded seats. Ellen closed her eyes and frowned as she recalled the last days at the clinic.

Ziggy had been waiting at the front door when Ellen's car turned into the drive. She looked edgy, her eyes darting tensely over Ellen's face and clothes, pausing for an instant on the tickets and passports she held in her hand.

'Look, Ellen . . .' she began, then her voice trailed off uncertainly.

Ellen waited quietly, expecting her to explain that she had thought better of their plan. In the brief pause, she asked herself if she would still go on alone, but couldn't decide.

'I'd like you to—ah—' Ziggy glanced around her. As if on cue, a figure slid out from between the shadowy trees that stood behind the small temple. A woman strolled slowly across the freshly mown lawn, her mouth spreading into a small hostess smile as she came close.

'Hi,' Ellen answered her unspoken greeting, glancing quickly over her body. She had dark hair and surprising blue eyes, but somehow she still managed to look like Ziggy—she had the same heavy-looking head, too-long feet, bulbous knees; the same gaunt arms with veins bulging beneath the skin.

Ellen looked away, screwing up her eyes and studying the sky.

'This is Skye,' said Ziggy. Snatching a quick breath, she plunged on. 'I said she could come with us, to India.'

In the silence a small bird chirped and splashed in the temple pond.

Ellen stared. 'What?'

'I said that she could come away with us.'

A short laugh burst from Ellen's mouth.

Ziggy carried on talking, extending the introduction as if they were all guests at a formal party. 'Skye's from LA—Hollywood. Her father's Richard Fountain. You know, the newspaper family. She was married to Al Macy, but you wouldn't know him. She's got plenty . . . well, she can pay her way, of course.'

Ellen looked at her blankly. Ziggy's words began to tumble over one another. 'We've been here—together. We've done therapy together. She found out I was going. I couldn't leave her behind, once she knew. Ellen, she's been here for years. I had to say yes.'

'Well *you* might have said yes,' said Ellen, 'but it's just not possible! We're leaving in less than a week. I've organised everything—for the two of us. There would be too much to do: vaccinations, passports, tickets.'

Ziggy waved an arm, wasted to the bone. 'Don't worry, we've got all that in hand. She's still got a valid passport and I've made extra bookings.' Ziggy met Ellen's gaze. A trace of her old spirit flickered briefly in her eyes. Then she looked down at her feet.

'Hell, Ziggy—' Ellen burst out angrily. 'This is mad. You're mad. Both of you.' She turned to Skye. 'What makes you think I even want to take you? I don't.'

Ziggy and Skye stared at Ellen. Their desperate silence gathered around her, making her feel rich and privileged, as if there were some link between her own firm flesh and their sallow baggy skin and jutting bones.

'Look, I understand,' said Ellen, 'but I just can't help. Surely there's someone else who could . . .'

They gazed at her with kitten's eyes, overlarge in their shrunken faces.

'Please don't leave me.' Skye's voice was soft and she spoke with a slow drawl. 'I've tried everything. I'll be here forever.' Bony fingers came up to cover her mouth. Ellen focussed on them, avoiding the woman's eyes.

'We have to take her!' Ziggy's voice rose, pleading. 'I said we would . . .'

Skye stood silent, her head bowed like a daisy awaiting the morning sun. Pared to the bone, her face bore the dignified, agonising beauty of a refugee, past hope.

She began to sob, thin shoulders shaking as she hunched over, her face hidden by a veil of long dark hair. 'I'll die here.'

Ellen stood stiffly, looking out at the distant trees of the forest beyond the clinic walls. She folded her arms over her chest, keeping her hands hidden, pushing aside the image of a pair of desperate arms reaching towards her, pleading for rescue, like someone caught in quicksand. She saw the hands clutching in panic at the air, then sinking slowly out of sight. Lost . . . because of her.

'You'll probably die anyway,' she said bluntly.

Ziggy smiled. 'I knew you'd want to help.'

Skye clasped her hands, eyes shining. 'Thank you. Oh, thank you.'

'Wait a minute—'

'You won't regret it.'

'For godsakes, Ziggy. This is crazy!'

'No it's not. You'll see. It'll be fine.'

The steward hovered anxiously by the empty seat beside Ellen. Finally he leaned towards her and spoke in a low voice. 'Ma'am? Your companions seem unhappy with the meal service. I wondered if there was some problem? I have no record of special meals being ordered.'

'Ah.' Ellen fought the impulse to stand and look over the back of her seat. 'In what way—unhappy?'

'Well, ma'am, they just say no to everything we offer. We have tried —'

'Don't worry about it,' Ellen interrupted. 'They don't eat. They're not well.' She sensed him recoiling slightly. 'It's all right; it's not catching.' She rubbed at the back of her neck, suddenly tired. 'How long till we land?'

'Four hours, ma'am. We'll be serving a light meal soon.'

'Could you bring me a drink—a Bloody Mary?'

'Certainly, ma'am.'

'Double vodka.'

Ellen stood up, aware of curious looks from the few other passengers awake in the first-class cabin. It struck her briefly that for once she was being stared at not because of who she was but because of who she was with—this pair of skeleton women who looked like refugees but who carried Louis Vuitton bags and wore couture suits which draped loosely over their ravaged bodies.

Ellen turned round to where they were sitting in the row behind. Their long limbs were draped uselessly over arm- and footrests, their bodies propped up by pillows. They looked like rag dolls that had lost too much of their stuffing. Skye had a magazine resting open on her lap. Her hand lay, claw-like, against a close-up of a woman's peach-skinned face. Seeing Ellen, she forced a bright look. Ellen felt like the class bully, invoking nervous friendship and respect from fear.

'We'll be landing in four hours,' she said. 'It'll be two a.m. local time. There may not be anywhere to eat till morning. So when they bring the next meal, please eat it. And—go to the toilet before you get off. Please.' She smiled quickly, suddenly embarrassed at treating them like children. But they were like children—weak and clumsy and vulnerable; defenceless against the world and themselves. Ellen shook her head, wondering how they would manage. It wouldn't be so daunting if their destination had been somewhere clean and organised—like Switzerland. But for reasons that now seemed vague and illfounded they had settled on India.

'Indian hill station' had started in the middle of Ellen and Ziggy's shortlist and worked its way up to the top, pushing aside Zurich, Johannesburg, Lisbon, Bali and the Isle of Man.

The travel agent had suggested Simla, in the foothills of the Himalayas. It had been the summer base of the British Raj, where officials' wives and children went to escape the piercing heat of Delhi, spending their time playing tennis, having garden parties and imagining breaking the rules. Their men would join them now and then. Small parties would gather to share Bombay gin and quinine tonic in the crisp evenings, and talk of Home . . .

Simla had kept them sane. Thank God for dear old Simla—quaint, respectable, upright and pretty. A little piece of England.

While scouring maps and travel guides Ziggy had discovered Mussoorie. It had the same clean, cool Himalayan air; the mountain views; English mansions and Swiss-style alpine chalets. But here, Ziggy read, Indian princes set up house with foreign mistresses; disgraced wives lived out their days in cottages perched on the edges of cliffs; playboys dallied along the Mall. There were stories of people being lost down gullies and lovers hiding out in abandoned ruins. There were rumours of murder and harems.

As a result, it seemed no-one asked too many questions. Mussoorie was known as a place for forgetting who you were, or who you were meant to have been. It was a place to disappear.

'It's perfect,' Ziggy had declared. 'There's even a Savoy Hotel.'

'You're kidding,' said Ellen.

'No, there is. Apparently, an English princess had a garden party there once.'

'Well, I still like the idea of Indonesia,' said Ellen. She shuffled pictures of coconut palms and white beaches. 'The Spice Islands . . .'

Ziggy looked up, dreamy-eyed, into the distance. 'My grandfather lived in Missouri. High up in the Ozarks. He was the original mountain man. Wild and funny, with a warm and loving heart.' Ziggy smiled. It softened the gaunt hollows of her face. 'I loved my old Pa from Missouri. I think it's a good omen.'

Ellen laughed. 'That's crazy!'

So Mussoorie it was.

When the plane landed stewards hovered around the three women helping them gather up hand baggage, hats, coats and magazines.

Standing by the door, Ellen felt a sudden impulse to run back to her seat. The aircraft was clean, comfortable and air-conditioned. The food was safe, and served with a smile by American stewards who had greenbacks folded in their pockets, and tanned faces spiced with familiar aftershave. But Ziggy and Skye were already making their way towards her. And behind them, the passengers from economy class stood poised to press forward. They stared openly at Ellen, as she stood there like some kind of priest, shepherding the two gaunt women out of the aircraft, laying a hand briefly on their pointed shoulders as they passed her.

At immigration, the officer looked at Ziggy's documents for a long time, his eyes flicking from the passport photograph to the face in front of him. Ellen stepped up beside her.

'Please wait behind the line, madam,' he said, waving her away.

Ellen returned to the queue and asked Skye for her passport. As she looked at the photograph inside, she found herself doing the same as the Indian official—trying to link the hollowed face that hovered beside her with the glamorous image of just a few years before. It was not only the roundness of the cheeks or the soft neck that had gone. It was the lift of the chin and the clear-eyed gaze. Something inside her—the taproot, the lifeline—had withered away and died.

Looking up, Ellen saw that a senior officer had arrived. Flicking her hair back, she looked directly at him as she came forward. She leaned close to him, cutting the other officer out, and offered a smile.

'I hope you can help us,' she said. She lowered her voice. 'These women are coming here for medical treatment. As you can see, they are very sick.'

'Sick?' the officer repeated sharply. 'Then why are they coming here? They should go home to America.'

'They cannot be cured in America,' Ellen explained, sadly. She pulled out a letter of discharge from the Marsha Kendall clinic. The officer held the paper in his hand, his eye lingering over the gold-embossed profile stamped in the top corner. The letter described the women's condition as a nervous eating disorder and noted that apart from the complications of lack of nourishment, they were free from disease.

'Eating disorder. Eating. Dis-order,' the officer repeated, as if waiting for it to make sense. He checked the names in the letter against Ziggy's and Skye's passports and nodded to his offsider, indicating that he should begin the rubber-stamping.

'Eating disorder?' he queried again. 'They eat, but stay thin?'

'No, they cannot eat.'

The officer shook his head. 'This is very unusual.'

'Yes,' agreed Ellen. 'Very.' She smiled. 'Thank you so much for your help.'

'It is a pleasure, madam.' The officer lifted his hand in a small salute and walked smartly away.

When they arrived at the luggage collection area, only two of their six suitcases could be found. Ellen glanced at her companions. They were drooped over their trolleys like wilting plants, beyond care. She went off alone in search of a Pan Am desk. At two in the morning, the airport was cavernous and empty, quiet and sparingly lit. Ellen passed a darkened bay of empty seats, pausing by the still form of a man in army uniform stretched out on the floor. His hat covered his face and his hands were folded comfortably over his wide chest; he might have been dozing by a swimming pool in his own back-yard. A sweeper woman wrapped in dull white cloth shuffled noiselessly by, her stooped body bent over as she flicked idly at the floor with a brush.

'Ah, excuse me—Pan Am office?' Ellen's voice boomed loudly in the abandoned air.

The woman turned, raising brown eyes set against smooth, honey skin. Then she smiled, uncovering a line of perfect teeth.

'Pan Am office. Luggage office?' Ellen repeated. For a second she couldn't help being Carter, totting up the value of those striking eyes, textbook teeth and slow, surprising smile.

The woman shook her head and held out her hand. Ellen looked at the calloused palm and rough skin as she pulled a note from her pocket and held it out. There was a tremor of contact as it changed hands.

Turning to go, Ellen glimpsed the woman studying the note, her body rising tall with surprise. It must've been a big one.

When she returned to the baggage area, Ellen saw Ziggy looking out for her.

'Ellen! We've found them!' she called. 'This lady helped

us.' She nodded towards a hugely fat Indian woman who stood beside Skye, giving out instructions as her husband and sons piled suitcases onto the three trolleys. The menfolk looked small and weak beside her, as if she had grown to her extravagant size by sapping their strength and sustenance. Skye stared openly, her mouth twisted with distaste, at the three rolls of naked flesh that bulged from the gap between the woman's short top and the skirt of her scarlet and gold saree. She held her head high, above layers of chin, and waved her hand regally, bearing a solid weight of flesh and gold bracelets.

'Is everything here?' Ellen asked, counting for herself, then smiling her thanks at the family.

She tried to concentrate, think ahead. In the past, she had always dreamed and wandered her way through airports, knowing that someone else had everything in hand. Cars would be waiting, security arranged, hotels primed, drinks cooled. All she had to do was pass the time, floating blank-faced behind big dark glasses, watching everyday passengers with faded make-up and creased clothes, while they watched her. This time it was different; it was up to her to plan and act. And now—thanks to Ziggy—she had two sick women to take care of as well.

Up ahead she saw an arrow pointing left towards Customs clearance. 'Let's go,' she called to Ziggy and Skye. Then she led the way down the long corridor, glancing behind her now and then to check that the others were still in tow.

They did look suspicious, Ellen realised. They looked thin, like drug addicts; and rich, like drug dealers—so it was not surprising that their baggage was searched. Their cases were lined up and opened. Clothes spilled onto the stained counter. Silk lingerie slipped through fingers; sharp-heeled shoes were balanced on palms. Books were flipped through, linings probed and toilet bags carefully emptied.

Ellen tried to avoid looking at Skye's belongings, not

wanting to know her tastes and interests—not wanting to know anything. She was just a name and a body. Ellen smiled wryly. It was the oldest hitch-hiking trick in the book. One person waits on the edge of the road, holding out a thumb, showing a leg and a smile; another hides in the bushes until a car stops and the front person is already climbing in. Then the second one advances casually as if they have been there all along. That's how two grows into a crowd.

For an instant Ellen met the eyes of the tired young customs official who was searching her baggage. He glanced quickly down at her breasts as he dropped her black lace bra back into her case.

'What is this?'

Ellen turned to see a man waving a small brown medicine bottle in front of Skye's face. She looked immediately guilty and turned to Ellen instead of replying.

'And this?' Another two bottles appeared, wriggled out from the narrow toe of a shoe. Then another, and another—each having been carefully concealed. Two more officials came over, one with gold tabs on his shoulders. He read the labels and raised hard eyes.

'Magnesium . . . sulphate?'

'Epsom salts,' said Skye quietly, looking down at the floor.

'What is it for?' asked the official. He opened one of the bottles, sniffed the contents, then tasted some off his little finger.

Skye seemed reluctant to answer. Staff and passengers stopped talking to listen.

Finally Ziggy spoke for her. 'It's a laxative.'

The men looked blank.

'It makes you go to the toilet,' Ziggy continued.

Laughter broke around her.

'But for that,' said the senior official, with mock gravity, 'you can rely on Delhi belly.'

There was more laughter, as he gathered up the bottles—

seven in all—and looked steadily at Skye, as if able to see behind her eyes.

'And tell me, why would you need to carry so many bottles of this material?' he asked.

'It's part of our illness,' said Ziggy, pointing at the clinic letter which lay open on the bench. He nodded, and one of his staff held it up for him to read.

'You have a prescription?' he asked Skye.

'No, of course she doesn't!' said Ziggy. 'You don't need one. You just get it at the drug store.'

His eyes seized on the word. 'Drug? Drug store?'

'Chemist,' said Ziggy.

The officer paused for a moment, studying the bottles. He glanced up at Ellen. 'You are responsible for these ladies?' he asked.

'Well—not exactly,' Ellen began, then shrugged, giving in. 'I guess so.'

She could see him looking over her clothes, noting that she was more casually dressed. A paid companion perhaps.

'I'm sorry, madam,' he said finally, facing Skye as he spoke, and frowning severely like a judge delivering sentence. 'The drugs must be confiscated.'

'They're not drugs!' protested Skye, wide eyes fixed on the brown bottles as they began disappearing into a paper bag. 'It's not illegal. He can't take them,' she said, turning to Ellen with pleading eyes. 'Tell him he can't!'

'Sure he can,' answered Ellen. She looked at the officer. 'She doesn't need them. Take them away.' A sudden thrill of power stirred inside her. She refused to meet Skye's gaze as the officials helped stuff their belongings back into their bags, before waving them on. The senior officer stood aside, his thumbs hooked through the belt loops of his khaki trousers. He rocked slightly on the balls of his feet, watching them through half-closed eyes.

As they wheeled their trolleys down a long, dim corridor,

the effect of the airconditioning faded, and with it the neutral feel of an international airport. Long spitlines of red betel juice slashed the walls. A giant cockroach rattled along beside them. And there, ahead, were the waiting porters in their ragged uniforms. They jumped eagerly to their feet. The delay at customs had isolated the women from the rest of the arrivals, and they appeared now like a gift straight from heaven: tired, helpless, female, foreign; pushing trolleys loaded with Samsonite cases and stuffed suitpacks. There would be good tips, folding American money—paper gold . . . .

'Stop here,' said Ellen. She went forward alone and chose the nearest, oldest-looking porter. 'I want some porters,' she told him. 'And a taxi.' She kept her face stony, sensing that she was upsetting the rules, but not caring; just wanting to get out.

The old man engaged three porters and applied himself to the task of escort, bringing along a faint smell of sweat, fried food and charcoal smoke.

'You have hotel booking?' he asked Ellen.

She nodded. 'Oberoi. Oberoi Maidans.'

'Oh . . .' he shook his head doubtfully. 'That is very far. Old city. You change. Hilton is very good.' His face brightened with thoughts of commission on three rooms—three suites, even.

'It's all arranged,' said Ellen firmly. 'I only want a taxi.'

The porter waved his hand magnanimously. 'No problem. Hotel car is waiting. This way, mem-sahib.'

He opened one of a bank of smoky glass doors. Ellen stepped outside. Hot air wrapped around her, holding her close, filling her senses, until she felt that she might dissolve away in its stillness, becoming just a wispy memory amid the fierce fumes and fragrances of an Indian summer night.

They rode in silence, Ellen in the front, the others side by side in the back. All stared, dazed, watching small cooking fires; wide tree trunks beneath spreading limbs; lone cows; and the dark outlines of trucks, cars, carts and bicycles. The shapes rose out of the gloom, like snatches of a dream—there for a moment, then swept away. Suddenly Ellen sat up, jerking wide-awake. God! Her eyes searched the shadows. There were bodies everywhere: spread out on the footpath; lying over carts and under rickshaws; on bare frame beds set outside huts and shops; in the gutters; on the edge of the road. There were hordes of them. Ellen swallowed on a wave of pity and fear. Did they have no homes to go to?

'All those people. Sleeping out there . . .' she said to the driver. Her voice trailed off.

'Yes, mem-sahib,' he answered politely. 'It is not yet morning.'

Ellen lay in the middle of the double bed and stretched out her feet, pointing her toes towards opposite corners. Then she rolled slowly over, feeling the cotton sheets pulling softly over her skin. Bright points of light pierced the curtains. Reaching for her watch, she saw it was nearly midday. She pushed aside a tinge of concern, telling herself that Ziggy and Skye could surely look after themselves for a few hours in a four-star hotel. She pictured them down in the lobby, huddled beneath the high Moghul arches, gazing uneasily out at the foreign sky. They would draw close to each other. Talking in low voices, reminding themselves that they had escaped. The clinic, consultants, visitors, cards and flowers—all had been left behind. And they were together; they had each other. Ellen screwed up her eyes as a bitter loneliness fell over her, a dead black weight. She had no-one, nothing.

She imagined Zelda and James carrying ragged two-hand sandwiches out into the noon sun. Sitting side by side, resting their backs against the warm walls of the hut; eating, not talking. Looking out over the wide blue sea that ran from strait to gulf to ocean—all the long way to America—where Mummy went.

Ellen bit against the flesh of her hand. Remember me. Please.

She imagined Zelda's voice. Daddy, when is Mummy coming back?

She's not coming back, angel. We have to get on without her.

Ellen lay still, barely breathing. A lizard waddled slowly across the ceiling. Perhaps. A thought crept in, thin and weak like the light filtering through the chinks in the curtains. Perhaps when Zelda was older, when she was more—separate. No longer a child needing a mother, but just another person in the house. Perhaps a time would come . . .

No. Ellen closed her eyes on a lurch of pain as James's words replayed in her mind.

'You're not coming back, Ellen. You know that, don't you?'

His eyes narrowed with anger, hatred, fear.

'We're going to make a life without you, Ellen. You will be gone. Finished. End of story.'

Rolling over, Ellen flicked open the room service menu and picked up the phone.

'Yes, madam?'

'Bring me coffee. Strong.'

'Yes, madam.'

'What's in the fresh fruit salad?'

'Mangoes.'

'And what's the fruit of the day?'

'Mango.'

'Ah. Okay, I'll have that.'

'Which one, madam?'

'Ah—mango. Of the day.'

'Yes, madam. Ten minutes please.'

Ellen stretched like a cat, arching her back. Then she closed her eyes and tried to relax. She ought to have breakfast and then take a swim in the pool. Soon enough she would be in charge again. Her mouth twitched. Ellen in charge! What a joke! Still, she was managing so far. When she was unsure what to do, she tried to remember the way Carter, James or the old, strong Ziggy made their plans and carried them out. Then she copied their style. Simple as that. And the more she pretended to be like them, the stronger and clearer she felt.

Her mind ran ahead over the plans. Tomorrow she had to get them all to the train station on time. Then there would be eight long hours of heat and dust as they rattled across the Ganga plains. At Dehra Dun they would switch from train to taxi. (She must remember to push aside the eager drivers while she checked the tyres of their cars.) Finally the three women would pile in with all their luggage. Then, at last, they would head straight up the side of the mountain, each long zig-zagging turn bringing them closer to the end of their journey.

Chapter 18

Ellen followed the old man, watching the bare tough soles of his feet moving noiselessly over the leaf-layered ground. The hillside dropped steeply away from the edges of the narrow path, disappearing into a smoky haze that hid the valley below. It was like walking through a dream.

The man turned to look back over his shoulder, smiling encouragement. 'Here! It is very close.' He pointed straight up.

They reached a cast-iron gate, hanging ajar between two crumbling grey pillars with remnants of carved plinths. The entrance merely marked a barrier for the path; there was no fence running off from either side, just more tall trees with sun-dappled shrubs beneath. Ellen paused to rest. The man came back and waited beside her, breathing evenly, gazing into the distance.

'What is your name?' asked Ellen, feeling the silence dense between them.

'My name is Djoti, mem-sahib,' he replied. 'But don't speak, just rest. This is very high altitude and you are not accustomed to it.'

Ellen glanced at him, taking in his worn workman's suit, the coolie rope lying over frayed shoulders, the rough hands and creased face. 'You speak very good English,' she commented.

'Of course,' he replied, grinning with pleasure. His teeth were brown and stained, but the smile lifted his face into an image of gentle beauty. 'I can read and write as well. I was a message boy. The mem-sahibs gave me notes to carry. Often they read them out to me, so that I could explain the message as well. Then I walked, studying the note and remembering the words. Soon I knew English!' He laughed, as if a clever trick had been played.

They walked on, Djoti talking back over his shoulder. 'I will be your message boy, too. You will need me for so many things. As you can see, there are no telephones, no taxis here. Everything is done by walking.'

It was true. The main road up from the plains ran through the village, which stretched from one hill peak across to another. Some of the hotels, boarding schools and mansions had vehicle paths going into their grounds, and several roads led away into the hinterland. But most of the paths were only wide enough for a horse or rickshaw, or foot. Here at the Landour end of Mussoorie, vehicles came only as far as the small hospital. Then you walked—slipping and crunching over fallen leaves—surrounded by flowering trees and singing birds.

It was a place coloured with shades of red and purple: mauve-flowered jacaranda trees, rosy-toned bougainvillea, hot pink rhododendrons, and the long-stemmed irises with deep purple heads. Here and there sweepers gathered up little piles of leaves and set fire to them, sending fragrant smoke curling into the still air. Ellen looked around her as she walked. In spite of the steep climb she felt light and relaxed. It was like strolling through a subtly tended garden, in a world of safe and friendly beauty.

It was mad, of course, Ellen realised. The house sounded ideal, but she couldn't imagine Ziggy and Skye struggling up and down the pathways. However, there was little choice. So far, all of the vacant houses had been unsuitable—too small, too close to the bazaar, too run-down, too . . . basic. And they could not stay forever at the hotel, giggling over the dusty toilet seats and old hunting trophies sagging above the grand doorways. Ellen shrugged. Ziggy and Skye would just have to be carried around. Their slim frames would make easy work for the coolies who passed their days bent double beneath loads of wood and metal.

As they came near to the house, garden flowers crept into the forest: cornflowers and yellow banksia roses peeping between vines and leafy shrubs. The peaks of the gables appeared first, dark green shapes between the treetops. Then she saw a long wall of tangled white-flowered wisteria, with shuttered windows peeping through. The path left them at the edge of a ragged lawn, facing a white marble fountain which was dry and clogged with fallen leaves. The house spread out in front of them, shaded by a long deep verandah hung with tattered green shade-cloth.

They walked up onto a patio paved with chipped tiles and stood among frayed cane chairs.

'It is very old, mem-sahib,' warned Djoti. 'A good cleaning was done yesterday. But it is not like it used to be.' He took a bunch of big, old keys from the folds of his clothing, opened up a pair of French windows and drew back the curtain. Ellen stepped inside and was greeted by stale musty air overlaid with the tang of floor wax and fly spray. She looked around the room, taking in the heavy drapes, oriental vases and dark polished wood; the Persian rugs, leatherbound books, framed portraits and the faded pastels of dried alpine flowers. She turned slowly on the spot, a dull, old pain rising in her throat. There were no castaway wine glasses and no clawmarks in the upholstery. The air was empty of floating fur. There were no cats, mewing and milling around. But still it called her back; beckoning with images of strewn teapots and cat collars, the touch of soft fur against her legs, and the bright kind eyes of a true friend.

Ellen could feel Djoti's eyes on her, like a beacon calling from far away, but she lingered with the vision of Eildon's abandoned parlour.

Dear Eildon, who had promised to take care of all her needs. Anything at all, he had said, standing in a dusty shaft of sunlight, holding Perdy in his arms—you just ask me. So she had sent him all her bills, collected in neat little bundles. Early on they were just for shoes, ribbons, tutus, yards of tulle, leotards and stockings; later there were much bigger ones, for special tuition, travelling, clothes, medical fees. He would mail them back to her with 'Paid in full' scrawled across the front. Sometimes there were little notes added—things like, 'Mama's Sheffield silver candelabra', or 'one Chippendale sideboard', or 'Remember the Audubon prints?' She would picture him wandering from room to room, happily picking out the next sacrifice, then ringing Carroll, the antique dealer. I've got a woman, she imagined him explaining, with a secretive smile. Damned expensive, I agree—but, hell, she's worth every cent.

And then he was gone. The bills mounted up, unpaid. No-one answered the phone. Finally there was a note from Carroll, saying Eildon had passed on, leaving all he owned to a pack of cats, for godsakes. Ellen had cried into her pillow all through the night, but she had never really felt him dead. Instead she sensed him with her, everywhere but nowhere, eternally ageing but never old, like God. And now she had found him here, half a world away.

She smiled at Djoti. The house felt warm and strong. 'I like it,' she said.

He wandered over to the window and pulled a silk cord to raise the blind. It came away in his hand and he stood looking at it with a sad frown. 'The family used to come from Delhi every season. They were English people. Then they didn't come. For ten years they have not come.'

'Then who is the landlord?' asked Ellen.

Djoti shook his head gravely. 'There is no landlord, mem-sahib. Only a message boy.'

Ellen returned to the house early the next morning. Ziggy and Skye came with her. They were in high spirits, trailing bright chatter and long, high peals of laughter as they were piggy-backed up the hillside. The coolies clasped their hands firmly under the women's thin thighs and leaned forward to keep their heads a polite distance from their passengers'. Lured by the hope of regular calls, light loads and good tips, they tried hard to impress with a steady gait and sober, downcast eyes. A long train of supplies and luggage followed: personal baggage, as well as food from the village bazaar, a cylinder of gas and a fridge. (There had been a dispute about the fridge. Ellen had paid the coolie double, expecting him to carry it with a mate, but he had insisted on taking it alone. Now he staggered along bent over beneath the huge weight, like a tiny beetle about to disappear into the dirt.)

Ellen walked beside Djoti, behind the line of coolies. She was conscious of her hands hanging free and empty at her sides. Already the sun lay hot on their heads and cicadas filled the air with their lazy hum.

'These are your neighbours.' Djoti pointed across to where the blue shape of a tin roof broke through the treetops. It stood out like the sail of a lone yacht in a wide sea of green. 'The Colonel and Mrs Stratheden. They were here a long time ago. They are old now and have come back home. And over there,' he pointed to a thin silver spire spiking the distance, 'that is the house of Ravi Nair. He is a very famous Indian movie star. Very handsome. Very rich. And no wife yet.' He glanced quickly at Ellen. 'People say he has spent maybe three million rupees building his house. The workmen covered every wall with mirror, and the ceiling also, in Ravi Nair's bedroom.'

Ellen groaned. 'Don't tell me, please. He sounds like some-one I know.'

Djoti smiled. 'You will like the old English ones.'

Choosing rooms was easy. Ziggy said she would prefer to know someone was nearby on the other side of the wall. Skye felt the same, so they each took one of the adjoining upstairs bedrooms. Ellen moved into what had been the master's study on the ground floor. She was glad of the isolation, but aware that she seemed all the more like a house mistress, tour leader—parent, even. She remembered the old school joke, as they picked up a teapot to pour. Shall I be mother? they'd ask, with a weak smile. Ellen used to say it too, forcing a light tone. But it always brought a twist to her stomach.

While the others were unpacking and settling into their rooms, Ellen stood in silence at the other end of the house, gazing out of her window. Right outside was a metal railing that ran along the edge of a steep drop. It was like being in a room at the very edge of a flat world where all that was real could be sucked away at any moment and vanish into the abyss.

Ellen opened up an old trunk and began to empty the room. Hunting trophies, guns, cricket memorabilia and books on birds and politics were all tumbled in on top of one another, until the room was stripped back to a bare and neutral palette. Then there was a quick knock, a light brush of knuckles against the open door. Skye stood there, her head ducked slightly to clear the doorway. Lengths of sky blue satin draped from her arms and trailed onto the floor.

'We thought of these,' she began tentatively, 'so we brought some for you, too. Satin sheets.' She gestured towards the garden. 'We thought that they would dry easily—you know, spread out on the grass.'

Ellen stared at the sheets, imagining how news of them would travel, in the footsteps of Ravi Nair's bedroom of mirrors. 'Thank you. Great,' she answered.

Skye paused, licking her lips. 'It's just . . . beautiful here. So many flowers.' She opened her mouth as if to say more, but then turned away.

Ellen stood watching her disappear, wraithlike, up the corridor.

Djoti arranged for his wife Prianka to cook for them. Her English was basic, but she had worked for foreigners before and had a range of simple menus. Their sons were employed to bring firewood and sweep the yard, their nieces to do the marketing and laundry. The little children helped in the garden.

'We are all here,' Djoti would say, spreading his work-worn hands and Ellen would smile gratefully.

As time passed she came to value the old man's help more and more. He always timed his suggestions to come just before a problem arose or a plan had to be made, but he gave the impression that she was the one who was thinking ahead. Their eyes would meet, both knowing the game.

'Mem-sahib, you are bothered by the shortage of water. American ladies like to wash too much.'

'Yes?'

'I have called the coolies to bring water, to fill up the second tank.'

'Good. Thank you, Djoti.'

'Yes, mem-sahib. You are right. It is wise to be prepared.'

He would move about the house and grounds like a commander troubleshooting among his troops: sending a child to accompany Skye gathering flowers in the forest; showing a boy where to climb up onto the warm tin roof to spread towels out to dry; advising Ellen to stand in the bath and undress, shaking out her clothes over the water, to find a flea.

At mealtimes he briefly attended the table to deliver short lectures.

'Please, mem-sahibs, I ask that you do not leave the windows open at night, in case many moths come inside.'

'Be very careful of snakes, especially near the water tanks.'

'Shake out your shoes before you put them on your feet.'

'Do not leave food around as it will bring the monkeys.'

'Always keep a candle by your bed in case of power cuts.'

'Keep away from dogs. They might have rabies and if you are bitten nothing will save you.'

Ziggy and Skye would listen avidly, lips parted with interest as he spoke. Ellen sensed that they welcomed every new danger or inconvenience as another leap further away from the safe, clean, predictable world of Marsha Kendall—proof that they had escaped, broken through to a brave new world where different rules prevailed. They could meet a tiger in the forest. They could get caught in a landslide. Or stumble off the winding path and disappear into the abyss. Anything could happen.

They could grow strong and well again. They could be happy.

There was no talk of food; of eating, swallowing, keeping it down. There were no scales for measuring changes in weight. There was only one full-length mirror in the whole house and it stood behind the door in Ellen's room with its face to the wall. Meals were offered, then cleared away without comment, whether eaten or not. Ellen never entered Ziggy's or Skye's room, and never waited, listening, outside the bathroom. She knew that after fruitless years of counting calories, being spied on in the toilets and having their rooms searched for drugs, they needed a new approach. This was their last chance. They would win or lose, or float between the two, but it would be on their own terms.

One morning Prianka's nieces brought Punjabi pyjamas and Kashmiri shawls up from the bazaar. They spread them out on the verandah and offered them for sale. Djoti explained that the traditional cotton clothes were more suited to the local method of doing laundry. The mem-sahibs dressed up, swapping tops and bottoms, laughing and arguing like children. Ellen wore plain blue. Ziggy, of the Paris catwalks, chose yellow pants and a wildly embroidered top. Skye strolled the lawns in a brown pyjama suit, swathed in an earth-toned woven shawl.

Prianka watched Skye from the door of the kitchen, floury hands patting a lump of pale dough. 'Very good,' she called, nodding approval. 'Beautiful. Indian girl.'

'She looks like a nun,' said Ellen.

'Or a holy man,' said Ziggy. 'She should try lying down on a bed of nails.' Her voice was innocent, eyes inscrutable. 'Or going for months without food.'

Ellen glanced quickly at her. Ziggy tipped back her head and laughed loudly.

Djoti joined in, chuckling between his words. 'Yes! Very thin, like a holy man. Here are two American sadhus . . .' His voice died out in a wheezing cough. 'You must go down to Rishikesh. The City of Saints.' He swallowed his mirth and forced out his last words. 'There you will be very . . . fashionable!'

Ziggy bent over with her hands on her hips, letting the last of her laughter out in short bursts. Then she leaned back against the verandah post and scanned the garden. A smile lingered on her lips. 'I'm going to start a new garden,' she announced. 'Right there, behind the fountain.'

The doors and windows of the house stood open, fresh sunny air breezing through the rooms and flapping the chintz curtains. Skye's flowers were crammed into vases, jam jars and coronation mugs, and dotted over any spare surface. They were strong, vibrant blooms, cut from the forest trees. They lasted well, holding their bright heads firm, and spreading a spicy pungence into the air.

Out on the front lawn, Ziggy leaned on a spade, watching

three teenage boys dig up her new plot. Two others were collecting stones for a border. She pointed and mimed instructions, but talked as well, even though Djoti had explained that they did not speak English. The boys added to the confusion by listening intently and saying 'Yes, mem-sahib!' before walking away with blank faces.

Ellen watched from an upstairs window, her face touched with warmth as she thought of how her friend was coming alive again. Though Ziggy was still thin and weak, she no longer hung around listlessly, watching the world through cynical, half-shut eyes. Instead, she smiled. She touched things, tentative fingers exploring shape and feel, as if she had been numb or blind for too long. And while she still refused most of the food that was offered her, she ate Prianka's chapatis—because, she said, they tasted of the earth, and not like food.

Led by her example, Skye usually managed to eat as well. She was still very quiet, but seemed happy enough, taking walks in the forest and picking flowers.

Seeing the change in them made Ellen feel stronger, safer, herself; as if the healing, once begun, had the power to carry her too. Looking down on the peaceful scene, she smiled. They had found the haven of peace they had hoped for.

Down in the garden, Ziggy moved to stand in the middle of the plot, looking around her, planning the layout of the plants. The boys stopped digging as Djoti appeared at the top of the path, peering over a large package cradled carefully in both of his hands. The morning sun gleamed off its fractured surface.

Ellen leaned closer to the window, her hands tightening on the edge of the sill. She swallowed, her pulse racing as she recognised the crisp folds of florists' cellophane.

She ran downstairs, picturing the small white card that would be pinned to the side. Stamped with the familiar 'Interflora' seal. A wild fantasy began, springing up unbidden like desert flowers after rain. There was James reading his message over the phone, his voice flat and stern.

Darling Ellen.

Would you spell that, sir? One L or two?

We can't live without you.

Is that all, sir?

Please come home. We can work it out together. I know we can. We love you, James and Zelda.

Okay, I've got that. I'll just read it back . . .

Djoti presented the bouquet to Ziggy with a solemn bob of his head. Ziggy's hands hung at her sides as she stared at the vague outlines of the flowers clustered inside the cellophane. Then her eye fixed on the card, marked with neat handwriting: Miss Ziggy Somers. Mussoorie. Try Savoy Hotel.

Ellen stood beside Ziggy, her eyes aching with mixed relief and disappointment. Djoti looked at her, awaiting instructions.

'Let's see who it's from,' Ellen said, her voice carefully calm, like a school nurse about to cause pain. She unpinned the card and turned it over.

'Darling Ziggy,' she read, 'please contact us. Your father can't eat for worrying about you. We miss our little girl so much. Ziggy, sweetheart, look at the flowers and think of me. Precious darling, I love you. Your dearest Mommy, Lucy.'

As she read the words, Ellen sensed a darkness running beneath the flow of warmth—something desperate, clutching, binding.

Ziggy waited, frozen, as the words fell around her. Then she took the bouquet and pulled open the cellophane. 'Orchids,' she said blankly.

'*She* wouldn't have chosen them,' Ellen cut in quickly, wanting to defuse them, to make them anonymous. 'I guess they'd be airfreighted from Singapore to Delhi.'

They both stared at the perfect waxen-skinned flowers. Miraculous survivors; boxed and packed in ice, they had travelled unscathed through heat and dust all the way to Mussoorie.

'How did she know we were here?' asked Ellen.

'I told her,' said Ziggy. Her voice was tight with anger. 'I didn't want to. I wasn't going to.' She reached in and touched the firm cool flowers. She closed her hand slowly into a hard fist, crushing the blooms and breaking the stems. Then she flung the bouquet into the middle of her half-made garden and ran away, face down, shoulders hunched.

'She does not like the flowers,' stated Djoti, his eyes widening with awe and dismay.

Ellen was silent for a moment, then she spoke. 'No, she does not like her mother.' She looked helplessly up towards the house. A few moments after Ziggy disappeared inside the curtains on her bedroom window were flung shut.

Skye appeared on the verandah, drawn by the sound of cane chairs scattering as Ziggy fled inside. She stood there silently, looking at the tumbled mess of orchids and the crumpled cellophane. Her face was stricken with fear and longing.

Ellen looked down at Lucy's card, abandoned on the lawn. She called Djoti over. 'I don't want this to happen again,' she said. 'From now on I would like you to bring all personal letters and deliveries straight to me, without anyone seeing.'

'Yes, mem-sahib,' said Djoti, bowing his head gravely.

'And please remove that.' She pointed at the remains of the bouquet. It lay on the ground, the flowers all twisted and wrecked, like the relic of an accident lying on the side of the road.

Chapter 19

Ellen resisted calling the doctor up from the mission hospital, hoping that the effect of Lucy's flowers and note would not last. But days turned into weeks, with Ziggy remaining silent, lying on her bed, staring at the ceiling. And Skye hung around her, drawn like a spider to her dark gloom. She left her bunches of flowers rank and festering in their vases. Her place by the dining room window waited warmed by morning sun, but she stayed all day in her room. Prianka set the table with places for three, but soon cooked only for one.

It was Djoti who suggested bringing the doctor and finally Ellen agreed. She waited for them to arrive by the fountain, beside Ziggy's abandoned garden patch. Their low voices could be heard as they came near. Then they appeared at the end of the track, stepping up onto the grass. Without pausing to catch his breath, the doctor came towards her. Crossing the lawn, he looked like a haggard party guest left over from the night before—bleary-eyed and pale, with uncombed hair. His clothes were neat in style, but crumpled and stained with sweat. Ellen felt him taking in the pallor of her own face. Her eyes, she knew, were red from lack of sleep.

'I'm Ellen,' she said flatly, drawing in her breath, readying herself for what she knew must come. The words of concern and then the outrage. How else could he respond to a woman keeping house up here with two others dying slowly around her? What on earth did she think she was doing? Bringing sick people away from a luxury clinic, where all that money could buy was available to cushion and comfort, if not to cure. She must be mad, stupid or cruel.

'Dr Cunningham. Paul.' The man spoke to Ellen's back as she led the way up towards the house. 'I'm sorry I couldn't come yesterday. It's been one of those times . . .'

Ellen glanced back at him over her shoulder. 'Are you all right?' she asked. 'You don't look too good.'

'I've been up all night,' he said, rubbing a hand over his face. 'A bad case. I've seen my share, but you don't really get used to it.'

'What happened?' asked Ellen politely.

'A woman came in from some village. Her baby had got stuck half-delivered.' He shook his head disbelievingly as he spoke. 'Well, it was more than dead; it was decomposing. She told me she'd walked four hours to get to a road, then a truck brought her to the turn-off about five miles from here. She walked the rest of the way.' He talked without a break, as if unable to find a place to stop. 'I couldn't get it out vaginally, so I had to do a caesar. I began with the normal incision, but found the baby was folded with head and breech both in the upper half of the uterus.' He broke off abruptly. 'I'm sorry. You don't want to know all this.'

'Will she live, the mother?' asked Ellen. Her voice was harsh, her mind filled with visions of a torn-open body drenched with antiseptic; bloody hands reaching for needles and thread; doctor's cloth-capped head bent over his work—a two-faced god, butcher and saviour.

Paul shrugged, trying for an aura of detachment. 'She's on intravenous antibiotics. Luckily she's got four other children.

They're all over five now, so they've got a good chance of surviving.' He finished with a tense smile.

Ellen led him inside. He paused on the threshold, looking around at the lavish furnishings.

'This isn't our stuff,' Ellen commented. 'We haven't been here long. Just about two months.'

He stood beside a muzzle-loading shotgun that hung slanted on the wall. 'I've heard of you, of course,' he said carefully. 'That two of you are unwell.'

'It was meant to be just me and my friend,' Ellen spoke quickly, facing him. 'Then another woman wanted to come. I was against it.' She bit her lip. She had meant to be calm and remote, helping him to mind his own business. All she wanted from him was some tranquillisers.

Paul leaned back against the wall and looked down at his feet. 'Just to sort out gossip from reality—your two companions are suffering from anorexia? Long-term? Chronic condition?'

'Ziggy's been in and out of hospital for three years. She's nearly died twice. Skye's been ill even longer.'

'Then they would have told you at the hospital,' Paul said bluntly, 'the outlook is bad. The chances of recovery are—'

'But when we arrived here,' Ellen broke in, 'it looked good. They seemed to be coming to life again. They ate—not much—but they were improving. Then Ziggy's mother made contact and it just seemed to bring them both down. Nothing I said made any difference. Since then, they've,' she laughed tensely, 'well, they've gone to bed. All because of a bunch of flowers from home.'

'I'm not an expert here,' Paul began. 'In fact, I confess when I come across it in the journals I think, here's one thing I can afford to ignore. But I've got the memory of an elephant. Sometimes it comes in handy. These flowers from home, for example, from one of the mothers. As I recall, anorexia is usually linked with problems in the family, often focussed on the mother.' Paul relaxed a little as the medical wordage spilled naturally into the quiet. 'The patients are often ambivalent about their sexuality. They want to starve away their flesh and become children again. The physical stress often stops them menstruating, which of course rewards the behaviour.'

'But that's not to do with the mother, necessarily,' said Ellen.

'Well, some studies have suggested the fear, if you like, of being female, is really a fear of becoming like their mothers.'

'You mean,' Ellen paused to swallow, 'they're afraid of being mothers?'

'Perhaps not afraid of being mothers per se; it might be something more connected with their own mothers. Fear of being, in some sense, taken over by their mothers. It's just a theory. There's not much real knowledge about the condition. But whatever *is* underneath it all, it's a powerful thing. They'd rather die than give in. Literally.' He looked straight at Ellen. 'Some of them do die. You know that, don't you?'

'Yes, of course,' said Ellen vaguely. 'They told me at the clinic.'

Paul studied her calm, detached expression, a puzzled look on his face. 'The strange thing,' he went on, 'is that they're so strong on one hand. It takes some self-control to starve your own body to death! But they're weak at the same time. A part of them usually wants to survive, but they just seem powerless to change course. That's why it's so difficult to—'

'What you said before . . .' Ellen interrupted. She stood in the doorway, blocking the way. 'That there are some women who can't cope with being a mother? They know what it means, but can't . . . do it?' Her voice was sharp and too loud. 'They want to, they'd give anything to be a good mother, but something's wrong and they just . . .' Her voice died to a whisper. 'They just can't.'

Paul frowned. 'There are always lots of issues in any set of problems,' he said carefully. 'But psychology's not my field. I'm a general surgeon.' He looked past her, up the stairs. 'Of course I'll do what I can to help.'

211

First they went into Ziggy's room.

'I didn't call a goddamn doctor.' The words were flung from the tumbled bed as soon as the light was turned on.

'He's come up from the mission hospital,' said Ellen, a warning note in her voice.

'Well, he can fuck off.'

Paul went to stand at the end of the bed, deaf to Ziggy's words as he looked calmly and frankly at her wasted arms lying over the quilt, her hollow cheeks, and fierce, over-bright eyes.

Without speaking, he walked out of the room.

Next door, Skye was crouched on her bed. As the doctor came close to her she stared up at him, her face torn between fear and longing.

'Just leave me alone,' she pleaded, her voice like that of a small girl trapped in the corner of the playground with her back against the wall.

'It's very clear,' said Paul when he and Ellen were downstairs again, 'that they can't stay here.' His voice hardened, denying his gentle brown eyes. 'We're short of beds down at the hospital. Our job is to look after the poor, who have nowhere else to go. I strongly advise you to leave now, before they become too sick to travel.'

'You mean, go back?' said Ellen, her voice hollow. Go back. The words held no meaning.

Paul nodded. 'Back to America. Or at least to Delhi.' His voice softened and he touched Ellen's shoulder lightly with his smooth, scrubbed hand. 'Look, it was worth a try. At least you know, as a friend, you've done all you can. In the meantime, tranquillisers will help. You can buy them at the bazaar. I'll write down the names of a few options.' He took a small notepad from his pocket and scrawled some words onto it. 'Heaven knows what they've got on hand. Go to the man next to the fortune teller, across from the pastry shop.'

'Pastry shop?' queried Ellen.

'Well, loosely speaking. I think they sell pizzas.'

Ellen laughed briefly. 'That's India . . .'

Prianka appeared with a tray of tea. She smiled at the doctor and spoke to him in Hindi. He replied, the foreign sounds lying easy on his tongue. Prianka beamed down at him proudly, as if he were her own creation. She placed the tray carefully on a low table, then bowed towards Paul and left them alone.

'Look at that . . .' Lifting the heavy china teapot, Paul turned it slowly around. 'We had one just the same—at home.' He held it, lingering, as if unwilling to let it go.

'Why don't you pour?' suggested Ellen, moving the cups closer to him.

Paul nodded, stifling a yawn.

They sat quietly, side by side on the old chesterfield, sipping the black spiced tea from gold-edged cups. Above them was a faded portrait of Queen Elizabeth. Trimmed with ermine and blue ribbon, she gazed serenely out over the room.

Behind the fragrant steam, laden with cardamom and cloves, Ellen caught the school toilet smell of carbolic soap, and beneath it, dried sweat. She glanced sideways at Paul. The crumpled open collar and unshaven chin created an air of dishevelment that contrasted with his lean, fine-featured face. She wondered—in spite of herself—how she looked. Uncut, unplucked, unmade-up. Probably just right for an eccentric dame with a couple of rich neurotic friends.

'Have you been here long?' she asked, suddenly wanting to know if, perhaps, he might have heard of her, seen her dance, seen her picture. Though he was of course a missionary. The word evoked images of black books, kneeling figures, plain food and smiling cannibals with bones in their hair.

'In India? Or Mussoorie?'

'Either. Both.'

'I was born in Calcutta. I came here about ten years ago.'

'You mean, you've lived in India all your life!' Ellen looked at him in open surprise.

Paul smiled. 'Almost. My parents were missionaries in Calcutta. They didn't approve of boarding schools, so I stayed there with them until I went to medical school in London. I hated England—the cold, and having to do everything at the right time. Well, one *ought* to, old chap!' He mimicked an Oxford accent.

Ellen laughed, feeling light and free, something inside her coming alive, tingling like frozen hands held up to a warm fire. She realised, suddenly, how this house of sickness weighed on her with its heavy spirits, while the burden of forgetting sapped away her strength. She longed to be free of it all. She watched Paul pushing aside his fatigue and enjoying being here, drinking tea with her. She wanted him to stay. Wanted him to take her away. Wanted him. 'And your parents, are they still there, in Calcutta?' Ellen asked lightly while she poured more tea.

Paul hesitated for a second before answering. 'No. They moved to Bangladesh. They were drowned in a flood there a few years ago.' His voice was steady and flat, but held a current of raw pain beneath.

Ellen closed her eyes on an image of two small figures, tossed like dolls in a mad mass of water. A dark engulfing tide . . . 'Oh, I'm sorry,' she said quickly, 'I wouldn't have asked . . .'

'I miss them,' he said simply.

The Swiss clock ticked loudly in the stillness.

'Are you married?' Ellen asked, to break the silence. Of course he was married, she told herself. To a sweet, serious woman, with a strong heart and comforting hands.

Paul glanced up, and she squirmed inside, imagining him thinking she might be thinking . . .

'No,' he said with a wry frown. 'Who'd want to live like this?'

He stared down at his hands, cradling the half-empty cup. They were fine, smooth-skinned hands, but they looked strong and steady. Ellen imagined them wrapped in surgical gloves. And his light brown eyes, like sea sponges, soaking up images of pain and horror. Dear God, a baby rotting in its own mother's womb.

Margaret's eyes used to be haunted, too, by her poor sad children. Only she seemed stronger, as if she fed off their agonies. Emergencies brought her to life, her heels tapping smartly as she gathered up her white coat and bag, while Ellen sat alone on a hard couch and watched her go—a hero of war sailing off to battle.

Paul seemed only sad and tired as if he were caught up in a game he disliked. He could not walk away, but longed for the end to come.

'Are you?' he asked.

'I'm sorry?'

'Are you married?'

Ellen stared at him. 'Yes. Well, not really. I'm—we're separated. Permanently.' Suddenly she wanted to tell him. 'I've got a little daughter. Zelda,' she said. 'She's—with him.'

Paul looked at her for a moment, with something like distaste clouding his eyes and thinning his lips. 'You must miss her,' he said with an edge of sarcasm.

Ellen looked down at her own hands, never bloodied, but guilty. She guessed at him thinking of lovers, dreams, plans and discontent. It's not like that, she wanted to say. You don't understand. No-one does. Not James. Not Ziggy. And Zelda won't either. Whatever James tells her, whatever reason he gives, she'll blame me, despise me, hate me . . .

'I'm sorry,' said Paul, draining his cup and standing up. 'I'm keeping you from your day.' He was the doctor again, calm and distant. 'I do want to stress the importance of leaving here as soon as possible.'

'Yes, thank you,' said Ellen mechanically. She followed him towards the door. 'Thank you for coming up here.'

'Not at all,' said Paul. 'Djoti can collect the bill.'

★　★　★

215

Ellen licked salt from a small heap in her hand, tipped her head back and took a slug from a bottle of tequila, then bit hard into a wedge of lime. She screwed up her eyes as the three tastes collided, fusing into a solid, fiery hit. As the burst faded, she let her head fall back, resting against the outside wall of the house. Nearby, huge moths clustered around a lighted window, beating their powdery wings against the glass. The glow of a single lamp spilled gently out onto the shadowy verandah, lying silver on the back of Ellen's dark head and glinting off the half-full bottle she held in her hand.

She breathed out slowly, feeling herself drained and empty, facing the blank wall of failure. They would have to give in, go back. But really—what else did she expect?

An image came to her, cutting through the years. Margaret, Mother, with her kind, pitying smile.

What else could you expect, Ellen?

The verandah post seemed to sway slightly, carrying the garden with it. Margaret hovered like a phantom conjured by the white fire.

Clumsy, useless, careless, dirty girl. You poor thing.

Her voice came through, beneath the silence.

No wonder your father went away.

'No!' said Ellen, shaking her head against the mocking ghost hovering above the silent garden.

Poor child. He just couldn't bear being around you. Even the sight of you made him feel ill. So he left.

The wind sighed in the treetops. Poor Margaret. Her life ruined, happiness taken away.

No! Ellen's hands gripped her knees, making pale, grasping shapes in the shadows. The fire burned clear and strong in her head, cutting through the old facades: the old agreements, judgements, sentences. It wasn't true. Couldn't be true. He must have had his own reasons. Something to do with Margaret. Or himself. Or someone else. No-one would leave everything they had and loved, because of a little baby. Only two months old.

Unless, Ellen thought suddenly, he was just like her. Trapped between love and terror. Another victim of some evil sickness that ran like a plague in the family. Perhaps he had torn himself away, dying inside, unable to make Margaret understand.

Ellen pictured the face in the wedding photo. The pale, blond man, standing meekly beside his young wife. It was hard to imagine him being forced, like herself, to leave, to get away. For the sake of the child that he loved.

She looked up at the moon, far off and silent, hanging like a jewel against the velvet sky. She would never know the truth about him, her own father. There was no-one to ask. Around the time Ellen had graduated from the Academy, Margaret had sold the house and moved permanently to England, leaving no forwarding address. Ellen remembered the sense of loss and panic and wild relief she'd felt when she'd realised that it was over at last. Margaret had gone away for good.

But she had taken her secrets with her. And the unanswered questions would stay with Ellen forever—a darkness inside her that she would never be able to leave behind. It was impossible, unbearable. The final, pitiless wounding.

Ellen stood up, facing the garden with unseeing eyes. A new certainty settled in her mind. She would not do that to Zelda. Zelda would know who her mother was and, one day, why she had had to leave. Whatever it gave Zelda, it was better than nothing, better than silence. Parents must not disappear. They can't, because the hole won't close behind them.

Ellen stayed on the verandah, half-awake, half-sleeping until the first light of dawn touched the sky. Then she went to her room and sat down at the desk.

'Dear James,' she wrote, her hand pushing sure but shaky across the page. 'I have to write. You have to let me. She's still my daughter. I love her.'

She looked up into the golden light. The paper was cool beneath her hand, like a soothing balm. Already she felt stronger.

She pictured how she would write—long letters sharing her news, her life, her self—carefully choosing the words, to make sure that nothing came out wrong. She even dared to imagine that one day Zelda would write back to her. One day, they would be together again.

The sounds of morning grew slowly around her: from the kitchen came the clatter of Prianka's pans; and outside someone was chopping wood. Upstairs, though, all was quiet. Ellen thought of Ziggy and Skye sprawled in restless sleep amid their tangled sheets. Remembering the doctor's advice that they would all have to leave, she looked around the room, dreading the task of packing up, moving out . . . Then a new thought came to her, strong and clear: if she could find a way to help Ziggy and Skye—if she could rescue them, instead of giving up and going back—it would be a sign that she was changing. That she was turning into someone who could be relied upon. Someone like Lizzie. A real mother.

The small seed took root and grew quickly, nourished by the warmth of her hope. It seemed fair and simple—a bargain with fate: if she could save Ziggy and Skye, perhaps Zelda would not be lost to her.

The next morning, Ellen walked into Ziggy's room and flung back the curtains.

'Get up,' she called over her shoulder. 'We're going down to the bazaar to do some shopping. There's a coolie waiting outside. Or do you want him to come up here?'

Ziggy lay with the fixed stillness of someone listening and thinking hard. She didn't answer.

'Fine,' said Ellen. She opened the window and waved at someone down on the lawn. 'He's on his way.'

Ziggy sat up slowly, scratching blankly at her tangled hair. She wore only a silk camisole, hanging limply over skin and bones.

Ellen pulled clean clothes from the cupboard and threw them at her. 'Put them on,' Ellen winced, swallowing on a wave of nausea. She put a hand on the wall to steady herself.

'What's wrong with you?' asked Ziggy.

'Nothing.'

'Oh? I saw a bottle on the lawn.' A small mocking smile played on Ziggy's face. 'Poor man's cocaine.'

'What?'

'Tequila. Where on earth did you find it?'

'Djoti got it from the Savoy.'

There was a light knock at the door. As Ellen went to open it, Ziggy's head jerked up. 'Don't let him in here!' she said. 'I'm not dressed!'

'Hurry up then.' Ellen's voice was hard and cold.

Ziggy watched from under lowered eyes as she dressed slowly, moving her body with the awkward gestures of a grounded seabird. 'Why aren't Djoti or Prianka going to the bazaar?' she asked finally. 'I hate it down there. It's dirty. There are beggars. I can't stand those old men poking tins at you.'

Ellen opened the door and waved in the coolie. He kept his eyes lowered and approached Ziggy cautiously, his hands poised at his sides.

'Mem-sahib?'

'Get out! Both of you.' Ziggy's face was pale with anger.

'No,' said Ellen calmly. 'If I have to call six more coolies and have you tied hand and foot, I will. But you're not spending another day lying about in here. You're coming out with me.'

Ziggy gazed at her, wide-eyed. 'But what are we going to do?'

'Buy some things. Visit the temple. Go to the bazaar. Ride the cable car. Whatever people do when they come to Mussoorie—or India, for that matter. You've hardly been outside this place apart from being in hotels. You might as well be back in America. So,' she paused for breath, 'I think it's time you just went out and—'

'Just a minute,' Ziggy broke in, holding up a hand as if to stem the flow of Ellen's plans. 'I know what you're doing. You think I've gone off the rails because of Lucy. And you think you're going to fix me up, by taking me to a goddamn Indian bazaar! Well forget it, Ellen. It won't work.' A tremor in her voice made her sound young and lost. 'I've been here before. Nothing works.'

Tears made pools of her big green eyes. The coolie stared down at his hands.

'Then it doesn't matter, does it?' said Ellen coldly. 'You can just come, and it won't make any difference.'

'Shit! You're not joking . . .' There was a short pause. Ziggy stared, her face rigid with amazement, as if she barely recognised the person who was speaking to her so firmly. Then she jabbed a finger towards the coolie. 'You!' she shouted. 'Go! You go!'

He didn't move.

'I told him you'd make a fuss,' Ellen explained, 'that you are unstable, crazy, and he should ignore you. I paid him extra.'

'Ah. Danger money.' Ziggy started laughing, a wild giggle that matched her feverish eyes. 'Oh that's good, Ellen. That's great, coming from you—'

Ellen turned and left the room. Ziggy stared after her, lifting a curled hand to pick at her face. A moment passed before she beckoned the coolie and stood with her feet apart, ready to be picked up.

They walked in silence down through the forest to where the road ended in front of the hospital. Ellen paid off the coolie and sent a boy to wake up a driver who lay asleep in his taxi.

'Yes, mem-sahib,' the driver said, blinking in the sun. 'What is your programme please?'

'We want to go to the bazaar.'

'Of course. No problem.'

Ziggy climbed into the taxi and flopped back against the seat. Ellen climbed in beside her, leaving a clear gap between them.

The driver watched them in the rear-vision mirror as he eased the car slowly down the steep, curving road.

They sat in tense silence. Who would speak first? In the old days it had always been Ellen . . . Looking up from her homework, abandoning her absent scribbling. Fixing eyes on Ziggy's head, watching her hands as she stabbed a needle into pink satin ribbon.

I'm sorry. Zig?

No answer.

Please, Ziggy. I didn't mean it.

A slow look up. Are you sure?

Yes. I'm really sorry.

A small nod and the hint of a smile. Okay, then.

Friends?

Sure. Friends.

The car moved slowly along, pushing into the market-day crowd. Ellen gazed out past faces pressed close to the window, at the tiny stalls that edged the narrow road. It was like travelling past an unbroken line of open cupboards, each one crammed with wares: bright-coloured sarees, bed quilts, sacks of spices, jars of sweetmeats, strings of bangles and cases of silver jewellery. There were regular outcrops of soft drink, standing in warm, dusty bottles. Limca. Thums Up. And what looked like some kind of Coke. A Kodak sign poked up behind piles of leather sandals. There was a faded poster showing Western-style jeans, worn by a Western-style Indian girl with a lean bare midrif. Beside her was a blacksmith's den, a dark, smoky cave with vague outlines and the muted glint of forged metal.

A cow stopped in the road ahead and refused to move. In the still air the car felt hot and close. Ellen wound down her window, letting in the sound and smell of the crowd. Ziggy covered her mouth and nose with her sleeve and closed her eyes. They were beside a shop that sold mountain-walking sticks. They covered the walls, hanging from long railings.

Some looked pale and new, others second-hand, with collections of metal badges and ornately carved ends. A photographic panorama hung in their midst, showing a sweeping vista of snow-covered peaks.

'Himalaya,' said the driver, noticing Ellen looking at it. 'You can see . . . this one . . . from Mussoorie. But not now. It's . . . like the same dusty.'

'Hazy,' suggested Ellen.

'Hazy. Yes. Hay-zee.'

'Dirty,' said Ziggy.

The cow ambled aside and the car moved slowly on.

'Take us to the old temple.'

'Yes, mem-sahib. It is very close. Actually it is here.' He pointed to a simple narrow gateway.

Ellen looked at it doubtfully. 'Is this the famous one?'

'Very famous temple, mem-sahib. Temple of Nanda Devi.'

'I'll go in and see,' Ellen told Ziggy. She glanced at the driver watching intently in his mirror. 'You wait here. I'll come back.'

She walked through the gateway and along an empty lane to where a door made of thick steel bars stood half open. She paused, peering into a shadowy gloom, musty with old incense. A figure stirred dimly in a swathe of orange. Then lights snapped on—a row of naked hanging bulbs, harsh and bright. An old monk sat in an alcove beside a bank of electric switches. He bowed his head and beckoned Ellen in.

'Please remove your shoes,' he chanted, standing and coming towards her. As she unlaced her boots, Ellen looked up at him. He was draped with layers of cloth—skirt, shirt, scarf, shawl, turban, shoulder bag—all in different shades of orange, thrown together with a striking casual style that would be the envy of any dresser.

The marble floor felt hard and cool through Ellen's socks as she padded after him towards a dim inner sanctum. There he reached for another switch and illuminated the shrine.

Ellen looked up into the face of a waxen-skinned goddess wrapped in gold cloth. Her slanted eyes were dark and bright, her lips caught on the edge of a smile. A garland of marigold flowers hung in a dense golden swathe from her slender neck. The regal head was tilted forward just a shade, giving her an air of benevolence that was strangely at odds with the long-bladed knife that she cradled in her arms. Melted red ghee ran like blood over her silver-coated feet and spattered the white wall behind. Bruised petals of bright flowers, pink, red and yellow, lay all around her.

'Nanda Devi is "she who gives bliss",' the monk intoned. 'The beautiful mother who removes sufferings and bestows her blessings. She loves all, but,' he turned to look at Ellen, 'her special favour is kept for the beautiful ladies.'

'Why does she have a knife in her hand?' Ellen asked. Her voice sounded loud and rude in the quiet dimness.

The monk waved his head, noncommittally. 'Of course, she has power,' he said, and shrugged. 'She has to be strong.'

Ellen looked up at the goddess. She pushed her gaze past the serene Madonna's beauty, reaching for what lay beneath: a wilder streak, an undercurrent of fierce strength and violence only just held at bay. There was nothing real about her, but somehow she spoke of life as it really was, embracing warm hope and bitter failure. The softness and the guts, the joy and fear. The good and the bad, both at the same time.

'Beautiful mother . . .' Ellen thought, searching the time-frozen face. Her words ran out into pictures, snapshot visions. Of herself, the mother, torn between love and fear. Of Zelda. Laughing with joy. Then the look of quick fear, the troubled eyes and wavering voice. Zelda crying. Zelda sinking, struggling, into the water. Then the good, strong mother taking over. Gathering up the child in her shielding arms.

'Beautiful mother,' Ellen said her name again. Creator and destroyer. Giver and taker of life . . .

'Prasad, prasad,' said the monk.

Ellen looked at him blankly. He put out his hand.

'Ah, sorry,' she nodded, and reached into her money belt.

The old man smiled and bowed. Stretching out a hand, he plunged the goddess back into the shadows.

Ellen pushed her feet into her boots, then walked quickly out to the light and warmth of the sun and the busy noise of the street.

She dodged through the crowd towards the car, but saw that Ziggy was not there, and neither was the driver. The vehicle seemed abandoned. Looking across the street, Ellen spotted the top of Ziggy's blonde head bobbing above the crowd. Moving closer, she heard her voice cutting through the chatter and laughter. 'I haven't got money. My friend is coming—she will pay.'

Ellen stopped and hid in the crowd. She watched Ziggy standing by a stall that sold sticky yellow cakes. They were piled up on plates set out on the counter, and more could be seen cooking over a small stove at the back. Beside Ziggy stood a toddler wearing just the ragged shreds of a pair of blue shorts. Ellen edged sideways until she could see more of him. A swollen belly stuck out above legs like sticks. Big dark eyes gazed up at Ziggy from a dirty face streaked with tears.

'The kid's hungry, for godsakes. What's wrong with you?' Ziggy was waving her hands and shouting. The stallholder looked around, grinning with embarrassment.

'One rupee,' he was saying, holding up a single finger.

Then the driver arrived beside her. 'Mem-sahib?'

'Give them some money,' demanded Ziggy. 'The other mem-sahib will pay you.'

The taxi driver took a coin from his pocket and put it on the counter. Smiling now, the stallholder held out two yellow syrupy cakes. The little boy followed them with his eyes as they went into Ziggy's hands. She held them gingerly, gazing at them. Seconds passed, and the child began to cry, a desperate aching whimper.

'No, don't cry,' said Ziggy, quickly bending to place one cake into each of the little bird-claw hands. 'They're for you. It's okay—for you.'

The boy stuffed the food in, chewing and swallowing, frowning with concentration. He gripped the cakes firmly, all the time looking around him as if expecting someone to chase him off or take away his prize. Watching him, Ellen realised he was older than he looked; his whole body was stunted by lack of food. But it was Ziggy who held her gaze. The woman was bent over the child, her own lips parted in something close to wonder as she watched the handfuls of food being crammed in.

Laughter broke out around them as the child held his hands up for more. An older boy appeared at Ziggy's side.

'Give me dollar,' he said, grinning widely. 'America. Richard Nixon. Very good.' Ziggy ignored him. She gestured to the stallholder, who handed over a large cake. The driver looked over his shoulder as he felt in his pocket for more money. Seeing Ellen, he waved her over.

Ziggy offered the cake to the child. He hesitated for just a second, as if imagining some trick. Then he grabbed the cake with both hands, hugging it close, and bolted away into the crowd. Ziggy stared after him, motionless.

An onlooker called out something to the stallholder, causing a ripple of laughter. The taxi driver looked uneasily at Ziggy.

'What did he say?' she asked him, spinning round.

'It is . . .' he shrugged. 'They are saying that you have given your cake to the beggar's child, but who is going to feed *you*?' He smiled and spread his hands. 'They are village people. They do not understand American things.'

Chapter 20

Looking out through the kitchen window, Ellen saw Skye sitting on the verandah, idly watching a line of coolies cross the lawn bent over under bulging sacks of rice. She held a scarf over her nose and turned her face away as the men passed by. Lately she had started complaining about smells—frying food, ripening fruit, smoke from the burning piles of leaves. Even the strong, sweet perfumes of the garden upset her.

Ellen pressed her lips into a grim line as she turned to face Prianka. 'How much rice,' she asked the old woman, spacing the words clearly, 'for, say, sixty people?'

'Sixty?' repeated Prianka. She held up ten fingers, then six.

Ellen shook her head and showed ten fingers, six times.

Prianka's eyes widened. 'Very big dinner!' Her face was alive with questions, but she made do with nodding towards the dining room and shaking her head. 'Too many. No good.'

'How much rice?' Ellen repeated firmly.

Prianka half-closed her eyes as she calculated. Then she reached up to the top shelves in the pantry, and brought down five giant cooking pots. They were white with the dust of years—unused since the days of English house parties and formal receptions. She pointed suspiciously at the sacks of potatoes that had arrived earlier in the morning.

'Aloo masala—sixty?' she asked. Ellen smiled encouragingly. Prianka frowned, unsettling the laugh lines that etched her face. 'Djoti. Come here,' she stated. 'Me—no understand.' Looking back at Ellen over her shoulder, she walked out into the garden.

At about five-thirty the first guests began to arrive. They hovered silently at the edges of the garden, hanging back until Djoti beckoned them on. By six o'clock, the back lawn was dotted with people. They stood in groups and pairs. Here and there a figure waited alone. Near the verandah, a line began to form.

Ellen looked down from an upstairs window, trying to estimate the numbers. The orange robes and turbans of holy men stood out among the drab rags of the poor and homeless that made up most of the crowd. There were a few holy women as well, inconspicuous in off-white sarees made of coarse cloth. The different groups milled and wandered, like guests at any garden party. Slanting rays of the waning sun shed a strange golden hue over the scene. A monotone of chanted prayer ran beneath the simmer of muted conversation. Old people, their gender lost in withered flesh and anonymous wraps, leaned on sticks or sat down on the freshly cut grass to rest twisted backs and crippled feet bound with stained bandages. Young men and women with stunted muscles and hollow cheeks turned weary eyes towards the kitchen. Mothers held babies to their scrawny breasts, while older children clung to grown-up legs and gazed wide-eyed up at the house.

Ellen kept back from the window as she scanned the crowd. Her eye settled on a wild-looking man with long hair matted into dreadlocks and caked in red mud. A line of yellow paint ran down the middle of his forehead onto the bridge of his nose. He was bare to the waist, every rib visible beneath loose skin rubbed with grey ash. He stood on one leg, calmly gazing into the distance, untouched by the gathering chill of evening. Ellen recognised him as a traveller—someone who had taken the vows of a holy man but who was not attached to an ashram. Djoti had explained that they wandered in perpetual pilgrimage from place to sacred place.

Ellen stared down at the traveller. In the life he had left behind he might have been a successful businessman: someone who struck big deals, travelled by air and stayed in the best hotels. Somewhere in India he probably had a family and a house, grandchildren, pets, television and a soft bed. And yet here he was, with all that he owned wrapped into a small cloth swag tied onto his walking stick. Free of the demands of family, friends, business, possessions, he was at last able to devote himself to his spiritual quest—wandering at will, visiting ashrams and temples to be fed, sleeping beside holy rivers and meditating in sacred caves until he reached the end of his days and left his body behind, abandoned like a husk in its last lonely shelter.

It seemed to Ellen both horrifying and enchanting, brutal and pure. As if in the lives of the travellers the desire to escape, to disappear, that held Ziggy and the others so tightly in its thrall, had been formally recognised. And in being recognised, transformed . . .

Leaning closer to the window, Ellen looked around for the young monk who had met Djoti and her at the door of the temple the previous day. They had stood on the steps while Djoti spoke in a low voice, watched by the beggars who were gathered about the entrance holding their empty tin plates and bowls. Ellen watched nervously as Djoti's voice rose, apparently pressing some line of argument. The monk kept shaking his head.

'What's wrong?' Ellen interrupted them. 'Does he think it's crazy?'

'No,' Djoti answered. 'It is normal for devout people to provide food for the poor. But it is done at the ashram—here.' He pointed towards a crumbling three-storey building behind the temple. Verandahs running the length of each tier were hung with lines of faded orange cloth, a hundred matching loincloths dripping dry. 'There is a courtyard. He says the monks will bring out a blackboard with your name written on it, so that everyone who comes to eat can bless you. If you wish, you can name the meal in respect for someone. Then the guests will bless them too. He is explaining to me that this is the way it is done.'

Djoti finished speaking and the monk nodded.

'No,' said Ellen. 'They must come to the house.'

Djoti relayed her remark. The monk looked at her and made no comment.

'Will they come?' Ellen asked.

Djoti shrugged. 'They will be invited.'

Ellen had wanted to know more but the monk had turned and wandered away.

A large bird swooped down over the garden and settled on top of the empty marble fountain. The young monk stood nearby at the edge of a small group, his hand resting on the shoulder of a child. As if her thoughts had reached him across the space, he raised his head and met Ellen's eyes. She smiled and waved.

The movement was small, but its impact spread and grew like ripples in a pond. A murmuring sigh spread over the crowd as everyone looked up and saw her there. Near the verandah an old woman sank to her knees and stretched up her arms. Others followed her example, kneeling and bowing their foreheads to the ground. Soon everyone but the young monk was bowing or kneeling.

Ellen stood at the window, frozen, her hand still half-raised. Then she jumped sideways and flattened herself against the wall. 'Shit . . .' she mouthed, seeing herself in mad impersonation of the Queen, the President, the Pope. Even Liberty would surely draw the line at this. Seconds passed before she peered carefully round the edge of the window frame and saw, to her relief, that the gesture was over. Chatter had started up again and people were beginning to move towards the verandah, holding out their food tins.

Stepping back from the window, Ellen relived the moment, turning it over in her mind like a half-familiar object. It brought back memories of being on centre stage. She remembered the feeling of the audience applauding, reaching out to her, wrapping her in warm, uplifting waves. But there was always a chilly current of doubt running beneath. She was a cheat. She didn't dance for them. They were just the backdrop, a part of the machinery. She didn't deserve their praise or their money. She looked down over the gathering. This was different. Here they had thanked her for their food and then turned quietly away. It was simple and clean, like a child saying grace.

Ellen turned away from the window to head downstairs. On the landing she met Skye, who looked as if she had just dragged herself out of bed. She stood there dressed in crumpled Punjabi pyjamas, lank hair falling over her sallow face and draping her bony shoulders. Daughter of a billionaire, she looked as if she belonged with the company gathered below.

'What's happening?' she asked, her eyes wide and anxious. 'All those people . . .'

'Dinner time,' Ellen said simply. 'Downstairs. By the way, have you seen Ziggy?'

Skye shook her head as she peered down over the banisters.

Ellen glanced into both of the bedrooms before giving up and going downstairs. Ziggy would be around somewhere, she told herself, and she wouldn't be able to help but see what was going on.

Prianka smiled at Ellen as she entered the kitchen. Djoti had explained to her that Ellen was holding a meal on behalf of the ashram. She and her daughters had worked hard all day, with

Ellen helping as well. Then one of the swami's own assistants had come, without warning, into her kitchen. He had lit sticks of incense and blessed the food, then the cook, and finally the whole household. Prianka had blinked away tears of pride, while Ellen had stayed in the corner, silent as a sweeper.

Now Prianka waved her hands to show that the mounds of rice were ready, along with the steaming pots of curried potato. She called Djoti's boys in from the verandah and gave them each a clean tin bucket which she ladled full of food. Ellen watched, unsure whether she should hang back, out of sight, or help serve her guests. Finally she took a bucket of curried potato from Prianka and carried it out onto the verandah.

She kept her eyes on her feet, watching how they moved steadily over the chipped tiles. Tread only on the pavement squares, never the cracks, she told herself, or the bears will get you. It was funny how that old fear ran so deep. More than once she had refused to dance on pavements, turning deaf ears to moaning photographers . . .

The holy men were to receive food first, and as they gathered at the verandah their steady chanting rose over the other sounds of the crowd. Most of them had deep food tins with wire handles, like billies. They set them out neatly along the edge of the verandah and Djoti's boys went along the line, ladling rice or pouring curry from the buckets. As they received their meal, the men stopped singing and moved away back to the lawn. There, as if tied to dining room ritual, they sat cross-legged in neat lines, facing the house. They relaxed and talked as they scooped up the food with the fingers of their right hands. Next came the holy women, their soft voices lifting the note of the prayers.

Ellen took the place of one of the boys who went to refill his bucket. Glancing quickly around she saw that Skye had not appeared and there was still no sign of Ziggy. She pictured them hiding behind curtains, peering out.

As she began to move along the line, tipping out serves of

the yellow potato speckled with bright red chilli, Ellen wished she had chosen rice. Then there would be just a single ladleful each, fair and even; with the curry she had to guess the size of each serve, aware of watching eyes. She kept erring on the generous side, but still felt uneasy. Prianka had assured her there would be enough, but only if it was shared out correctly.

The spicy steam rose up over the smell of sweat and something else that Ellen recognised—a thick and musky perfume which belonged to the past, along with the smell of dope and hazy rooms full of loud music. Bob Dylan. Van Morrison. The Eagles. She traced it back, knowing that while people and events disappeared, perfumes lingered, carrying their joy and pain through the years. She leaned closer to the edge of the verandah, following the smell. There it was—stronger now. Yes . . . patchouli. It came from a small bottle labelled Spiritual Oil. You dabbed it on your wrist but it soon spread through everything you owned—the black leotards, even the white school towels.

Anointed with patchouli, she and Ziggy had sneaked away from the Academy after dark, following Ziggy's wild and dangerous plans, appearing at parties, dances, clubs, private meetings. They were beautiful, they had their pick of men at any gathering. They showed off, collecting admirers, but only to impress each other. They knew they were strong, invincible. The world was their oyster, their plaything.

We'll be strong again, thought Ellen. Come on, Ziggy. Wake up, damn you. I want you back. I'm going to bring you back.

Ellen tried to avoid meeting the eyes of her guests—she didn't want to attract their attention but nor did she want to appear piously humble by looking down at the ground. Instead, she kept her eyes on the children, who stood back waiting for their elders to eat first.

Her gaze lingered on a little girl whose stick legs were smeared with fresh diarrhoea. She watched as a boy began to cough. Convulsions shook his frail body, again and again. Then he bent over and dropped bloody phlegm from his mouth onto the lawn.

Ellen paused, the bucket hanging in her hand. She reached into herself again, feeling for the old wound, testing the pain. She pitied the children, she realised, and was outraged at their state. But she didn't feel the fierce protectiveness that would have been aroused by the sight of a plump, smiling baby in a clean cradle. Neither, though, did she feel the dark impulse that was its shadow side: the desire to crush, hurt, damage, disappoint. It was as if, having already found the world harsh and painful and ungiving, the beggar children had survived a vicious but inevitable rite of passage. It was over and done with, and now they were safe—or already lost. Either way, Ellen realised, they were nothing like Zelda. And nothing like the lost child that haunted her dreams, sobbing alone in a cold and empty room. As she watched the beggar children, a sense of release fell over her like a sweet, warm rain. She could smile at them freely and touch them without fear.

Glancing into the bucket, Ellen saw there was barely enough left for two serves. For a moment she paused, torn between making two small ones, or a single that would be way too large. The next in the line was a young man, with lean arms reddened by brick dust. He's got a job, she thought. Did that mean he'd worked all day and still couldn't afford to eat? Or perhaps he shouldn't be here, pretending to be a beggar? Either way, he looked much too thin to be hauling bricks around. Ellen emptied the bucket quickly into his bowl and headed for the kitchen.

Ziggy met her in the doorway, coming out with a full bucket of curry. For a second neither spoke or moved—they just stared at each other. Ellen breathed out slowly, wanting to smile with relief. Ziggy was joining in, helping. The plan was working.

Ellen pointed back towards the place she had left. 'Take over down there,' she said simply. 'I've run out.'

Ziggy nodded and limped off down the line. She could barely carry the bucket, but she pushed on. The crowd hushed at the sight of her, appearing like a goddess—a beggar's body reincarnated with golden hair and clothes of yellow silk. One of Djoti's boys ran up to help her, but she waved him away. As she struggled on, a hundred eyes fixed on her, keen with recognition, as if she symbolised, somehow, all their own weakness and the stubborn hope that kept them going. They welcomed her with smiles as she bent to fill their plates. And she smiled back, her blonde hair falling over her face and trailing through the food.

The next morning, Ziggy joined Ellen in the dining room. Her hair had been brushed and she wore clean clothes. When Prianka came in with a plate of fresh chapatis, Ziggy took one and put it on her plate. It lay there for a few moments before she began tearing off small pieces and slowly eating. Ellen tried not to watch, busying herself with pouring tea.

Neither spoke about the evening before. The memory of the smiles, the grateful words and the licked-clean bowls of the children lay between them, a bright, friendly presence.

When all the food had been cleared away, Skye shuffled in, barely dressed in a crumpled robe. She sat down at the far end of the table and looked at Ziggy and Ellen with silent, questioning eyes.

'We'll be doing it again,' Ellen stated, breaking the quiet. 'Next Friday.' She waited for Ziggy's response and smiled as Ziggy nodded her approval.

Skye stared in disbelief. 'But they're so dirty. The smell . . .' She tried to collect herself. 'I mean, I'm not against helping people. My father always said, one tenth is for sharing around. But we don't have to ask them here.'

'Yes we do,' said Ellen. 'It's for us, too. It helps us to help them.' Ellen faltered. God, she thought, I sound like a Sunday School teacher.

Skye laughed, a small doubtful sound. 'Well, I'm not going to have anything to do with it,' she said. She lifted her chin in a show of defiance, but the gesture looked wrong, ill-fitting, like something borrowed.

Ellen looked down at her hands, thinking. What would Carter do? Or James? How did they always manage to get others to follow their plans? Her next words came out calmly, with a firmness that surprised her. 'You'll have to. There'll be no staff to do the work—I've given them the day off.' Ellen glanced at Ziggy before ploughing on. 'So, the coolies will deliver the raw food. We—three—will prepare it. And at six o'clock, ready or not, our guests will arrive to be fed.'

Skye stared at her, speechless. Ellen could see her thinking through what had been said. The idea of having fifty hungry scarecrows arrive to find no food was impossible to contemplate, but the thought of preparing, cooking and serving food was almost as bad.

'Ziggy—*you* say something!' Skye's voice rose thin and sharp.

Ziggy lifted her eyebrows, but said nothing.

'Well, I certainly won't be here.' Skye grasped the arms of her chair, as if to draw strength from its solid frame. 'I'll call a coolie, and—I don't know, I'll . . .' Her voice waned. Everything had been left up to Ellen since their arrival. Skye didn't even have any cash. The only thing she could really do would be to stay upstairs in her room or hide in the forest. But it wouldn't be beyond Ellen to send coolies to find her and drag her back.

Skye stared at Ellen's face, anger burning in her eyes. 'You're mad,' she said, her voice harsh. 'There's something wrong with you. You're—'

'Shut up, Skye,' said Ziggy in a low voice. She had a round glass paperweight in her hand and she rolled it back and forth over the table, making the flowers trapped inside do little cartwheels in a patch of sun. She looked up at Ellen. 'I think it's a good plan.'

Skye started to cry. 'I'll be sick,' she said.

Ziggy held the glass ball still and looked up. 'So what's new?'

Ellen smiled, warmed by Ziggy's support. She had a sudden vision of them standing together, she and Ziggy, side by side. Neither of them stronger or weaker; neither one in charge. But equal instead. A new beginning . . .

When the next 'feeding' day came, Ellen and Ziggy rose early. Skye got up, too. She hovered around, reluctant to help with the preparations, but unwilling to be left alone.

Ellen gave her the task of peeling vegetables. Skye sat on the verandah with a bowl on her lap, holding potatoes under water to avoid their starchy smell and flinching at the touch of the clammy white flesh. More than once she prepared to get up and walk away, but the empty lawn stretched out in front of her, a reminder of what was to come.

Meanwhile Ellen and Ziggy worked in the kitchen.

'Do you think they'll mind having the same again?' Ziggy asked Ellen as she stood over the stove roasting Prianka's spices.

'What?' asked Ellen, beginning to laugh. 'You mean it should be à la carte?'

Ziggy grinned.

'Have you eaten today?' Ellen asked carefully.

Ziggy didn't respond.

'You should, you know,' said Ellen.

'I would if Prianka was here, with chapatis.'

'Take a look in the fridge,' said Ellen, smiling over her shoulder, 'she brought some in this morning.'

By six o'clock the expected crowd had arrived and the women began serving food. But more people kept appearing, edging quietly out of the forest and drifting onto the lawn. Ellen watched with dismay as the original number seemed almost to double. There would not be enough food for them all. She felt sick inside, as if she had deliberately set out to betray these poor, hopeful people. But at least, she noted, the scale of the crowd seemed to have pushed Skye into action—she moved steadily down the line, her face fixed bleakly on the task in hand, like a child facing bitter medicine and wanting to get it over with as quickly as possible.

The beggars stared openly at Ziggy and Skye—wealthy foreigners with bodies wasted from hunger. They bowed their heads as the women approached, giving the respect due to people who have chosen the way of mortification—though the grand house was a far cry from a bare, cold cave.

Ellen tried to stay out of sight in the kitchen. She cooked all the rice in the house and boiled up dhal and vegetables and anything else she could find into another makeshift curry. But still there was not going to be enough, and it would take hours for coolies to bring more up from the market. The orderly gathering would turn into chaos, spurred on by hunger and disappointment.

Something would have to be done, Ellen realised. Perhaps the ashram could be paid to feed the rest of the people, or some little cafe taken over and a helpful rice merchant found. Either solution could probably be made to work. She pictured Ziggy becoming weak again, joining Skye in expecting someone else to take charge. But now, Ellen told herself, the time had come for Ziggy and Skye to wake up, to look after themselves. To show that they had been rescued.

Ellen left the kitchen by the back door and went to her room. She tried not to think of the children waiting quietly for their turn and unaware that by the time they came to the verandah and held up their little bowls, with shy smiles, the food would all be gone.

She sat down on the bed and stared at the wall, patterned with neat lines of even-petalled roses. Someone came in, quick steps drumming against the thin carpet. Skye's French perfume clouded the air.

'We're going to run out of food,' she said.

'I know,' answered Ellen.

'You've got to do something,' said Skye, urgently. 'They're
. . . hungry.' The word sounded strange, coming from her, as if
she had plucked it at random from a foreign language dictio-
nary. 'And the children waited till last.' Her voice was high and
shrill, edged with panic.

'I can't do anything,' Ellen stated. 'There's nothing left.'

'But . . .' Skye stared at her mutely, struggling with the idea
of empty shelves, empty fridges, in a world of no supermarkets.
A magic world—clean, foodless—in which no-one could eat.
But then she remembered the children, waiting with their
dented tins and chipped bowls, refusing to give up hope.
'There must be something,' she said, pleading.

'Well,' said Ellen flatly, 'see what you can do.'

'But,' Skye's eyes widened with outrage, 'you set all this up.
You've got to deal with it.'

'What's Ziggy doing?' Ellen found herself asking.

'She's serving the last of the food. *The last bucket*. What are
we going to do?'

'That's up to you. You and Ziggy.' Ellen traced a pattern on
the floor with her foot. Her eyes fixed on her toes, following
them round and round. She refused to look up.

Eventually Skye walked out. Alone once more, Ellen put a
record on the old player, a mindless waltz that covered the
muffled sounds from outside. Then she lay down on the bed
and closed her eyes.

Some minutes later, Skye walked back in. 'All we want to
know,' she said bluntly, 'is do we have money? Cash?'

'Yes, plenty,' said Ellen. Reaching into her shirt, she pulled
out her money pouch and handed it over without looking up. 'Rupees and dollars.' Skye took the money and
disappeared.

The record ended, lilting music giving way to the soft
scratchy beat of the needle as the turntable spun fruitlessly on.

Time passed, and the house and garden grew still and quiet. Finally Ellen got up and walked slowly outside.

The lawn was empty. Valuing every thread and shred they owned, the eighty visitors had left nothing behind them but the marks of their feet on the grass. The kitchen was also empty, the stove a weak glow in the gathering dark. Then she saw them, the two figures on the far end of the verandah, sitting quietly with their backs to her, looking out towards the top of the track, where the last of the visitors must have disappeared from view just a short time before.

Ellen approached them slowly. They said nothing as she came up to them. 'Did you think of anything?' she asked, forcing a light tone.

'Yes,' said Ziggy, sounding slightly surprised, 'we did. We stood on the verandah and asked if anyone spoke English. And this weird old guy came up, all dirty and ragged. But wearing orange, you know, like those monks. And he said,' she looked down her nose and tried a plummy English accent. '"How may I assist you?"' She smiled up at Ellen, overtaken by the telling of her story. 'I mean, he was half-naked, and his skin was covered with something . . .'

'Ash,' added Skye. 'He was wearing ash on his skin. Like a caveman.'

'Anyway,' Ziggy took over again. 'I told him to translate for us, and we spoke to the man from the ashram. He said the children and others who missed out could go down there because the ashram kitchens would be open for a busload of pilgrims due back from . . . Where did he say?'

'Gangotri,' Skye replied in a soft voice. 'The holy place where the Mother Ganges bursts forth from the earth.'

'Yes, that's it—Gangotri. So, off they all went. We paid the ashram. Everyone seemed happy.'

'Good,' said Ellen. She felt awkward, unsure of how the others viewed her. She sat down beside Ziggy and bent her head, letting her hair fall forward. It still smelled of the

239

morning's cooking—fried onion and rich spices. Suddenly, she felt hungry. She let her mind wander freely over images of hamburgers-with-the-lot, New York cut steaks, red-hot nachos. And the meat of a freshly caught crayfish, rolled in James's seasoned flour and pan-fried over an open fire. Eaten in sight of the sea from whence it came. Food of the gods.

A few minutes later a beam of light appeared, swinging through the trees, then flashing across from the top of the track. It was Djoti, coming towards them with a hurricane lantern swinging from a wrist. His wide, white smile greeted them before his face could be seen.

'Mem-sahibs,' he said, holding out a covered cooking pot. 'I heard that you ran out of food.'

'I don't think that would have helped much,' said Ziggy, eyeing the pot. But there was no sarcasm in her voice and her smile was warm and easy.

Djoti waved her words aside. 'They are at the ashram. No problem. But you are here and you too must eat.' He sat cross-legged on the verandah nearby and beckoned for the others to join him. 'My own sister has prepared this for you.' Lifting the lid of the pot, he leaned over to breathe the fragrant steam that curled up into the crisp air. 'Dhal. Lentils. I warned her, not too spicy, and no chilli at all.' Then he undid a cloth bundle, revealing a pile of chapatis still warm from the fire.

Ellen moved to sit beside him. Ziggy followed—and then Skye as well. Together they made a small circle around the steaming pot. The yellow light of the lantern threw their features into sharp relief.

Ellen took a chapati and handed one to Ziggy. Skye waited for a few moments, her hands lying still in her lap, then she reached out and picked up a chapati for herself. Copying Djoti, she tore a piece off and used it to scoop up some dhal. She placed the food in her mouth, wordless and solemn, like a young girl at her first communion.

Ellen kept her eyes on her own hand, afraid of breaking the

spell. She sensed Skye chewing and swallowing, then her hand returning to the pot for more. She looked at Djoti, wondering if he knew what he had done by bringing food here now and offering it to Ziggy and Skye at a time when painful images of unchosen hunger were so strong and clear in their minds.

Djoti met her gaze and gave a shadow of a smile. He felt in his pocket and brought out a handful of tiny red spikes. He popped one into his mouth and offered one to Ellen. 'Chilli,' he said. 'Really, chilli is needed.'

Everyone ate, slowly and steadily.

Ellen turned towards Ziggy, wanting to catch her eye, but the blonde head was bowed as if she were deep in thought.

Finally Ziggy broke the silence. 'You know why so many people came, Ellen? The man from the ashram told us news had spread of the arrival of a foreign swami—that means teacher. They said this swami had students who were dedicated to overcoming the power of the flesh. They were happy to see us today, serving for you. But it was you they wanted to see.' She looked at Ellen. 'I'm not kidding. He was serious.'

Ellen laughed. Her eyes watered with the bite of the chilli on her tongue. 'You're joking.'

Ziggy's face was bright with interest. 'No. It's true.'

'Well, what did the man from the ashram say?'

'He said stranger things have happened many times.'

Djoti nodded his head slowly. 'Here we are close to the abode of the gods, the eternal snows, and their children the sacred rivers. Strange things will happen. No-one could disagree with that.'

Ellen looked at him, but his face was a mask. She shivered, feeling the cold fingers of the deepening dark reaching in through her clothes.

Chapter 21

Each evening, now, they sat cross-legged on the verandah, gathered in a close circle around a simple meal of chapatis and dhal. Sometimes Djoti joined them, but usually they sat alone in an easy, tranquil silence.

Both Ziggy and Skye ate the food that was offered them, and sometimes even asked for more to be brought from the kitchen. Ellen watched them cautiously. Now and then she was tempted to tell herself that she had succeeded—that Ziggy and Skye were recovering from their illness—but she feared that this second honeymoon might come to an end, just as the first interlude of optimism had done. As a precaution, she reminded Djoti that he should continue to bring all mail and messages only to her, and that if flowers or parcels arrived he was to take care that no-one saw him with them.

As a result, whenever she was alone she found herself waiting, hoping, for Djoti to come. Sitting in her room reading, or listening to the old records, she would keep glancing up at the window or across to the ready-open door. Then, when he finally did appear in the hallway, or approach her in some quiet corner of the garden, she would stiffen with quick panic and hope. Several letters came for Ziggy and Skye, simply addressed 'Care of Mussoorie, India', along with telegrams and cards. There was another bouquet of flowers from Lucy. But nothing from James—just a huge, yawning silence, an empty hole in every day.

Ellen wrote 'Return to Sender' on the letters and cards and threw the cool, slender lilies down the hill. Telegrams were different. She tried to skim read them, just enough to get an idea of their contents. They were mostly from Lucy, though one came from Skye's father. They didn't contain urgent, serious news, only tirades of love and worry, so she fed them to Prianka's ever-burning kitchen fire. She felt guilty, watching the words burning away, but reminded herself that it had to be done.

Meanwhile, new life spread through the house. The upstairs windows hung open and butterflies danced in and out past the fluttering chintz drapes. Ziggy returned to her garden, taking over the digging herself as her strength grew. Skye went back to her walks in the forest, usually with a crowd of children following her, weaving a trail of bright laughter behind them. On other days she wandered around the house, looking at books and playing tentative snatches of jazz on the tuneless piano. One morning Djoti arrived with a silver-haired porter, brought over from the Savoy Hotel. The man spent hours wistfully bent over the piano, tuning it by ear. He declined Prianka's offer of tea and worked on until he was finished.

'Thank you, madam,' he said gravely, as Skye pressed more than a year's wages into his hand. 'It was a pleasure. One time, I had many pianos to look for. But those days are no more coming.'

He crossed the lawn, heading for the track, with a small smile on his face as her music followed him away.

Each week they continued to hold the open meal. They cooked for sixty and arranged for the ashram to prepare for the overflow. Everyone seemed happy with this arrangement. The beggars, holy men and women, parents and their children all stood on the lawn and watched the foreigners, while a system evolved for deciding who should be among the sixty that would be served. It ran smoothly, except that Skye insisted all the children eat first.

Most rumours found their way to Prianka eventually, and it was she who told Ellen how the stories about her had changed. Now the people said the foreign women were thin because they had been very ill. The Swami Mem-sahib had cured them with her wisdom and goodness. It was plain to see: every week they grew stronger and healthier. Nanda Devi, Beautiful Mother, had answered their prayers.

'It's true,' Ziggy said.

'Don't say that,' Ellen protested quickly.

'You saved our lives,' added Skye. 'No-one can deny that. We were stuck in that clinic.' Her blue eyes opened wide, haunted by the painful memory. 'And we'd be there still. Either that, or we'd be down in the churchyard with our toes turned up.'

'Well, you've got Ziggy to thank. It wasn't my plan,' said Ellen. But beneath her own words she heard another voice. A silent song of warmth and hope.

You did help them. You rescued them. The people say you are good.

Skye began to follow Ellen around. She would wait for a quiet moment then lick her lips and draw in air—a quick, tense gasp—as if about to speak. Then she'd breathe out in a slow sigh and start waiting again for another chance.

Finally Ellen asked her what it was that she wanted.

'Nothing,' Skye answered in a small voice.

'No, it's not nothing. Otherwise you wouldn't keep starting to say it. Just tell me.'

'Can I?' asked Skye, a cowering child asking approval before daring to help herself.

'Sure. Anything.'

'Well, when we were at Marsha Kendall,' Skye began, 'the consultant, Dieter, said I was ill because of . . . you know the usual things. My parents were very strict. In our family you weren't allowed to cry or say you wanted something. You always had to be neat and polite and calm. Momma wanted Poppa to be proud of us, me and my brother. He worked so hard, got so rich and famous—she figured he deserved good kids.' Skye paused, waiting for Ellen to wave her on. 'Anyway, Dieter said I might have gotten along okay, except I married someone just like my Poppa. Al was very successful—he sold real estate in Hollywood—and strict, with himself and me. He used to swim for miles each morning and always looked in top form. I tried to be like him. So we'd match, I guess. I went to the beauty parlour, exercise class. Took a tennis coach.' She laughed ruefully. 'You know that thing in the *Reader's Digest*— Build Your Word Power? I did it all, for him. And then he—' she swallowed painfully, 'he left me for another woman. I saw them together. I was shopping at the Centre, you know, where there's that pet shop. And there they were, looking at some little kittens. She was slim and young and beautiful. She had a fabulous smile. You just stared at it, and wanted to see it again. Well, Al moved into a new house with her. He left me. Sure, he gave me lots of money. He still does, each week.' She laughed, a small bitter sound. 'It's like he still owns me a bit. In a way I hate him, but I love him, too.'

She was silent for a moment. There was the little gasp as she got ready to go on. 'You know, when I read about someone's husband getting killed in a crash, I envy them. I think at least you'll never have to see him leave you for another woman. Because when that happens, you feel like nothing. You can't do anything. In the end, someone would say, white wine or champagne? And I wouldn't be able to answer. I wouldn't even know which one I wanted, for myself!' She stopped, abruptly, as if the storehouse of words had suddenly run dry.

'Why did you want to tell me?' Ellen asked gently.

'Well, after the time with Dieter I know all about how Momma set me up to feel like I had to please other people all the time. I understand that. What I want, now, is to just forget everything that ever happened. I want to blot it all out and start again.' Skye's eyes were wide with longing. 'I want you to show me how to forget.'

Ellen looked down at her feet. Any moment, she expected to hear Skye crying, but when she looked up, the woman's face was alive with strong, bright hope. It gave an impression of the beauty that would be there if she were happy—the blue eyes burning clear against fair skin, set off by dark brown hair. Hell, Ellen thought, she's expecting the answer. She really thinks I'm going to come out with it, just like that.

'Skye,' she began, trying to find some help to offer, 'I'm not a therapist. I don't really—' Then a thought came to her, just a point of idle interest, but at least it would fill the empty space. 'Tell me what happened to your brother.'

'Nicky came back from college one Christmas and told us all that he was gay, homosexual. Just like that, in the middle of dinner. Poppa nearly choked. Momma cried. So, of course, they threw him out of the family, cut him off cold. We didn't see or hear of him for years. Then, not long after I was married, I saw him at a charity ball. I picked him out of the crowd a mile off. He always stood up so tall and straight, like a boy scout. He introduced me to his wife, and showed me a photo of his kids that he had in his wallet.'

'So he wasn't really gay?'

'Not at all. But it worked. He got away from us and didn't look back.' A wistful tone entered her voice. 'I could tell, you know, he was really . . . happy.'

Later, Ellen joined Ziggy on the verandah, breathing the garden fragrance of the evening, overlaid with roasting cumin and coriander wafting from the kitchen.

'I was talking to Skye,' Ellen said vaguely, 'about her family.'

'They're poisonous creeps,' spat Ziggy. 'Her parents, anyway. I never met her ex-husband, or the precious Nicky. But old Patty and Richard—Mr and Mrs American Dream—they used to come to the clinic in a hired limo and sunglasses, they were so ashamed. They've completely screwed Skye up.'

'Who paid for her to go to Marsha Kendall?' Ellen asked.

Ziggy shrugged. 'She did herself, I think. She wouldn't have wanted to use her folks' money. She got a big divorce payout. Al's loaded—sells dream homes to stars, then sells them again when they get divorced. Good business.'

They were sitting side by side, looking out into the trees, as they had from their nuns' bedroom and the wired-in balcony at the clinic far away.

'Families seem to cause a lot of trouble,' said Ellen. 'Look at you and Lucy. You're so much better away from her.'

Ziggy was silent for some time. 'When we were at the Academy,' she said finally, 'you told me, once, that your mother hated you.'

Ellen stiffened beside her, and turned in surprise. 'What?'

'You did,' said Ziggy. 'You said she blamed you for your father going away, when you were born. You were crying when you told me. Then, straight afterwards, you said it wasn't really true.'

Ellen laughed tensely, her lips drawn back into a too-wide smile. 'It wasn't true! I mean, it was true that my father left because he didn't want a baby around. Crying and crapping everywhere. Some men just don't want all that. But Margaret . . .' Ellen looked around while she spoke. 'She loved me. She always gave me presents, took me on outings. She was very protective; she always had to know exactly where I was. People said we were too close because there were just the two of us.' Ellen paused. A soft smile lit her face. 'I remember when she first sent me to ballet classes—it was her idea, you know, in the very beginning—she bought me a whole new set of things.

Leotard, shoes, wraparound jumper, matching hair ribbons—
the lot. The other girls were so jealous. Later, of course, she
travelled around, lecturing, and then moved abroad. I didn't see
her so much.'

'You hardly saw her at all. She never once visited you at the
Academy. Not in six years!' Ziggy looked sideways at Ellen.
'And that old man with the cats, he paid your bills. There was
something weird about it. Everyone said so. Of course, I always
stood up for you, and Margaret. But . . .'

'Well, Eildon just wanted to pay. He was all alone in the
world. He kind of adopted me.'

'Yes,' Ziggy stated baldly. 'Because you were like an orphan.'
She chewed at her lips with a tense frown, then launched on.
'Look, Ellen, I only wondered, when you started talking about
Zelda that time at the clinic. Perhaps it had something to do
with Margaret. I didn't say anything; you were so upset. But
there might be something there, you know . . .'

'You're as bad as Skye,' said Ellen, with a short laugh. 'You've
spent too much time with Dieter.' She stood up, stretching
with a lazy air, and began to wander away.

'You also. Told me. Once,' Ziggy called after her. She spoke
carefully, pausing over each phrase. Ellen stopped, but did not
turn around. 'That Margaret got very angry with you. About
something you'd done. And she gave you an injection. By
force. You were terrified. You thought she was going to kill
you.'

Ellen walked on, shaking her head as she went, as if to stop
the words from finding a way in.

'Afterwards, you had nightmares for months.' Ziggy's voice
followed her.

When she reached the edge of the lawn, Ellen headed on
down the track. Winter was coming and the forest was cold
towards the end of the day. After a while she stopped walking
and sat down on a fallen log. She stared at her boots pressed into
the dark earth. A red centipede crawled slowly up the side of the

rubber sole and onto the leather upper. A myriad of arms moving together in perfect timing. Were there a hundred? Ellen leaned closer and began to count. Two four six eight ten. Twelve . . . But still, she saw it. She couldn't escape it—the image of the bag standing open on the lounge-room table, spreading its sharp smell across the room; Margaret's head bent over as she searched through it, rattling small bottles and things in crackly packets.

'Roll up your sleeve.' Margaret's voice, muted and sad.

Tap, tap. Finger flicking the top of a small glass vial, settling the liquid held inside.

'No. Please.'

'It's the only way to calm you down.'

Snap. The top breaks off. Then the sharp needle drops down, ready to drink.

She looks up, faceless—her face is lost. But her hand, big and clear, holds up the syringe, needle to the sky, and pushes up until a bead of liquid sits poised on the tip of the spike.

Now she's ready. Her arm swings round. It swings round, the needle angled ready.

'No. No! What's in it?'

She smiles. It's poison.

'You're going to kill me . . .'

'Don't be silly.'

She's careful. Takes a swab and rubs the skin clean. Infection is her enemy. She hates dirt. She hates clumsiness. She hates, hates, as she jabs and sticks—and empties the syringe into the thin, white arm.

Afterwards, there are red marks that match her big strong fingers.

I feel sick.

The room dims, fades away.

Gentle Jesus, meek and mild I don't want to die.

I don't want to sleep.

I don't want to wake up.

★　★　★

Djoti was waiting for Ellen at the top of the path. A tremor of concern passed over his face as he saw her eyes, raw with unshed tears.

'I have something,' he said, reaching into his pocket. 'A telegram. For you.'

Their eyes met as he handed it over. 'I hope it is something good,' he said simply.

He hovered beside her, unwilling to leave her alone. She was about the age of his oldest married daughter, who lived in a distant village. He hated to think of her facing troubles far from home.

'Mem-sahib, if you want something, you will find me. I will be here,' he said, and waved towards the house.

Ellen watched him go.

The telegram was thin and crisp in her trembling hand. She tore the envelope open and snatched out the folded slip of paper inside. Her mind was a blank, like the moment before an explosion . . .

Do not write stop you promised stop Zelda will not receive any letters stop you must forget her stop James Madison

You must forget her.

Splinters lodged in Ellen's fingers, and the palms of her hands were hot with new blisters. She squatted by a heap of firewood as she loaded one arm with split logs. As the pile grew, she tipped the weight back against her body. Rough wood pressed through her thin shirt, into the tender skin of her breasts. The last piece of wood fitted just under her chin. Pressing her heels to the floor, she lifted the load and carried it into the woodshed.

All afternoon she worked, dripping with sweat in the chilly air, filling her mind with the slow mechanical dance—back and forth, up and down. If she didn't keep moving, she thought, she would stop forever. She imagined lying in bed, as the others had done, refusing to eat; starving herself into numb, senseless release. Escaping from the pain of her memories—the searing emptiness that was Zelda, lost.

Sinking into nothingness. Disappearing . . .

The thought filled her with icy terror; a deep fear that pounded wildly in her heart. Pausing at the door to the woodshed, she rubbed her hands roughly over her face, as if to prove to herself that she was still there, alive, breathing sweat and gathering grime.

She had to keep going, she told herself, returning to the hard, steady work. Ziggy and Skye still needed her, still wanted her. She was the kind mem-sahib in the big house who gave food to the poor. The people loved her. She could not let herself fall apart and become nothing again. She had to find a way to cover her pain and go on.

Chapter 22

The snow came early, lying softly over the villas and mansions of Mussoorie and covering the grime of the slums behind the bazaar. Down at the hospital, the missionaries started giving out bags of rice and coarse grey army blankets left over from Earthquake Relief. The news spread quickly and soon the clinic grounds were crowded with ragged beggars, homeless families, and even a few holy men and pilgrims.

On the lawn of the Swami Mem-sahib's house, Djoti set up a row of 44-gallon fuel drums, with holes spiked around the base to let in air. When the day of the open meal came round, wood boys lit the makeshift stoves so that the guests could gather round them for warmth. If snow was falling, or sleet slashing icy against the sides of the house, the people still came—running out of the shelter of the forest, bent over beneath their blankets, clutching tins and bowls. But they left with the food, going back to eat in their makeshift huts and meagre hideouts.

Often the sun shone, and the women of the house put on layers of Kashmiri wool and walked up to look at the mountains. The forest was cold and gloomy, and they hurried up the pathways between the stranded gates and pillars, panting out long clouds of vapour. But when they reached the open plateau, bright sun burst over them, warming cold red cheeks and noses and tanning their faces a deep golden brown.

The chill banished the haze, turning the abyss into a gentle green valley, and unveiling the secrets of the distant horizon. Through the clear air, they could see rugged mountain ranges of bare brown rock with dark scatterings of forest. And beyond, the sparkling vista of the boundless Himalaya. It lay like a vision spread before them—crystal-white peaks and crags, shadowed with purple, set beneath an azure sky. They visited a lookout platform, where they took turns to peer through an ancient telescope. An old man lived in a tiny shack beside it, taking money from tourists during the day and guarding the place by night. He welcomed them solemnly each time they came, and stood beside them as they each gazed into the distance.

'God,' he would say, pointing towards the mountains. 'Home of God.'

The cold air was champagne in their lungs, stirring up laughter and giving rise to plans for snowmen and handfuls of ice down the fronts of jumpers. Long high screams cut the air as snow met pale winter skin, then melted, trickling down between warm breasts.

These days spent on the plateau fuelled their hunger so that as the sun sank towards early evening they ran, sliding and falling, down the track to the house. There, they gathered in Prianka's kitchen to eat warm chapatis, and the hot rice pudding that Djoti claimed was the all-time favourite of every real Englishman.

They soon finished the books that belonged to the house, but Ellen discovered an old library down at the Mall, near the Savoy. They had to line up, solemnly presenting passports and giving signatures and money before a purse-lipped Indian woman bestowed on them their Borrowers' Identity Cards.

She warned them that books would be examined on return and checked for damage.

Under her roving eye, Ellen, Ziggy and Skye moved quietly between the glass-fronted cases of old leatherbound books, careful not to disturb the dusty ghosts of the wing-backed reading chairs or the neat lines of ageing English journals set out on the polished tables.

In the evenings they sat in the lounge under the eye of the smiling Queen, laughing over titles like *Every Inch a Briton* or *Dear Land, Dear England*. Then there was *Men and Ghosts* and a thick, dense tome called *The Origin of the Idea of God*. They talked and read, and Skye played aimless streams of languid jazz, while the fire burned high in the grate. They felt easy and careless, cut off from the trials of the outside world. Ahead lay the next open meal, the next few chores, the next trip down to the bazaar, the next mountain walk. Further ahead lay the spring and then the summer—time stretching into the future in a smooth unbroken line.

In the early mornings a different mood prevailed. The three gathered in the sunroom, sitting cross-legged in a circle, as if preparing to eat—but they were silent and tense, facing the colours of dawn with inward-looking eyes.

Ellen was the leader. They waited for her to begin, to ask the questions that would lead them back . . .

The daily ritual had begun with Skye. It had been Ellen's attempt to help her find a way to forget, to escape from her past. Ziggy had wanted to take part as well and it had soon become something that involved all three.

'Who do you see?' Ellen would ask, to begin.

'I'm with Nicky,' Skye's voice was tinged with surprise. 'We're arguing. It's about something he did and blamed on me.'

'Where are you?'

'In the garden of our summer house, up in the hills. It's spring. There are flowers everywhere; blossom on the trees; plastic cups left out on the lawn. Red and yellow . . .'

Next there was Skye's father, sitting on the couch, watching himself making statements on television. Then her friend Caroline in the school dormitory, undressing beside her thin, hard bed.

Ziggy saw Lucy piling her arms with shopping. Ellen remembered Carter eating bean sprouts from a jar while talking on two telephones.

When each of them had spoken they sat in silence, the wind tossing in the treetops. Then, carefully, they took the pictures apart and cut out all the people. Gardens stayed. Televisions talked on. Food, shopping, cars, beaches, airports—they all remained. But they were emptied. The people all gone. Uprooted, unravelled, torn out.

Then life moved calmly on. The wind blew through the grass where they had stood. On vacant sofas, squashed cushions became smooth and plump again. Boxes of shoes and bags of new clothes grew dusty in the corners of rooms. The air was clean and voiceless.

That piece of the past was gone—or, at least, pushed further away.

At the end of each meeting, breakfast was set out ready in the dining room. They came to it with calm faces and steady eyes, feeling stronger, safer. Another sandbag stacked up against the swamping tides of the past.

It wasn't easy. Lovers, parents, brothers, sisters—Zelda—came back, and back again. Sometimes it was almost impossible to wipe them away. But the three women, seated together, fought their way on. Fear, pain, sadness, hope, love, strength—everything inside them—was distilled into a single strain of pure, iron will.

And gradually, as the winter wore on, the meetings grew shorter and shorter. Then they ended.

'Who do you see?'

'No-one. No-one at all.'

'Where are you?'

'Nowhere. I've gone away. Finished.'

Now nothing could touch them. They rested easy in the sweet balm of forgetting. Walking light and easy, with the winds of time blowing free and empty behind them.

One warm morning they all sat out on the verandah drinking tea from clay cups. A hint of spring showed in swelling buds on the bare trees and thin spikes of green piercing the blank earth.

A flash of bright red moved between the trees near the head of the track.

'Someone's coming,' said Skye, looking quickly around at Ellen.

A turbanned figure, leaning forward against the weight of a bulging backpack, appeared at the edge of the lawn. Fine, fair features suggested it was a woman and, in spite of the turban, a foreigner. Ellen, Ziggy and Skye stared silently at her over their cups.

'Hi,' the woman said as she came up to the fountain. Her greeting was bright and friendly, but it seemed to use up all the vitality she could spare. She kept her face down as she laboured up the steps and unloaded her pack. Then she sat on the floor, leaning against the wall, and closed her eyes.

Ellen glanced questioningly around, but the others shrugged. Neither knew her.

'Excuse me, are you looking for someone?' Ellen asked as she went to stand beside the stranger.

There was a short silence before the woman spoke.

'I've come up from Rishikesh. I was staying at an ashram but I got thrown out. I heard there was a place here.' She spoke in a flat voice, like someone reading lines for the first time. 'My name's Kate.'

Ellen frowned at her, uncertainly. She glanced up at Skye. 'Ah—better ask for some more tea. Look, Kate, I don't know what you've heard, but this is just a private home . . .'

Kate looked up, her eyes rimmed with red beneath puffy lids. One iris was blue-green and the other brown—like a fairy's cat. Lost.

'I want to see the swami, the one in charge,' the woman murmured.

Skye giggled.

'There's no swami,' said Ellen bluntly. 'It's not an ashram or hostel or anything like that.'

'I *have* to stay here,' Kate insisted.

'There are some cheap hotels down in Mussoorie,' Ellen said. 'There'll be rooms.'

'I haven't got any money,' Kate said quietly.

Ellen smiled, relieved. 'No problem. You can have some money. We'll give you some. Stay for some tea, then I'll get a boy to take you down.'

In reply, Kate slid slowly sideways onto the wooden floorboards and curled up like a foetus.

'Don't send me away. Please.' She flung out her arm, pleading. It lay over the floor, a pale line tracked with needle marks.

Ellen stared down at it, a sick feeling rising inside her. She got up and walked to the far end of the verandah.

Ziggy and Skye followed her. They stood together, looking back to where the woman lay curled up alone on the floor.

'She's a junkie,' whispered Ziggy. 'You can tell a mile off.'

'What does she think this is?' hissed Skye. 'The Red Cross? A damn dosshouse?'

Ellen glanced at her, surprised at her vehemence. It didn't seem so long ago that Skye had been weak and helpless herself.

'She looks ill,' said Ziggy.

'We could send her down to the hospital,' suggested Ellen. 'That doctor—Paul Cunningham—he could do something with her.' She shook her head, smiling thinly. 'But then, I don't think he'd be terrifically impressed if we did that.'

Ziggy looked up thoughtfully. 'I think she should stay,' she said firmly. 'We've got room. We've got time.' She turned to Ellen. 'You might be able to help her. Like you did with us.'

Skye snorted. 'You can't help junkies. She'll be shooting up in the bathroom. And stealing things.'

'She looks pretty bad,' said Ellen doubtfully. 'We don't even know who she is.'

'Who cares?' argued Ziggy. 'We'll hire someone to follow her around, like they did at Marsha Kendall.'

'You're kidding!' Ellen protested.

'No, you're right,' answered Ziggy, undeterred. 'We'll try something else, something completely new.'

'No way. Forget it,' said Ellen, watching Ziggy's face. 'I'll get Djoti to sort it out. She's not staying. It was enough putting up with you two being ill. I'm not going through it again.'

'But look at us!' Ziggy exclaimed. 'Look how well it's turned out!'

They eyed each other, sharing a sudden sense of closeness. They were happy. They had found out all about each other and then forgotten it together. Now they were like a new kind of family. Separate and free, yet close and happy.

The curled body on the floor coughed, disturbing them.

'I'll get Djoti,' said Ellen. 'He can deal with her.'

But when Djoti was summoned he was shocked. 'She is American!' he said.

'No she's not. She sounds English. Or she's Irish or something.'

'She is a foreign lady.' Djoti was firm. 'If you make me take her away, I can only report with her to the police.'

'You can't do that,' said Ellen quickly.

'Then,' Djoti shrugged, 'what can be done?'

Finally, it was decided that Skye would move in to share Ziggy's room and Kate would stay. Now that there was a stranger in the house, Ziggy thought it would be wise to pack away all the ornaments, memorabilia and other moveable treasures that cluttered the rooms. While Kate was asleep and Ellen and Skye were out walking, she spent an afternoon piling everything into tea chests and trunks and supervising Djoti's boys while they stowed them away in the attic.

When Ellen and Skye returned, they were shocked at the transformation. Skye demanded that the vases be brought back out and complained that it no longer looked like a home. But as they wandered through the bare, purged rooms, they found a new sense of ease. It was as though the pervading presence of the family from Delhi—with all its entanglements and inevitable sorrows and joys—had forced them to remain as visitors, lodgers, passers through. Now, at last, the place was theirs.

They took turns to nurse Kate through the long days and nights of withdrawal, wiping away sweat, pouring water between clenched teeth and holding her tight as she jerked with pain and floundered on the edges of a dark, engulfing terror.

When the worst was over, Ellen sat with Kate in the mornings while she brought out her past, piece by piece, following Ellen's voice, answering her questions. She named people, places, things that had happened. Then stripped it all bare and carefully sealed it away.

Slowly she grew strong again, and a new light burned clear in her eyes.

'You see?' Ziggy said. 'I was right. I knew you could help her.' She and Ellen were standing on the verandah, watching Kate weeding the vegetable garden.

'The things you do and say—they really work,' Ziggy continued. 'That's three of us now.' She screwed up her eyes thoughtfully.

Ellen was silent. Part of her warmed to Ziggy's praise, but behind it she sensed something growing. A plan, or a path. And whatever it was, she suspected it would soon be set firm. Then, slowly but surely, it would become the only way ahead—

Ziggy's way. Ellen frowned and pushed the thought aside. That was how it had been in the old days, she told herself, but things were different now. She turned to Ziggy and offered a grateful smile.

One cool, misty evening, just a few weeks later, Ellen saw Kate sitting under a tree at the edge of the garden. A sense of stillness clothed her body; an aura of calm undisturbed by the slow, smooth movements of her arms and the rise and fall of her chest as she breathed deeply. Her face was a tranquil mask. Ellen watched her from a distance. Minutes wore into an hour, with no sign of their passing, as if time were nothing more than a flicker in the flame of a candle.

'It was yoga,' Kate explained later on, when Ellen asked her what she had been doing. 'I did classes when I was at the ashram. It takes some practice, but after a while you can kind of slow down your mind.' She grinned wryly. 'Otherwise, I just think and think at a hundred miles an hour! All the time—unless I'm stoned.'

'Can you show me? Us?' asked Ellen.

Kate frowned doubtfully. 'Well . . . I dunno. I'm really a beginner. I hardly know anything. And it's not the kind of thing I'm good at. You know, being in front of people.'

'It doesn't matter. You can just show us what you know,' insisted Ellen. She looked into Kate's eyes as she spoke. Was it Carter who said that when you want to persuade someone, you copy the inflection of their own voice? And you smile, of course, drawing them towards you.

'Well, if I did,' said Kate tentatively, 'it might be easier if we were inside, somewhere . . .'

Ziggy helped them empty the last remaining pieces of furniture from the sitting room. They kept only a few cushions dotted along the edges of the Persian rugs, and they tied back the heavy drapes to leave clear the view to the distant mountains.

The following evening Kate sat in front of the bank of

windows, facing the women who were spaced out around the room. Skye was in the far corner, gazing sullenly into the distance, reminding everyone that she had not chosen to take part.

Kate was shy and tense. She gave vague instructions and made stilted movements. But even so, some small sense of an underlying harmony came through. It was something to do with finding stillness through movement. And it was linked with the power of silence.

Ellen took hold of each morsel, savouring the alien tastes. Effort without strain and punishment. Success without measure or audience. She pushed for more, but Kate was like a tourist with a half-memorised phrase book. The real language, the life and soul of it, lay way beyond her grasp.

At the next open meal, Ellen asked Djoti to bring her the young monk from the ashram.

'I would like to study yoga,' she said, through Djoti.

'Of course,' the monk replied. 'You may study with our own yogi, who is a master of knowledge.' He spread his hands apart. 'Day and night you may study with him—because you are held up by the people. You are already a teacher. It is right for you to follow the path of enlightenment.' As he spoke his eyes followed Kate, who was moving along the food line with a bucket of rice, looking ahead to Skye for guidance. The newcomer to the house was still thin from months of poor food and a bout of hepatitis. But her eyes were bright and her cheeks touched with the rosy promise of health.

On the way back from one of her visits to the temple ashram, Ellen was walking, mechanically dodging her way through the market crowds, when she found herself face to face with the doctor from the hospital.

'Oh, hi,' said Paul.

They both moved back to a more formal distance.

'How are you?' Ellen asked. He looked well, no longer tired, and there was a cheerful smile on his face.

'Fine. And you?'

'Fine.'

'It's been ages.'

'Sure has.'

They both nodded, then looked around them, as if to fill the silence with the things they could see.

After a moment, Paul spoke again. 'I came across your neighbour, Mrs Stratheden, the other day, down at the bank. I asked if she knew how you were getting on. She said you'd turned the place into a hippy commune.' He laughed and shook his head. 'I can tell you, she wasn't too pleased.'

'It's not a commune!' Ellen protested. 'One more person has moved in with us. That's all.'

'You don't want to worry about it,' Paul said. He signalled that they should walk on together. 'Edith wouldn't be happy unless you were British, old, and served cucumber sandwiches at teatime.' He looked sideways at Ellen, his eyes taking in her profile. 'But perhaps you do?'

Ellen grinned. 'No, that's not Prianka's style.'

'Well anyway,' said Paul, 'whatever you're doing up there, it seems to work. I've seen your friends at the bazaar. You wouldn't recognise them.'

'No,' said Ellen, 'it's turned out well.'

They walked side by side, taking slow, even steps, their strides well matched. A donkey cart passed, filling the narrow roadway and pushing them closer together. Amid the smell of dust and dung, Ellen caught the sharp tang of disinfectant. It came to her like a distant warning, whispered from far away.

'So what next?' Paul asked. 'What're your plans?'

Ellen shrugged. 'I don't know,' she said, thinking immediately of Ziggy. 'I guess we'll just stay on and see.'

'Well, then perhaps our paths will cross again,' Paul said. He paused, running his finger around his collar and squinting up at the cloudless sky. 'I get a day off occasionally. Perhaps we could—' he broke off, and smiled a little awkwardly. 'Well, we could have lunch. There are some terrible cafes to choose from.'

'Sure. That would be nice.' Ellen nodded and smiled. She remembered how she and Ziggy used to make promises, so freely, to the men they met on their stolen nights off from the Academy. Agreeing to dances, parties, dinners, cruises—knowing all the while that rehearsals and classes and sheer exhaustion would be more likely to fill their time.

Here and now, it was different. In a way, Ellen could choose to do whatever she liked. On the other hand, she knew, there was no place in the life they had made together for visiting friends, or having lunch with a doctor met by chance in the bazaar. New friends made new memories; they began new volumes of hope and pain. And these were the very strands of life that they had all worked so hard to break; the bonds they had severed, so that they could begin to live again.

When they reached the path that led to the hospital, Paul turned to look at Ellen. She kept her face carefully blank, aloof. She sensed him reading her eyes, puzzled by her sudden remoteness. Perhaps he had offended her. A shadow of doubt narrowed his gaze. 'Well, goodbye then,' he said, and turned to go.

Ellen walked on alone, guessing that he would not, now, come up to the house to see her. Nor would he send a message with Djoti. He would leave her alone. Behind a dull feeling of loss, she felt a sense of relief, knowing that she could return to the house, to Ziggy and the others, with a clear, quiet mind and an empty heart.

By the following winter, there were five people in the house. Ruth had turned up one cold afternoon, following a rumour of a Western woman guru. She claimed to be on a spiritual quest, though she seemed more like an ordinary tourist. She was full of life and laughter and Ziggy and Skye persuaded Ellen to let her stay for a while.

She livened up the long evenings by the fireside with her stories of life on a sheep station in outback Australia. Her schooling had been done by correspondence, in odd moments between droving and shearing, and she knew even less about the world than Ellen and Ziggy (whose dance classes had left little room for science, geography, history or current affairs). But Ruth just laughed at her ignorance, her mistakes, her own jokes, and carried everyone along with her.

Ellen would listen quietly, taking in the soft Australian drawl and casual manner that brought back the abandoned spirits of Lizzie, Doctor Ben and other islanders. Sooner or later she would find herself picturing Zelda. Two years on, she must be taller, stronger, with more words, new ideas, plans and inter-ests . . . With Ruth's easy voice bubbling on and on it was hard and painful to force memory into blankness. But Ellen made herself stay and listen, refusing to allow defeat. It was like hold-ing your hand in the flame. Eventually, the nerves would wear out into numbness.

When it was agreed that Ruth could stay, Ziggy suggested that she and Ellen take her aside and tell her the rules of the house—no letters, no photographs, no foreign clothes. And no talking about home or anything to do with the past, except in the special times with Ellen. There were obligations as well—chores, serving at the open meals, attending yoga classes.

As she listened, Ruth's eyes grew bright with intrigue. 'I knew it wasn't just any kind of house,' she said.

'Every family has its rules,' said Ellen. 'It's nothing more than that.'

Ziggy made no comment.

Ruth looked at Ellen with serious eyes and an embarrassed smile. 'You'll laugh, I know, but the other day I remembered who you reminded me of. My little sister used to have all these teenage dolls. Sindy, Barbie. There was a Twiggy doll, too. Mum used to order them from Melbourne. Then my aunt sent one over from the States. It was a ballerina doll, and she came with all the different outfits. I don't remember the name she had. But,' Ruth laughed, mocking herself, 'you remind me of that doll. It's bizarre, I know, but you really do.'

Ziggy gave her a small, cool smile. 'Remember,' she said, 'we don't talk about the things we've left behind. Sisters, dolls . . . who cares?'

Chapter 23

Ziggy came into Ellen's room with two cups of tea balanced on a small lacquer tray. Under her arm was a roll of paper with ragged, yellowed edges. They sat side by side on the bed and Ziggy opened out an old map of Mussoorie. 'We'll have to find a new place,' she said, sipping her tea, looking at Ellen over the rim of her cup. 'I've got two in each bedroom and the box-room as well. Kate's moved out to the shed.' She glanced down at the map. 'What we need is a really big house with lots of servants' quarters. Our staff could live out, and we could put people in there. Or we might even be able to find an old boarding school. There seem to be plenty of them around here.' She looked up, waiting for a response.

Ellen didn't reply, but felt in her pocket and pulled out an envelope. 'This came today.'

Ziggy opened it and quickly scanned the letter inside. It was handwritten on a large thick sheet of watermarked notepaper. A thoughtful frown grew on her face. 'Jerry McGee. That name rings a bell. Who is he?'

'You've been in the jungle too long!' Ellen joked. 'He was the lead guitarist in The Shout.'

'He wants to send his son, Jesse,' mused Ziggy. 'I wonder how old he is?'

'Jerry McGee must be well over forty,' Ellen answered. 'I guess Jesse could be around twenty. How would he have heard of us, do you think?'

'Who knows? Maybe Carter told him. You can be sure he's been in touch with Lucy, keeping tabs on us. Next thing he'll be asking for commission, for referring clients!'

Ellen smiled briefly, then stood and began pacing around the room. 'I don't know, Zig,' she said finally, nodding towards the map spread open on the bed. 'It's already getting so—settled. All these people here. What if we wanted to go away somewhere? Do something else?'

Ziggy stared at her. 'What else would we do? Go back to the States and spend our time swimming and playing bridge? Going to fashion promos and first nights? Reading the investment pages? We're too old to work. We'd just be . . . nothing.' She leaned forward, her eyes lit with enthusiasm. 'Here we're really doing something.' She paused, looking closely at Ellen's face. 'Especially you. You're saving people. Saving their lives. Doesn't that mean something to you?'

'Sure it does,' said Ellen. 'It's just, you know, I don't want to take on too much. People come here and expect me to help them. They count on me. Sometimes I feel trapped. It frightens me.'

It was true. When she thought about the growing household, and her place at the head of it, she couldn't work out how it had all come about. She felt torn between the warm realisation that she was needed, admired, and a creeping fear that sooner or later she would be exposed as a fraud—a nobody, pretending to be someone.

'People have always counted on you,' Ziggy continued. 'Carter, the Academy, Karl. It never worried you before.'

'They just wanted me to dance, or model, or whatever. To *do* something. These people want me to *be* something. Someone. It's not the same. I don't want to let them down—'

'Listen to me,' said Ziggy firmly. 'People turn up here because they've heard something about you. And they stay because they can see that it's true.'

Ellen laughed. 'You make me sound like a circus freak.'

Ziggy shrugged, grinning. 'I can't help that! And I disagree with you—it's not that different from what you've done before. In fact I think it's all to do with the same thing—you know, that "special quality" that Carter was always going on about. And the critics—what did they call it?' She put on a false, theatrical voice. 'A privacy of the soul . . . Elusive, unknowable, possessing a strange and captivating power. Remember?'

'That was all crap,' said Ellen.

'No it wasn't. It isn't. It's real. Ask Kate, Ruth—any of them. Trust them, if you can't trust yourself.'

There was a short, tense silence. Skye's piano beat a faint ragtime. Ziggy leaned over and put her cup back on the tray. 'By the way, we need to go down to Mussoorie to open a new bank account.'

Ellen looked up. 'Why? There's plenty of money in mine.'

'Yes, but people want to make some kind of contribution. Or their families do. And if we charge something, we can use the money to improve things here instead of paying for everything ourselves. It's the only way to go.' She waited for Ellen to nod before continuing. 'Anyway, they say most treatments work better if they cost people something, in real terms—money, in other words.'

Ziggy stood up, turning slowly around as she stretched long, slender arms towards the ceiling. Ellen's eyes travelled over her body and face. It was Carter's 'outdoor girl' reclaimed—a vision of blonde-haired, green-eyed health and beauty. It was hard to imagine she had ever been starving to death. Watching her, though, Ellen felt a vague sense of foreboding, as if Ziggy's growing strength had somehow sapped her own and left her weak and defenceless with no power to choose.

'I'll leave the map with you,' Ziggy called back over her shoulder as she crossed to the door. 'Have a look at the different areas. I think we should find somewhere with a road, for cars, I mean. Don't you?'

'Yes, sure,' said Ellen.

'Night, then.'

'Night.'

'Sleep well.'

'You too.'

Ziggy turned back. Their eyes met as they remembered the nuns' room with its big cold window and how they used to giggle in the darkness, telling stories, sharing fears, until Ziggy decided it was time for them both to stop.

Okay, now I'm going to sleep.

Yes, goodnight, Ziggy.

Good night.

The air dense with silence. Shallow breathing, the only sound.

Are you awake, El?

Yes?

Guess what I saw this morning . . .

Ellen stood by her window, watching the snow falling; a white pattern sliding endlessly down over a dense, black sky. The house was quiet, the last voices stilled into silence and the last laughter folded away into sleep. Keeping her thick woollen socks on, Ellen climbed into bed and wriggled down, pulling the blankets up around her ears. She closed her eyes and carefully relaxed her body, ignoring the cold that lay like bloodless hands around her head.

A strong wind rose, hurling snow against the glass and howling around the corners of the house. Ellen pulled the covers up higher, muffling her ears against the noise. It rose and fell as the wind tossed and turned, roaring and moaning, then dying away into a breathless lull. Suddenly Ellen threw back the covers and lay still, her ears straining. For a long time she could hear nothing. Then it came again, a small sound cutting through the night. The faint cry of a dog caught out in the storm. Ellen lay rigid, fighting a wave of sudden panic and an impulse to jump up and escape. I hate dogs, she told herself. That's all. I didn't like James's dog . . .

She found herself drawn to the window and stood there, bathed in the cold that spread in through the glass, while her eyes searched the darkness. Something stirred in the back of her mind, far off and faint, like the first rumbling of a train coming. She continued to stare out the window. It was coming, slowly. Coming nearer, louder, sharper. Drawn on by the snow lying white on the ledge and beating across the black sky in long lines. And the dog crying out of the frozen night. The small desperate cries, faint beneath the howling wind.

Sweat broke out on Ellen's face. Her heart pounded. Her breath came in ragged gulps as she fought to bring down the cover of safe, white blankness—to get away . . .

Wait. A still small voice came into the storm. *Listen.*

No! Run!

For a moment Ellen hovered, caught at the crossroads, where two journeys met: one, the well-beaten escape route; the other, a thin, sharp line leading into the unknown . . .

You're strong, now. Separate. Free. You're ready.

Ellen let her head fall forward, resting against the ice-hard window, closing her eyes. She imagined herself in the quiet of the ashram temple. The words of the yogi falling steadily into the stillness, leading her on . . .

One is all. This is the knowledge. Concentrate on one single point, the bindu. Begin the journey inward, withdrawing the mind from all that is without.

She began to reach back, pushing through the tangled layers of memory.

Eliminate all thoughts, feelings and perceptions.

Transcend the limitations of mind and senses. Find absolute

calm. Look, listen to the object of concentration. A word, a colour, a sound.

A cry in the dark . . .

The sun slanted across the snowy garden, casting a golden light over the ice-coated shrubs. Ellen threw the ball once more and Sammy ran after it, leaving a trail of small, shallow footprints behind him.

'Fetch it back,' called Ellen, but Sammy looked at her over his shoulder, wagged his tail and ran off towards the forest with the ball in his mouth.

'No, Sammy! Come back here!' Ellen shouted, running after him. 'Here, boy. Good boy!'

The dog slid under the fence and trotted off between the tall pine trunks. Ellen glanced anxiously down at her school uniform, then plunged after him, pushing through snow-laden bushes.

'Sammy! Come back!' she cried, her voice sounding thin and weak against the muffling snow. Then she stopped, realising that he was enjoying the chase. She glanced back towards the house, biting nervously at her lip. Then she forced herself to stand still and whistle, long and calm, again and again.

Finally Sammy returned, with his tail drooping and head hung low. He looked up at her reproachfully as he dropped the ball at her feet. Ellen grabbed his collar and picked him up. 'Silly dog,' she said, in a wavering voice. 'You'll get us into trouble.'

Hugging him close against her chest, she ran back towards the house. Sammy lifted his cold nose and nudged at her chin. 'Naughty dog,' Ellen said, smiling as a hot wet tongue flicked over her cheek. Then a jolt of fear shot through her body. There was a red shape in the driveway. Margaret's car. She stood frozen for a second, then pelted across the lawn, heading for the front door. 'Don't let her see,' she prayed. 'Please.'

But Margaret was there, looking down at her from an upstairs window. She looked frightened, like Ellen, but angry as well. Her face was pale and tight with hard, hooded eyes. Ellen stared up at her, holding tightly onto Sammy as he squirmed and whined in her arms. Margaret disappeared. For a moment Ellen looked out towards the road, thinking of running, taking Sammy and getting away. But she was only a child. They'd just bring her back. It would make things worse.

She stood outside the front door, still holding Sammy, but trying to be neat and orderly. Her plaits were pushed behind her shoulders. Her clothes smoothed down. Her feet placed carefully side by side. As the handle turned, she looked up, watching the crack appear and widen. Margaret's face was stiff and empty. Ellen shrank inside, but stood rock still.

'Where were you?' her mother asked mildly. 'I looked inside and in the garden.'

'Sammy went into the forest,' said Ellen, struggling to sound polite and calm. 'I had to go after him.'

'I have told you,' said Margaret, 'not to leave the house when I am away. Haven't I?'

'Yes, Margaret.' Ellen looked down at her mother's feet, at the sharp-heeled shoes of ox-blood red. She shivered.

'You could have fallen somewhere. I wouldn't have known where to look for you. Ellen, you're eight years old.' Margaret's voice was sad; disappointed again. 'You have to be taught a lesson. Come inside.'

Ellen took a step towards the doorway.

'Put the dog down.'

The child looked up.

'Put it down,' repeated Margaret.

'But he—' Ellen's voice stuck in her throat '—he always stays inside. I'll put him straight in the laundry.'

Margaret stood over her, filling the doorway. 'You come in. Leave the dog outside.'

'But it's snowing.'

A long arm reached out, taking hold of Sammy's collar and dragging him free, yelping and struggling, before hurling him to the ground. He landed on his back, short legs waving. Then he rolled round onto his haunches and sat up. His tail wagged, but there was a puzzled expression on his face.

Margaret caught Ellen by the shoulder and pulled her inside, slamming the door behind her. 'When will you learn to do as I say?' she asked, her voice rising as anger broke through.

Ellen stared at the closed door. A soft whining began and a light scrabbling of claws against the wood.

'Go to your room,' said Margaret, coldly.

'Please. I'll do anything. I'll give up my allowance for a whole year. I'll clean everything. I'll never be naughty again. Please . . .' Tears rolled down her cheeks. She clutched at the back of Margaret's jacket as she walked away. 'He'll be freezing!'

'You have to learn, Ellen.'

'No! No!' A long scream began inside her, uncoiling like a giant snake, and choking her as it came out. It went on and on, filling the air.

Then Margaret reached back and slapped her hard on the side of her face. 'Stop it.'

Ellen pressed a hand against her stinging cheek and tried to be calm. Perhaps if she was quiet and good Margaret would change her mind and let him inside. She probably just wanted to give her a scare. 'I'm very sorry, Margaret,' she said meekly, and walked slowly upstairs to her room, shutting the door noiselessly behind her.

She crossed to the window. Down on the front step she could see Sammy, still sitting, looking up at the closed door. She raised her hand, ready to knock on the window and call him over. Then she realised it would be better if he gave up waiting to be let in and ran off to find a warm place to hide. Later, when Margaret allowed her, she would go outside and whistle for him to come back.

She sat on the bed and looked down at the floor, studying the soft pink carpet with its pattern of little teddies and rocking horses. She began to count them, following the lines away towards the door and across to the window. She tried to guess how many rows of teddies there were in the whole room. How many rocking horses, with their dumb, smiling mouths . . .

Time passed and the sun went down, shadows spreading into the room. Outside, Sammy began to bark. Sharp, angry sounds that turned into long, mournful howls. Ellen screwed up her eyes and pressed her hands over her ears, but still the cries came through.

She went back to the window. Snow was falling, slanting in long lines against the gathering dark. The trees of the garden were black, spiky shapes. And there was Sammy, a small smudge against the snow.

'Go away,' pleaded Ellen. Run to another house. Get into the woodshed or the bathing hut. But he was waiting for her to come down and let him in. To rub the snow from his back and lift him into his warm, soft basket.

Finally she decided to go downstairs. She found Margaret in the lounge room, sitting under the standard lamp, reading one of her medical journals. A pool of warm light fell over her face. As Ellen came in, she looked up with a mild questioning face, as if nothing was wrong.

'It's snowing,' said Ellen.

'Yes?'

'Sammy's waiting outside the front door. Please let me bring him in.'

'No, Ellen. The dog will stay outside. Perhaps that way you'll learn something once and for all.'

Ellen stared at her, bitter anger in her eyes. 'But you gave him to me. You bought him for my birthday.'

'I bought him *at* your birthday,' Margaret corrected her, 'to keep you company while I was away, so that you wouldn't ask to play outside, or visit friends after school. So that I would

274

know exactly where you were. And I could phone you. And you could phone me. If anything went wrong.' She paused, letting her words sink in. 'Instead, I find you out in the forest.' She looked back at her journal. 'Clearly, the dog was not a good idea.'

'You're going to let him freeze.' Ellen's voice was soft with horror. 'You want him to die.'

'Control yourself, Ellen.' Margaret turned a page and read on.

'No!' screamed Ellen. 'I hate you! I hate you! I wish you were dead.'

In the silence, Sammy howled. Margaret raised her eyes slowly. 'What did you say?'

Ellen stared at her, paralysed with dread, searching for words that might drag her back from the edge . . .

Sorry. I'm sorry. I won't do it again. Margaret. Mother. I'm sorry. I love you. The words were there, circling in her mind— but this time she could not make them come out.

'All right,' Margaret sighed, with a look of resignation as she left the room. She returned with her medical bag already open.

'Roll up your sleeve,' she said, as she searched through the bag.

Ellen watched a small glass vial appear, along with a syringe and needle. 'What is it?' Fear rose inside her.

'It's the only way to calm you down.' Margaret snapped the top off the vial. She filled the syringe and held it out, poised, ready.

'No. Please.' Ellen stood motionless, watching Margaret come towards her. 'You're going to kill me, too,' she said, her voice soft with horror.

'Don't be silly.' Margaret grasped her arm and rubbed it with a swab. Ellen watched as the needle pierced her skin, lifting thin flesh as it angled in.

She listened into the night, to the sad whimpering cries of

the dog waiting out in the snow—while the blank clouds gathered over her, taking her away.

Goodbye, Sammy. Goodbye, little dog.

My only friend.

Morning came, flooding Ellen's bedroom with sunshine. The window was a patch of clear bright blue. She dressed carefully in her school uniform, standing by the window, looking down over the empty garden.

She went downstairs and ate her breakfast, steadily chewing and swallowing, trying not to look at Sammy's bowl lying empty by the back door. Margaret was ready for work, dressed in a red suit with a matching waistcoat. She was silent and distant, hidden behind dark glasses and crimson painted lips.

As they walked out to the car, Ellen stopped for a moment and looked around her. Only bird footprints marked the white lawn. The car had been left out overnight and snow lay thick on the roof and bonnet. Margaret had already scraped the windscreen clear. Ellen stood numbly, waiting for the passenger door to be unlocked. Then she climbed in and sat staring straight ahead as Margaret began to reverse slowly up the driveway. There was a bare patch where the car had stood. In the middle was a little black dog, curled up where it had huddled next to the lingering warmth of the engine.

Ellen jumped out of the car, stumbling to the ground, then staggering onto her feet. She caught an impression of Margaret's face, lips parting in surprise. Then she was standing over Sammy, looking down at his black fur frosted with ice. She reached down with a trembling hand to touch his head. It was cold.

'Sammy . . .' she whispered. She pulled at his little paws, but they were stiff, frozen. Dead.

She walked back to the car. Carefully, she shook the snow from her shoes and straightened her socks. Then she climbed inside.

'I'll pick you up from school,' Margaret said. 'Wait for me outside the office.'

'Yes, Margaret.'

'And don't be late.'

'No, Margaret.'

Ellen stared into the darkness. The night had quietened; the lost dog moved on, or found a home. The storm was weakening and a faint moon hung high in the frozen sky. But Ellen saw only Margaret's face, lost for so many years . . . She studied the slanted green eyes and pale brows. Saw how lipstick ran into the corners of her mouth, and small white hairs grew along her upper lip. The inside of her nose was a deep pink, with tiny broken veins. Her teeth were small and sharp, laid bare to the gums when she smiled.

The close-up face faded and another picture grew to take its place: Margaret stretched out in the sun beside a swimming pool. Behind her the door to the changing shed stood open; it was painted a fresh light green to match the shutters with their little cut-out hearts. Dry towels hung from the hooks inside. Bright swimming costumes trailed over the floor.

Margaret stretched out her long hairless legs and wriggled her toes. The sparkling water threw up white highlights that danced on her tanned skin. 'I'll give you another swimming lesson,' she said, lifting a turbanned head.

Ellen looked at her from the door of the shed, one foot jabbing nervously against the tiled floor. She smiled tentatively, wanting to be held in her mother's smooth arms and to hear her voice close up. But she knew how Margaret would draw back with distaste if she got scared and swallowed water and started splashing and coughing.

'Come on.' Margaret slid into the pool and held up her arms. Ellen let herself fall into them, dropping down into the cold water, breathing the smell of suntan oil, chlorine and hairspray.

Margaret held her up with both arms and told her to do dog paddle, the way she'd been taught. 'Keep your head up! That's it. Good girl!' She held Ellen away from her body. 'Now, kick your legs.'

Ellen grinned, trying hard and feeling the buoyancy as she moved forward. 'I'm doing it!' she called out.

Margaret pulled her arms away, letting Ellen go. The child turned to her in panic, struggling to paddle and kick as she began to sink.

Margaret laughed. 'That's it. Kick! Paddle! Go on. Kick!'

Then her voice was gone, taken over by the close clicking sounds of underwater. Ellen's cheeks bulged as she tried to hold her breath, waiting for the arms to come back for her. But they didn't come. She struggled, beating the water with her arms and legs. Then her foot found the bottom and she pushed up, lungs bursting, desperate for air. But something was pressing against her head, holding her down. She reached up, scratching and tearing at long, strong fingers trying to prise them away from her head. But they went on pushing. Down. Down.

Somewhere behind the struggle and the terror was the knowledge that ran like a white hot spike to her core.

It was Margaret.

She was doing it. At last.

Then the hands pulled away. Ellen rolled over, looking up towards the surface, gleaming gold, rippling against the face of the sun. It was beautiful, like heaven, or the face of God.

Ellen stumbled through the dark house to Ziggy's room. She stood in the doorway, her shoulders heaving as she sobbed silently.

'Ziggy!' she gasped. 'Ziggy, wake up . . .'

Ziggy stirred and stretched. 'Hmmmm?' She opened her eyes and sat up, feeling for the lamp switch. 'What's the matter?'

Ellen shook her head and lunged across to the bed. 'Help me,' she whispered, and fell into Ziggy's arms. Her whole body shook as she cried openly.

'What is it?' Ziggy demanded urgently. Ellen gave no answer, so Ziggy just held her tight for a few minutes, rocking gently. 'It's all right, angel. Let it out. Let it go.' She slid over to one side of the bed and eased Ellen down next to her. Then she pulled the blankets up over them both and hugged Ellen close, smoothing her hair with long strokes.

Finally Ellen was quiet. They lay side by side on their backs, hair tangled together, blonde and dark, like wisps of the sun and the moon. Ziggy tried the lamp, and found that the power was off. She fumbled with a match and candle, making small, close sounds in the darkness. A light flared.

'I remember everything,' Ellen said in a low voice. 'About Margaret—things she did to me.' She tried to go on; instead she began to weep quietly, making small whimpering noises.

Ziggy said nothing, but reached over and took hold of her hand. The room was quiet, timeless. The candle flickered, sending shadows skittering over the ceiling.

Finally Ziggy spoke. 'Do you want to tell me?'

Ellen shook her head. She wiped her face with her hand and took a deep breath. 'It's not just what she did to me. I mean, it was a long time ago. It's over. Finished. But . . . now I know. All the time, with Zelda. It was her—Margaret.' She pulled away from Ziggy and spoke into the stillness of the shadowy room. 'Zelda was the little girl. And I was the mother. Margaret. It wasn't me. It came from her.'

Ziggy nodded in the half-light. For a long time she said nothing. 'But that's all over with too,' she said at last, in a steady voice. It's finished. You have to leave it there where it belongs.'

'No,' said Ellen, rolling over onto her elbows and looking down at Ziggy's face. 'It's not finished. There's still Zelda. If I'd known this before, everything would have been different. I could have changed things. I'm sure I could. I wouldn't have left.'

'But you did,' said Ziggy firmly. 'You left her behind. It's done. There's no looking back.' She half-sat to face Ellen. 'Perhaps it's good that you've remembered it all. I'm sure it is. Now you can leave it behind once and for all. Seal it off. It doesn't exist.' She grasped Ellen's shoulder, digging her fingers into the bone, using pain to add weight to her words. 'That's the rule. It's worked for all of us. It's worked for you before. Hell, it's your own rule, Ellen!'

'This is different,' Ellen began, but Ziggy cut her off.

'No, Ellen. It's not different. Not at all. This is *your* chance to be strong.'

'No,' murmured Ellen. 'I'm not strong. I'm not going to be strong.'

'Yes you are. You have to be,' said Ziggy, her voice softening. 'We'll help you.' She lay back and pulled Ellen's head down to rest on her flat breast. Her voice rose into the stillness, seductive in its velvet, soothing tone. 'We'll help you, Ellen. *We're* your family now.'

In the first light of dawn Ellen crept away to her own room. She pushed a heavy chair up against the closed door, wrapped herself in blankets and sat down to write.

She laid it all out. The story of Margaret and Ellen. And Ellen and Zelda.

Then she wrote a brief covering letter.

Dear James,
This is all true. Believe me, it is. Everything is different now. I have to come back.

After breakfast, Ellen announced that she was going down to the temple ashram. It was the one place where she always went alone. Ziggy searched her face, then nodded and kissed her goodbye. Sensing pain or trouble, the others watched her mutely, unsure how to respond.

Ellen went to the ashram, as she had said she would. But on the way back she left the path that led up to the houses on the hillside and went instead to the hospital.

At the main entrance, the villagers moved aside to let her through. As she passed them, the tang of antiseptic cut through strains of cooking oil, garlic and sweat.

'Yes, mem-sahib?' An Indian woman greeted her through a window in a makeshift wall tacked up around a counter in the hallway. 'What is it that you want?' As she spoke, she wrestled with a padlock that secured a wooden casing over the dial of a big black telephone.

'I'd like to see Dr Cunningham,' said Ellen. 'Not for a consultation. It's a personal call. It won't take long.'

'Please wait in the parlour.' The woman waved towards the room across the hall.

In spite of the crowd waiting around the front door, there were only two people in the parlour. They sat in opposite corners, separated by clusters of mismatched dining chairs and low tables. Ellen nodded politely at a well-dressed Asian woman, who she guessed was a visiting boarding school mother. Diagonally opposite, an old Tibetan man kept his head bowed, staring at a magazine held upside down in his big rough hands. Ellen sat in the middle and looked around the room. The walls were covered with health messages and religious texts. Her eye settled on a photograph of the mountains, with a caption printed across the sky:

He giveth snow like wool.
He casteth forth his ice like morsels.
He sendeth out his Word and melteth them.
Psalm 147

It made no sense to her, and yet it was strangely comforting. Melteth. Melteth them. She touched the thick pad of her letter through her cloth shoulder bag and felt a current of warm hope.

'Mem-sahib?' The receptionist leaned into the parlour. 'Come this way, please.'

She led Ellen down long corridors, past patients in green hospital pyjamas. Some loitered, idly watching people pass; others hopped by on crutches, or held onto the walls and shambled painfully along. Ellen kept her eyes away from open doorways, imagining what medieval horrors lay within: people with elephant's feet; cysts the size of heads or babies; raw, come-as-you-are deformities, untended by plastic surgeons; paw-handed lepers . . .

They reached a door marked Laboratory.

'Wait in here. Doctor Paul will come soon,' said the woman, and waved her towards a swivel chair set beside a glass-fronted cabinet.

'Would you like some tea?' A young Indian man wearing a once-white jacket peered at her over a tray of specimens— tubes of dark blood and yellow urine; clay pots of runny brown stool. On the desk beside him sat a glass lab beaker full of milky tea.

'No,' said Ellen, forcing a smile. 'No thank you.'

'Please be comfortable,' said the technician, and returned to his work. Ellen turned to the cabinet and looked along a line of large preserving jars. Lumps and cysts and long, curled worms floated wanly in their pools of formaldehyde. On the next shelf were pickled foetuses, tiny semi-formed babies, dwarfed by coiled remnants of umbilical cords. She bent to look closely at the perfect miniature hands, the peaceful closed eyes, delicate necks and blooming heads. She saw the networks of blood, a delicate tracery showing through pale translucent skin. One baby was deformed, all its features twisted and blurred. But it still looked almost human, and friendly.

Paul came striding in and stopped short at the sight of her. 'Ellen!' he exclaimed. He glanced over her face, taking in her red eyes and skin shadowed with fatigue. 'What are you doing in here? Are you ill?' In a moment of silence, memories of their last meeting ran between them.

'I'm sorry,' Ellen stood up quickly. 'They said to wait in here. I . . . I wanted to see you.'

Paul ran his hands through his hair. 'Of course. Yes. Have you been waiting long? They didn't tell me.'

'No, just a few minutes,' replied Ellen. 'I wanted to ask you something. I thought you would know, and . . . it won't take a minute.' She spoke quickly, feeling awkward and tense.

Pulling back the neat white cuff of his coat, Paul glanced at his watch. 'Look, it's nearly lunchtime,' he said. 'They usually bring me something in my rooms. Just the hospital food, but it's not too bad. Or at least I'm used to it. Would you like to? I mean . . .?'

Ellen eyed him uncertainly. 'I don't want to take up your time.'

'It'd be a pleasure,' he said, spreading his hands in a gesture that included the room, the work, the hospital. 'For a change . . .'

Ellen shrugged. 'Why not?' The fledgling warmth stirred again inside her. She relaxed, letting a smile grow on her lips. She wasn't meant to be here anyway, so there was nothing to stop her from staying for a while. And she wanted, suddenly, to be away from the house, to be carried along another path by events that came from outside. 'Thanks. I'd like to.'

Their eyes met and held for a brief moment.

'Salim!' Paul called across to the lab technician. 'I'm going to have lunch. Could you ask Mandi to send food for two?'

The man nodded. 'Certainly. I'll do it.'

Ellen followed Paul down another corridor. An Indian nurse called out to him and ran up with a clipboard. He scanned a page of notes quickly and scrawled something across the space at the bottom. Here, in his own kingdom, he looked completely at ease, a stethoscope dangling from his neck like a medal of state.

'Thank you, doctor,' said the nurse, her eyes flicking over Ellen's face and body as she took back the clipboard.

'Here we are.' Paul took keys from his pocket and opened the door at the end of the corridor. He stood aside to let Ellen pass. 'Home sweet home.'

He followed Ellen in, going straight across to a washstand to scrub his hands and wrists with soap and water. Ellen looked around the large, light room. It was simply furnished, with a desk, wardrobe, table and chairs. There was a neatly made single bed as well. On the floor beside it lay a thick black Bible, ragged with use. A few framed photographs hung on one wall and books covered another, set out neatly on tiers of planks and bricks. Brightly coloured Indian rugs were scattered over the floor, softening the feel of the room. But still it reminded Ellen of an office, a boarding room, or their own house up on the hill.

'You live here full-time?' she asked.

'I used to have another place,' Paul replied. He poured fresh water and beckoned Ellen to take her turn at the washstand. 'But now I'm the only doctor, I have to live in.'

'I only saw Indians. Are there other . . . ah . . .?'

'White men?' joked Paul. 'No. Now and then there are. But at the moment I'm the only foreigner.'

There was a light tap on the door and a woman came in, her head bent over a loaded tray. They both watched while she set out bowls of food on the table, adding a jug of water and two brass beakers. She looked up at each of them in turn; a pointed stare, as though they were guilty children.

When she was gone, they sat down. A sudden awkwardness fell over them.

'Let's give thanks,' said Paul.

'Sure. Yes.' Ellen folded her hands in her lap and looked down at her plate. There was silence. She waited for a minute or two, then peered carefully up. Paul was already tearing pieces off his chapati.

'There must have been a revolution in the kitchen,' he

commented, as he passed Ellen a plate and a chapati. 'They've actually sent cutlery. So you can take your pick.' He ate in the local style, using his hand to dip bits of chapati into a bowl of curry. 'Monday's always channa. Split pea. It's not bad.'

'It's very nice,' said Ellen politely.

They ate in silence, chewing self-consciously and smiling with the corners of their mouths when their eyes met.

'How's it going up there?' Paul asked. 'I hear your numbers have swelled again.'

Ellen nodded. 'Actually we're thinking of moving to a bigger place. We really need more room.'

Paul nodded, but made no comment. He went on eating. Ellen chased a dribble of gravy down the back of her hand with her tongue.

'What can I do for you, then?' Paul asked, a doctor again.

'It's really not much,' Ellen replied. 'I've just got a letter to send back to Australia. It's way too long to telex, but it's very urgent, and important. I wondered if you knew any way for me to get it there? Quickly?'

'Usually I'd say no,' said Paul. 'But I'm going to Delhi on Friday myself. I'll take it for you if you like. I can probably get it onto a Qantas flight, one way or another.'

'Oh, that'd be great,' said Ellen. 'Thank you.' She looked down at her finger, scratching at loose paint on the table.

'Are you all right?' Paul asked. 'You look . . . tired.'

Ellen glanced up at him. He looked so gentle and kind and wise. For a moment she wanted to tell him everything . . . 'Yes, I'm fine.' She pulled out the letter and a bundle of money and laid it on the table. 'I'd better be going. I hope that's enough. I'm really grateful.'

'That's okay.'

'It's very important, the letter.'

'I'll guard it with my life.' Paul said, raising his hand in a mock pledge.

Ellen smiled slowly, surprised again by a feeling of warmth

within. It was almost as if the memories that had flowed out in the night had opened up something inside her—a long-sealed well.

'Actually, I'm leaving,' Paul said. 'Leaving Mussoorie.'

Ellen held her smile. 'You mean for good? Tomorrow?'

'No. I'm going down to Delhi to set some things up. I finish here in a month. Then I'm moving to Bangladesh, to take over at the hospital my father started.'

'Bangladesh,' Ellen repeated the word. 'Where is that? Far away?' The thought of Paul leaving roused a bright flash of hope. If he could leave, so could she. She could go back and find Zelda—see her own daughter, meet her face to face.

'It used to be East Pakistan.'

'Oh, another country!' Ellen said without thinking, then flushed with embarrassment.

'There's a Doctor Laska taking over here. I'm sure you'll find him helpful.'

'Yes. Well, goodbye.'

'Don't worry about the letter. I'll see to it. And,' he smiled kindly, safely, 'if you ever come east, look me up.' He reached into his pocket and pulled out a small white card, which he handed to Ellen. 'That's where I'll be.'

The card was printed with neat plain type:

Doctor Michael Cunningham MB. BS. (Lond)
D Obst. RCOG
Bagherat Community Hospital
Bagherat
East Pakistan

'Michael Cunningham. Your father . . .' said Ellen.

Paul nodded. 'He always said I'd take over from him.'

There was a short silence. Paul smiled wryly. 'Sometimes I wonder if I had any choice.'

'You didn't want to be a doctor?' asked Ellen.

'It's not as simple as that. It's more that I just didn't ever really consider doing anything else. And now he's dead it only seems more important.'

Ellen nodded. 'You must have admired him.'

'Yes,' said Paul, frowning thoughtfully. 'Yes, I did. But then children do, don't they? Boys want to be like their fathers. And girls, I suppose, look up to their mothers . . .'

Ellen stared at him for a moment as images jostled in her mind. Margaret, mother. Zelda, daughter. Herself, in between—both daughter and mother. And strands running between them all—anger and joy, love and fear . . . A knot of pain tightened in her throat. She forced a smile and searched for something to say. 'But tell me about where you're going. Is it a nice place?'

'It's low-lying land, prone to flooding—always has been—but the balance was tipped when they cut down the forests upriver in Nepal. Now the rain just runs off the hillsides and swells the rivers, and when they reach the delta they burst their banks. They didn't like it in Calcutta, being washed out all the time, so they built a big levee, which only made things worse in Bangladesh. The rivers wash over the land, taking the soil away and dumping loads of sand on the farmland. Whole villages get washed out to sea. Huts, animals, crops. People.' He broke off suddenly. There was a short silence, cut by the sound of a wailing child.

Ellen fixed her eyes on his face, remembering what he told her the morning he came to the house. 'Your parents,' she said carefully.

Paul nodded. 'Bagherat is on higher land, but they were visiting a tribal village. Doing a bit of medicine, a bit of health teaching, and a bit of preaching, I imagine.' He smiled sadly. 'You know, the local people used to worship the rivers. Especially the Ganges. She was the holy mother, giver of life. Now she's turned on them, as far as they can tell. They live in constant fear of her.'

Ellen looked down at the floor. 'It must be strange for them,' she said. 'Trying to work out how that could be.' Holy mother. Giver of life. Angel of death.

'That's the world,' answered Paul. 'It's a strange place.'

He stood up and began piling plates back onto the tray. Ellen added hers.

'But you're going to help them?' she asked.

Paul shrugged. 'You don't make headway in a place like that. You just play ambulances at the bottom of the cliff. Giving vitamin injections to hungry babies. Doing corneal grafts on people who've gone blind because there was no medicine to cure a simple eye infection. That kind of thing. I guess it's help of a sort.'

Silence grew around them again. Ellen picked up her empty water cup and studied the pattern engraved in the brass. A frown tightened her face as she looked up. 'Don't you ever get tired of it all?' she asked. 'Helping other people. Trying to fix things you have no control over?'

'Sure. All the time!' Paul grinned. 'But just when I reach the point of wanting to walk away, something always seems to happen. Like this . . .' He reached into his pocket and brought out a small cloth purse with a drawstring top. He handed it to Ellen. 'Pull the shorter strings.'

Ellen did as he said and the purse opened. Inside was a small slip of paper. She took it out and turned it over. It looked like a clipping from a child's schoolbook. On the printed blue lines were two words roughly handwritten in a foreign script.

'A woman turned up here this morning,' Paul explained. 'I remembered operating on her two or three years ago. Her name's Paminda. She had a long stay in hospital, and while she was here she became completely fascinated with books, papers, forms—anything with words on it. When she left, she told me she was going to learn to read and write. It's two days' walk at least from her village, but she came back here to show me that she'd kept to her word.' He nodded towards the slip of paper. 'It's her name. Written with her own hand.'

288

'And before she came to the hospital she'd never thought of going to school?' Ellen asked.

'Before she came to hospital,' replied Paul, 'she was blind.' He held out his hand to take back the purse.

Ellen felt the softness of the homespun cloth, weightless, as it left her palm.

'So you see . . .' Paul added nothing more, as if it were clear that in the slip of folded paper and the fine stitched cloth lay the seeds of hope, the means of finding the courage to carry on.

Somewhere in the hospital a bell rang. Paul glanced at his watch.

'I should go,' said Ellen, standing up. Her eyes fell on the letter, lying on the table. 'Thanks for your help.'

'Not at all,' said Paul. 'Any time.'

A look travelled between them, sharp with regret. Time had passed, and they had missed the place where their paths might have met.

'Well . . .' Ellen searched for a final word. 'Good luck, with everything.'

'Thanks. You too.' He followed her to the door.

She felt his eyes on her as she walked steadily away along the dim corridor.

Chapter 24

Ziggy and Ellen sat side by side in the back of a taxi, looking out at the passing scenery. The last of the snow had melted and the hillsides were green. In the villages on the outskirts of Mussoorie, old men sat outside, enjoying the early sun.

The taxi driver leaned out of the window to check the way ahead. 'Road no good,' he said.

'Keep going,' Ziggy insisted. 'It's just around the corner.'

'No good road,' he repeated.

'It's okay,' said Ellen. 'We can walk from here.'

They climbed out and set off along the narrow track. Tall trees almost met above their heads and thick undergrowth crowded the verges.

'We'd have to get the road fixed,' said Ziggy, 'and there are a few other things too.' She turned to Ellen, her eyes bright with excitement. 'But just wait. It's fabulous!'

They rounded the corner and saw the first outhouses. They were roofless and the walls were half broken down. Charred remains of cooking fires marked the earthen floors.

'Don't worry, the rest of it's not like this,' said Ziggy. She walked on quickly, then stopped and pointed ahead. 'There.'

They stood on the edge of a natural amphitheatre. It scooped away from them: a wide shallow bowl of grazed grass, dotted with native shrubs. On the far side, the ground rose up to meet the facade of a grand old house with Greek pillars and arched windows. It was set on the edge of a cliff with only sky behind.

'The agent told me it was classic Regency,' said Ziggy, 'whatever that means . . . And the arches are supposed to be Moghul.' She turned to Ellen. 'Isn't it wonderful?'

'Oh yes,' Ellen breathed. 'It's—like something from a dream.'

They walked down into the bowl of grass and up towards the house. It stood over them, solid with the secrets of years; its feet set firm in mountain rock. But the windows gaped open, glassless; doors lay on the ground. The cracked, peeling walls were scrawled with graffiti.

'It's almost derelict,' Ellen said doubtfully.

'Just cosmetic,' Ziggy responded in a firm voice. 'The walls are solid. And so is most of the roof. A couple of years ago there was an earthquake disaster and the Red Cross used it as a relief centre. They fixed up the plumbing, put power on and roofed-in the servants' quarters over there.' She pointed to two long buildings, each of which had an identical line of small windows.

'That's a lot of servants,' Ellen commented. 'I thought you said it was some kind of colonial office base.'

Ziggy grinned. 'It was. The Royal Trigonometric Survey. But the man in charge was, let's say, a little eccentric. Rumour has it that he had a harem out here.'

'You're kidding,' Ellen protested.

'No, I'm not. That's what the agent said! And of course it's haunted as well.' Ziggy watched Ellen's face for a moment or two. 'You like it, don't you?'

'It's beautiful,' Ellen replied. 'The way the pillars stand up against the sky . . .'

'So we'll take it? We should be able to get it done up ready to move in by next winter. Even the name's perfect. Everest House. We'll get some stationery printed—'

'No, stop!' Ellen interrupted. 'I just said I'd come and see. That's all. I'm not ready to make a decision.'

'Yeah, sure.' Ziggy smiled confidently. 'Anyway, we have to do something. More people will come. Even if you say no, they'll still come.'

Ellen raked her fingers through her hair, dragging it away from her face. She frowned into the distance. There was a long silence, dense with unspoken words. Ellen felt herself floundering, helplessly caught up in the momentum of Ziggy's plans. At the same time she still clung to the slim and secret hope that the letter from James would eventually arrive and offer her a way back into another life. The life of an ordinary person. A mother . . .

'Well,' she said finally, 'I guess if I had to leave, you and the others would just have to manage without me.'

'Don't start that again!' Ziggy waved Ellen's words aside and beckoned her on. 'Come in here . . .'

They stepped into the cool shadows of the entrance hall, walking over clumps of fallen plaster, bird droppings and pieces of blackened firewood.

'There are good workmen around,' said Ziggy, talking back over her shoulder as she led the way. 'They say that movie actor, Ravi Nair, had a lot of work done on his place.' She opened a door into a pool of dusty sunlight. 'We could ask him.'

Ellen followed her into a big, light chamber. It began, like any room, with the corners leading into two straight walls, but it swept away into a perfect curve, with a line of stark windows that seemed to open right against the sky. Near the door was the bare black hole of a fireplace and the outline of a missing mantelpiece etched into the peeling plaster.

'See that?' Ziggy waved a hand towards a narrow geometric frieze that ran along the top of the walls. 'It's like a Greek temple!'

Ellen went over to one of the windows. Outside, there was barely room to stand; the land dropped so steeply away to the valley floor thousands of feet below.

Ziggy came up behind her. 'Think how it'd be, living here. It's far enough away from Mussoorie for privacy, but still close enough for visitors to come. It's like a private kingdom. We'll get a proper kitchen and a real cook. We'll have the gardens replanted. Get a fountain put in. Statues.' Her words wafted down over the world spread out below them. 'We'll get a long lease. It'll be our own paradise.' She let her arm fall lightly over Ellen's shoulder.

For a while, neither spoke. Then Ellen glanced down at her watch. 'We should get back.'

She turned to go, but Ziggy grasped her elbow.

'Wait. I've got something for you.' There was a note of tension in Ziggy's voice. 'It came by some special service, so the postmaster brought it up himself. I signed for it. Djoti wanted to give it to you but I said I thought it'd be better if I did.' She held out an envelope. 'It's from James.' She looked keenly into Ellen's eyes. 'I guess you must have written to him again.'

Ellen stared at it, without moving. 'Open it.' Her voice was strangled in her throat.

'Shall I read it?' asked Ziggy quietly.

Ellen nodded dumbly.

Ziggy slit the envelope and removed several folded papers. She opened them out. 'It says . . .' Ziggy took a deep breath, then read on without a break. '"Dear Ellen. When you left, Zelda kept asking when you were coming back. At first I gave vague answers. She was young and I thought she would soon forget. But she didn't. And there was nothing I could say to explain to her. In the end I told her you had been killed in a car accident. It seemed the best thing to do. That way she would never have to know why her mother went away. I'm sure you can understand the importance of that.

"What you've written makes sense of a lot of things. But it's

293

too late for us, Ellen, and too late for Zelda, too. You can't come back. I could never allow it. I don't want to threaten you, but I have to make myself clear. Attached is a copy of the letter you wrote when you left. On the basis of this confession a court injunction was issued, forbidding you to make contact. A copy of this is also enclosed.

"I am sorry, but I have done what I believe to be right. For Zelda's sake. She is only a child. I'm sorry.

"James."'

Birds called into the quiet with thin, shrill cries, like echoes of screams.

'The—documents—are here,' said Ziggy, looking quickly at the other pages. 'And there's this.' She held out a photograph.

A little girl leaned over an iced cake with flaming candles. Her eyes were sparkling with excitement; her round cheeks puffed, ready to blow, to make a wish.

Ellen jerked forward, closer to the image, but her hands stayed frozen at her sides.

'God, she looks like you,' said Ziggy softly.

Behind the girl stood a man, frowning with pride. His hand was draped casually over Zelda's red T-shirt, fingers touching the bare skin of her neck.

Ellen gasped—a short harsh sound. Her eyes wandered over the picture, seeking every detail—always coming back to the bright dark eyes. 'She looks okay, doesn't she?' she said finally. 'She looks happy.'

'Sure she does,' said Ziggy. 'She looks great.' She tightened her arm over Ellen's shoulder and drew her away from the window. 'Let's go home.'

'No.' Ellen shook her off. 'I don't want to.' Her voice was hoarse with pain. 'I can't bear it . . .'

'Yes, you can.' Ziggy's words were smooth and even. 'You just have to keep on going. It's the only way.'

'No,' Ellen moaned. 'I can't.'

Ziggy grasped her shoulders and pulled her round until they

were face to face. 'Look at me,' she demanded. 'I'll be with you. I'll help you.' She breathed in deeply, calmly. 'Nothing has changed.' Her voice soothed, as if she were the mother. 'We'll just go on, as we were.'

Ellen stared into Ziggy's eyes. They were bright and clear, like beads of green glass. She saw love and sympathy there, glowing warmly. But there was something else as well. Pushing through from behind, sharp and strong. Ellen frowned, searching the green depths. Whatever it was, she was sure she had seen and felt it before . . .

Then it came to her. An image of Lucy's face, her eyes charged with the bright glow of her dreams as she mapped out the path that Ziggy's life would take. Ziggy had been her puppet, handed a script and pushed onto the stage, while Lucy basked in the glow of her daughter's success—until Ziggy proved defective and the dream became a nightmare. In turn, Ellen realised, Ziggy had now set a stage for her. Carefully, gently, she'd helped Ellen take on the role of swami, teacher, leader: the one whose name drew strangers to the house, just as Liberty had once drawn crowds to fill theatres and stadiums.

Ellen turned back to the window, gazing down over the treacherous slope. She tried to think clearly, to push through the dulling cloud of pain and confusion. Had her friend betrayed her, used her? Or did she simply know what was best—for them both? Either way, Ellen knew Ziggy needed her to go on being what she was. Ziggy felt safe, successful, standing behind her creation. Ellen could choose to deny her. She could break free. But for what? To do what? Glancing down at the photograph still clenched in her hand, Ellen felt a sharp slash of pain. There was nothing else, no-one else, for her.

A sudden weariness engulfed her. She looked down across the rocky scree away below her—tempted by the vision of a final journey, the inexorable falling, down and down. Then she felt Ziggy's arms wrapping around her, holding her tight, pulling her back.

'It's all right,' Ziggy murmured, her voice buzzing close in Ellen's ear. She rocked her like a baby.

Ellen rested her head on her friend's shoulder. She felt a stillness growing inside her, as tears ran slowly down her face.

They drove back to Mussoorie in silence. Ellen grasped the papers and photo in her hand but stared straight ahead, jolting stiffly with the movement of the car. Ziggy sat close to her, snatching quick sideways glances at her face. Soon they reached the edge of the town and began to wind their way through the jostling chaos of the bazaar. In the car, the air was tense, choked with silence. The driver watched them curiously in his mirror.

Ellen's face was blank and cold. Eventually she spoke. 'You can set it all up. We'll move in.'

Ziggy breathed out slowly and smiled. 'Oh, by the way,' she said, after a few moments, 'when you see Djoti, can you tell him you got the letter from me? You know how he is—he takes his duties so damned seriously . . .'

They left the car where the road ended, and walked on up the track towards the house.

The forest was cool and soothing. Ellen moved slowly, reaching for the strength that lay in the weight of the leafy branches, the thick dense moss and the relentless years of the forest's growth, measured in rings and hidden by bark. Ziggy followed. Their muffled footsteps joined in a common rhythm, then broke away into separate mismatched beats. They panted, working hard against the climb until they reached, at last, the hand-clipped edge of the lawn.

Alone in the middle of the freshly mown grass stood the slim figure of a grown-up boy, or a young man. A bulging backpack stood nearby—stranded like a lost craft, adrift in the expanse of green.

'He's just a kid!' said Ziggy.

The boy's eyes passed over her and fixed on Ellen. For a long moment he stood still, as if afraid to move. Then he walked slowly towards her without speaking.

'Hi,' said Ellen as he came close. His eyes were shiny with hidden tears, hungry with longing. She smiled, her own eyes blurring. 'I'm Ellen.'

'I know who you are,' he said.

'And who are you?' she asked gently.

'Jerry McGee's son,' he answered.

'Jesse,' said Ziggy.

He nodded, looking down at his boots, scuffing the lawn. 'I didn't want to come. I wanted to go home instead.'

Ellen said nothing. She put her arm around his shoulders and led him slowly up towards the house.

Ziggy shouldered his pack and followed on behind.

The people say you are good. They say you are wise and strong. You need nothing. But they need you.

Ellen drew the words around her—all the things that she knew had been said. She bound them together into a shield to cover her pain, a suit of armour to hold her together.

She hovered in the shelter of the trees, on the edge of the deep, wild forest. Across the lawn stood the house. The ground floor was all closed up and darkened, ready for the night, but the upstairs windows were still open, spilling lamplight into the flutter of moths held back by Djoti's screens. Soft evening voices floated down towards her. Women's voices, whispering comfort and safety, soothing pain. We're still here, they said. We need you, you need us. That's all there is.

New tears stirred in Ellen's eyes. She left the leafy shelter of the trees, stepping up onto the lawn and moving on past Ziggy's neat garden. As she came closer to the verandah she saw the ragged lines of shoes stretched out on each side of the doorway. Kate's leather sandals, several pairs of embroidered

Indian slippers, Ruth's thongs, Skye's boots; and, right at the end, the American gym shoes of Jesse McGee.

It was true, she told herself. These were her people. This was where she belonged. She had to go on. She would go on. Buoyed up by their hopes, held safe within their dreams.

PART FOUR

Chapter 25

Zelda woke slowly. Sleep ebbed from her body, leaving her feeling stranded, abandoned. She looked around the plain room, with its pastel curtains, white china and blank television screen. It could have been anywhere.

Over by the door her backpack stood like a limbless torso propped against the wall. Her eye lingered on the worn canvas stained with campfire charcoal and engine grease from the back of the jeep. On the flap was the sketchy outline of an American flag, a patch of coloured threads almost worn away. It had been James's pack; the one he had taken when he left home, went to college, went everywhere. There was a time, he'd said, when that pack was like a part of him. He had given it to Zelda to take on her first school camp, lifting it up onto her narrow shoulders and adjusting the straps. It was big and soft, with just her toothbrush, nightie, sleeping bag and torch inside. You look like a tortoise, he'd said, and kissed her on the cheek.

The old pack stood there, solid and shabby; a single relic washed up from a wreck, a remnant of all that was lost. Zelda turned and buried her face in the pillow. James is dead. He's gone. Mum is alive. She's here. The words were like a mantra, binding together pain and hope into a single strand: barbed-wire laced with velvet ribbon. It twisted inside her, snagging in her heart and rising like fear—or joy—in her throat. She lay still, her eyes fixed on the blank ceiling, tracing the spidery cracks that ran through the plaster.

Mind over matter, she told herself. Be brave. Be Daddy's girl. You can't feel a thing.

Slowly the pain settled into a dull shadow in the pit of her being. It would rear up, she knew, when it chose: slicing through half-formed words; leaving her breathless, her heart hammering. And bringing with it a sense of urgency. All those hours on the plane she had listened to the engines droning on and on, eating up the miles. Taking her away. Bringing her closer. Closer . . .

Now they were in the same country. Ellen, Mother, Mum. And Zelda. In India.

India? She remembered Drew's voice on the phone, sharp with barely concealed pain. What the hell do you know about India?

Keen's Indian Curry Powder (a daring sprinkle into the sausage casserole), Indian cricketers; Indian ink; the hitchhik-ers from the mainland in their Indian skirts and leather thongs (hippies, James called them. Goddamn freaks). And Lizzie's 'Stamps For India' saved up in a jar. Ragged shapes, with torn pieces of brown envelope still clinging to their backs. The mis-sion sold them to stamp collectors, she said, and sent money to the Little Sisters of Our Lady of Perpetual Help. Indian nuns, who swept like angels through the slums of Calcutta collect-ing unwanted babies and taking them away to be washed, fed and lined up in rows of matching cribs.

Zelda closed her eyes and recalled her arrival in Delhi. She saw again the hot night streets sprawled with sleeping bodies, looking like the aftermath of a catastrophe. Policemen stand-ing in the shadows, with dark skin, dark clothes, dark guns—their eyes too white. She saw the lights of the taxi swinging over the sentry box, with 'Delhi Police' painted on the side. Their motto: 'With you for you always.'

With you, for you, always. It sounded like an epitaph, or a line from a suicide note; something scrawled across the mirror in the room of a crime.

Zelda showered quickly and dressed in clean clothes. Then she drank a glass of water carefully laced with iodine. It tasted of swimming pools and doctors and made her think of Rye. Two days before she had left the island, a package had arrived at the post office. Inside was a cloth bag, containing the bottle of iodine, a tube of insect repellent, a mosquito net, medicines, money belt, maps, lists of hotels, and names and phone numbers of people to call on if she needed help. There was a book as well: *India—A Travel Survival Kit*. It covered everything, from finding bed bugs to choosing safe food. Zelda had looked up Delhi and Rishikesh and found notes scrawled in the margins. The bold, sloping handwriting matched the style of the accompanying letter—Rye's three pages of warnings and advice:

It would've been better to wait and make enquiries.

People don't stay put in India, they move on.

You'll get to Rishikesh and she won't be there. Then what will you do?

Zelda had read it all with growing anger. Who did he think he was? What did he think *she* was—a dumb deckhand who wouldn't know what day it was? She understood the risks. But she also knew that she had to get away, quickly, before the world grew real again. She had wanted to tear up the pages and toss them into the stove, but hadn't been able to, because of all the useful information, and because—near the end of the letter—he'd remembered the colour of her eyes.

Take care, Zelda, he'd written. *I hope you find her. Yours, Rye.*

Zelda stepped out into the warm air of the corridor. This part of the hotel was old, and the corridor was more like a long patio, with heavily shuttered arches that opened to the outside. Distant laughter found its way into the dimness, along with the creeping heat. At the end of the passage was a small open lounge, set up with a smoking stand, padded leather chairs and a glass cabinet full of old books. As Zelda passed by she glanced along a line of framed photographs that hung on the wall. They showed scenes of the British Raj: croquet games, polo, picnics and hunting parties. In one of them, a white man in a pith helmet knelt victorious at the front of a crowd of forty Indian beaters, trackers and assistant hunters. There was just the one slain animal—a limp tiger, stained with dark blood.

Finally she came to a wide, carpeted staircase. She descended slowly into the cool five-star air of the lobby. Muted music played into the stillness and potted palms drooped pale, static fronds. There were small groups of people sitting here and there on leather couches set out in facing pairs. Zelda sensed eyes following her as she passed, but she kept her gaze fixed on the reception desk. She wished she was wearing normal clothes—jeans, shirt, boots—but Rye's letter had recommended light-coloured clothing with long legs and sleeves. Modest and cool, well protected from insects. Dana had dragged out a cream linen suit and Cassie had declared it perfect. But it was too perfect, Zelda realised. She looked like a leftover colonial, or someone who belonged in a Mills & Boon novel.

The man behind the desk looked up as she approached. A badge on his jacket said 'Day Manager'.

'Good morning, madam. Did you sleep well?' he asked, with a polite smile.

'Yes, thanks,' said Zelda. She always slept well. While others cut ferns and dry grass for camp beds, she could sleep on bare earth, with just a hollow carved out for her hip. 'I want to change some money,' she said, glancing up at a clock mounted on the wall. It was nearly midday. The book said you should always change money after 11.00 a.m., otherwise you got the previous day's rate, plus a loading (proving you were not a serious traveller). 'I have cheques in American dollars,' Zelda explained. She pulled several out of her wallet and handed them over.

'You wish to cash all these?' asked the day manager.

'Well . . .' Zelda paused, uncertain, 'yes.'

Slowly and carefully, the man began to fill out forms. Zelda gave up watching him and glanced down at a newspaper spread open on the counter. Noticing that it was in English, she leaned over to look more closely. It was an advertising page, covered with small entries in columns.

'We are not hoping for snow in June in Delhi,' one piece read. 'We would be happy with a smart Punjabi top bracket industrialist. If he lives in Delhi it will be a bonus. The lady is 28, 5'2" petite, sensible and rich. Write Box 91564, *Times of India*, New Delhi 2.'

Zelda's eye jumped on, picking out phrases from the long lists.

'Suitable match for beautiful Sindhi girl, 32, working Air India, caste no bar. Reply with horoscope indicating place and time of birth.'

'Wheatish complexion, good looking, having very slight limp.'

'Divorcee (issueless) smart graduate girl, 30.'

'Very, very attractive Brahmin girl, smart, homely, religious, 34, green card holder, invites alliance from well-settled boy in America/India.'

The manager glanced up, noticing her interest. 'I am searching for a wife,' he said solemnly, 'for my second son. He is a doctor.'

Zelda smiled politely. A tall, slim girl. Age 21. Strong, healthy. Good swimmer. Skilled deckhand, scallop splitter. Can dance.

The manager began counting out wads of money, his fingers flicking easily over the notes. 'Sign here. And here. And here.'

'Thanks,' said Zelda. She rolled up the money and stuffed it into her pocket. 'Can you tell me, please, how I can get to Rishikesh? As quickly as possible?'

'Rishikesh?' the man repeated. A slight frown crept onto his brow. 'You are travelling alone?'

'Yes,' said Zelda. 'But I'm visiting my mother. She lives there.' Her quick smile covered a twist of apprehension, a swell of excitement. Visiting my mother. She lives there. It sounded so close, so ordinary, so real.

Please be there . . .

'Ah,' he relaxed again. 'Then you will have no problems.' He shook his head sadly. 'Some young girls come to India and they travel alone. Rishikesh is a famous Hindu city, as you know. There are many temples, dharmshalas, ashrams. But there are some bad places there. People take advantage of foreigners.' A puzzled look came onto his face. 'But your mother? She has not arranged for your journey?'

'No,' said Zelda quickly. 'It's a surprise visit.'

'Ah, I see,' he said doubtfully.

'But I have other friends there, too,' Zelda added. 'Friends of the family.'

'Good, good.' He seemed reassured. 'Please excuse me, but what is your standard of travel?'

'Sorry?'

'The day train is cheaper, but there is no airconditioning. You cannot reserve a seat, so it will become very crowded. It will take about eight hours. You will get off at Hardwar, and take a taxi to Rishikesh. It is not—'

'What time does it leave?' Zelda interrupted. Her foot beat a tense rhythm against the floor.

'For today it has left already. Tomorrow there is no train. You must wait until the next day after.'

'That's too long,' said Zelda simply.

'Then, you have no choice. The night trains are reserved a long way in advance at this time of the year. So you must take a taxi all the way. It may cost about fifty dollars.' He paused, waiting for her reaction. She nodded encouragingly. 'It may take about eight hours.' He looked at her sternly. 'You cannot drive at night. So, today you rest. Tomorrow morning, you can leave.'

Zelda was silent, frowning. The man laid his hands firmly on the counter.

'Okay,' she said finally, 'I'll do that.'

He nodded gravely. 'I myself will choose your taxi and driver. I recommend that you leave early, while it is not so hot. Settle your bill tonight, and I will call you at 6 a.m.'

'Thank you very much.' Zelda watched his face as he wrote a note in the register. He looked tired, but there were deep laugh lines around his eyes. 'I hope you find a good wife for your son,' she said.

He looked up, surprised. 'There are plenty of good wives,' he said. 'That is not a problem. Only my son—he wishes to choose his own.' He shrugged hopelessly and Zelda found herself shaking her head in sympathy. She searched for something to say.

'Perhaps he will know best . . .'

'That is what he tells me!' The man spoke in a tone of mild surprise, then shrugged and waved a hand as if to push the problem away. 'And what else can I do for you?'

'I wonder if you could tell me where to eat?'

'Yes, madam.' He was on duty again. 'You can take lunch in the coffee shop over there, or there is room service if you wish.'

Zelda nodded, turning to go. 'You'll make sure everything is organised with the taxi? It's very important for me to get there tomorrow.'

'Of course. Why should I not?'

The coffee shop was decorated with lime green paper grapevines. They trailed stiffly over striped awnings and white-painted lattice, working overtime to endorse the elegant sign that hung in one corner: The Terrace Patisserie. The tables faced a bank of French windows, opening onto a real terrace covered in real flowering vines. But the outside air shimmered in the fierce heat and the place was deserted.

A waiter shepherded Zelda towards a small table set with heavy silver cutlery and bright green napkins. 'Is someone coming?' he asked.

'No.'

He left her with a menu. Zelda glanced quickly over it without interest. She was hungry but could think of nothing she wanted to eat. Looking up, she noticed a small Indian child standing near her table, staring intently with big, solemn eyes. She was dressed in bright clothes, all brand new, still creased from their packages, and all at least a size too big. Her dress had slipped to one side, baring a thin brown shoulder.

'Hi,' Zelda smiled at her, then looked around for her parents. The only other guests were a large blonde woman and a bald man with a red beard. They were engrossed in the menu. Their voices wafted over.

'Kids like pancakes—they all do. Let's get some of them,' the man said.

'I don't know,' replied the woman, frowning as she pulled the menu closer. 'I think an egg and toast would be more healthy.' She looked up suddenly and called out, 'Sally? Sally?' Her eyes searched the room, before settling on the little Indian girl. 'There you are! Come here, darling. Come on, over here.' The girl stood where she was, her face torn with confusion.

'Go on,' said Zelda, turning her to face the woman. 'There you go.'

The child looked from Zelda to the blonde woman and back. A waiter came over and spoke softly to her in a language she appeared to understand. She ran forward and clasped her arms around his leg.

'Please excuse me, madam,' he said to Zelda, and bent to peel the thin limbs away.

The blonde woman arrived and swept the child up into her arms. 'Here we are, sweetie,' she said. 'Daddy's getting pancakes and ice-cream for you.' She smiled down at Zelda. 'Isn't she adorable?'

'Yes,' said Zelda.

'She's our new daughter,' the woman explained, bowing her blonde head over the dark, wispy curls.

'My name is Amanpree,' the child chanted, in a singsong voice. 'My name is four years old. I like play ball. I like help carry water.'

'Clever girl,' the woman crooned, her head pulled back, chin pressing into the folds of her neck, as she watched the little face. After a moment she turned to Zelda. 'I'm Maree,' she said. 'That's my husband Steve. We're from Australia—Sydney. Where are you from?'

'I'm Australian too. I come from Flinders Island.'

Maree looked blank. 'Can't say I know it.'

'It's between Victoria and Tasmania.'

'Ah, yes. I remember it now, from the weather map on telly.' Maree put the child down and pointed her towards Steve, who beckoned with a piece of bread, held out like a carrot. 'We came here to collect our adopted daughter.' She laughed nervously. 'I don't usually talk to strangers but—I'm so happy. We've waited years for this. I can't believe we're here. With her.' Her eyes grew shiny with tears.

'Where did you—get her from?' asked Zelda awkwardly.

'Sacred Heart orphanage,' said Maree. 'It was all set up in advance, of course. At first we wanted a baby. But so many are ill, you know. Some even die when you get them home. And then, of course, the older ones get left. No-one wants them. It's awful for them, watching the little ones being chosen all the time. So anyway, they sent us a photo of Sally— Amanpree. Her mother's dead. Her father's in prison. Maree had no-one. We fell in love with her, straightaway.' Maree leaned down and lowered her voice. 'Steve's over the moon.

He built a new room on the house, made her a rocking horse, toys—everything.' She smiled again, letting her joy spill openly. 'We always wanted to be parents . . .' She pulled herself up. 'I'm sorry—carrying on like this. You're?'

'Zelda.'

'On holiday?'

'No. Actually, I came here to meet my mother.' Zelda paused. For a moment she wanted to explain that she didn't know this mother yet; that she had been only a little girl like Sally Amanpree when her mother went away. Not dying. Just leaving. Leaving her behind, like nothing at all . . .

'She lives in India?' Maree asked. Her blue eyes were bright with friendly interest.

'She . . . moves around,' said Zelda vaguely. 'Of course I have to make my own life—work and all that. But we try to get together when we can.'

'Course you do!' breathed Maree. 'I bet you can't wait to see her. And she must be dying to see you.'

'Oh yes,' said Zelda smiling brightly. 'We write, of course. But it's not the same.'

'No, it certainly isn't!' agreed Maree. 'Well, all the best to you both. I hope you have a wonderful holiday together.' She looked up at the sound of cutlery clattering to the floor. The child was standing on a chair, picking up knives and spoons and dropping them one by one. Steve was studying the menu. Maree raised her hands in a gesture of delighted helplessness. 'Kids!'

Zelda watched her go. She lifted her own menu and studied the lines of writing. They wavered in a thin wash of tears.

'Yes, madam?' a waiter spoke over her shoulder.

'I'll have pancakes and ice-cream,' said Zelda. 'Please.'

'Sorry, madam, it is afternoon now. Breakfast menu is finished. If you wish pancake, I suggest masala dhosa. Indian pancake.'

'Okay. Good.'

When he left her, she sat still, staring down at her green-edged plate.

'Miss Zelda Madison?'

She jumped at the sound of her name. 'Yes?'

A bellboy handed her a slip of paper. 'Fax, madam.'

Zelda took it from him, staring blankly at the page. There was a message written in a long, looping hand that stretched out across the space:

Thinking of you, darling, as you set out on your 'long walk'.
Be brave. Be strong. Be yourself.
Your ancient friend,
Cassie.

Zelda folded the paper and closed her hand around it, drawing strength from the old woman's words. Cassie knew. She understood. During the days at Dana's house she had listened openly to Zelda's phone calls—the stumbling explanations, long silences, noiseless weeping.

'Who was that?' she would ask, when Zelda finally put the receiver down.

Zelda would stare at the ceiling, tears running down her cheeks as she answered. 'It was Drew. My boyfriend. He's my best friend. I love him. James loved him.'

'It was Lizzie. Drew's mother. She loves me too.'

'They want me to stay. They want me to wait.'

'Don't wait,' Cassie would say, in a voice as firm as rock. 'Now's the time. Begin your journey. You'll find what you find. There's nothing else to do.'

Zelda smoothed out the fax and placed it beside her plate. It was a charm, a talisman, that would travel with her. *Be brave. Be strong. Be yourself . . . With you for you always . . .*

Zelda sat in the back of the taxi, with her pack lodged beside her. She wore sunglasses and her Akubra pulled well down as a barrier against the world outside. Safely hidden, she stared out at

311

the wide tree-lined streets. Here and there a late sleeper lay, swathed in cloths, face hidden. Beggars waited patiently, like statues, only just alive. Holy men chanted tranquil prayers. As they drove on, the streets narrowed and stillness gave way to a pattern of bustle and movement. Stallholders stoked up small burners. Students in white shirts gathered in groups to drink tea from clay cups, while ragged children hovered around them.

By seven o'clock the roads were already busy, jostling with loaded oxcarts, bicycles, trucks and old buses with barred windows. Motor scooters weighed down with whole families wove dangerously through the traffic: fathers driving, with one or two children perched in front; the mothers riding side-saddle behind, with the ends of their bright sarees streaming in the wind.

Zelda took out her bottle of iodine water and took a long gulp. As she did so, she glimpsed the driver watching her in the rear-view mirror. He grinned, flashing white teeth.

'He is a good driver,' the day manager had said. 'We have chosen him specially. Actually, he is a relative of mine. He speaks good English. The money you have paid is the full fare, but if you like you may give him a tip. But no more than twenty or thirty rupees.' He had paused to look sternly at the driver. 'He will take you to the Holy Ganges Hotel in Rishikesh. Now you relax please, and enjoy your journey . . .'

After nearly an hour had passed, Zelda noticed that the road was widening again. Soon the city thinned out, giving way to farmland and small villages shaded by leafy trees. The air was hot and dusty, but smelled strangely sweet. They overtook a line of trucks laden with green cane.

'This one sugar,' the driver called over his shoulder. 'Sweet one.'

They passed whole fields of heavy-headed sunflowers, brown faces fringed with yellow, all turned towards the climbing sun. Then there were squares of brown, ploughed earth, marked with splashes of hot pink, turquoise, red and amber— peasant women in bright skirts and shawls. They hovered in the fields, like small flocks of exotic birds.

Around mid-morning the driver pulled in at a small road-side cafe. 'Inside?' he pointed. 'Tea. Cold drink. Toilet.'

Zelda nodded. She fought with the catch on the door and climbed stiffly out. Her clothes were layered with dust and fused to her sweaty skin. Faces, eyes and long-limbed bodies appeared noiselessly and hovered around her. She paused, glancing back at her pack inside on the seat.

'Okay, no problem,' said the driver. He pointed at a small boy who had climbed onto the bumper bar. 'He will take care.'

'Thanks,' said Zelda. She headed for the cafe, aware of the many lingering stares stretching after her.

Inside the cafe it was dim, but not much cooler. A ceiling fan revolved lazily, keeping the flies moving. Behind the counter stood an old man in a faded pink turban. It was wound loosely and sat on his head in a precarious pile. He waved his hand towards a short line of dusty bottles. 'Limca? Thums Up? Soda?'

Zelda pointed at a yellow drink and held out some money.

'You come from?' A voice came from behind her. She turned to face a young dark-skinned man. His eyes latched onto hers. They were almost black.

'Flinders—' She stopped. 'Australia.'

'Ah,' he nodded gravely. 'America. George Bush.'

Zelda smiled politely. Wiping the top of the soft drink bottle with the sleeve of her jacket, she began to drink down the sweet yellow fizz. She turned to head back to the car.

'Mem-sahib! Mem-sahib!' The old man called out urgently from behind the counter. 'No. No.'

Zelda stopped. He was pointing at the soft drink and shaking his head. She frowned, puzzled, and reached in her pocket for some more money.

'Bottle. No take,' said the young man helpfully. Their eyes met again. This time he slid them carefully down to Zelda's breasts, and back. She swallowed the drink quickly and put the bottle down on the counter.

'Yes-my-friend . . .' the man called after her as she walked away. Laughter followed her out into the dusty heat.

The eight-hour journey became ten, somehow, without anything particular going wrong.

'Are we nearly there?' Zelda kept asking. 'How much longer?'

The driver just wobbled his head on his shoulders, non-committal. 'It is far. Delhi. Rish'kesh. Far. But please, enjoy your trip.' He spread his hands, abandoning the wheel. 'You are recreating —yes?'

Finally, forest thinned again into fields and buildings cropped up along the sides of the road.

'Rish'kesh coming,' the driver announced. Then, without warning, he swung off the road into a wide tree-lined driveway.

The Holy Ganges Hotel was like an office block with a decorated entrance. Its walls were drab yellow and streaked with dust. Rows of windows gazed blearily down. Faded pots of tired cacti stood at the edges of a set of wide stairs that led up to two glass doors.

The taxi driver took Zelda's money with a nod and motioned her away from the car. 'Boy will bring,' he said, pointing inside.

'No, it's okay, I can manage,' said Zelda. She dragged out her pack by one strap and heaved it up onto her shoulders. 'Thank you very much. Goodbye.' She sensed him gazing after her as she climbed the steps. *Always use a porter.* Rye's words came back to her. *It's mean not to. They need the work.* She glanced awkwardly behind her, and caught sight of a boy running towards the car. He stopped still, his thin arms dangling, as he stared at her with wide, disbelieving eyes. She looked quickly away and hurried on.

The lobby was deserted. She put down her pack and stood still for a moment, letting the cooler air soothe her sticky skin. Then she went to stand by a wide counter, bathed in harsh blue light shed by a bank of fluorescent tubes. A big black phone stood alone on the counter. As if in response to her, it began to ring. No-one came. It rang on and on. Just as it stopped, a man rushed in. He looked from Zelda to the phone, as if surprised that she had not picked it up.

'I have a reservation,' Zelda began. 'My name is Zelda Madison.'

'Yes, mem-sahib. We are expecting you. Yesterday. But no problem.' He lifted a large book onto the counter and opened it. 'I will arrange your room. First you must register as a Foreign Guest. Passport please.' He glanced up. His eyes travelled quickly over her face. 'You have come from Delhi,' he stated. 'You are tired.'

'Yes,' answered Zelda.

He slammed his hand down on a bell and looked up expectantly. The boy from outside appeared, arms still dangling. The man handed him a key hung on a large brass ball. He glanced at Zelda. 'Special room, only for you. River view.'

'Thank you,' said Zelda. 'Is there a shower?'

'Of course. Even hot water, I hope.'

Zelda stood in the shower, letting water run over her face. Remembering Rye's warnings, she kept her mouth tightly closed, imagining amoebas swimming around like little fish, looking for a chance to break in. The hotel soap was red, small, hard and smelled of the school washroom. She scrubbed herself all over, then turned off the water and stepped back out into the warm air. She paused by the phone and dialled the number given for room service.

While it rang she pictured herself, standing there. Zelda in India. Wrapped in a towel like an American actress . . .

'Yes,' she said coolly. 'Room 12 here. Could you send someone up with a bottle of Limca, please? Thank you.' She paused with the receiver in her hand, then reached for her passport wallet and wriggled out a small white business card. Mr Ranjit

Saha, it said. 97 Veer Bhadra Road, Rishikesh 249201 Phone 516. She dialled the numbers quickly, to avoid preparing a speech. Instead, she recalled Rye's note: *Ranjit's an old family friend and knows everyone. Call him when you arrive.*

Her head jolted up as a voice came onto the line. 'Hello? Hello?' She cut into a long line of foreign words. 'Is Mr Ranjit Saha there please?'

Silence.

'Ranjit Saha?' Zelda repeated.

'I'm sorry. Ranjit Saha is not at home, madam. Please ring tomorrow. Good evening.'

Zelda gripped the receiver with clammy hands. Tomorrow. It felt like a week away. She couldn't bear just to wait, doing nothing, now that she was here. But there was no other plan, no lead to follow; no choice but to let the time drag by.

She sat down on the bed and looked around her. There was nothing of India in this hotel room either, unless you counted a faded poster of a Bengal tiger. It gazed bleakly over icons of Western living: a laminex dressing table, brocade bedspread, fringed lampshade. But the carpet was stained, the walls were soiled above the bedhead, and loose wires poked from the side of the lamp.

Well, here I am at least, thought Zelda. In Rishikesh.

Rishikesh. City of saints. And Ellen.

'Filed from Rishikesh, India.' Zelda saw the words in print, small and black against newsprint yellowed with years.

'LIBERTY' FINDS NEW FOLLOWING.
FILED FROM RISHIKESH, INDIA.
A decade after the American ballet
superstar vanished amid rumours of

She knew every word, every letter. She could see the ragged shape of the torn-out piece of newspaper. A big, cornerless continent.

She crossed to the window and looked down over a patch of sparse garden, dotted with bright pink flowers. By leaning out she could just see a bit of the river, almost lost in a white haze. The shadows were soft and long, the daylight fading.

She looked up at a knock on the door. Quickly dragging on some clothes, she opened it slowly. A young man in a maroon uniform stood there smiling.

'I am someone,' he said.

'Sorry?' Zelda frowned.

'I am send someone with Limca.' He eased past her, carrying a tray and a bottle.

'Thank you,' said Zelda. She signed the tab and handed him a tip. *Always tip*, Rye's letter had said. *Just a rupee or two. If you don't, things will stop happening.*

The man nodded. 'I'm coming back,' he said brightly. 'Bring glass and open bottle.'

The dining room was like a big abandoned theatre, looking out through a bank of windows onto a wide stage set with mythic props: hills painted in soft mounds against a pastel sunset sky; and a river—a wide, still swathe of pure spun silver, edged with mist. The holy Ganges.

Zelda walked past rows of empty tables until she came to the window. There she leaned her head against the warm smooth glass and gazed out at the scene through a thick cloud of mosquitoes that clustered around an outside light.

While she watched, a tall orange-robed man emerged from the shadowy garden and approached the river's edge. In his hands he held a light—a small yellow flame. It burned steadily in the still air, only wavering as he began to swing it slowly from side to side. He lifted his face towards the last glow of the sinking sun and began to sing. His voice came through the glass like a distant echo. Zelda tried to find words in the sounds, but there was nothing she could name.

317

'It is puja, the time of blessing.' A voice came from behind her, close and soft. Zelda turned to face a young Indian woman dressed in a bright silk saree. 'It takes place at dawn and sunset,' the woman continued. She spoke with a slight American accent. 'He is the hotel priest, holy man. He offers prasad, the blessing, on behalf of everyone here.'

Zelda nodded. 'The river is very beautiful,' she said.

The woman bowed her head, as if accepting the compliment for herself. Then they both watched in silence while the priest scattered yellow flowers into the river. The ragged heads dipped and twirled as the waters carried them away.

'I shall leave you to your meal,' the woman said, and turned to go.

'Wait,' Zelda said suddenly. She reached into her pocket and pulled out a folded envelope. 'I'd just like to ask you something.'

The woman raised her eyebrows slightly and shrugged. Zelda carefully unfolded her newspaper cutting and pointed at Ellen's face. 'I'm looking for this person.'

The woman studied it for a moment, then laughed. 'But it's you!'

'No—' Zelda began.

'Ah. Your sister then. She's here? In Rishikesh?'

'I don't know,' answered Zelda. 'She was when this was taken, but it was twelve years ago.'

The woman frowned. 'Foreigners come here to stay in the ashrams. But most don't stay long, they just come and look, and go. There are exceptions of course. Some stay for a while. Some even take sannyas.' She bent over the photograph to look more closely.

'Sannyas . . .' Zelda repeated. She cast her mind back over the books on India she had read in Dana's house, and the long discussions they'd had—speculation about Ellen, led by Dana and Cassie.

'It was a leftover of the hippy thing.' Dana felt sure. 'She'd have hung out there for a bit, and then moved on. I bet she's been back in the States for years.'

Cassie disagreed. 'If she was there, she'd have been discovered for sure. Her face was so well known. I think Zelda's right—India's the place. But what do they mean by "Liberty finds new following"? It sounds political, or religious. Or philanthropic perhaps—doing good works, helping the poor . . .'

The discussions always finished up in the same place, with Cassie shrugging her shoulders and spreading her hands. 'Whatever happens, it's a wonderful adventure. Remember that, Zelda. In the end, it counts for a lot.'

The Indian woman tilted the photograph towards better light, then looked up with a frown. 'Why is your sister in the newspaper?' she asked. 'Has she done something? Against the law?'

Zelda chewed at the side of her finger. She offered no reply. Faint drumming and singing could be heard in the distance. Nearby, metal clashed behind the doors to the kitchen.

The woman carried the photograph over to a lamp. Zelda followed her, waiting in silence for her to speak.

'When you take sannyas, you give up your worldly life for-ever,' the woman said finally. 'You follow the spiritual path. Some foreigners have achieved it. But—not her, I think.'

'Why?' Zelda asked quickly.

The woman pointed a long, slim finger at a corner of the photograph. 'This bit of her dress. It's made of Indian cloth, but it's rich cloth. It looks like Benares silk. The sannyasins all wear simple handloom khadi.'

'Well, there must be other things that foreigners stay here and do.' Zelda's voice quavered.

'Perhaps,' the woman answered. 'Of course, I don't live here in Rishikesh. I'm only visiting my sister.'

'Well, if my—this person—was here, how should I try to find her?'

'First, in the morning, go down to the bathing ghats. Everyone

goes there for puja. You may see her, if she's here. If she is devout.'
She looked away, as a waiter arrived with a menu. He bowed his
head at the two women, then cast his eye gravely over the empty
dining room. He chose a seat at the end of a long table and
motioned Zelda towards it.

'Bon appetit!' The woman smiled and swept away, trailing
bright silk over her elbow.

Zelda looked around the room. All the tables were long, as
if people usually came here in large parties. Like at the island
golf club, where all the locals used to meet, laughing and talking over porterhouse steak and tinned mushrooms in butter
sauce. Drew, Lizzie and Sharn—even James, sometimes.

James. Dad. His face rose before her. Strong, lean, tanned.
Wet with seaspray. Windblown hair standing up like a wild
crown. She closed her eyes on rising tears. That was the old
James, the one she knew and loved so much. She tried to hang
onto him, but the questions began piling up, building into a
dark cloud of confusion and anger. He'd said Ellen was dead.
Why? How could he? What right did he have? Zelda opened
the menu and studied the foreign words: Puri bhaji. Kashmiri
dum alu. Raita dahi. But the questions kept coming. Why? For
so many years. While Ellen was alive. Her own mother . . .

Zelda pictured the Ellen and baby photograph, trying to
reach back towards it, through the years. She'd been nearly four
years old when Ellen left. Quite big. Somewhere, there should
be memories of the things they'd done together; pictures from
her own head. But there weren't. Over the years she had tried
many times to uncover some deep-hidden remnant. All she
ever found was a strange, unsettled feeling. A sense of something that she wanted, yet pulled away from. It was probably the
idea of someone being dead, she thought, mixed with them
being your mother, once alive. But it had always bothered her
that there was nothing more. A few years ago she had talked to
Lizzie about it—after all, Lizzie had been there when Ellen and
Zelda were together, and when Ellen had disappeared.

'You missed her so much,' Lizzie had explained. 'I reckon you just blocked out your memories. And James wanted you to forget her, too.' She had paused, frowning. 'He said no-one was to talk to you about her. I argued with him—it didn't seem right, or healthy, to me. But he was grieving, too.' The shadow of a smile had softened Lizzie's lips. ' "*You* be her mother," he said to me. "It's what Ellen would have wanted." '

Zelda closed her eyes, torn between warmth and pain. Lizzie had done and had given so much. And James too—he had tried to be everything his daughter needed. But still, an empty space had opened up behind her, yawning wider with the passing years. A ragged hole, letting in cold winds of doubt and discontent. She felt like a cutout figure with nothing but blank space behind her. Well, almost nothing—there were just a few meagre clues; scraps gathered here and there, saved up like the relics of a saint . . .

The waiter, hovering at her elbow, broke into Zelda's thoughts. She pointed quickly at a couple of dishes on the menu and waited while he wandered towards the kitchen. Then she returned to Ellen, running over her collection of clues and facts—all the things she had ever been told.

Mother, she began. Ellen. Ellen Madison.

Dancer.

American.

Killed in a car accident on the mainland. (She was away shopping, but James didn't know what she'd bought. 'Are you sure?' Zelda had asked, years later, hoping for a clue to some last thought. A cuddly toy, a puzzle, a little four-year-old's dress?)

'She died quickly,' James had said. 'Without pain.'

Another time, he'd added that she'd been buried there, on the mainland. He'd wanted to get it all over with as soon as possible. He wasn't interested in funerals and gravestones—Ellen's memory would live on in the hearts of those who loved her.

There was only one thing more: a piece of paper. A death certificate. But that had only come out when Drew's grandma died in her bed, ten years ago.

'What about Mum?' Zelda had asked James. 'Where's her certificate? Drew says everyone has to have one. Can I see it?'

Silence. Then a long breath in, James's eyes widening. 'Sure. Sure you can. Not here, not now. But I'll—get a copy of it for you.' As he spoke, his words began to come quickly, tumbling out. 'Your own photocopy that you can keep. Because I do understand, Zelda. You need to know, to see.'

He kept his word. A few weeks later he gave Zelda a copy of the document.

Cause of Death: Exsanguination. Following ruptured spleen, perforated bowel, uncontrolled haemorrhage.
Due to Motor Vehicle Accident.

Zelda had read the words over and over. Then raised her face, blank with horror, sickness rising inside her. Exsanguination. It sounded like something dark and final, carried out by the Devil.

James had just shrugged, hopelessly. 'She bled to death, in other words.'

He'd opened a bottle of bourbon and stared out of the window as he slopped some into a glass. It was a sign that the talking was over. He wanted to be alone with his thoughts.

Alone with his lies.

Zelda stared down at her hands, fiddling with the cutlery laid out on the white tablecloth. 'Holy Ganges Hotel' stamped on the handles.

So many lies made up over years and carefully preserved. Even a fake death certificate. Why? Was it so important that Ellen did not exist? Or was it just something begun in anger or pain; something that, once born, had to continue. Deceit enslaving truth forever . . .

What *else* was untrue?

'Tell me about Ellen's family,' Zelda remembered asking one Christmas, summoning her courage to push through James's wall of silence.

'What do you mean?' he responded, with a puzzled frown as though her words made no sense.

'My grandma and grandpa on her side.'

Zelda fixed her eyes on James, refusing to look away. Finally he was forced to speak.

'There's nothing much I can tell you.'

'There has to be. You must know something.'

James sighed. 'Well, Ellen was an only child. Her mother, Margaret, was divorced soon after Ellen was born.' He looked down at his book, indicating that the conversation was over.

'Well, what's she like?' Zelda persisted. 'Margaret.'

'*Was*, not is. She's dead now. I never met her.'

'Not even at the wedding?'

'No. I told you. Only a few friends came to the wedding. No family. Especially not her.'

'Why especially not her?'

James grunted, leaning to poke the fire.

'I want to know,' Zelda urged him. 'I'm not a child any more. I'm nearly sixteen.'

James weighed up his thoughts behind lowered eyes. 'Okay,' he said finally, 'you want to know. I'll tell you.' His voice was harsh. 'Then you'll see—delving into family history is a murky business and best left alone. Ellen would never face it, but the fact is her mother was a mean, twisted old bitch. Rich, selfish and all screwed up about the fact that her husband walked out and left her with a baby to bring up alone.'

He paused.

'I guess,' Zelda said carefully, 'it would have been very hard for her.'

James snorted. 'Sure. But pretty tough for her husband too, trying to live with a baby in the house, all the time

323

knowing it wasn't his. No, sir. This baby was begun while he was away.'

'You mean . . . ?'

'That's right,' James continued. 'The outcome, you might say, of his wife's adultery. And with his best friend!' James shook his head slowly. 'A double betrayal, you see . . . The story goes that he couldn't stand the sight of the baby because he loved his wife so much. He just couldn't bear it, so he left and never came back. Margaret blamed the baby—Ellen—of course.' In the quiet, the fire hissed and spat. 'It's sad and ugly. I told you.'

'Poor Ellen,' said Zelda. 'Growing up knowing that . . .'

James leaned across the table to pour himself a drink, glass chinking glass. 'Don't you worry about that, Zel.' His voice softened. 'She didn't know. I only found out a couple of years ago. Margaret died in some nursing home. Apparently she made them promise to send her papers to her long-lost daughter. They traced us somehow. Once upon a time you could cover your tracks, but that was before computers took over. Still caused them a heap of trouble, and all for nothing—just a pile of old letters.' He paused, frowning thoughtfully, then stood up and went into his bedroom. He returned with an envelope. 'And there was this photo,' he said, handing it over. 'You can have it, seeing you're so interested.'

Zelda opened the envelope and slid out the print. Her eyes met dark bright eyes that matched her own. She didn't need to ask.

'That's him,' she said. 'Her real father. My . . . grand-father.' The words felt strange on her tongue.

'Harlan,' stated James, with a faint sneer in his voice. 'His name's on the back.'

'He looks like me—us,' said Zelda, her eyes travelling the man's face, over and over.

James made no reply. 'Typical Margaret,' he said, changing the subject. 'That'd be her though. Couldn't bear to die without one last mean act. And dressing it up into a pile of excuses, and all that "I'm really sorry" crap.' He laughed bleakly and spread his hands. 'How can you be sorry for being a total bitch for a whole lifetime! And what's the point anyway? Dumping it all on Ellen, when they'd had nothing to do with each other for years.' He stared at his hands, clenched into angry fists.

'Why didn't they?' Zelda asked. She made her voice light and casual, hoping James would keep talking, without noticing her urgency.

'Oh, Ellen went away to school. They grew apart I guess. That's a dancer's life. No room for people.' James glanced around the hut, his gaze lingering on the window that looked down towards the sea. 'That's why we had to come here. Best thing I ever did.'

And that was that.

Poor Ellen. Blamed. Unwanted. Not even knowing why.

Plates of food slid onto the table, steaming and colourful on shiny stainless steel. Zelda barely noticed them. She gazed out at the darkening river. Silent. Calm. Holy Mother.

What had it meant to Ellen, she wondered, to be caught up in such a sad, dark story? And what would it mean to her, now, to learn the truth of what lay behind it? She thought of Harlan's photo—the laughing man—held safely in her bag beside her cheques and passport. When I find her, she thought, I'll tell her, show her.

She smiled, imagining the lost daughter appearing from nowhere. Filling in the gaps in Ellen's own past—the murky events that had placed their mark on her life. Bringing news of an unknown father. And telling of a mother who was dead, but who had wanted to say she was sorry . . .

For a long time Zelda sat with her thoughts, watching the mist fall like a layer of secrecy over the water. The deep, eternal river.

Chapter 26

In the frail light of the coming dawn everything looked dark and flat. Only the flowers pushed their colours into the grey-black frieze: deep gold marigolds, hot pink roses and white jasmine. They hung in long garlands, festooning the stalls that lined the walk from the street, down towards the ghats. Here and there a naked bulb hung, throwing a patch of yellow light over small piles of incense, neatly folded towels and baskets full of empty plastic bottles. Zelda wandered slowly along, breathing in the cool air—sweet with incense and fragrant flowers, but undermined by something stronger, dustier, animal . . .

Two large iron gates guarded the entrance to the ghats. They stood wide open, letting in a steady stream of people. Men, women, children, holy men, beggars. Zelda headed down towards them. She scanned faces as she went, peering from under the lowered brim of her hat. They were all dark-eyed, dark-haired; all Indian.

Now and then her gaze lingered: on an old woman with pure white hair, and a man whose dark skin was dappled with patches of light pink. Then she stopped still, staring openly as a man strode towards her wearing only an orange loincloth.

His rib-marked chest was daubed with coloured ash and he carried a metal trident, gripped in a sinewy hand. His face was almost lost behind a matted beard and wild hair; but bright eyes burned through, piercing the distance. He looked like an emissary from some strange, unknown realm. Zelda spun round, watching him until he disappeared from view. A slow current of wonder stirred inside her as she turned back towards the gates and joined the pressing throng.

The path led on past another line of stalls. In each one, a figure sat cross-legged on a small dais. There were men dressed in orange robes with stripes of paint on their faces, and women wrapped in plain white. They bent over stones, grinding and mixing coloured powders. Zelda paused to watch as a young man stopped by one of the stalls and leaned forward to receive a spot of red in the middle of his forehead. His hair clung wet to his bowed head. He pressed his hands together, then bent to place a few coins into a metal dish. His eyes brushed Zelda's face as he straightened up. She looked quickly past him, studying the trees in the distance. At the edges of her vision she sensed him pausing, looking. Still looking . . .

She walked on. Her eyes roved steadily over the crowd, left to right, right to left, before stopping, startled by a big red face framed with blond hair. Zelda pushed closer.

'Hi!' she called out, with a smile. She was almost within reach of the man's wide shoulders and his bulging biceps straining against faded denim shirt-sleeves. He turned to look at her, but then just nodded briskly and walked on, frowning as he fiddled with his camera. Zelda knew what he meant. Don't remind me I'm a tourist, he was saying, like the mainlanders who visited the island each summer. Rack off and leave me alone. I'm trying to pretend I belong.

She pushed towards the edge of a wide paved terrace that stretched away to meet the river bank. Out of the flow of the crowd, she sat down on a cement step and propped her head on her elbows. A big black crow waddled up to her, stabbing the air with its beak. Not far away, a holy man stood in a stone pavilion, chanting prayers. His voice floated clear and strong in the still air, passing over sleeping beggars laid out beneath their cloths and reaching across to where bathers waded in the grey river. Little piles of clothes dotted the shores nearby. People squatted between the boulders, drying themselves or wrapping long cloths into neat sarees. Others picked their way back towards the terrace, with towels draped over their arms and plastic bottles full of river water in their hands.

A group of white marble gods and goddesses looked down over the scene from a pile of boulders arranged in the middle of the terrace. They stood tall against the ashen sky, with long flowing robes and hair. Zelda found them oddly familiar, like characters from a book of Greek myths—noble heads, serene faces, smooth clear skin. She looked away, into the face of a small child with big brown eyes. On the edge of a smile, her lips froze. The child's cheeks were pierced with nails. One through each—a dirty iron spike disappearing into puckers of soft flesh. Matted hair hung in clumps, draping over thin shoulders that were covered with scars. Criss-crossing scars, like the marks of a knife slashing, or a cutting whip.

'Give rupee. Give rupee,' the child said, holding out a small clay pot.

Zelda stared at her, mute with horror.

'Rupee,' the child repeated, shaking the pot. Her lips parted in a smile, cracking open a crusting sore and showing white baby teeth. She stepped closer.

Zelda jerked back. 'Yes, yes. Okay.' She dug a hand into her pocket and pulled out a note. A monkey hand shot out and snatched it. Then the child bolted away, bent over, hugging her hands to her chest.

'Oh God.' Zelda swallowed on a wave of sickness. 'Jesus . . .' She looked down at her hand, recalling the brief touch of dry hot skin, and rubbed it against her jeans, as if the seeds of something horrible might have stuck there, ready to grow.

The others materialised like seagulls gathering around a picnic—ragged scarecrow children with thin arms and big dark eyes. They stared at her pocket and waited in silence. Zelda stood up and backed away. They followed, a creeping mass oozing the smell of unwashed skin and greasy cloth. Flies came with them, feeding on sores and eyes gluey with pus. A fly landed on Zelda's face. She felt it there, wet.

Her hand moved towards her pocket, as she tried to remember what she would find inside. Not much, she knew. She had tied most of her cash in a cloth and tucked it down inside her boot. What she did have in reach was in big notes; no small coins. And there were so many hands held out her way. She looked around desperately. Beyond the children, she noticed other faces turning towards her. A small crowd was gathering, people leaving their prayers and abandoning their path to the river. A low murmur spread, drawing more eyes, more faces. To what? Zelda spun round to check behind her, but there was nothing there; only empty steps and black, stalking crows. She stared over the heads of the crowd, fixing her eyes on the distance. The peaceful forest beyond the river . . .

It's me, she told herself calmly, denying her racing heart. They're looking at me! What have I done?

The murmuring grew into a loud but muted hum, breaking in over the prayers of the priest. The crowd was growing, swelled by bathers coming up from the banks, some barely dry and still dressing.

Zelda scanned the faces nearest her. They didn't look angry. A few people pointed at her and nodded or shook their heads. But mostly she met eyes lit with surprise, or intrigue, as though she were an alien creature, dropped out of the sky. But that was crazy; she was just another tourist . . .

Zelda looked down at her feet. Scuffed, worn boots. One toe marked with the map-like stain of squid ink. She felt the voices, faces, eyes gathering together, like a wall closing her in. She sensed it growing and gaining strength. Somewhere inside she knew it had to be broken, before it grew solid around her. Her heart pounded, urging her to run. Her breath came quickly, snatching at air that seemed too thin. She turned and half-stumbled up the steps, scattering birds, only to find there was a stone wall ahead and no way out. She turned to one side, steeling herself to push through the crowd. But as she plunged forwards it melted away ahead of her. She forced herself to move steadily on along the opening path.

It's like passing a fierce dog, she told herself, you pretend you aren't there and it hardly sees you go . . .

Then an arm shot out, grabbing at her shirt. Zelda stifled a cry as she jumped away. She fixed her eyes on the metal gates and half-ran towards them. A young child was pushed into her path, but she skirted it and kept going.

At last she was free of the crowd. Feeling the weight of eyes fixed on her back, she walked towards some iron railings. But then she realised they were not the gate but the doors to another terrace. She faltered, glancing quickly around her. A white face caught her eye—the creamy, freckled skin of a young woman dressed in a white saree. She had wide, clear eyes, grey like the river. They settled on Zelda for a moment, then flicked down to the ground. Zelda hurried towards her, but as she drew near, the swathed figure turned and walked away.

Following close behind her, Zelda watched the hem of her saree dragging, grey, in the dust, and the movement of her sandals slap-slapping over the pavestones.

Zelda felt the moment when the crowd let her go—the gaze shifting, faces turning away. She faltered, as if the power that moved her had been suddenly withdrawn. Now she was floundering, free. Only the steady movement of the woman's sandals drew her on, down off the pavement and away over the dusty ground.

Outside the ghats, the woman crossed a busy street and turned down a narrow laneway. There, she stopped. Zelda moved round to face her. 'Ah, I'm sorry to come after you like that. But I . . .' The woman went on staring blankly ahead. Zelda breathed out slowly. She tried again. 'I guess I must have done something. I don't know what. Unless . . .' She frowned doubtfully. 'I gave money to this kid. She was—she had scars. She had nails in her face.' As the words came out, she barely believed them herself.

Reaching into the folds of her saree, the woman pulled out an exercise book and pencil. She began to write, quickly but carefully. After a while, she handed the book over.

'I have taken a vow of silence,' Zelda read. 'The girl is the child of a holy man. An ascetic. Through the discipline she accepts, she will be reborn a saint. It was right for you to bless her.'

Zelda stared at the book. She felt like someone fighting off a dream, clutching for something that felt real. She found the woman's grey eyes, and tried to hold them fast.

'So why did they all crowd around me?' she asked. 'What were they saying about me?' She thrust the book back. A pale hand took it and began to write again. Zelda watched the words as they appeared.

'I don't speak Hindi, so I cannot say. Perhaps they recognised something in you.'

'I don't understand,' said Zelda.

The woman shrugged. 'We all hold seeds of the Divine,' she wrote. 'In our Selves.' She gave a small smile.

Zelda stared at her, then nodded politely and glanced past her, down the laneway. She wondered if she should just excuse herself and leave. But it was still too early to call Ranjit and there were no other leads to follow.

'I'm Zelda,' she said finally. 'I've just arrived here, in Rishikesh. I'm searching for someone. I wonder if you could help me?'

The woman nodded and wrote again. 'I am Anandi. My name means joy. I am here to help you.'

She waited for Zelda to read and look up. Then she grinned—a cheeky smile that transformed her face. For a moment, Zelda expected her to laugh and say she had only been joking. Instead she studied Zelda's face and wrote again. 'Have I seen you before?'

Zelda shook her head. 'I only came yesterday. I've been at my hotel.' Anandi nodded and turned towards the gates, motioning for Zelda to follow.

They walked side by side through the streets. Zelda gave up trying to remember the route they took, telling herself she would just head back towards the river, later, and find her bearings from there. She tried to think of questions that could be answered without words.

'I didn't see any foreigners down at the river,' she said. 'Well, only one. Are there many here?'

Anandi pointed to the sun, still low in the sky, and mimed being asleep.

'Foreigners come later?' Zelda suggested.

Anandi nodded.

'Perhaps I should have waited, then,' Zelda said, slowing her steps.

Anandi shook her head and gestured towards the end of the street.

'Have you been in India long?' Zelda asked, as they walked on.

Anandi nodded briefly, without shifting her gaze.

'Are you American?' Zelda asked.

Anandi glanced at her and gave a small dismissive shrug. Zelda fell silent, suddenly embarrassed at the harsh sound of her voice; words, and more words, piling on top of each other.

Eventually they reached a sprawling collection of pale yellow buildings—modern, but already aged, like the Holy Ganges Hotel. They passed under an archway of ornately carved marble, its detail harshened by layers of grime. It looked out of place, as if it had been borrowed from somewhere else.

332

Anandi pointed at a painted sign that said: Shaktiananda Ashram. A second sign was tacked on below: Please talk softly and a little, only when necessary.

Anandi led Zelda through a compound. They passed quiet groups of men dressed in faded orange gowns, and a few women clothed, like Anandi, in dull white. Some nodded greetings, but most seemed lost in thought. Zelda made herself move calmly, slowly. Her eyes, alighting on each face she passed, were all that betrayed her restlessness. She wanted to do something: phone Ranjit; go to the police station—anything to start the search. Rounding a corner, she almost collided with an old man. He was hobbling along, his head bent over a bundle grasped close to his chest.

'Sorry,' said Zelda automatically as they passed. Then she stopped and turned round. A baby peeped at her over the man's hunched shoulder. A blonde-curled, pink-cheeked, blue-eyed baby. One small grubby hand waved in the air, the other grasped a stained feeding bottle of bluish-coloured milk. Zelda stared, motionless, until Anandi took her arm and pulled her on.

'My mother came here,' Zelda said. 'I don't know when she arrived, but she was here twelve years ago.' She spoke quickly, the sight of the baby unleashing a new urgency. 'I'm looking for her. She must be about forty years old, and she—looks like me. At least she used to, when she was my age. She's American. Her name is Ellen Madison.'

Anandi stopped and reached for her book. 'Don't be concerned. You will find the one you are looking for,' she wrote.

Zelda clutched at her shoulder. 'What? Do you know her?' she asked.

Anandi smiled mysteriously and kept walking.

They passed a building with 'Dining Room' written outside, above the entrance. Double doors stood open and the clatter of steel and the sound of chanting came from within. Zelda paused to peer in. Rows of people sat on the floor with metal plates in front of them. A blackboard stood in one corner; it bore writing in English and Hindi: 'Today's meals have been given as a gracious love offering by Mr Madhu Sudhanan Nair, of Bombay, in loving memory of his parents.' A man moved along the rows; pouring something that looked like brown porridge onto the plates. An earthy smell, like warm, damp sacking, drifted out. Zelda felt suddenly hungry, and sick at the same time.

Anandi led them towards a big central building that was decorated with moulded plaster painted in bright pastel colours. Before going inside, Anandi pulled the cloth that covered her head further forward and slipped off a pair of leather sandals. She glanced at Zelda's hat, nodding approval, but frowned down at her boots.

'Ah, will they be safe here?' Zelda asked awkwardly as she loosened the laces. Leaving your boots was like hanging up your pack in the bush. You felt naked and unsafe. Anandi waved her words away and hovered nearby while Zelda removed her roll of money and pulled off her boots.

They stepped inside, bare feet silent on cool stone tiles; small figures, in a big empty hall. The air was still, and heavy with fragrance. The high walls were white and dotted with hand-painted posters bearing pieces of text like framed Bible verses on a Sunday School wall:

Think like a genius. Work like a giant. Live like a saint.

The desire for pleasure and power is a great barrier to spiritual peace.

He alone can command who obeys.

At the far end of the room was a shrine, with incense burning in front of a life-sized statue of a man clothed in a red cloak. Anandi took Zelda's hand and led her towards it. Still some distance away, she crouched down and touched her head to the floor. Then she wrote, bent over her book. Her saree slipped back, uncovering a head of red curls. Zelda looked at the shrine, but thought of her boots left alone outside and hoped that they were still there. Anandi looked up and handed over the book. Her grey eyes were clear and deep.

'This is our teacher, our guru,' Zelda read. She glanced up. A faint smile touched Anandi's face. 'His wisdom is truly amazing. You don't need to look any further. Everything you seek is here.'

Zelda fixed her eyes on the words. Words. They surrounded her, coming from the walls, from the book, from her own mind.

Everything you seek is here.
Be brave, be strong, be yourself.
With you for you always.

She handed back the book and walked away. Behind her she could hear Anandi's pencil scratching over the page. It was still going when she stepped outside, blinking in the bright morning sun.

Ranjit's house looked quiet and empty but the door was opened to her knock, and a man in a white uniform led her through a dark corridor into a shadowy sitting room. He offered to take her hat, but she held it on her lap.

'Mr Saha will come soon,' he said, and left her.

Zelda leaned back in a cushioned wicker chair. It creaked loudly in the quiet. A potted palm hung close to her face. She peered through the fronds at walls hung with dark paintings and small windows smothered with heavy velvet drapes. A solid old clock ticked away on a mantelpiece draped with lace.

A boy came in, as silent as a cat. Avoiding Zelda's eyes, he set a glass of soft drink and a bowl of some kind of snack on a table beside her, then disappeared.

Zelda sipped the drink slowly, remembering Rye's warning about only drinking from bottles that you open yourself (and only bottles which have printed labels). Her hunger roused by the sweet drink, she picked out a small handful of what looked like peas and put them into her mouth. Chilli spiked her tongue as she swallowed quickly, choking and coughing.

'Welcome to Rishikesh.' A cool voice cut through her spluttering.

Zelda looked around. A man stood behind her chair. She could barely see his face in the gloom. She sprang to her feet.

'No, please,' the man said. 'I'll join you.'

He sat opposite her, leaning back and resting his hands on his knees. 'Rye has written to me,' he stated bluntly. 'He tells me you are searching for your mother, who was here in 1981. I'll tell you now, she will be gone, long gone.' He raised a hand to cut off any interruption. 'I'll explain. The sixties and seventies—that was the time for coming to Rishikesh. Even the Beatles were here, sitting at the feet of the Maharishi. Briefly. Movie stars as well. Even sisters of movie stars. Oh yes, we were fashionable.' His voice was light, but edged with cynicism. 'It was even worse in Goa, but believe me we had our share. Americans, Germans, French—you name it—running around pretending to be devotees, wearing no clothes, taking drugs, having sex with anyone. This is a holy city. It was not suitable. And their children! Pitiful! I tell you, if your mother came here then, you should thank God you were left behind.' He paused for breath, his lungs wheezing. 'Fortunately most of these hippies have gone. Back to their lives of luxury and materialism, where they belong.' He paused, and softened his voice. 'I'm sure your mother has done this too. She was here in 1981, you say—well, that was the tail end of it all. After that the party was over.'

'But there are some foreigners here,' Zelda said plaintively, close to tears. 'I've seen them.'

'Yes, yes,' Ranjit answered. 'There is always some new attraction. Some guru arises with a fresh plan. But only the young people come. You know, they're taking their trip round the world, after school and before college—exploring life.' He frowned. 'How old would your mother be now?'

'Forty-four,' said Zelda quietly.

Ranjit spread his hands. 'Then she would only be here now if she has become a devotee. There are a few serious ones, genuinely spiritual people. But if your mother is one of those, then forget it. She has taken vows, given up her worldly life, and that includes you, too.'

The clock ticked loudly in the silence. A late rooster crowed, far off. Zelda lifted her glass to her lips, trying to look calm. Her hand trembled. 'I don't think she has taken sannyas,' she said firmly.

'Then I fear she is not here,' said Ranjit.

'Okay,' Zelda responded, forcing a light tone into her voice. 'Then I have to find out where she was, to see if anyone knows anything. I just have to begin with some kind of lead . . .'

Ranjit laughed. 'That's impossible. I'm sorry, but it is. These ashrams are not like your American colleges. People drift in and out. Some have sold their passports to buy drugs. They take new names.' He snorted. 'The names of gods—it appeals to them. Saraswati, Yuddhistra, Abhimanyu. No. The only thing I can suggest is that you go to the American Embassy in Delhi.' A shaft of light touched the side of his face.

Zelda could see him searching the shadows for some sign of her response. She found a bleak smile.

Ranjit spoke again. 'It's dark in here because of the furnishings. I have many old cloths and silk paintings. Very valuable. They cannot stand the daylight.' He waved a hand at Zelda's glass. 'Another lime soda?'

'No. Thank you.'

'You are a good friend of Rye?' he asked, but didn't wait for a reply. 'I knew his father. He was a great man. We climbed mountains together.' He stopped for a few moments, overtaken by memories. 'I was on his last expedition, the ascent of Nanda Devi. I think of that peak now, like a big stone, a monument to him, his own gravestone. After all, he's still there. You have met Rye's mother as well?'

'No,' answered Zelda. 'Actually I don't really know Rye. We only met once.' The evening at Dana's house seemed a long time ago, a whole world away.

'Ah,' said Ranjit wisely. 'Once can be enough, eh? His mother writes to me about him. All the ladies fall in love with him. But he? He only cares about the sea!' Ranjit frowned. 'Mountains I can understand. But just a big piece of water!' He shook his head. 'So anyway, be careful. In case he breaks your heart.'

Zelda stared at him. Her search for Ellen had pushed aside other things. Thoughts of Rye—or Drew, for that matter. But Ranjit's words still cut her. All the ladies fall in love with him. Swept away by his talk of beautiful eyes . . .

'I don't think there's any danger of that,' said Zelda curtly. 'I don't even like him. I didn't ask him to write to you, either.' She stood up.

Ranjit chuckled. 'Now you are angry.'

'I'm not angry,' Zelda said, but her voice quavered. 'It's just— I—'

Ranjit leaped to his feet. 'Please, forgive me. I didn't mean to upset you. Rye, he's—'

'Look, I don't care about Rye. I just want to find my mother.' Zelda strode towards the door and opened it. Bright light flooded the room, spilling from a sunny patio. 'Shit, wrong door,' she muttered. She turned, to find that Ranjit had followed her. 'I'm sorry. Excuse me.'

'Wait.' He moved round to study her in the light. She rubbed her eyes roughly with the back of her hand. 'Oh my goodness—' His voice broke off and he walked away from her.

'What?' asked Zelda. 'What's wrong?'

'Nothing,' said Ranjit firmly. 'Nothing at all. I thought for a moment . . . Never mind. Please sit down again. It's nearly lunchtime.' He attempted a thin smile. 'My wife is a wonderful cook.'

'Thank you, but I have lots to do,' said Zelda. She moved

towards the other door. Her foot caught the spindly leg of a small table and tipped it over.

'Look, I think I can help you, after all,' Ranjit said. Zelda stopped. The table lay on its side, ignored, between them. 'I have contacts, I can ask around at the ashrams. Speak to the librarians. Someone might remember your mother. In fact, you should come here. You don't have to stay in a hotel. Rye would not like it.' Ranjit clasped his hands together, almost pleading. 'Let me help you. I think you need proper advice.'

'Thank you,' said Zelda, frowning. She felt disconcerted by his change of tone—his sudden eagerness to help—and she wanted time to think. 'I have to go to my hotel first. I'll come back this afternoon.'

'No, you need not go,' Ranjit protested. 'I can send someone for your things.' He edged between her and the door. 'It's not good for you to wander around Rishikesh by yourself. Please! Don't go.'

'I'll be okay,' Zelda insisted. She slid out into the hallway and put on her hat.

'Good, yes—wear the hat, then,' Ranjit said. 'It's—hot. You are not used to it. You need sunglasses as well.'

In answer Zelda took a pair from her pocket and put them on.

'You will come back?' asked Ranjit. 'Straight away?'

'Yes. Okay.'

The taxi was waiting outside. Ranjit stood in the doorway while Zelda climbed in. He smiled fleetingly as he waved goodbye.

Midday sun beat down over the town. Stallholders, rickshaw drivers, beggars and holy men huddled in small patches of shade. Here and there a figure braved the heat, bending to sprinkle the earth with water to settle the dust. Zelda looked into the rear-vision mirror, waiting to catch the eye of the taxi driver. Then she mimed drinking and pointed towards the side of the road.

'Drink?' the driver suggested. 'Yes, cold drink?'

Zelda nodded and the car swerved to a standstill. The driver shouted out the window at a boy who was leaning drowsily over the counter of a small stall. The boy called something back, shrugging his shoulders and waving at a line of different coloured drinks.

'It's okay, I'll go over,' said Zelda.

She picked the yellow drink again and handed over some money. The boy frowned at the note and took it over to the taxi driver to get some change. Zelda leaned on the stall and drank slowly. She looked back up the road in the direction of Ranjit's house, wondering again why he had changed his attitude so suddenly. Was he just feeling guilty because she had been upset? Would he really help her? And should she trust him? He was tough, rude . . . Zelda frowned. What did she expect? Rye had betrayed her; betrayed James. Why turn to a friend of his?

She leaned round to place the bottle back on the counter. Bright flowers caught her eye—marigold wreaths, hung over a line of framed pictures. The first was a painting of a goddess with dozens of arms fanned around her head. Beside it was a modern photograph of an Indian man with long hair and a wide smile. He wore big, square-framed sunglasses. Dabbed on the glass, over the middle of his forehead was a fresh spot of red paste. The next picture was a photograph too, half obscured by the offering of flowers. The boy saw her looking, and obligingly lifted them aside. Zelda froze.

It was her own face. Her own dark smudgy eyes looking back at her. Brows like black wings, pale skin. The Charlie Chaplin face, James called it. Black and white.

'Nanda Devi. Nanda Devi,' said the boy, jabbing a finger at the photograph.

'Nanda Devi?' Zelda echoed. Her voice was thin and light, a

wisp carried in a breeze. She felt faint, far off, swirled in the haze of a dream. She licked her lips and spoke again. 'Who is she?'

God, she thought, *what* is she? Some kind of saint? Goddess? Weird. Mad. But the face was calm, serene. The eyes were kind. The lips, gentle. The hands, restful.

'Rishikesh?' Zelda whispered.

The boy wobbled his head from side to side, a perfect blend of yes and no.

'I'm looking for her!' Zelda's voice rose. 'Where is she? Tell me!'

The boy shouted across to the taxi driver. Words were exchanged and they both laughed. The boy pointed towards the car, then at Zelda, and finally back towards the picture hanging in his stall. 'Twenty rupees,' he said. 'Go. We go.'

Zelda's eyes widened. 'Twenty rupees to—go to her?' she asked. The boy's head wobbled again. She bent down and shoved clumsy fingers into her boot to find her money. Dragging out a thick wad, she snatched off two notes and pushed the rest into her pocket. The boy watched, wide-eyed, as it disappeared, then he closed his fist around the notes she offered him and jumped into the front seat of the car. Zelda took her place in the back.

As the car drove off, the boy turned round to look at Zelda. He grinned, showing big white teeth, and pointed at her sunglasses. 'You give me.' He mimed putting a spot on his forehead and broke into loud laughter. 'Me big man. Me god!' The driver laughed too.

'Is it far?' Zelda's voice cut in. 'Long way?'

The driver glanced at her in the rear-vision mirror and shook his head. 'No far.'

Zelda took off her hat and leaned her face against the dirty window. Her mind was jumbled with half-formed thoughts. Ellen . . . Draped with flowers like a goddess . . . That was why they knew me, stared at me, down by the river . . . That's why Ranjit Saha recognised my face . . .

After a short drive through the crowded streets the car slowed and stopped. They were outside a high, white wall topped with creepers. Only the upper storey of a white-rendered building could be seen above the border of green. It had a long line of small shuttered windows, like a school or a hospital. There was a plain narrow gate in the wall with a simple sign: House of the Beautiful Mother. Please enter.

Chapter 27

Pink marble stepping stones marked a path through a sea of white gravel, carefully raked into long swirling lines. A row of small trees followed the same track, casting a narrow swathe of shade. Birds perched on the branches, twittering into the quiet air.

Zelda looked up, scanning the facade of the building as she walked. It was three storeys high, with a long line of windows on each level. They were all closed up behind blue wooden shutters, except for one on the top floor. There, a curtain hung half-drawn, and a length of cloth or towel draped out over the sill. It was the only sign that the place was not abandoned. Zelda paused, frowning, as she glanced around the courtyard. Everything was neat and tidy; no litter, no outside chairs, no bicycles, no teacups left out. No signs of daily life. From the distance came a mournful cry, like the wail of a newborn child.

Ahead, the stones and gravel gave way to a forecourt of marble flagstones, bearing a group of life-sized statues. From a distance they reminded Zelda of the ones she had seen at the ghats, but as she came closer she recognised the bowed, draped head of a Mother Mary. The stone face was fixed in a look of calm joy. In her lap lay a baby Jesus, unswaddled, with arms and legs waving free. Near them was an old worn statue of a plump Indian child. He grinned playfully, stretching out an arm, snapped off at the elbow. Beside him stood the tall, elegant figure of the many-armed goddess, long hair flowing around her shoulders and slender limbs fanning out around her head. There was one other statue but it faced the entrance to the building. Zelda continued, heading towards it, then stopped, suddenly, as a lean brown hand reached over the stone shoulder, rubbing away bird droppings with a white cloth.

'Excuse me,' Zelda called. The hand disappeared. An Indian man in a pale blue uniform jumped out and stood stiffly beside the statue.

'Good afternoon. How may I help you?' he chanted.

As she reached him, Zelda nodded a greeting. She glanced at the statue, then moved round to face it front on. It was as if a mirror stood between her and the carved figure—a strange mirror that turned flesh to stone and leached away the colours of life into shades of marble white. They stood shoulder to shoulder, even height, and eye to eye, a look filtered through dark sunglasses. Zelda's lips parted as she leaned forward, her warm skin touching the cool, hard pallor.

'Beautiful Mother,' the man stated, flicking his cloth along the stone arm. 'She not here.'

He pointed towards the entrance to the building, drawing Zelda's attention to a wide imposing door of painted wood bound with brass. In front of it sat a peacock, its gleaming blue chest and long iridescent feathers a streak of wild colour against the calm stone.

'Paper is there.' The man's finger jabbed the air. 'You take paper.'

Zelda walked quickly up a set of wide shallow stairs and entered the shade of a portico. To one side of the door she saw a container of pamphlets mounted on the wall. Leaning over the bird, she pulled one out. It was made of thick soft paper, in pale blue. A gold embossed profile of Ellen's head filled the centre, like the Queen marked on a stamp. The fine, detailed work showed tendrils of hair and the sweep of long eyelashes.

As she unfolded the paper a fragrance escaped. An elusive aura—spicy, sweet, but light and clean—unlike anything she could name.

Her eye scanned the page. 'Summer Program . . . Hotel accommodation in Mussoorie . . . half-hour drive . . . alpine views . . . arrive at Everest House . . .'

'Okay?' The man called across to her. 'You go. Mussoorie. Taxi. Okay?'

'She's there?' shouted Zelda.

'Yes.' He waved an arm towards a hazy line of steep mountains in the distance. 'There.'

Zelda ran down the stairs and on, abandoning the marble stepping stones and crunching over the gravel. The paper felt warm in her hand, already damp with sweat.

The road wound steeply up the mountain side in a long series of hairpin bends. At each corner was a cluster of billboards advertising honeymoon suites, luxury apartments, hotels, restaurants—all in slightly odd English. Their bright paintwork was overlaid with white dust from the road, making them look old and shabby. On the long sloping ramps between corners were other signs, simply written in plain black and white.

Someone Risk on You, Be Gentle

Avoid Accident

Better Late Than Never

The same slogans appeared again and again, stamped with the mark of 'India Roads Division'. Zelda read them each time, searching the ominous warnings for thin strands of hope.

Better Late Than Never.

She glanced down over the edge of the road—a sheer drop

to the valley floor only a foot away from the wheels. Leaning her head back against the seat, she closed her eyes. She knew the contents of the pamphlet word for word. It was really a timetable, listing names, times and places. Meditation. Yoga. Breakfast, lunch, tea, supper. Periods set aside for what was described only as Programme. Then there was something called Satsanga at 7.45 p.m. daily in the Great Hall, with Beautiful Mother.

With . . . Beautiful . . . Mother. Zelda had read and reread the three words. There could be no confusion. At 7.45 p.m. today, at Everest House, Ellen would be there.

Beneath the information about Satsanga there was a note in small lettering: Visitors wearing blue clothing (including blue denim) will not be admitted. Perfumes, other than Shahastra, may not be worn.

That was all, no explanation, and no other information about what the House was. The only real clue was at the top of the page. The gold-lettered heading: Shahastra—The Way of Unknowing.

Unknowing. It sounded mysterious, calm, restful. Thoughts going backwards—first you knew, and then you didn't. Didn't know that James was dead, a swollen face on the stained wood floor. Didn't know that he had lied, and gone on lying for years. Didn't know that Ellen had not been killed, but had just gone away. Didn't know, didn't care, didn't ever have to cry . . .

Zelda sat forward, looking up the side of the mountain into the hazy blue sky. She tried to think ahead, to leave the painful thoughts behind. She imagined herself strolling up to the front door of Everest House. A fantasy. I've come, she'd say. The true daughter. The only true daughter. Only? A new thought came to her. Perhaps Ellen had other children. There might be half-sisters, half-brothers, or even a step-father. Why not?

Zelda frowned. She would have to be careful. There was too much she didn't know. Just lie low, James used to say. Always lie low till you know the lie of the land.

Ranjit's face came to her. She remembered how he had reacted on seeing her in the light, and his insistence that she wear her hat and sunglasses and come back to him without delay. He didn't want her to be recognised as the daughter of Beautiful Mother, that much was clear. But why, she wondered, with a nagging sense of misgiving. What was it that lay behind his concern? Knowing there were no answers to the questions, she tried to push them aside.

The road seemed endless. The sound of the car grinding slowly on and on filled Zelda's head, driving out thought. The air, coming in through the open windows, grew steadily cooler. The trees grew taller, greener. Then, at last, groups of buildings appeared ahead: small boxes tacked roughly onto an almost vertical hillside. Below them, the mountain slid away into a sea of haze.

'Savoy?' the driver asked.

'Savoy?' Zelda queried. 'Savoy Hotel?'

'Yes, madam. Everybody go to Savoy.'

Savoy. The name conjured up images of cigarettes in long holders and martinis at sundown; vistas of faraway wealth and romance. She remembered their source, the novels of F. Scott Fitzgerald: *Tender is the Night, The Beautiful and Damned, The Great Gatsby.* Zelda had read them all, along with everything else by him or about him that she had been able to order from the island's library. It had begun after she'd complained to James about her name.

'They call me Zelda-the-welder,' she'd said. 'All the kids at school do.'

'Well don't blame me,' was James's reply. 'It was your mother's idea. I'm afraid you were named after Scott Fitzgerald's wife. Who was he? Some trash writer. Dead and gone now, like his wife. She was a dancer before she married— that was the connection, for Ellen. In the end she went mad, poor old Zelda. And she was burned to death when her lunatic asylum caught fire.'

From that time on, Zelda had treasured her name. Chosen by her own mother. She'd pictured a tiny pink baby, cradled against soft breasts. Zelda and Ellen. Mother and child.

'Mussoorie,' announced the driver, as the car swung left into the midst of a busy bazaar. Stalls lined the roadside, offering the usual Indian clothes and brightly coloured soft drinks as well as Kodak film, woolly jumpers and an array of gifts and souvenirs.

Zelda glanced at her watch. 'I'm in a hurry,' she said.

The driver took both hands off the wheel to indicate his helplessness. The road was jammed with people: couples strolling hand in hand; large family groups lining up for photographs; men in loaded donkey carts; coolies balancing huge suitcases on their heads; boys herding goats. The taxi crept on past a Swiss patisserie and a white-domed temple, before grinding to a standstill outside the Kashmiri Emporium.

'Wait. Wait here,' Zelda called suddenly and jumped out of the car. The driver smiled at her indulgently as she turned and ran inside. He seemed surprised when she emerged only a few minutes later. She was carrying a dark brown shawl and a set of matching pyjamas.

'Okay, thanks,' breathed Zelda, bending to push her money back into her boot as the car edged on.

Tall old trees and a faded sign marked the entrance to the Savoy Hotel. The car laboured up the steep drive, passing a building that looked like a toy railway station. A uniformed guard stood at attention outside. Above his head, a sign read 'Savoy Post Office'. It marked the boundary to another world, where purple irises coloured the verges and leafy boughs met overhead. Green turrets appeared first, then an array of red tin roofs and green-fronted gables. The taxi swung round into a parking bay overlooking tennis courts, tea gardens and long covered walkways. In a gravelled courtyard below, men in dark green uniforms and hats were sweeping large pieces of red carpet. Above them, a boy moved like a monkey over the tin roof, spreading out lines of white towels to dry in the sun.

A tired old porter shambled up to the car and opened Zelda's door. 'Welcome, madam.'

He bowed gravely, wearing his courtesy like a shield—something to protect him against the indignity of girls like this, who arrived wearing faded jeans and sunglasses. He knew without needing to glance into the car that there would be a grubby, overstuffed backpack. A far cry from the leather cases and metal-bound trunks that had once made up his loads; the neat luggage of English princesses, Indian statesmen, maharajas, colonels, ladies.

Zelda stood back, averting her gaze as he struggled to shoulder her pack. He led the way across to an open doorway and directed her inside.

The room was dim and cool. Zelda found herself facing a long high partition broken by a row of hatches covered with metal grilles. Above each hung an engraved brass sign—Cashier, Reservations, Miscellaneous—like a bank in a cowboy movie.

'May I help you?' A voice came from somewhere behind Reservations.

Zelda stepped up to the hatch and peered through the grille. 'I'd like to have a room, please,' she said.

'Do you have a reservation?' The voice floated out, faceless, male; maybe Indian, maybe not.

'No,' answered Zelda. 'I was just hoping . . .'

'Of course. No problem.' A hand waved, flashing gold. 'We guarantee accommodation at all times for Everest House visitors. We have over a thousand rooms. Whatever you need, we can provide it. Special diets. Laundry service. Taxis to Everest House, wait or return.'

Zelda frowned. 'How did you know I was going there?'

The man laughed. 'Who else comes here? Indians on holiday only. And a few old colonialists living in the past. Passport please.'

Zelda handed it over. She looked at it spread open on the counter. The photograph was a bad likeness. She had been caught by the flash, staring wide-eyed like a roo in the middle of the road. The light had glanced off her face making it washed out and shiny.

'Thank you. Take one of these.'

The passport slid back to her, along with one of the blue pamphlets. Zelda looked at the gold head, stamped like a seal. Shahastra. The Way of Unknowing.

'I've got one, thanks,' she said.

A big brass key replaced the pamphlet. 'Room 69. The boy will take you.' As he spoke, he brought his hand down to strike a bell.

Zelda turned to go.

'Just a minute,' the man called after her. 'The name was Madison, wasn't it? I think there's a telegram for you.' Papers rustled in the shadows, then a blue envelope was pushed through the grille. 'Here you are. It's come via Rishikesh, forwarded by a Mr Saha.'

Zelda looked at it for a moment, anxious thoughts crowding her mind. She picked it up and went outside. Ignoring the hovering bellboy, she tore open the envelope.

Sender: Drew Johnstone.

Her eyes seized on his name, then scanned ahead.

Dear Zelda come back stop I want to marry you stop say yes and Lizzie will prepare for wedding stop you have to decide now stop once and for all stop I love you stop Drew

Zelda stared at the words, reading them again and again, as if unable to grasp their meaning.

Come back. I want to marry you.

She tried to relive the old dream, to feel the warmth that used to grow inside her as she imagined how it would be: how she and Drew would build a house together, a place to begin their new, shared life; how they would tell Lizzie the good news; and how she would cry with joy as she swept her new daughter into her arms. Now you really can call me Mum, she would say, as she'd been waiting to say for so long.

But it all seemed so distant now—like a scene from a life that belonged to someone else. Zelda reread the words: 'you have to decide now stop once and for all stop'.

you have to . . .

Mixed emotions tangled together inside her—dismay and guilt, bound together by anger. All she had wanted was some time alone, to go in search of her mother. Now this telegram had found her. It was just a slip of paper and a few lines of words, but she felt its power—sensed it taking hold of her, drawing her back towards the old, known world.

Looking up, she saw the bellboy watching her. He smiled as he met her gaze, his teeth blazing white against dark skin.

'Good . . . morning . . . madam,' he said. 'I hope you liking visit India.'

India. Zelda breathed out slowly, a sense of relief spreading through her as she thought of the great distance that lay between her and the island. She was in a foreign land, far from home. She was following her own plan and she didn't have to let it go. It was up to her to make the choice.

Be brave. Be strong. Be yourself.

She folded the telegram into a small square and buried it deep in her pocket.

The old porter walked ahead of Zelda and the bellboy. He was tall but thin, and moved slowly under the heavy pack. A long staircase rose up ahead of them. Zelda glanced sideways, hoping the boy might help the old man, but he was busy swinging the key from his little finger.

They passed a succession of doors and windows, mostly

closed and shuttered. Then they came upon a pair of jean-clad legs, stretched out on the floor, protruding from an open doorway. The porter stepped over them without changing his gait. The bellboy did the same. Zelda paused and looked down. A blonde-haired woman lounged in the doorway, smoking.

'Hi,' said Zelda.

The woman nodded, blowing out smoke, and raised her hand. 'Get them to check your loo,' she said, raising her eyes slowly as if anything more would be too much effort, 'before they go.'

'Thanks,' said Zelda. She glanced back over her shoulder.

The woman raised an eyebrow and dragged on her cigarette. 'You're welcome.'

The boy opened a pair of French windows and waved Zelda inside. She walked past him into an old-fashioned sitting room complete with open fireplace, heavy couch and armchairs, coffee table, and big, polished writing desk. It was like a part of an English country house but without all the soft touches. No flowers, no lace cloths, no pictures; just the big solid furniture and worn carpets. A mouldy-mouthed deer with long hooked antlers gazed down over the room from a vantage point above the fireplace. The noble head had sagged over the years, but some handyman had winched it back up. A wire around the throat; a bush facelift.

'Okay? You like?' asked the boy, with a flourish of his hands that took in the room.

'Oh yes!' answered Zelda. She did. It was not like a hotel; it felt real, as if the cupboards might contain real clothes, and the desk, real letters. 'But, ah—what about the toilet?' She smiled lamely. 'Does it work?'

She followed the boy through the bedroom and into a light bathroom. It was lined with white tiles, dulled and crazed with age. Chicken wire covered the windows instead of glass, but generous curtains graced the edges. The boy lifted the lid of the toilet, disturbing dust, and yanked on the flushing lever. It came away in his hand. A small trickle of water ran from the cistern. The boy shook his head, frowning with regret.

'Don't worry,' he said. 'I will fix.' He led Zelda back into the sitting room, and waited for his tip. Then he grinned and slid away.

The old porter gave up trying to balance Zelda's pack on the carved suitcase stand and unloaded it onto the floor.

'You are going to Everest House?' he enquired politely, as Zelda hunted for more money. 'It is a popular destination for our guests.'

Zelda turned towards him, surprised by his English. 'Do you know her? The Beautiful Mother?'

The porter nodded. 'Of course.'

'What's she—like?' Zelda asked. 'Have you seen her?'

'Certainly,' replied the old man. 'I am acquainted with her since many years. She resided at Landour. There was a big mansion there, with a piano, even.' His enthusiasm broke through his formality, softening his shoulders and freeing his hands. 'She assisted everybody, Indian and foreigners also. She gave them food, made them well—whatever they needed.' Zelda read his face as he spoke. His eyes were bright, and creased with the memory of a smile. 'I myself—one season I was too ill to work—I went there. Everyone admired her. Truly, they loved her.' He talked on, swept up in his words and barely looking at Zelda. 'Then she went away to Everest House with all her people. They required even a bigger mansion, because many foreigners came and they wanted to stay. But—' he paused, 'it is a great distance to walk from here, so we have not seen her for a long time.'

Zelda moved round to face him as he spoke. She took off her sunglasses and then her hat.

The man continued. 'And in winter, when it is very cold here, they remove themselves to Rishikesh, to another—' His voice broke off. He looked quickly into Zelda's eyes, but then searched her face, hair, body. The silence lengthened. 'You . . .'

His voice faltered, but he swallowed and pushed on. 'Excuse me. You resemble her.'

'She's my mother,' said Zelda. He stared at her, dumb-founded. 'She's my mother,' Zelda repeated. 'I'm her daughter.'

For a long, timeless moment he stood as if carved from stone. Then he bowed his head suddenly and half-ran from the room.

Zelda gazed after him. Words came to her, snatches of the things he had said: 'Everyone admired her.' 'She helped everybody.' 'Truly, they loved her.'

A smile touched her lips, the words filling her with warmth.

Zelda crouched in the empty bath and washed herself quickly under the cold tap. The water braced her skin, leaving her feeling clean and alive. Afterwards, dressed in the pyjamas and wrapped in the shawl, she stood barefoot in front of the tall mirror that hung inside the wardrobe door. The handwoven cloth was slightly rough against her skin. It smelled strange and foreign—pungent with natural dyes and faintly tinged with the incense that had been burning in the Emporium. She lifted the shawl and covered her head, pulling the cloth forward to shade her face. The cheekbones were hidden, the chin disguised. The black and white of hair and skin were diffused into something softer, less striking. It was not her.

She removed the bundle of notes from her boot. For a few minutes, she wandered around the room, trying to decide where she could hide it. Then, in one of the drawers of the writing desk, she found a Directory of Services. 'Please do not leave valuables in the room', it said. 'They may be deposited in the Manager's safe. Enquire at Miscellaneous.' She glanced at her watch. There was enough time to go down, and she could arrange a taxi while she was there.

As she walked into the sitting room, the French windows opened. A line of green-uniformed men filed in, nodding to her without speaking. The first carried a tall pile of snow-white towels, topped with rolls of toilet paper and bars of soap. The next carried cushions and an armful of folded cloths. A faint smell of camphor surrounded him. He was followed by a man with a padded velvet chair and an ornate lamp. A last figure appeared, almost hidden beneath a bright mound of flowers.

Zelda stood still, watching in silence as they moved around the room, putting down their loads. Quickly, silently, like set decorators at work between scenes, they transformed the room. A gold brocade bedspread covered the couch, an embroidered linen cloth graced the coffee table, and a lamp was set up to throw a rosy light over the velvet chair. The flowers were the final touch, placed on every table and ledge: great pitchers of irises and pink azaleas, drooping wisteria and curling jasmine. As soon as the men were finished, they left. No hands held ready for tips, and no words. Just warm quiet looks, as if they were welcoming an old friend.

The road to Everest House was new—wide and smooth—but there were no houses, huts or farms along the way; just thick forest, overgrown with tall flowering trees and a tangle of shrubs beneath. The light was fading quickly; the haze that hid the distance was now a thick grey shadow creeping towards night.

Zelda checked the shawl, draping the edge further forward over her face. She remembered how Anandi had gazed blankly into the near distance and tried to do the same. She had a new taxi driver. He didn't try to meet her eye and hadn't spoken— even when the hotel manager had explained that she wished to be dropped close to Everest House, but not in sight, and to be picked up again in the same place, two hours later. He had merely nodded, and when he stopped the car on the side of the road to let her out he just nodded again and settled back to wait.

Zelda walked quickly on towards the corner. She felt strangely calm, but still found it hard to think, to make a plan.

At the corner she stopped, finding herself on the brink of a wide, natural amphitheatre. It scooped away from her in a deep bowl, sweeping down to where the land ended abruptly, cut off against the sky. There, on the edge of the cliff, loomed a big white building, its marble columns and gabled facades gleaming softly in the dimness. White lights shone from the windows, bright and welcoming. Zelda guessed it was the Great Hall, the place of Satsanga.

She turned her head to catch the faint sound that carried up from the building. It was singing, or chanting, accompanied by drums and bells—soft but strong, like a heartbeat over the land. A breeze fluttered her shawl, making it brush across her cheek. She began to walk down the hillside, moving through a pattern of low shrubs dotted with big pale boulders. It resembled a natural garden, tended but wild. It seemed familiar . . . She breathed in slowly. It looked like the island, with its wind-sculpted heathlands and outcrops of granite rising up like ancient signs—the backdrop of her life, calling her home.

Chapter 28

The glow of a near full moon lit the way down through the rockgarden. Zelda walked slowly, picking her way between boulders and low shrubs. Crushed leaves spread a green sap smell into the air and sharp twigs snagged at the ends of her shawl. Crows kept watch from a distance, dead still.

As she drew nearer to the hall, Zelda saw that there were other buildings behind it, spread out along the edge of the cliff. They were all dark, with unlit doors and windows making patterns of black against grey stone walls. A high iron fence separated them from the rock garden, the road and the forest; the hall was like a giant gatehouse, offering the only way into the compound.

Reaching the roadway, Zelda noticed that the music and singing had stopped. Her leather sandals slapped softly over the stone paving as she headed on towards the hall.

The wide front doors were closed. Zelda paused in the entrance, looking up at a high scalloped archway. Clusters of spirit lamps burned at each side, with clouds of insects dancing in the light of the yellow-blue flames. The glow lit up a white facade inlaid with a decorative frieze: flowers, peacocks and trees drawn in flowing lines and studded with jewel tones of lapis lazuli, jade, carnelian. It was like a fairytale palace, set on the edge of the tangled forest; an illusion that would vanish with the coming of dawn.

At the edge of the lamplight loomed the shadowy bulk of a huge stand stuffed with pairs of shoes. Sandals, boots, thongs, velvet slippers, even high heels. Zelda slipped off her sandals. She frowned, puzzled, as she wedged them in between two pairs of Reeboks. It was not yet seven o'clock but she was obviously late; everyone was already inside. There was no crowd to get lost in; she would have to open the door and walk in by herself. She adjusted the shawl, making sure it shaped her face. She wrapped the loose ends close around her body against the chill of the night air. A peacock cried nearby, a single haunting wail. As if in reply, a loud chanting started up in the hall. The song reached out to her; the voices of the ones inside—the ones who belonged—taunting her, while she stood alone in the night.

Her feet carried her under the towering archway, up to the tall, blue doors. She pushed at them with both hands, but they didn't move. Then she noticed the outline of a smaller entrance, cut into the lower portion of one of the main doors. She tried pushing here and this time a crack appeared. It widened steadily and silently, drawing her in. She stepped up over a ledge. And she was there . . . inside.

It was cool and dim, the air heavy with the strange sweet-spicy perfume—Shahastra, the fragrance of Unknowing—and beneath it, the oaky smell of burnt charcoal. Still there was no-one around. She was in an empty vestibule with a cloth-draped table set to one side. Zelda glanced over it as she passed. It was covered with little packets of incense and broken charcoal; a basket piled with single stems of pale blue orchids and another of peacock feathers; then there were painted blocks like small building bricks, each one decorated with flower motifs and clearly marked with a price in rupees and dollars. Ahead was another pair of closed doors.

The chanting was close now. A steady drumbeat under strong clear voices—many voices. Zelda thought back to the sound of thirty people singing hymns in the island chapel. A thin, tenuous sound almost lost in the wheeze of the foot-pump organ. She fixed her eyes on the doors. There must be hundreds of people gathered in there.

Tension clamped her throat as she forced her steps onward. Reaching one of the doors, she pushed gently. It swung open.

Sound swelled to surround her in the semi-darkness. For a moment she stood there, gazing over a sea of people seated cross-legged on the floor, their heads and shoulders swaying to the beat of the drums.

'This way.' A voice cut through the chant. An arm circled her and pushed her gently across to her left. Another arm found her there and guided her towards a faintly visible patch of space on the carpet.

Copying the shapes around her, Zelda sat down crossing her legs, straightening her back and resting her hands on her knees. Then she drew herself up, stretching her neck, to see to the front of the hall.

In the distance, a bluish glow lit up a small stage. There was a glass table piled high with large pale flowers. That was all she could see. Around it were only shadows.

Without warning, the music stopped, the final drumbeat left behind by the last lingering note of the song. In the silence, the light grew—smoothly, steadily—cast by rows of spotlights dotted across the high ceiling. Zelda half-knelt, ignoring glances from the person beside her. Now, at last, she could see . . .

Beside the table was a glass chair. A figure was seated there, cross-legged. At first Zelda saw just a silhouette, then light etched in the features of a woman—dark brows, dark hair, pale skin. She stirred in her chair and smiled a warm welcoming smile. Her gaze passed over the crowd, beginning with the people close to her and moving out towards every corner of the room. Slow breaths and whispers ebbed and flowed, following the movement of her eyes. Zelda slumped back to the floor and bowed her head. Sweat crept over her scalp, tingling. In the rigid frame of her body, her heart pounded wildly. Words, unspoken, matched the rhythm. It's her, it's her, it's her . . .

There was a sudden rustle of clothing and the clinking of bracelets as all around Zelda people began rising to their feet. They moved towards an aisle that ran down the centre of the room. Many held flowers in their hands: blue orchids on long slender stems. Some carried wooden bricks, like the ones on sale outside. Others held small packages or folded papers.

Zelda stood with them and let herself be carried along as they shuffled slowly forwards. She leaned and peered between heads and shoulders, but the dais was cut off from her view. Instead she caught sight of an area close to the front and set a little apart in which all the people were dressed in blue— different blues and different clothes, but no hint of any other colour. Where the blue group met the rest of the crowd there was a line of people dressed in plain dark tunics. They sat perfectly still, but their eyes raked the crowd steadily, back and forth.

As she drew near to the blue-lit dais Zelda kept her face down, hidden by her shawl. Ahead of her, bodies were forming into pairs, moving to the front in turn. She glanced up, watching how they approached the glass chair, bowed their heads and placed their gifts in large baskets laid out at each side. Then they returned to their places at the back of the hall.

Zelda felt a figure beside her, joining up with her, without touching. Soon it was their turn. They moved forward over an empty space and bent down towards the basket. Zelda's hand stretched out, empty. Reaching past the basket towards a bare slender foot. Shaking fingers, almost there. Skin brushing skin . . . A dark blue arm shot out, ready to push her hand away.

'No. Leave her.' The voice was low, calm, warm. Zelda lifted her face, raising dark bright eyes.

Here I am . . .

Her arm froze as slow shock coursed through her body. The eyes. The eyes were deep, icy blue.

The woman leaned forward in her chair, lips parting. A tremor travelled over her face.

Zelda stared, unmoving. Her companion returned to the crowd, leaving her there, poised over the basket. Whispers stirred around her, but she heard nothing. One thought chased through her head, chilling her body in its wake. It was not her. Not Ellen.

The woman jumped up, tipping the glass chair back. The room moved with her, a swelling tide as people scrambled to their feet. She composed herself quickly, her face falling back into lines of calm, her lips forming a small, steady smile. People in dark tunics moved to surround her. They side-stepped, facing the crowd, as she drew them away, across the front of the hall and through an archway, out of sight.

Zelda backed into the crowd, ignored, just a thin wraith veiled in anonymous brown. She wove her way to the rear of the hall and edged out through the doorway. Then she ran, throwing open another door. It slammed behind her with a loud bang that echoed down a long dim corridor.

She stopped and looked around her, realising she had taken the wrong door. She ran on, uncaring. The image of the woman's face rose before her. It was a strange face, defined with make-up so that from a distance she looked like Ellen. Close up she was someone else. But she had sat at the front, she was Beautiful Mother. It made no sense . . .

Zelda's pace slowed to a walk. She passed an alcove filled with blue flowers and a wall decorated with panels of carved ivory. There were paintings as well. Brief glimpses reminded her of the statues in Rishikesh. There was the plump playful child and the many-armed goddess; images of both, surrounded by Indian emperors, jewelled elephants and princesses with bare breasts.

Large double doors lay ahead of her now. Zelda faltered, glancing over her shoulder. She had no plan, no idea what to do next. A big part of her wanted only to get back outside into the clear open air. But she knew that the statue in Rishikesh was Ellen, and so was the picture at the drink stall, and the gold profile stamped on blue paper. In spite of the stranger in the hall, Ellen *was* the Beautiful Mother. Somehow, somewhere, she was still to be found.

The doors snapped shut behind her, trapping her in near-darkness. The air smelled of stale spice and Shahastra. Moonlight leaked wanly through cloth blinds, and somewhere far ahead a lamp burned with a blue light. Zelda paused while her eyes adjusted to the gloom. A strip of black carpet marked out a path down the middle of a long room. In the shadows to each side, eyes glinted. Pale limbs held stiff poses, and circles — faces—stretched away in long rows.

Reaching back to the door, she felt around the frame and found a switch. It clicked on a bank of dim spotlights, casting down weak yellow beams. Zelda turned slowly, staring around her. The room was crowded with large dolls—hundreds of them—arranged on tiered stands that rose up on both sides of the carpet almost to the roof. They were child-dolls; you could tell by their clothes and their oversized heads, round cheeks, small mouths and flat chests. Strange, sombre children with haunted eyes. Nearly all of them were girls.

Zelda turned her head from side to side, fixing her gaze on one figure after another. They looked as if they had been made by hand: modelled from white clay, then dressed and painted. But they didn't appear to be the work of a single artist; some of the bodies were well proportioned and realistic, others were distorted and clumsy. Nearly all had carefully detailed faces, though: lips painted with the sure stroke of hands used to applying lipstick; eyelashes familiar with the touch of a mascara wand; cheeks delicately blushed; bones highlighted. The hair was done well, too—hair of all kinds: real hair, rope hair, painted hair. Blonde and dark; curly and straight; short and long.

Zelda moved silently along the thick carpet. The sound of her breathing marked time with the beat of her heart—living sounds, out of place in this chamber of stillness. There was an aura of reverence, as if an ancient tomb full of religious statues had been uncovered. Or models of the dead, unveiled in some tribal burial ground.

The stands were roped off from the walkway with a velvet cord. Zelda ran her hand over it as she walked slowly along. The dolls were dressed in pieces of Indian cloth. The silks and cottons had been tie-dyed, embroidered, printed and painted, and transformed into the raw material of T-shirts, jeans, sweatshirts and skirts—ordinary clothes, of ordinary children, from the real world. One doll even carried a newspaper, hand-written on folded pieces of rice paper. Another held a cat; another, a bird with real feathers.

As she moved down the walkway, Zelda realised that the collection must have been gathered over a long period. The figures she had seen first were bright and new, but further on they became increasingly dusty and laced with cobwebs.

There was another pair of doors at the end of the room. Near them, Zelda stopped, her eye caught by a small black and white face and a little girl's body, made of dusty whitewashed clay. She was almost naked, dressed only in a white bathing suit painted with a brightly coloured design of starfish and seahorses. Dark hair tumbled around the thin shoulders, matted into strands as if it was wet. A striped towel hung over one bent arm. Her eyes were dark and dimmed with dust. In the blue lamplight she looked cold and abandoned. Leaning closer, Zelda saw that the doll wore a bracelet, a painted gold chain with a nameplate set in. She bent to wipe away the dust. A cold, prickling sweat broke over her as the first letter emerged. Painted in a fine looping script—*E* And then the rest following: *L L E N.*

Ellen.

Zelda stood back and let her eyes move slowly over the doll. The image felt oddly, strongly, familiar. Not the bathers or the towel, but the child's body, her wet hair, her face. And the look in the eyes—the longing backed by fear. The strange fear that pushed and pulled, both at the same time.

I want you.

I'm afraid of you.

Go away.

Don't leave me.

The child was Ellen. But in some way that could not be named, Zelda sensed it was herself as well. She wanted, suddenly, to take the doll, wrap it up and carry it safely away. But it would be just another relic, another clue, nothing more.

She grasped the velvet cord with her hand, the ridges pressing into her flesh. Her toes pushed into the carpet, feeling beneath the softness for the firm, solid floor. But still, nothing seemed real: the Grand Hall with its high arches and perfect symmetry; the room of dolls and the child Ellen; the corridors lined with rich paintings and lavish flowers; the air tinged with fragrance. They wove together into an aura of calm, beauty and harmony. Shahastra. The Way of Unknowing. It held out the promise of a refuge from life—an escape from pain, lies and stories that had no end.

But even as she felt herself drawn by the vision of rest and release, Zelda sensed a darkness lying beneath it. She imagined the state of unknowing to be like floating on a calm sea. The water all around you, a blue mirror reflecting the sky. The lullaby sound of gentle waves lapping the shore. The sun warm on your skin . . . But below you, in the depths, was a different world: a wild place where all that you had tried to push down and hide away from still lurked, ready to rise up and attack you.

Zelda stepped up to the heavy doors and pushed her way out—glad to escape the gloomy hall with its ghost-like dolls, and the smell of Shahastra that seemed to be filtering into her mind.

Finding herself in another corridor, she half-ran on towards a well-lit foyer. Then she stopped still and pressed herself against the wall. There were voices.

'Here we all are.' A woman spoke in a light, strong voice with an American accent. 'The founding members—me, Skye, and that's Kate, with Ruth standing behind—'

'And that's her,' a male voice cut in.

'Yes.' There was a short pause. 'That's her. It's an old photo, but she hasn't really changed much. We stopped allowing cameras, so you'd have to go by the paintings for anything recent. But if you saw her, you'd know. She's got that kind of face . . .'

'Was it taken here, the photo?' the man asked.

'Hell, no,' the woman scoffed. 'That was some old place we had on the other side of Mussoorie.'

Zelda leaned round until she could just see the two people standing with their backs to her in front of a line of framed pictures hung on the wall. The woman was tall and slender, with long straw-blonde hair streaked with grey. She was swathed in a sea-green saree. It hung down to the marble floor, in heavy folds of rich silk. The man wore a plain dark suit.

'And who's that, standing behind her?' He jabbed a finger towards the edge of the photograph.

'What? Oh that! Just some old Indian servant. I don't know what he was doing getting into the shot. In fact, I never really noticed him there before.' She held up a hand to mark off the edge of the picture. 'I think he could be framed out.' The woman turned side-on to smile at her companion. She had eyes to match her saree; a magazine face with finely chiselled features only lightly blurred with age.

'Well how long can you go on—like this?' the man asked carefully. There was no reply. 'Ziggy?' he prompted.

'Well, I'm not sure,' she answered, turning back to the wall. Her voice softened, so that Zelda had to strain to hear. 'Skye's doing a good job.' The lean shoulders shrugged. 'Maybe we can gradually bring her out—as her own person, I mean, and let the other just . . . fade away. You know, without making a big deal about it.' A willow arm rose, showing off a sparkling watch. 'Satsanga's finished by now. We should go over there.'

The two crossed the foyer and disappeared.

Zelda leaned back against the wall, replaying their words and trying to make sense of them. Ellen had been here at Everest House; that much was clear. And now she was gone. They were going on without her.

You knew this might happen, Zelda reminded herself. Everyone knew—Lizzie, Drew, even Rye. She pictured his words, written in the bold sloping hand: You'll get there and she won't be there. People don't stay put in India, they move on.

She walked towards the photograph, but before she reached it her eye was caught by another picture—a bright pastel painting in romantic Indian style. It was Ellen, the Beautiful Mother, floating in a cloudy blue sky. She looked happy and peaceful, in a place beyond damage and death. Like Lizzie's saints, Zelda thought, Perpetua and Felicity, their bodies devoured by lions, but their brave souls still burning bright. Or Christopher, protector of travellers. Jude, saint of the impossible. Anthony of the lost and found.

With you for you always. But dead. Gone.

Zelda scanned the room, looking for a way out. A single feeling swelled inside her. She had to get out, get away, before it burst, and swallowed her up . . .

She ran back through the hall, ignoring voices, faces, arms; pushing on with her head down, her shawl torn loose. Out past the shoe stand, she ploughed through a milling crowd, then stumbled on through the rockgarden, her bare feet grazed by boulders, twigs snagging at her clothes. She fled into the forest, with its damp leaves, smooth limbs and dark mushroomy floor—safe at last in the calm silence.

The taxi driver jumped up in alarm when she knocked against the window. He switched on the headlights. In a moment, he took in her scratched face, bare feet and torn clothes. Zelda saw him glance away down the road, as though he was planning a means of escaping his connection with her. Quickly she opened the back door and slid into the seat.

'Let's go,' she said flatly. 'Back to the hotel.'

The driver turned round to look at her.

'I left my shoes,' she said, forcing a smile. 'And I walked in the forest.'

He frowned doubtfully, then turned back to start the engine. He drove fast, clearly wanting to get the journey over as quickly as possible.

'Forest no good,' he said accusingly, after a few moments of silence. Zelda didn't answer. She sat stiffly on the seat, tipped askew by a broken spring, looking straight ahead as she watched the road rise up out of the gloom.

Soon the glow of cooking fires and the lamps of village huts dotted the darkness. The driver braked suddenly to avoid a wandering cow. After that he drove more slowly, his hand poised over the horn. Zelda wound down her window and breathed in the smell of wood smoke. Laughter travelled on the air, and the low hum of quiet, end-of-day talk. A boy herded a few goats along a narrow path, heading home.

Zelda rested her cheek on her arm. Home . . . The smell of wet wool drying by the fire. The old black kettle hissing on the stove. Fish spitting in the pan. Legs stretched out into the hearth. Jokes and stories over a glass of bourbon.

I'll go back, she told herself, to the island where I belong. I'll live on the boat, work the pots, save up and buy a bit of land. But then Drew's face came to her, painfully clear, and she closed her eyes, overcome with sudden despair. Everything had changed—she couldn't go back. But there was nothing for her here, either . . .

The driver glanced over his shoulder at her as he steered the car round into the driveway of the hotel. Then he jammed on the brakes, slowing the car to a crawl.

'Hah!' he exclaimed, leaning forward over the steering wheel. The road ahead was crowded with men, women and children. They were not guests, or staff; their lean bodies were draped with the pale uniform cloth of the poor, all colour and pattern leached out by years of wear. Flowers burned golden in the thin light—dozens of marigolds woven into long wreaths, like the ones that had been hanging in the stalls down at the ghats.

It must be some kind of religious festival, thought Zelda. She sank low in her seat, grateful for the darkness that would hide her from peering eyes. The slow movement of the car was like a mesmerising song. She wanted it to go on, carrying her with it forever and leaving thought, action, feeling—everything— far behind.

After a while, the driver began hammering on the horn, sending people scrambling for the verges. They stood there, shoulder to shoulder, ignoring the taxi; their eyes were fixed on the lights of the hotel glimmering through the shrubs.

Ahead, two huge iron gates were closed across the driveway. Some distance in, with his face turned away from the crowd, stood a uniformed guard. He spun around at the sound of the horn and stared mutely at the approaching taxi. The driver leaned out of the window and shouted. The guard shouted back. After a short wait, a group of green-uniformed hotel staff joined the guard. Shouting and waving back the crowd, they pushed open one of the gates to let the taxi in.

The reception building was surrounded by guests and staff talking excitedly as they watched the crowds waiting on the other side of the gate. Zelda pointed to the far end of the carpark. The driver nodded his approval of her plan and let her down in the shadows of a dark old tree. He took her money without comment and drove quickly away.

Zelda paused for a moment to get her bearings, then took a circuitous route back to her room, avoiding the main walkway. She moved quickly. All she wanted was to get to her room. She felt it there, waiting for her like a comforting friend. It would take her in, and let her rest.

Near the door she faltered at the sight of a garland laid out on the threshold. But the curtains were drawn back and the interior was safely dark. As she put her hand on the door, she paused again, remembering that she'd left the key at Reception. She glanced across at the window, checking how it was fastened. At the same time she tried idly to turn the knob. To her surprise the door opened. She sighed with relief as she slipped inside.

The air was sweet with the perfume of flowers. There was incense as well—a tiny red spot burning in the darkness. As her eyes adjusted, Zelda picked out the shape of the rose-shaded lamp and reached to turn it on. From somewhere in the shadows came a rustle of movement.

'Who's there?' she asked. Her voice was thin and sharp. The light snapped on. She spun round to see a figure standing in the doorway to the bedroom—an old man, with white hair and leather-brown skin. For a long moment he studied her face, then he smiled widely and held out one hand.

'Zelda,' he said. 'Zelda.' He repeated her name slowly, as if savouring the word on his tongue. 'At last you have come. After so many years.'

Zelda stared at him silently. His words were like a healing balm, a kind wind. She let them wash over her and waited for more.

'For years I prayed that you would come.' He spoke in a low quiet voice—an old voice that cracked and rustled like dry leaves. His Indian English poured out easily, rising and falling in a smooth and fluent song. 'I burned incense for you. I asked for you in dreams. Then I gave up. And now you are here. And you . . .' His voice died away and he stood there silently. His arms hung loose, but his hands kept moving restlessly. 'You look just like her—the day she first arrived here!'

'Who are you?' asked Zelda, faintly. 'You know me?'

He nodded. 'I am the old message boy, Djoti,' he said. He

paused, as if running through a choice of things to say, hunting for a place to begin. He sighed, still smiling, and spread his hands. 'There are many things I want to tell you. Too many things. I—'

'Do you know where she is?' Zelda broke in.

'Of course. I'm going to take you to her,' said Djoti.

Zelda stared at him, eyes wide with mixed fear and hope. She opened her mouth to speak, but Djoti held up a hand. 'The house where she is living is a long walk from here, through the forest. It is not possible in the dark. Tomorrow morning we will go.' He looked at her sternly. 'Believe me, there is no choice.'

Zelda licked her lips and breathed out slowly. 'Okay. But just don't—I mean—' Her voice grew brittle. 'Don't say it if it's not true—please.'

Djoti touched her arm, a brief but firm gesture. 'You will see her,' he said. 'Otherwise, why did you come? After all this time? If not to be together.'

A silence grew between them. The sound of laughter could be heard in the distance. Zelda spoke. 'I didn't know she was alive until a few weeks ago.'

A few weeks. A thousand years.

Djoti nodded. 'Your father told you she was dead.'

Zelda stiffened. 'How do you know?' she asked.

Djoti shrugged. 'I was the message boy. Letters, telegrams— everything passed through my hands. And Ellen, she also—'

'What letters?'

'She wrote to your father, asking if she could send letters to you. She wanted also to visit you. But she was not allowed. Your father, he would not agree to it.'

Zelda stood rock-still, every part of her focussed on the old man's words. Djoti moved around the room, picking things up and putting them down, as if the small movements would defuse the power of her gaze. Finally he picked up a cushion and hugged it to his chest, smoothing the velvet cloth with his rough hand.

'There were legal papers as well,' he said. 'So she had to accept it. But it was very hard for her. She did not want to tell anyone, but slowly I made her talk to me. You see,' he smiled apologetically, 'my own daughter is the same age as her. She lives in a village far from here. I always hoped that she would never have to face trouble with no friend to stand beside her. And also,' his voice softened, 'I am a father. I can understand how it would be, to lose your child.'

'She didn't lose me,' Zelda said quietly. 'She went away.'

Djoti was silent for a moment. 'Even so—she loved you.' He nodded his head, to add weight to his words. 'She did.'

Zelda watched him with hungry eyes.

'She had one photograph of you as a little girl,' Djoti continued. 'It was taken on your birthday. It was her most precious possession. In the end, I think it was the only thing she kept, of herself. Everything else became the Beautiful Mother. That was what she chose. It was a big sacrifice. I admired it, of course—it is what a great teacher must do—but I missed her. And,' he frowned uncertainly, 'to be honest, I felt it was not the right thing for her. Her own self, I mean.'

'You have to tell me,' Zelda said slowly, 'who—I mean what—is she? I don't understand. I went to Everest House to see her. But someone else was there.'

'It is a big story,' Djoti motioned for her to sit down. Zelda lowered herself into the velvet chair without letting her gaze leave his face. He sat opposite her on the couch.

'You know, people have been arriving for hours since they heard the daughter of Nanda Devi was here,' he said. Now his voice was light and casual, like someone describing the weather. 'Of course the hotel will not let them in.'

'I saw them,' said Zelda. She pictured the ragged crowd—the friends of Ellen. 'They didn't notice me,' she commented. 'They didn't even look into the taxi.'

Djoti nodded. 'The hotel manager didn't want them waiting there. He said you had already retired for the night. But the people are still hoping you will come out. And who knows? Maybe you will.'

'What do they want me to do?' Zelda asked doubtfully.

'Nothing,' said Djoti. 'They just want to welcome the daughter of Nanda Devi. You see, let me tell you . . . When she lived here in Mussoorie at the other end of the village, the part called Landour, she helped so many people. There are children standing outside, at this moment, who would have died if Ellen had not helped their mothers with food, medicine or money. That kind of thing cannot be forgotten. Also, she studied at the temple ashram and learned their language. So she talked to them and listened as well. She was their friend. And they were the ones who began to call her Nanda Devi. Some others who spoke English gave her another name as well. Beautiful Mother. That was many years ago. These village people have not seen her for a long time now, but they still remember her.' He paused to settle himself further back on the couch. 'You see, when she moved to Everest House, she stopped going out. They did not meet her any more in the bazaars, or the ashrams. They did not pass her in their villages. I myself did not see her for a long time. I used to work for her when they lived at Landour, and for a little while at Everest House as well. That was before they set up the ashram in Rishikesh and started going down to the valley for the winter. It was Ziggy's idea. She was one of the original group and she was in charge of running everything. She wanted the visitors to be able to get religious visas. Then they could stay in India as long as they liked, with no problems. And that was why they opened the ashram down in Rishikesh, the holy city.

'I could not move up and down, summer and winter, with them. I was too old already for such a way of life! And I have my own family as well. So I had to go my own way.' Djoti paused, looking down at his hands, clasped together in his lap. 'But it was more than that. Ziggy did not like me being around. She made sure that I got left behind. Ellen—she wanted me to stay.' His face creased, suddenly showing his age. 'But at that time she was leaving behind personal things. All that mattered was her students. She gave them everything. There was nothing left even for herself. And nothing for an old Indian man. So I lost sight of her. But I didn't forget her, either. I never saw her. Only the pictures.' He laughed briefly. 'You know, in the bazaar they sell cups with her face painted on the side. And even dolls! They must have been made far away, because it is true they have her face, and they are dressed in her blue clothes—but the hair is red! My wife, Prianka, she saved some rupees and bought one. But I made her put it away. Who is she to us? I asked. Our old friend is not her. She is gone. And we have enough gods already to keep us busy!'

Zelda shared his smile, his plain words bringing with them a sense of relief. Suddenly the telephone rang—a rude noise that shattered the peace of the room. The two stared at it, but neither moved. Finally it stopped. Djoti leaned across and switched off the light. 'In case someone comes,' he murmured.

In the darkness small sounds swelled and sharpened. Djoti leaned back, making the couch springs creak.

'Go on,' said Zelda.

'Yes. So then, not long ago a boy came to me and said Nanda Devi is in the hospital. I rushed to see her, but they told me she was not there. For most of my life I was a message boy, so I know how to find out what lies behind simple words. The truth was this: she had been brought there from Everest House, at night. No-one was allowed to see her. She had her own people washing her, cooking for her. The nurses said she was very ill. The doctor called it a breakdown. Like a car? I thought. Even an old car does not break down if it is cared for properly. If that is the situation, I said to Prianka, how will they look after her now?' Zelda saw the outline of his head as he nodded slowly. 'Some time passed. I heard that she was not recovering. It was a big problem for us. We kept thinking of her, lying there. Hidden away. We had to do something. So—'

Djoti's voice grew warm with triumph. 'We stole her! That is what we did. There were three sadhus to help me. We had to create a small problem of flooding in the hospital, to call the nurses away. Then we wrapped her up in a cloth, like a person who is dead, and the sadhus carried her away. I watched them from the forest. It was very hard for them. They wanted to hurry, but they had to walk slowly, like priests.'

Zelda sat forward in her chair, urging him on.

'We took her to a small house in the hills,' the old man continued. 'Colonel Stratheden—it was his hunting lodge, but then he died and it was forgotten. We took her there nearly two months ago. So—you see? You went to Everest House to find your mother. But she has disappeared! Vanished into thin air!' He laughed softly. 'They want her back, of course. They have asked everyone where she is. All the ashrams, dharm-shalas, hotels. Even in Delhi, Calcutta, Goa as well! My friend at the Post Office, he knows it all. So you see, she cannot stay around here.'

The couch creaked again as Djoti turned towards Zelda in the darkness. She saw the gleam of his smile. 'And that is why you have come!' he said. 'That is why you are here!' His voice ended on a strong, clear note. It resonated in the darkness, long after the silence took over.

'But, is she . . . all right?' Zelda's voice sounded strange to her. It seemed impossible to be speaking of Ellen as if she were real and close, after so long.

'She suffered from dreams,' said Djoti. 'They were not bad dreams, but they upset her very much. Because, you see, for many years she did not have dreams. No dreams at all. She studied yoga for a long time and yogis can control their mind totally, even when they are sleeping. Ellen had this power. Complete control. It was because of this that she could help the foreign visitors with their problems. But then, I think, her body became too tired. She could not eat, she was in pain. She was exhausted but she was afraid to sleep, because of the dreams. She knew she was losing her strength. Her mind wanted to be free again. It filled her with fear. So for days she would force herself to stay awake. This is how she was when she came to the hospital. But they drugged her.' His voice rose with indignation. 'She always hated drugs. And hospitals. Even the smell of disinfectant. Ever since I knew her, she hated these things. So I was glad to take her out of there. Instead of nurses and doctors, she had her old friend Prianka. They rested together by the fire in Colonel Stratheden's lodge. Prianka stayed with her every moment, caring for her like a small baby. She stroked her hair, cooked her food and fed her by hand. Rubbed away the pains from her body. Prianka loved her. And who,' Djoti laughed softly again, 'who can resist the love of an old woman?

'I visited her whenever I could and it was then that she talked to me about her dreams. They were long dreams, like stories. Some were about you, Zelda. Others went back to when Ellen was a little girl, living in America. These ones, especially, upset her. She could not escape from the idea that her mother blamed her for something she had done wrong. It haunted her. But she could never think what it might have been.' A note of anger entered Djoti's voice. 'What could a child do, I ask myself, to turn a mother's love into something dark and hurtful? There is no answer to it, I told Ellen. You must turn your mind to your daughter, Zelda. Because somewhere in the world, she is there. Your mother—who knows?' He pulled himself to his feet. His figure made a darker silhouette against the black-grey window. 'And I was right, because you have come. But now I must leave you to rest. Tomorrow I'll return.'

'No,' said Zelda, jumping up beside him. She felt suddenly that he was the only link with the morning, the only proof of the promise of dawn. She grasped his arm. 'Don't leave me here. Please.'

'But I must,' said Djoti, his voice lifting with surprise. 'I am expected at my home, a long time before this.'

'Take me with you,' pleaded Zelda. 'I could sleep there, somewhere. Then we'll be together, ready to go in the morning.' She leaned over and switched on the light, so that she could see Djoti's face.

He laughed, his eyes sweeping the room. 'I don't think you understand,' he said. 'My home is a hut. There is no electricity, no taps with water. We sleep on beds laid out on the floor.'

'But I lived in a hut,' Zelda insisted. 'We used to have rain running in under the doors and wind blowing the smoke back down the chimney. It was very small—built so close to the sea that Dad reckoned you could cast a line from the front window . . .' She tried to smile, but her lips quivered and tears filled her eyes.

'Don't cry,' said Djoti, just like Cassie.

But his voice was too kind. Zelda turned away as tears spilled down her face. Behind her, she sensed Djoti's stillness. Then she heard him moving around the room, picking up her things and stuffing them into her backpack. When he was finished, he shouldered the load and went to stand by the door.

Chapter 29

Close to Landour the forest paths were bare earth, swept clean. Dotted along the way were piles of dead leaves and shrivelled flowers smouldering slowly, sending fragrant tendrils into the still air of early dawn. The small fires were all untended, suggesting that there were sweepers nearby; ever-present, but always just out of sight.

Further into the forest, the path grew rough and slippery, but the same flowers coloured the treetops, and birds— already awake—chattered as they flapped among the high branches. Djoti walked ahead, but kept glancing back over his shoulder.

'Look out. Don't fall,' he warned. At the edge of the path, the ground fell away steeply; a long unbroken slope running down to the valley floor. 'People have died, you know,' he said. 'Horses as well, have fallen down the khut.'

As they walked, Djoti pointed out the signs of distant houses: wide plumes of smoke, gabled rooftops, foreign trees. He paused to show her the blackened ruins of a once-grand mansion. Young lovers, high-caste Indians, had run off together, he said. They had taken refuge here, but lightning had struck and they were burned to death. Now only their ghosts remained, singing their love to the night . . .

Neither Djoti nor Zelda spoke about themselves, or Ellen, as they walked, both sensing that the journey should be peaceful and calm—a time of transition—sheltered from the sharp winds of pain and hope and remembering.

By mid-morning the last of the Landour houses were long gone and the path began to cut steeply uphill, winding round short, jagged bends. Soon they were breathing too heavily to speak at all. Zelda paused to take off her jumper and tie it round her waist. It was an old jumper, with worn-through elbows, but she liked the colour—blue-grey, like a wintery sky. Early in the morning she had lingered over her backpack while Djoti and his relatives waited outside to let her change in private. She had dressed first in the brown pyjamas, but then decided against wearing Indian clothes. Instead, she had taken out her jeans, boots, bush shirt, hat and the blue jumper. She had pulled them on, gaining a sense of reassurance from the touch of worn denim encasing her legs and the weight of the leather belt lying firm on her hips. Around her neck she had tied James's old scarf, its edges frayed and bleached by sun and wind. The traveller was gone. She was Zelda-the-welder, Jimmy's kid, Drew's girl, from Nautilus Bay.

Djoti had frowned as he handed her a clay cup of sweet spiced tea. 'Are you a boy now?' he asked. But he nodded approvingly at the solid boots. 'The road is rough. You will need them,' he said, though his own feet were bare.

Zelda watched Djoti's back as they climbed. 'He's an old man,' she told herself. 'You should be miles ahead of him.' She rubbed at a stitch in her side, trying to knead away the pain. Then she started counting steps, like she used to, trying to keep up with Drew. Fifty. Fifty more. Just another fifty to go. Bit by bit, you ate the distance away. By the yard it's hard, James used to say. By the inch it's a cinch.

Djoti stopped suddenly and turned around. 'We are there,' he said.

Zelda stared at him. 'What?'

'Look through those trees. There it is. The hunting lodge of Colonel Stratheden.'

Zelda looked past Djoti's head, following his outstretched arm. There were trunks, leaves, shrubs, and sky above. Then, almost lost in the background, she picked out the straight lines and angles of a raw wood building.

'It is only small,' Djoti explained, 'and it has no paint.'

Their eyes met. Zelda floundered in a wave of panic. The end of the journey had come too soon.

'You just go forward,' said Djoti quietly. 'I will wait here, for some time.'

'No,' said Zelda quickly. 'You should take me . . .'

Djoti gave no answer, but stepped off the narrow pathway and waved her on.

The path led her round a sharp corner into a small clearing. In the middle stood a grey-weathered cottage with split shingle walls and roof. At the windows hung wooden shutters, gaping open on sagging hinges. Bleached white skulls, with pairs of long, twiggy antlers, were nailed in a line along the front wall. Above a rough plank door hung two rusty guns, their barrels crossed. Zelda walked closer, her shirt snagging on the wild plants that had taken over the untended garden beds. With a sharp movement she pulled her arm free of a clinging vine. It flicked back, knocking one of the swinging shutters. The short bang emptied the air, leaving a gulf of silence behind.

Zelda glanced back down the path in the slim hope that Djoti was coming after all, but he was nowhere in sight. The quiet drew her on, like a vacuum that had to be filled. She followed a small track that led round the side of the building. Pausing by an open window, she glanced in at a line of washing hung up to dry. A shirt, pyjama trousers, underpants, socks—all in different shades of blue. She moved quickly on, stepping heavily now, wanting to disturb the quiet; to be found, seen, first.

At the corner she stopped. Long dark hair draped the back of a tall figure bent over a patch of freshly dug earth. Pale arms flexed as they pushed a shovel into the soil.

'Djoti?' A voice floated back. 'Is that you?'

In the silence the body straightened and turned. A pale arm rose, wiping across the forehead, leaving a trail of earth behind. It froze there, like a shield held up against a bright light.

'No, it's me.' Zelda's voice broke the stillness. Far overhead a bird cried out. In the distance another called back.

Their eyes met, held—then tore away, searching over face and body, before fusing together again. A mask of tears swam in between them, blurring vision. Slow steps carried them close, a steady dance led by a silent song.

They knelt, knees touching, in the soft dark earth. It cradled them like the sands of the seashore—a white beach on a far-off island—long years ago. And the sun lay gentle over their heads, the source of warmth and life—the mother.

Ann Clancy

The Wild Colonial Girl

MEET THE NEW HEROINE OF COLONIAL
AUSTRALIA—KATE O'MARA

Feisty, spirited and independent, Irish orphan Kate
arrives in the colony of South Australia determined to
make a new life for herself. Wanting the security that only
wealth can bring, she shoves her derringer in her pocket,
cracks the whip over the bullocks and sets off on a
rugged outback track for the adventure of a lifetime.

What she doesn't count on is love . . .

In the bestselling tradition of Colleen McCullough and
Nancy Cato, *The Wild Colonial Girl* introduces a
captivating and unforgettable Australian heroine.

Beverley Harper
Storms Over Africa

Richard Dunn has made Africa his home. But his Africa is in crisis.

Ancient rivalries have ignited modern political ambitions. Desperate poachers stalk the dwindling populations of the game parks.

For those of the old Africa, the old ways, nothing is certain.

But for Richard—a man used to getting his own way— the stakes are even higher. Into his world has come the compelling and beautiful Steve Hayes. A woman he swears he will never give up. A woman struggling to guard her own dreadful secret.

Richard has no choice. He must face the consequences of the past and fight for the future. To lose now is to lose everything . . .

Storms over Africa is a novel of desperate struggle and searing passion.

Di Morrissey

Tears of the Moon

TWO INSPIRING JOURNEYS
TWO UNFORGETTABLE WOMEN
ONE AMAZING STORY

Broome, Australia 1893
It's the wild and passionate heyday of the pearling
industry, and when young English bride Olivia Hennessy
meets the dashing pearling master, Captain Tyndall, their
lives are destined to be linked by the mysterious power
of pearls.

Sydney 1995
Lily Barton embarks on a search for her family roots
which leads her to Broome. But her quest for identity
reveals more than she could have ever imagined . . .

TEARS OF THE MOON IS THE STUNNING NEW
BESTSELLER FROM AUSTRALIA'S MOST POPULAR
FEMALE NOVELIST

'. . . a sprawling saga . . . skilfully atmospheric'
THE BULLETIN

J. Radford Keir

The Site

Ex-cop Kerry Staines wanted a fresh start. What he found in the little country town of Mallen was . . .

THE SITE
Cursed for 10 000 years, a place where black legends and white spirits meet.

THE SITE
Where a young girl lies murdered, her soul restless while the guilty go unpunished.

THE SITE
Where a maximum security prison is planned, on ground that holds the town's shocking secrets.

But Mallen's shameful past will not stay buried, and Kerry Staines is going straight to hell . . .

Anne Hilton-Bruce
Somebody's Watching

A CHILLING STORY OF OBSESSION, DECEIT AND
DANGEROUS LOVE FROM THE AUTHOR OF
SOMEONE CAME KNOCKING

It seemed like the perfect place to start a new life. When
Mary Sutherland arrives in the small town of Fullers
Wells, she wants to escape her past and forget her grief.
Her job at the local school guarantees her
accommodation, but when she sees the vast, empty
house she realises it wasn't quite what she had in mind.
But the house has a dark past of its own, which soon
begins to cast a shadow over Marty's life.

In Andrew Rees she finds an unlikely and, at first,
unwilling housemate. He is in Fullers Wells on a mission
to find his ex-wife's killer. And he thinks he knows where
to find the answer. But there are forces at work beyond
both their control.

Somebody's watching and somebody knows the terrible
truth . . .

'Anne Hilton-Bruce is shaping up as the Australian Mary
Higgins Clark'
COSMOPOLITAN